DEBRA WHITE SMITH

Lorna

HARVEST HOUSE PUBLISHERS

EUGENE, OREGON

Published in association with the literary agency of Alive Communications, Inc., 7680 Goddard Street, Ste. #200, Colorado Springs, CO 80920. www.alivecommunications.com.

Cover photos © Jim Whitmer Photography; Martin Diebel / fstop / Getty Images; iStockphoto

Cover by Dugan Design Group, Bloomington, Minnesota

LORNA
Copyright © 2008 by Debra White Smith
Published by Harvest House Publishers
Eugene, Oregon 97402
www.harvesthousepublishers.com

Library of Congress Cataloging-in-Publication Data
    Smith, Debra White.
    Lorna / Debra White Smith.
       p. cm. — (Debutantes ; bk. 2)
    ISBN-13: 978-0-7369-1930-2
    ISBN-10: 0-7369-1930-9
    1. Debutantes—Fiction. 2. Houston (Tex)—Fiction I. Title.
    PS3569.M5178L67 2008
    813'.54—dc22

                                2007046200

Printed in the United States of America

08 09 10 11 12 13 14 15 16 / LB-SK / 11 10 9 8 7 6 5 4 3 2 1

ONE

The shadowed silhouette hovered just off the garden walkway. Lorna Leigh slowed her steps along the illuminated path and glanced over her shoulder. Inside her parents' brightly lit mansion a crowd of Houston socialites and politicians enjoyed the aftermath of the mayor's inauguration. Again she looked toward the shadowed figure ahead. His back to her, he appeared to be watching the full moon and the ebony sky alight with glistening stars.

Lorna halted. Should she go back inside and take the front door? She preferred vanishing out the back to making a public exit. That way her dad wouldn't realize how short her stay had been...and neither would anybody else. She'd enjoyed all of this bash she planned to.

She'd promised her dad to put in an appearance. So Lorna had come, she'd shaken hands, she'd smiled. Now her fingers ached from all the times her ring had been forced into her skin by overly exuberant Houstonites. And if she had to smile again, she was sure her aching lips would crack. Lorna had done her duty; she'd paid the price for being the daughter of a prominent Houston merchant. Now she was her own woman again...unless she was interrupted...

or attacked by the man on the path before she made it to her Jeep. She shuddered.

Common sense told her the man was probably an attendee who'd come out to get fresh air. Furthermore, she was so close to the ultra-modern home that someone would hear her screams if the guy were a psycho and up to no good. Logic insisted her fear was senseless, but it had been an integral part of her psyche for four years now, and no amount of counseling had put it down. Someone once told her that courage wasn't the absence of fear. Courage was going forward in the face of fear. Gripping her little sequined bag, Lorna tiptoed toward the gap in the shrubbery that led to the parking area.

As she neared the silhouette, she practiced controlled breathing and assured herself the guy hadn't heard her. The fragrant summer night carried her on its spirit. The humid air was welcome after the refrigerated ballroom. So was the full moon that riveted the silhouette. Tonight it was more lustrous than any manmade chandelier. Tiny moonbeams flickered across her sequined dress like fireflies. Lorna ran her fingertips along the sequins and wished she could absorb the shimmer for those mornings she couldn't glow if she tried. And that was nearly every morning these days.

She forced herself to ignore the silhouette and moved along the stone path lined with lights strategically nestled in foliage. The path wove through the labyrinth garden, but her destination was close. The parking lot lights jutted toward the sky just on the other side of the bushes. In her urgency to get to her Jeep, she picked up her pace and her high heels clicked against the stones. Lorna stopped, held her breath, and decided to make her final dash. *Nearly home free!* she thought.

But just then the man emerged onto the path and looked straight at her. "Oh, hello there. I *thought* I heard someone," he said.

Lorna stopped and gazed into the face of the very reason she'd been trapped all evening. "It's you!" she blurted. "The new mayor!"

And what a mayor he was. Even during the boring formalities Lorna couldn't help but notice what the press was buzzing about. Michael Hayden looked more like a cover boy for *GQ* magazine than a politician. Last year he'd been featured in *In Town* magazine as Houston's most eligible bachelor. According to the press, he was still as single as he could get. No wife. No fiancée. No girlfriend. Not even a mild flirtation in the wings...or anywhere else for that matter.

"Yes, it's me. Who were you expecting? An ax murderer?" he said through a smile that was as familiar as the latest edition of the *Houston Star*.

"Uh..." Lorna hedged and didn't dare admit that was in line with her imagination. Trying to cover the awkward moment, she asked, "What are *you* doing out here?"

"Shhh," he whispered and peered toward the tree-lined perimeters. "I don't want anyone to know I escaped my own party."

Lorna snickered. "I'm trying to escape your party too."

"Well, that's not very neighborly." He shook his finger at her nose. "I'll have you thrown into jail first thing Monday. What's your name anyway?" he asked without taking a breath. "Did I already shake your hand tonight? You look familiar, like someone else I... um...know of."

"Yes, you already shook my hand." Lorna lifted her right hand. "And it's all shaken out."

Michael chuckled. "Mine too. I'm ready to get this gig over with and move on to doing my job." He waved toward the mansion. "I think the press is more interested in my love life than whether or not I'm going to be a good mayor. They're driving me nuts! A year ago *In Town* magazine pestered the living daylights out of me and then labeled me an eligible bachelor." He waved away the honor as an annoyance. "I must have been temporarily insane to let that happen, but they wouldn't leave me alone. And now the media's at it again!"

Lorna crossed her arms and glanced toward her parents' house.

"I feel your pain," she admitted and relived the days she was close...
so close...to winning the U.S. Open. The press had seemed omni-
present. She'd been so certain of victory, yet so tired of having
microphones crammed into her face. Then the evening before the
final match a nightmare had been unleashed into her life. She'd
been so shaken she forfeited the game the next day...and the championship...and ultimately walked away from pro tennis.

She gazed toward the velvet horizon. No matter how appealing
this man was, he was still a man, and she wasn't ready to go there...
and didn't know if she ever would be.

"Well, try not to enjoy your party too much," she said through
a mild grin before stepping around him. She glanced at Hayden
and got the impression he wasn't quite as ready to end the chat as
she was.

"Wait a minute!" he exclaimed.

Halting, Lorna faced him again and was impressed anew with
how sharp he looked in his dark suit. Out of nowhere came the
urge to straighten the crook in his tie—like she'd seen her mom
do for her dad. Lorna curled her fingers around her purse strap and
resisted the unexpected urge.

"You look *so familiar*," he said. "All evening I kept thinking..." He
leaned closer, peering into her eyes. "But it can't be," he continued
and waited for her response. "I don't think I ever got your name in
there." He waved toward the house.

Lorna hesitated and looked down. Fewer people recognized her
these days. Sometimes she went weeks without anyone suspecting
she was a former tennis star. Yet as many times as she'd heard that
comment, she still hated having to answer it. It always led to the
same conversation about why she'd walked away from the pros
and whether or not the guy responsible was in prison.

She lifted her gaze to Michael's.

"I didn't mean that to sound like a pickup line or anything,"
Michael explained.

A laugh burst from Lorna. That was the last thing she'd expected him to say. "I didn't take it that way."

"Do you have to act like the idea is so hilarious?" He crossed his arms in mock offense. "What? Do I look like the type who couldn't pick up a gal if he wanted to?"

"No way!" Lorna exclaimed and then lived through the aftermath of hot cheeks.

A flicker of interest played in his dark eyes.

"It's just that you're at your own party," she rushed. "And you're the mayor."

"And that's how we started this whole conversation, isn't it? Yes, I'm the mayor." He rested his fingertips against his chest like an elementary teacher. "And you are?"

"Lorna Leigh," she said and extended her hand. Inwardly she winced through the handshake while anticipating the dawning light that would begin in Michael's eyes.

"I'm not believing this!" he exclaimed. "I knew you resembled her, but I couldn't believe... You're *Lorna Leigh*? The tennis star Lorna Leigh?"

"Yep," Lorna admitted.

"You live in Houston?"

"Yes. All my life. Oliver Leigh is my father." She waved toward the multimillion-dollar home.

"Why haven't I known this before now?"

"Maybe because I keep a low profile," she admitted. "And my parents honor that." While Lorna had submitted to southern high society traditions—including her own debutante ball—she'd steadfastly refused to allow her image to appear in the newspaper...or any other press hoopla. She enjoyed her privacy...period. Especially after what had happened.

"Oh my word! I'm not believing this *at all!*" he repeated and sliced both hands through the air. "I rooted for you all the way to the last minute, and then you just disappeared. You forfeited."

Lorna's face went cold and her lips tightened as the silent question hung between them. After the attack, she'd dealt with the police and the necessary details. Then her father had quietly told the press that if they involved Lorna in the story they'd be hit with lawsuits that would keep them occupied or put them under for years. They'd complied. And once the police rounded up the other women who'd been attacked by the same guy over a year or so, the lawyers had an airtight case against the creep. Lorna's testimony hadn't been needed or given. Today the rapist was still in prison.

Michael's silent question went brittle and crumbled. "Sorry," he mumbled, lowering his eyes. "It appears I've pried where I'm not wanted."

"It's okay," Lorna rasped, but anyone listening would have known it really wasn't. Even though she'd done a lot of recovering, she was a long way from comfortably explaining to a total stranger how she'd come within seconds of being raped. While the final sexual violation had been stopped by her friend Heather, the violence and fight had bruised and shattered Lorna. Without the stability of the Lord, her family, her two best friends, and counseling, Lorna didn't know how she'd have survived.

She pointed a rigid smile toward Michael and said, "Well, it was nice meeting you. I hope you have a good, uh, mayorship."

His chuckle was marked with regret. His eyes said he *still* wasn't ready for the conversation to end.

Nevertheless Lorna turned toward the path and targeted the gap in the bushes that led to her vehicle. All she'd wanted was to escape the mayor's party, and somehow she'd landed in something close to a flirting session with the man himself.

A carefree, tropical tune filtered from her sequined handbag. The distinctive ring indicated the caller was one of her two best friends: Heather Winslow or Brittan Shay. Lorna debated whether to take the call or wait and return it once she got into her rig.

But then Mr. Mayor was in front of her with a determined smile that wouldn't stop. "You know, I never got your phone number," he quipped and eyed her like she was a slab of the marble cheesecake that had topped the evening meal.

"Just a minute," Lorna hedged and fished the phone out of her bag. "Do you mind if I take this first?" She flipped open the phone and didn't wait for his reply. If nothing else, taking the call would give the hint she was in no way interested. Her father would never forgive her if she made the new mayor mad, but...

"Lorna here," she said into the receiver and eyed the man again. His engaging grin revealed twin dimples that added to his appeal.

Well, maybe "in no way interested" is a little too harsh, she decided. Despite her resolve to never trust another male or her own judgment regarding them, Lorna's resolve softened around the edges...right along with the meltdown going on in her stomach.

His smile increased, and he silently waved like a little boy who sensed he was gaining ground.

Realizing she'd been staring, Lorna looked down. Only then did she comprehend Brittan's "Hello! Hello! Lorna? Are you there? Hello, Lorna? Can you hear me?"

"Yes, I'm here. Whazzup?" she replied and imagined the half-Chinese chick with her no-nonsense expression.

"Heather and I are at her place. Have you heard the latest news?"

"No. What gives?" Lorna swiveled until her back was to the mayor. She gazed across the shadowed garden toward a fountain that burped water out the top of an urn held by a young girl.

"The pastor of a church in Houston has been arrested. He's accused of being part of a child pornography network."

Lorna's eyes bugged. "You're kidding? Do you guys know him?"

"No. But my brother does. Adam said his publicity firm has done work for the church. He's shocked and thinks the pastor is innocent. And, of course, the pastor is saying he didn't do it."

"What's his name?"

"Trent Devenport. Do you know him?"

Lorna allowed the name to linger in her mind while she raked her memory. "No, I don't," she finally said.

She went silent and wondered where this was leading. A year ago she and her two friends had created quite a stir in Houston when they'd secretly solved their first "detective" case. The three of them had uncovered a hacker who'd created a cyber-virus that periodically shut down Houston's banking systems. They'd alerted the press with a document that revealed the criminal—a college dropout genius who was more interested in turning his talents to cyber-mischief than earning a living. Along with the clues they left at the newspaper office was a single-stemmed red rose. The press had dubbed the mysterious detective "the Rose." Houston had been abuzz.

Later that summer the mayor was murdered. After working the case the debutantes again left the clues and their hallmark rose at the *Houston Star's* offices. After discovering who was behind a bank robbery and finding a kidnapped girl, they'd likewise received major press coverage. For weeks "the Rose" was on the tip of everyone's tongue. Except for Heather Winslow's fiancé, Duke Fieldman, no one in Houston knew who "the Rose" was. The "not knowing" kept talk flying.

All three women knew if they were going to continue their detective hobby, they needed to lie low, cling to their socialite personas, and make certain no one suspected three of last year's wealthiest debs were really serial sleuths. Although not fond of the high-society social scene, it was the best cover they could ask for. So after the flurry of "the Rose" activity, they'd dedicated themselves to making the social rounds and resisted taking on a new case for a season...long enough to ensure they weren't detected.

Lorna figured her friends were thinking it was time for "the Rose" to bloom again.

"Heather and I would like to check this guy out and see if he's innocent," Brittan continued "We're seriously wondering if— Are you alone? Are you still at that mayor business? Should I save this conversation for later?"

"No, yes, and yes," Lorna answered. She shot a glance toward Mr. Mayor.

He stood with his hands in his pockets and gazed at the moon as if the giant, glowing disk held the answers to life's momentous questions.

"Okay. Look. Why don't you just come over to Heather's place as soon as you can escape. We need to talk...possibly make plans. Comprende?"

"Right. I'll be there in..." Lorna checked her watch, "about half an hour," she finished before saying goodbye and disconnecting the call.

When she turned around Michael had stopped his moon-watching and switched to Lorna. His smile was less flirtatious, more enthralled.

"Sorry 'bout that," Lorna stated.

He pulled a Palm Pilot from a belt clip and said, "No problem. Let's see, you were just about to give me your number."

"I was?" Lorna hedged.

"Well, I *hoped* you were." He lifted his brows and waited.

"What do you want it for?" Lorna asked. She dropped her phone into her bag and slipped the slender strap on her shoulder.

"I thought I'd give you a call for dinner one evening," Michael said.

"You work fast," Lorna replied and forced her melting stomach to stop. The last fast-working, good-looking man Lorna trusted had tried to rape her.

But this guy's the mayor, she reasoned. *He couldn't have been elected with a bad past. It would've come out in the news.* "We just met," she said and realized she was sounding less and less convincing.

"I've known you for years," Michael insisted. "*You* only just met me."

Lorna narrowed her eyes and wondered if Mr. Mayor was more awestruck by someone he viewed as a celebrity than anything else. "Would you be asking for my number if I weren't Lorna Leigh?" she asked and purposefully moved past him toward the parking lot.

His silence answered her question, and she thought she'd shaken him until he appeared at her side. "Yes," he replied. "I watched you all evening—even before I knew who you were. You never noticed?"

Lorna stopped, crossed her arms, and examined his eyes for any trace of dishonesty. Truth be known, she *had* caught his eye a couple of times, but she'd never imagined he was *purposefully* looking her way. In any social gathering, you catch the eyes of a dozen people several times before the night is over.

"And I didn't even *remind* you of Lorna Leigh?" she challenged, even though she already knew the answer.

"Uh…" Michael's gaze wavered, and then he looked her squarely in the eyes.

In the evening light his dark eyes and complexion reminded Lorna of a mysterious sheik in a mystery novel. You never knew what that type was up to.

"Like I already said, I *did* notice the resemblance," he admitted. "But I never imagined—not in my wildest dreams!"

"So you're asking for a date?" Lorna queried and wondered if the Houston paparazzi would trail them if she were to agree. The last thing she wanted was media coverage.

"Well, yes." He shrugged. "Unless there's someone else…"

"No." Lorna shook her head.

"No, you aren't interested? Or no, there's no one else?"

"No one else," Lorna admitted.

"Me neither," he admitted. "Not for a long time. And I don't normally work so fast, but you're disappearing into the night here, and

I feel like my chances after this will be zero." He once again looked at Lorna like she was the most delectable morsel he'd encountered in years.

Her stomach started churning. "All right," she heard herself agree before reciting her cell number.

He punched it into his Palm while grinning like he'd just won the U.S. Open. "I'll call soon, okay?" He leaned closer and extended his hand.

"Okay," she agreed. "I share my home with my friend Brittan, so don't be surprised if she answers the phone." Lorna placed her palm against his. After a lingering handshake that was every bit as unnerving as a soft kiss, she wondered if she'd gone stark raving mad.

TWO

Lorna settled onto Heather's leather love seat and placed her bottle of Diet Coke on a coaster on the teak coffee table. Heather eyed the Coke and glanced away. Lorna hid a smile. Her friend was one step removed from needing therapy over her vegetarian, health-nut ways. Lorna was sure her caffeine-laden diet drove Heather crazy.

She'd probably blow a fuse if she knew I ate a Kit Kat on the way here, Lorna decided. After that episode with the mayor, she'd needed something to steady her nerves, so she'd stopped at a convenience store and got the cola and candy bar. Somebody once told her that drinking a Diet Coke while consuming a candy bar canceled out the chocolate's calories. She picked up the cola and guzzled the fizzing liquid. She needed all the canceling she could get these days.

"Okay, here's the latest newspaper." Brittan Shay adjusted her narrow-framed glasses and leaned forward in the chair opposite Lorna. Her snug-fitting jeans and casual T-shirt made her look closer to 18 than 23, as did her lack of makeup and cropped hair. Brittan extended the *Houston Star.*

Lorna set her soda down and grabbed the paper.

"That guy looks as innocent as Tigger," Heather said as she

pulled her tabby cat into her lap. He yawned and rubbed his head against her arm.

Lorna examined the front page. "Houston pastor arrested for child pornography" claimed front and center. A photo of a shocked-looking blond man was featured beneath the title. Lorna adjusted the paper and skimmed the article while Brittan and Heather filled her in on the details.

"He's got a wife and twin boys," Heather said.

"They're only four," Brittan added.

"Look at the end," Heather insisted. "You'll see the quote from his wife, Katie. She thinks the material was planted on his computer."

"That is possible," Brittan supplied.

Lorna lowered the paper and eyed her friend. Brittan knew more about computers than Lorna had forgotten.

"If you want to ruin someone, it only takes an hour alone with his computer. You can go online and visit smutty sites, and then have someone else 'accidentally...'" she drew invisible quotes in the air, "discover the links by 'stumbling' into their computer's history."

"Now that's really encouraging," Lorna drawled and glanced toward Heather's computer on the corner desk.

"That's why it's important to have some kind of program that blocks *any* user from accessing those types of sites," Heather stated.

"Yes, but if you're good and know what you're doing, you can hack past almost all those." Brittan crossed her slender legs and leaned forward.

"So we're all sitting cyber-ducks?" Lorna queried.

"All depends on how big of a hunter is after you." Brittan never blinked.

"I feel so sorry for this guy," Heather said. Tigger jumped from her lap, and Heather pulled her legs into the chair. Her casual lounging pants appeared far more comfortable than the sequined torment Lorna wore. She squirmed against the snug fit and wished for something floppy and soft.

"You guys are sure he's innocent?" Lorna put the paper on the coffee table, carefully avoiding contact with the flickering vanilla candle.

Heather and Brittan exchanged a glance. "Adam is an ace at diagnosing character. My gut tells me he's right," Brittan said while Heather nodded.

"We were talking about snooping around and seeing what we could find out, and then seeing if we can make a difference." Heather smiled.

"Sounds like it could be fun," Lorna agreed. "I don't have a lot on my agenda in the next few weeks anyway. If he's innocent, we save a reputation. If he isn't, what have we lost?" She lifted both hands.

Another of Heather's six cats meandered across the palatial room toward the coffee table. This one was a yellow-striped character named Lucky. After one glance at Lorna, he paused, deliberately showed his teeth, and hissed.

"Lucky!" Heather scolded. "Why do you want to be so mean?"

Lorna mimicked a feline howl and hissed back at him.

The yellow cat lowered his ears while his tail hair puffed out.

"Now you're terrorizing him, Lorna!" Heather stood and stepped toward her pet.

"Maybe Lucky's met his match," Brittan said through outright laughter.

"Lucky and I are *not* a match!" Lorna insisted. "Nor am I a match with any other cat!" She fingered the faint scar on the back of her hand—a battle wound from 14 years ago. Her grandmother's Siamese, Goliath, had attacked Lorna because he was jealous of the attention Lorna was getting. She'd hated cats ever since, and they seemed to know it.

Now in his mistress' arms, Lucky growled and glared at Lorna; Lorna yowled back at him.

"Heather's going to throw you out if you don't stop," Brittan warned.

"I'm not scared of Heather." Lorna wrinkled her nose. "And I don't think Lucky would be scared of Godzilla. He's just acting scared to get Heather's sympathy. That cat is possessed! He growled at me the whole time I drove him to the vet last year. He never even gave me a chance. Why'd you name him Lucky, anyway?" Lorna questioned. "He's been neutered and declawed. That's lucky?"

Brittan chuckled and picked up the paper.

"I found him in the middle of the road, and he's *lucky* he didn't get run over." Nuzzling the feline, the blonde settled back into her chair.

Heather's ruby engagement ring glistened like a popping blaze, and Lorna thought of Heather's fiancé, Duke Fieldman. After Lorna, Brittan, and Heather left the newspaper reporter their hallmark roses along with convincing evidence, Duke "solved" several cases. Now he was the *Houston Star's* leading investigative reporter.

"So what does Duke think about this guy?" Lorna asked and pointed toward the paper. "I noticed he didn't write the story."

"No, Mike Mendez did," Brittan supplied, never lifting her gaze from the paper.

"Aka 'the Mike,'" Heather supplied. "You know, that tall, Latin dude who was with Duke at our party last Christmas."

"Tall? Latin? Good looking? Jazzy personality? Didn't notice," Brittan teased.

"I guess I *really* didn't," Lorna admitted and scrounged around her brain for a trace of this Mike person. But the only Mike she encountered was Mayor Michael in his black suit with his incredibly beautiful dark eyes pleading for her phone number. Lorna swallowed and wondered when he'd call. She reached for her sequined bag, pulled out her cell, and made sure the ringer was on loud.

"Duke and Mike both think he's guilty," Heather added. "They say there's too much evidence."

"I told Duke he was being too hasty. And well..." Heather looked away.

"Uh oh," Lorna chimed in as she slipped her feet out of her backless spikes. "Is there trouble in paradise?"

Heather shrugged. "No trouble. We just disagreed. And he told me he thought it was a waste of our time."

"And you said?"

"Nothing." Heather's blue gaze never wavered while a sly smile tilted her lips. "I just silently decided to prove him wrong."

"There's no greater wedding gift than showing your man he's wrong," Lorna teased and wiggled her toes against the Persian rug's soft pile.

Heather tilted her head from side to side. "I wouldn't say *that*. It's just...I *do* think he might be wrong." She deposited the squirming cat on the floor. "And I think this would be a good case for us. We've been lying low a while now. No one would suspect us if 'the Rose' went back into full swing."

"Question is...if we *do* exonerate this pastor, who do we leave the rose and clues with this time?" Brittan asked. "Duke knows who we are. That takes the fun out of leaving it with him."

"Maybe for *you*," Heather replied and picked up her tea mug. She sipped the greenish liquid and eyed her friends over the rim.

Brittan snickered. "So you'd love nothing more than to organize the facts and leave them with Duke...just to be able to say touché?"

"Touché," Heather repeated.

Lorna laughed. "I'd *love* to see his face."

"So would I—*literally*," Heather said and checked her wristwatch. "He was supposed to be here by now."

"Maybe he was held up by a breaking story," Brittan said and dropped the paper back on the table.

Her face glowing, Heather eyed Brittan. "Or maybe your dad's publisher finally called him from New York. You know he's on the verge of selling a novel to them."

"Yep." Brittan adjusted her glasses. "Dad told me last week that he was pushing through Duke's latest proposal. I haven't said anything because I didn't want to steal Duke's thunder. But I think this one will fly. Dad's really impressed with Duke's work at the *Star*... and with him in general."

"Aren't we all," Heather purred.

"Oh brother!" Lorna groused and rubbed her forehead. "Save us, will you?"

"That's okay. You'll fall in love one day," Heather predicted. "And when you do you'll be as starry-eyed as the rest of us."

"Speak for yourself!" Brittan exclaimed.

Heather pointed at Brittan and shifted her finger from side to side. "If you aren't careful, you'll fall harder than even Lorna does."

Michael Hayden suavely strolled through Lorna's mind again. She wondered if there were any way she could squirm out of the date she'd all but promised him. She reached for her cell phone and changed the ringer to silent.

Maybe I could just plead temporary insanity, she mused and wondered if it was really a case of *permanent attraction.* She placed her cell back into her bag.

But before she could resist, she imagined herself straightening his tie and pressing her lips against his cheek. On the brink of delicious chills, she went for her cell phone again and changed the ring back to loud.

No going back, she decided. *No more cold feet. If he calls, I'm in.*

"What's the deal with you and your cell?" Brittan questioned.

Lorna looked from Brittan to Heather. Both eyed her as if she were up to something sneaky...or at least something odd.

"Oh, I, uh, I was just, um, making sure the ringer was on."

"So you checked it three times?" Heather asked as she removed a scrunchy from her wrist and looped it around her hair. "Come on! Whazzup? Who's calling? Or who do you wish was calling?"

"Um…" Lorna didn't usually hide information from her friends. They'd been a threesome since they bonded on the tennis court at a blue-blood junior high school. But for some reason she didn't want to tell them about Michael. Not yet. After all, he was *the mayor.* The fewer people who knew right now, the better. If Heather leaked the information to her mother, Marilyn Winslow would take it straight to Lorna's mom. Then there'd be much ado about something…or maybe nothing…if she and Michael didn't hit it off.

"So if we're going to do this," she pointed toward the paper and swept aside her friends' queries, "where do we start?"

Brittan and Heather exchanged glances. Lorna dropped her cell back into her purse and reached for her Diet Coke.

"We were talking about infiltrating the church," Brittan explained while eyeing Lorna's purse. "You know, show up as attendees and see where that takes us."

"I guess somewhere in the mix we need to snoop around his office," Lorna mused. "All highways seem to lead to snooping— when it comes to us anyway."

"Don't you mean 'all *roads*'?" Heather's eyes sparkled; her lips quirked. "It's all *roads* lead to Rome, anyway."

Lorna waved her hand. "Whatever. You know what I mean. You get my drift. You comprende. Why be so picky?" She downed a swallow of pop.

"I'm sure by now the police have confiscated his computer and anything else they might use as evidence." Brittan stared into the air and never acknowledged the friends' playful exchange.

"Still, we might find something they overlooked," Lorna said.

"Right," Heather agreed before her attention drifted to Lorna's sequined bag. "I'm all for snooping."

When they'd worked the mayor's murder last year, the three

friends had posed as plant delivery people, marched into the mayor's house, and talked to his wife. Brittan had retrieved information from the man's computer while Heather and Lorna kept Mrs. Mayor and the housekeeper occupied. They could do something similar at the church.

Michael Hayden dug through a stack of keepsake *Sports Illustrated* magazines until he found the magic one...the copy with Lorna on the cover for the U.S. Open. She held her tennis racket like a warrior ready to do battle. Her intense gaze beckoned her challenger, "Come on, show me whatcha got!"

"Or is she saying, 'Eat my grits'?" he mumbled under his breath and then laughed out loud.

Michael stood and meandered from his magazine stash in the den's corner to the couch. He plopped down. His apartment was near the top of a high rise in downtown Houston, not far from City Hall where the previous mayor was gunned down.

"Here's hoping it doesn't become a tradition," Michael said and then dismissed the ridiculous notion. After the mayor's assassination, Michael had won the next election to become one of the youngest mayors in Houston history. He had no plans to get killed... or place himself in situations that would lead to such.

He focused anew on the *Sports Illustrated* dated four years ago. Lorna had been about 18 then. She'd seized the spotlight with her combination of feisty determination and spunky good looks. At the time Michael had been an assistant to the city manager, and, at 27, too embarrassed to admit he had a serious crush on Lorna Leigh. After all, she was barely out of high school, and he was a grown man. And one with a broken heart at that. Michael had blamed his pining for Lorna on his wounded heart's lack of discretion. Lorna had somehow become the epitome of the perfect woman for him, a woman who would be as determined to keep her word as she was to win on the court—unlike his former fiancée, who'd flouted their engagement and fallen in love with his best friend.

He thought of the piles of fan mail he'd received after that most eligible bachelor fiasco. Michael wondered if all those women were crazy enough to think he'd even *consider* responding to them. Most discreetly threw themselves at him. One mentioned she had a fiancé she'd drop if Michael were interested. *Like I'd respond to a woman who was unfaithful to the man she* did *have,* he reasoned. He shook his head and eyed the *Sports Illustrated.*

A long, low meow floated from the hallway before Michael's cat sashayed into the room. A former tom who'd been "relieved of his manhood," Socks had adopted Michael two years ago. Never a cat person, Michael had tried to shoo the annoying kitten from the parking garage, only to find him there the next morning, even more piteously hungry. Next thing Michael knew, he was in his apartment, serving the waif albacore tuna. Now Socks nearly refused to smell anything less than the best.

Michael scratched Socks' ears and placed the magazine on the coffee table. He checked the page notation for the story on Lorna and flipped to the full-page spread. Michael smiled. She looked better tonight than she had on the court...less intense...more approachable.

"No, angelic," he said and recalled how the garden shadows accented her understated beauty.

He rubbed his chin and wondered what had happened to make her forfeit the championship and walk away from tennis. He imagined several scenarios...none of them pleasant. Her expression had taken on a fragile, shattered quality when he'd asked about the past. Michael wanted to kick himself for opening his big mouth. Picking up the magazine, he slumped back into the couch's soft folds and skimmed the article he'd already read more than once. He checked his watch and glanced out the picture window. The

Houston skyline blazed with lights. He wanted to call Lorna now, but he didn't dare. Eleven o'clock was too late.

But maybe I could get away with a text message, he countered and eyed the collection of model airplanes claiming the floor-to-ceiling shelves near his big screen TV. *If she's up, she'll read it. If not, she'll see it first thing in the morning.*

He'd gotten home from the party 30 minutes ago. Michael had barely changed into his pj's when he remembered the *Sports Illustrated* story on the U.S. Open. He'd left his suit, cell phone, and shoes in a crumpled heap as he went in search of the magazine. Now he tucked the publication under his arm and hurried back into his bedroom to find his phone right where he'd left it—hooked to his belt, which was still in his pants. He tossed the magazine onto the bed, retrieved the pants from the floor, and wrestled the phone from its holster. He was halfway through the text message, asking Lorna for a date tomorrow night when he stopped and plopped to the side of the bed. He eyed the photo of Lorna and then the thin-line cell phone.

A thrill zipping through his gut urged him to send the message *now.* The voice of common sense reminded him how reluctant Lorna was to give him her number in the first place, and maybe he should at least wait until tomorrow night. Michael admitted he'd pushed hard to get her number. He normally moved a little slower and with a lot more class. But it was hard to have class when your dream woman materialized before your eyes in a beautiful garden.

"I did well not to babble." He chuckled, snapped the phone shut, and rubbed his thumb across the case.

So I'll wait until tomorrow night to call. Maybe set up a date for early next week. No pressure. No sense in scaring her off. Maybe we could meet somewhere outside Houston so no media spots us.

Michael nodded, scooped up the magazine, and plopped back onto the pillows. He held Lorna's photo close to his face and couldn't believe he was on the verge of a date with her. Finally, after all these years, Michael was thankful he was single. He'd never dreamed he'd ever consider calling that whole engagement upheaval God's will. But for the first time he wondered if it just might have been.

THREE

Brittan Shay pointed the Glock 30 at the target and pulled the trigger in rapid succession. Five bullets pelted the bullseye. The sixth and seventh strayed to the first and second rings just outside the center. Brittan grimaced as she lowered the gun. She hadn't practiced in a week, and her last few rounds revealed the lack of polish. Hopefully she wouldn't need to use the weapon she was licensed to carry concealed, but she didn't want to take any chances.

Her cell phone vibrated against her shorts pocket. Brittan sneezed. The smell of gunfire always reaped at least one sneeze. She rubbed her nose, set her Glock on the bench, and reached for her phone. Caller ID indicated Heather Winslow.

Brittan flipped open the phone and said, "Hey, girl."

"Hey yourself!" Heather replied. "Whatcha doing?"

"I'm polishing up my shooting." Brittan settled onto the wooden bench inside her family's pistol range. "I haven't practiced in a week, and I can tell." She picked up the pistol and aimed it at a knot in the wood across the range.

"I've been training at the dojo—going through my katas—getting ready for our church trip tomorrow."

The friends laughed.

"Have you heard anything from Miz Cell Phone today?" Brittan cradled the phone between her shoulder and ear, picked up a soft cloth lying on the bench, and polished the petite gun's barrel.

"Not a peep," Heather replied. "She's probably too busy turning her cell phone ringer on and off to call us."

Brittan laughed. "What was the *deal* with all that?"

"It's a man. Gotta be."

"You think so?"

Heather snorted. "Did you see the way she looked at us? She had 'man' written all over her. Whoever he is, he must be a doozy."

"Well, she *was* at the party for the mayor." Brittan squinted at the target and then shifted her gaze to the pillared mansion in the distance. "I'm sure there were plenty of men there."

Heather gasped. "You don't think—"

"No, I don't. I never do actually." Brittan laid aside the gun.

"Ha, ha," Heather responded. "She was at the *mayor's* party," she stressed.

"And the mayor *is* single," Brittan replied. She leaned against the wall and welcomed the cool breeze that wafted through the pistol range. "And not hard on the eyes...and on Houston's most eligible bachelor list last year."

"Hmmm. It would make sense she wouldn't mention him. He's pretty high profile right now. Given the way she thinks, she's probably not going to mention him unless something comes of it."

"You're probably right," Brittan agreed.

"You know her parents are pressuring her to marry that IBM heir?"

"Yes. But I think Lorna would rather drink arsenic-laced ink."

Heather laughed again.

A mockingbird fussed in the distance, and Brittan spotted him dive-bombing a squirrel beneath an oak.

"Can you even *imagine* them together?" Heather asked. "He's about six feet shorter than she is and acts like he thinks he's that singer...what's his name...ah, Prince. Forget 'Purple Rain,' that IBM guy's a purple pain!"

Brittan snickered. "Yep, and the only thing that matches with those two are their fortunes."

"Did you hear her on the phone last night at all?" Heather asked.

"No. I never even heard her cell ring. So unless she had it on vibrate and I missed it, I don't think she talked to anyone. She was still in bed this morning when I left."

"Keep me posted, okay? I'm, like, *dying* to know what's going on."

"I'm sure she'll get around to telling us soon."

"She'd better. This secretive thing breaks all the rules. What are you wearing to church tomorrow?" Heather asked without taking a breath.

"Clothes," Brittan drawled and glanced down at her shorts and T-shirt.

"Oh really? I thought maybe you were going to wear curtains."

"Not this time. Curtains are getting old," she said through a smile. "Actually, I'm going with something really low-key and nondescript. Maybe that new Chanel pantsuit I got last week at Neiman's."

"Yes, you look good in that, and it's not too flashy. I'll do something similar and keep it loose in case I have to..."

"Kick somebody's teeth out?" Brittan interrupted.

"Well, we *are* going to be snooping, and you just never know."

"Now that's a fine attitude to have the first Sunday you visit a church," Brittan stated. "Hello, my name is Heather, and if I don't like your sermon, I'll whack your nose off."

"Well, that's better than shooting them! You'll have your gun, I'm sure."

"Yes. I've learned you never know what we'll get into. Better safe than sorry."

※ ※ ※

Lorna slammed the final match serve into her opponent's court. He lunged for the ball but missed. "Yes!" she said and lifted her racket into the air.

The puffing 20-year-old struggled to regain his breath and then approached the net the same time Lorna did. With a wry smile he extended his hand. A droplet of sweat trickling from her temple, Lorna shook his hand. She made it a point to regularly play Sergio Juarez because Sergio was a semi-pro on the verge of making the pros. As long as she could occasionally beat him, Lorna knew she wasn't losing her edge.

"You've still got the meanest serve in the south," he said.

"And you're not so bad yourself," Lorna encouraged. "What's the latest on the tour?"

"I try out again next month. Wish me luck."

"Luck." Lorna gave him the thumbs-up and strode toward her duffel bag sitting at courtside.

She caught a glimpse of Sergio and realized the younger man had followed her. Lorna offered a vague smile and reached inside her duffel for the towel that would soak up some of her Texan sweat.

"Want to join me for lunch?" he asked, his voice a bit hesitant. "It's the least you can do after beating me." His smile revealed white teeth against a "genetic tan" that the sun had darkened. His shirt and shorts were every bit as white as Lorna's tennis gear and nicely contrasted his dashing darkness.

On the verge of laughing him off, Lorna realized the Puerto Rican's black eyes were full of an expectation she'd never noticed. *Yikes! How long has* this *been going on?* In her mind they'd been nothing more than country club pals who took turns smearing each other into the tennis court. She'd never imagined anything more than a light, slightly competitive friendship.

And that's all it's ever going to be, she decided. Sergio was four years younger than she. If Lorna ever did get interested in a man, he would be someone more mature, someone who'd already secured a solid career, someone more like...Michael Hayden.

Lorna patted her face with the towel and then dropped it back into the duffel bag. Before she got on the court, Michael still hadn't called. She picked up her duffel, pulled her cell phone from the bottom, and noted there still had been no calls.

"Thanks for the invitation, Sergio," she said, "but it's probably best for us to keep our friendship on the tennis court."

His eyes clouded. "Well, okay. But if you ever change your mind..."

Lorna kindly smiled. "I'm an old woman compared to you. I'm sure there are scores of sweet young things who'd *faint* if you'd only ask them." She threw in a friendly wink and strode toward the court's exit.

Michael Hayden sat in the country club's coffee shop and peered toward the tennis courts. He'd not thought of "accidentally" running into Lorna at the country club until this morning when he was putting the final polish on the wings of his Cessna Skyhawk. He'd recalled her father owning The Pines, one of the finest country clubs in Houston. By the time he pulled the plane back into the hangar, Michael remembered a meeting with Lorna's father late in his campaign. Oliver Leigh had announced that morning he was endorsing Michael's candidacy, and he'd also given Michael a complimentary lifetime membership to The Pines. Michael's mind mulled over a blurry memory of seeing a brunette on the tennis court that day and thinking she favored Lorna Leigh. It had been a Saturday morning. He hadn't connected the dots until last night.

This morning Michael decided to take his chances, hang out at the country club, and see what he could see. And what he saw in the distance made him smile—except she'd been playing some guy who was tanned beyond belief and a bit trimmer in the middle than Michael. He sucked in his gut. Even from 50 yards away the man looked like he was interested in way more than tennis. Michael wrapped his finger through the coffee mug's handle and squeezed. Last night she said there was no one special in her life.

But that was last night, he thought. *Lots can happen in 14 hours.* He pushed aside the untouched apple turnover, signed his bill, stood, and decided to up his speed from slow and cautious to just cautious. Michael walked through the occupied tables, casting a few greetings as he went, but dodging those who might engage him in conversation. The parking lot was near the gym where the lockers were. He figured Lorna was heading there.

By the time he stepped into the June sunshine, Michael knew his assumptions were correct. Lorna was heading straight for the gym. Her nice, long strides indicated her height...and her grace. Michael trotted forward and calculated her distance from the parking lot. If he hurried, he'd reach his Mercedes about the time she passed it.

He intermittently focused on Lorna as he maneuvered through vehicles until he arrived at his car. After digging his remote out of his pocket, Michael pressed the button that unlocked the vehicle. It chirped.

Lorna looked his way just as he "casually" glanced toward her. Her eyes widened. She slowed.

Forcing his breath to an even rhythm, Michael put all he had into a "surprised" smile and said, "Well, hello there! Imagine meeting you here."

FOUR

Lorna stopped and limited her gape to three seconds, although her mouth wanted to hang open for a good 10. She'd been vaguely aware of a man rushing across the parking lot, but she'd been so distracted over the Sergio business she hadn't realized it was Michael. Considering the way he'd hustled toward his car, Lorna assumed the guy must be in a hurry. She'd have continued walking toward the gym except Michael rounded the front of his Mercedes and approached her.

She fretted with her ponytail and wished she'd taken the time to put on at least a scrap of makeup this morning. *I must look as limp as a dust rag,* she thought. *Or is that a dishrag? Oh, who cares!* Michael now stood in front of her, and Lorna didn't have *time* to care about a word choice. *Malaprops are me,* she mused.

"I was planning to call you this evening," he said and eyed her like she was his personal pot of gold.

"Oh really?" She tried to force her breathing into a normal pattern, but her lungs rebelled. She settled into a shallow pant.

"I was going to see if you'd like to have dinner one day next week."

The sunlight revealed what last night's shadows had hinted at. His eyes were chocolate brown…a rich, delicious chocolate that would make a woman's mouth water. Hers was.

"Next week?" she repeated and reminded herself that just last night she'd tried to shake him off like she'd done with Sergio. But a lot could happen in that time. She'd been checking her phone nearly every hour on the hour since she'd gotten up this morning.

"Yes, but…" He hesitated and glanced toward the country club's main entrance.

Lorna was hard pressed not to lean forward and say, "But?" *Maybe I'm more ready for a relationship than I realized,* she thought and added, *a* healthy *relationship.* The mayor was certainly promising. A few days might determine just *how* promising.

"I think they've still got the brunch buffet on. At least it smells like it anyway. Are you hungry by chance?"

Lorna glanced toward his vehicle and then back to him. He wore a sports shirt, pleated shorts, a pair of sneakers, and looked every bit as good as he had last night in "his mayorship" uniform. "Are you sure you have time?"

He waved away the worry. "Oh yes. Everything can wait." Michael pointed his remote at the vehicle and pressed a button.

A thrill zipped through Lorna in sequence with the automatic lock chirping.

"Well, if you don't mind then, I'll head on to the gym, shower, and change." She shifted her duffel bag to her other hand, pulled her T-shirt away from her damp torso, and didn't think she could fake looking cool. "I've been sweating like a cow—I mean sow," she corrected.

Michael's laugh was as melodious as a brook that gurgled through the woods and nourished the earth. Lorna recognized the traces of loneliness nibbling at the corners of his mouth; in his eyes she saw a hint of past pain. She wondered if his story was as heartbreaking as hers. *Maybe I'll find out before too much longer.*

"So do you want to meet in the restaurant?" He jutted his thumb toward the two-story brick building that featured an upscale restaurant, meeting rooms, a lounge, a coffee shop, and a few hotel suites.

"Yes. Will you give me 30 minutes or so?"

"Sure." Michael beamed.

※ ※ ※

Brunch was delightful—so delightful Michael didn't want the encounter to end. He suggested they play a round of golf. Even though Lorna protested she was no good, she was now close to beating Michael—just like he figured she'd beaten that guy on the tennis court.

The deciding factor in who won the game was Lorna's final putt. The odds were as long as the ball was from the hole. The ball lay on the edge of the green, and Michael calculated it to be a good 13 feet from the cup. Plus there was a slight rise between the ball and target.

Michael stood by, holding the flag. He watched Lorna's face. She was as intense as she was on the cover of his *Sports Illustrated* magazine. He recalled his mother once telling his sisters they should *never* beat a boyfriend in anything—even if they were leagues better—due to some kind of unspoken female code Michael wasn't sure he understood. Whatever it was, he didn't think Lorna played by that code *at all*. While they were having loads of fun together, the woman played to win.

And I like that, Michael noted with a smile. So far he liked everything about Lorna Leigh, right down to her carefree ponytail, her girl-next-door freckles, and the sporty scent she wore. Whatever it was, the fragrance made Michael want to move closer...close enough for a kiss.

Lorna hit the ball. Michael leaned forward and held his breath.

He wasn't sure he enjoyed being beaten any more than Lorna would, but he still wanted the ball in the cup. It rolled over the swell in the green, and her calculated angle sent it straight to the hole. The ball plopped in as if it were steel and there was a magnet at the bottom of the cup.

She lifted her hands and shouted, "Yes!"

Michael dashed to Lorna. Raising his hand, the two shared a high-five. "That was a *killer* shot!" he exclaimed.

"Can you believe it?" she replied.

"I thought you said you weren't any good!" he accused and gently punched her upper arm.

"Are you kidding?" Lorna shifted her club to her left hand and started walking toward the cup. "That's the best game I've played. You must be a good luck charm."

As Lorna grabbed her ball and Michael replaced the flag, he hummed a few bars of an old Elvis tune. He began singing, "Come on and be my little good luck charm…" He spontaneously grabbed Lorna around the waist and twirled her toward the golf cart. She expertly followed his lead until they paused for a final spin near the passenger side.

Lorna plopped into her seat. Laughter lightened her green eyes, accentuated her dimples, and for the first time Michael couldn't recall the name of the woman who'd dumped him. What a blessed state of amnesia that was!

"So what other Elvis tunes do you know?" she asked.

"Not many. My dad is a Beach Boys nut actually," he said.

"My mom *loved* the Beach Boys," Lorna exclaimed. "She used to play all their albums on the weekend. Do you know 'Barbara Ann'?"

The two spontaneously began the classic tune while he walked to the driver's side. They sang in unison like two long-time friends relishing fond memories. Michael sat down, released the brake, and steered the vehicle toward the bridge that led back to the clubhouse.

When they both faltered over a few words, he glanced toward Lorna and they laughed some more...until Lorna squealed and Michael jerked his attention back to the path. A tree was straight ahead! He jerked the steering wheel but not quickly enough to miss the object. The cart slammed into the tree.

Lorna hollered again as she was tossed to the earth. Michael's grip on the steering wheel was all that stopped him from a similar fate. He turned off the ignition and zoomed to Lorna's side.

She lifted her head and sang, "You've got me rockin' and a rollin'!" Then she collapsed back and giggled hysterically.

"You're *crazy!*" Michael exclaimed and extended a hand to help her up. But when she placed her hand in his, she gave a hard yank that brought him tumbling to the warm grass beside her.

"Hey you!" Michael wailed. "That's not very neighborly."

"That's what you get for being such a *bad* driver." She wrinkled her nose.

"Well, that's what happens to women who beat me at golf," he responded. "I take them out on the fairway and dump 'em."

"Isn't that illegal?" Lorna sat up and pulled her knees up, resting an arm atop one. "And, like, how are you going to do the mayor thing from jail?"

"Like, how are you going to do the mayor thing from jail?" Michael mimicked and made a sour face. He couldn't believe how quickly the two of them hit it off, how relaxed the afternoon had been, and how much he needed everything that had happened exactly the way it happened. After being in the spotlight for so many weeks and having to stay "on" professionally, he was due an afternoon of relaxed fun...and who better to relax with than Lorna Leigh!

Wow! What a woman! He gazed at her in awe. She was more than he'd ever imagined. *More* than his dream woman.

Lorna's cheeks grew a delicious shade of pink, and she studied a blade of grass she was twisting.

Okay, Michael thought, *I guess I was a little too obvious.* He'd thrown "slow" away at the coffee shop and just stomped "cautious" into the ground. Michael gazed around the tree-lined course, searching for any signs of an audience. A group of players was one hole ahead and another was merging toward the tee behind them. As much as Michael wanted to press his luck and move a little closer, he decided to save something for their second date.

"Are you two okay?" a concerned voice floated from down the course. Michael's attention snapped to a cart zooming straight toward them. The gray-haired man driving looked too much like Lorna's father not to be him.

Michael was gripped by unexpected intimidation...like he was 17 and picking up a girl for the prom while her dad sat on the front porch with a shotgun. He shook himself. He *was* the mayor and Oliver was one of his biggest fans.

Lorna gasped and then gaped toward the cart. "Oh no! That's my dad! What's *he* doing here?"

"Maybe he owns the place or something?" Michael replied and smiled toward Lorna's dad. "We're fine!" He waved.

Lorna hopped up, brushing off her capris like a first grader caught playing in the mud in her best Sunday dress. "What am I going to do?" she fretted. "He wants me to marry IBM, and here I am with *you.*"

Michael stood and looked her eye-to-eye. "IBM?" he asked under his breath. "Is that the guy you were talking to on the tennis court?"

"No. That's Sergio Juarez. Tennis semi-pro," she explained and then blinked. "You saw me on the tennis court?"

Michael hid a wince and said, "Wow! Would you look at that nice blue sky?"

"Lorna!" Oliver exclaimed as he stopped his cart within feet of theirs. "I had no idea! Are you okay?"

"Yes, just fine, Dad." Lorna lifted both arms, ran in place, and said, "See? Good as new."

Oliver leveled a glare toward Michael. "Hayden, what in the devil are *you* doing here?" He stepped out of the driver's seat, hurried forward, and pumped Michael's hand. In his khaki shorts and matching shirt, he looked more like a wildlife expert than a business tycoon.

"We were just enjoying a round of golf." He released Oliver's hand and motioned toward Lorna.

"Michael and I met each other last night at the party and just happened…" she dubiously eyed Michael, "to run into each other a while ago. So we did brunch and decided to do a round of golf too."

"Oh." Oliver shifted his gaze from his daughter to his mayor. Then he swung around and looked at the golf cart and tree. "I hope you're better at driving a car than you are at driving a golf cart," he groused as he turned back with a mischievous glint in his eyes.

"I guess I *did* get a little carried away," Michael admitted and slipped his hands into his pockets. "I haven't been able to relax in weeks, and Lorna helped me unwind. Maybe I was closer to unraveling than I realized," he added.

Lorna giggled.

Oliver's bushy brows flexed. He shot his daughter an "Is there something you failed to tell me" look and finally focused on Michael. "If you weren't the most gifted young man I've ever met, I'd have you for dinner," he grumbled through a begrudging smile.

"Thanks…I think," Michael replied and crossed his arms.

"Like I told you, I have high hopes of you landing in the White House," Oliver continued and eyed his daughter anew before addressing Michael once more. "If I *did* eat you for dinner, it would be the same as eating the president." His lower lip protruding, Oliver shook his head. "Not good," he murmured.

Lorna snickered.

Michael joined in and sensed a wealth of silent communication erupting between father and daughter. Even though he wasn't IBM, Michael had a hunch that particular "sin" just might be pardonable.

FIVE

Brittan sat in the church parking lot and gaped at the Sunday morning paper. The lead story in the Lifestyle section featured a photo of Lorna at a restaurant with Michael Hayden. The two sat at a table and smiled into each other's eyes over their coffees. The headline read, "Houston mayor spotted with former tennis pro." Brittan identified the restaurant as The Pines Country Club where Lorna spent many Saturday mornings playing tennis.

She propped the paper against the steering wheel, reached for her cappuccino, and sipped the sweet liquid while skimming the article—nothing more than a bunch of speculations mingled with the recounting of the city's fascination with the mayor's love life.

"So this is what you were up to most of yesterday," Brittan mumbled and shook her head. *Lorna will not be happy when she sees this!* she added to herself.

Her cell phone's "Shout to the Lord" ring interrupted Brittan's musings.

She set aside her coffee and fished the phone from her bag's side pocket. Brittan had barely placed the phone to her ear when Heather asked, "Have you seen it?"

"Yes! I'm sitting here at the church reading it right now." Heather had called an hour ago and told Brittan about the paper, so she'd grabbed her unread copy on the way out of the penthouse she shared with Lorna.

Brittan glanced toward the large church. The front was wall-to-wall panels of glass. A white steeple jutted toward the clouds. The landscaping took art to a new level. Last night the three friends agreed to arrive at the church around ten-thirty. They planned to pose as separate visitors in order to snoop different areas of the church.

This morning when Brittan got up Lorna was already gone. No note or anything. She hadn't answered her cell phone either. Now Brittan figured her friend must've met the mayor for breakfast somewhere. She narrowed her eyes, examined the photo, and wondered if Lorna was enjoying the secrecy as much as the tryst.

"Hello? Are you still there?" Heather asked.

"Yes, still here," Brittan replied. "Just thinking. Lorna was gone this morning when I got up and never told me she was going anywhere. It's not like her."

"Like I said yesterday, I think she wants to make sure the relationship is a go before she tells us. She's been through a lot with men, and maybe she's gun-shy."

"I'm sure you're right." Brittan closed the paper.

A flash of sunshine on chrome caught Brittan's attention, and she noted a black Honda zooming into the parking lot. The vehicle had barely stopped before Lorna emerged, slammed the door, and walked toward the church entry. The three friends had agreed to rent vehicles to come to church…just in case something happened and someone felt "inspired" to jot down license plate numbers. This way they were covered.

"Hello?" Heather prompted. "Did I lose you?"

"Nope. I'm still with you. Lorna just drove up, and it distracted me," Brittan replied and dropped the paper into the Town Car's passenger seat. "Where are you anyway?"

"Five minutes out," Heather replied.

As usual Brittan had been early, Lorna was exactly on time, and Heather was five minutes late.

"I guess it's time for the fun to begin. We'll talk to Lorna after church about what she's been hiding, okay?"

"Works for me," Heather agreed and disconnected the call.

Brittan looked down at her black Chanel pantsuit and then examined what Lorna wore. Her friend was dressed in a casual cotton skirt, a T-shirt, and a pair of spike sandals. While the outfit looked as understated as all get out, Brittan had been with her when Lorna had paid the earth for it. She wore a straight, blonde wig and no makeup—perfect for covering her identity and giving her a care-free, college girl look. Because Lorna kept such a low profile, she was rarely recognized these days unless someone was a diehard tennis fan. Considering this morning's paper, Brittan was thankful her friend had opted for the wig. The *last* thing they needed was for half the church to recognize Lorna.

She reached to her slacks waistband and patted the Glock 30 safely concealed in a holster that rested next to her body. The black gun measured just over 6½ inches, but it packed a mean punch and fit Brittan's grip perfectly. Brittan felt far safer with it than without it.

"Let's go," she whispered and opened her car door.

Lorna strode into the church's cool foyer with Michael on the brain. After spending yesterday afternoon together, they'd met for breakfast this morning. As much as Lorna wanted to keep telling herself to take it slowly, anyone with one eye and half a brain could see that Michael was *not* taking it slowly. Even though she'd only met him, he'd known of her for years. Frankly Lorna was beginning to think his interest in her had been much more than that of a casual fan.

She didn't see the photo in the paper until Michael showed it to her and profusely apologized. She hadn't made a big deal out of it outwardly, but inwardly she'd been on the verge of yanking out her hair and then the hair of the person who'd stolen the shot. Lorna and Michael both speculated that someone must've used a camera phone and then run with it to the *Houston Star*. The whole ordeal made her cut short their breakfast date, race home, don a wig, and remove her makeup. The last thing "the Rose" needed was to have someone recognize her.

"Good morning," a female voice floated in from some distant land, and Lorna snapped her brain to the task at hand. "Welcome to Houston Heights Community Church."

"Thanks." Lorna focused on a slender woman whose hair was as blonde as her wig. She smiled, accepted the church bulletin, and scanned the foyer. Summer sunshine blasted through the front glass and cloaked the wooden cross on the west wall in a golden veil. Large vases of flowers dominated the corners. The smells of new carpet and fresh hymnals suggested all was well financially with this congregation. The look of hollow distress in the eyes of passersby hinted that at least some of the members were as shocked by their pastor's arrest as was the rest of Houston.

Hopefully, "the Rose" will help right that, Lorna thought and noticed Brittan entering from the other side of the foyer. Her friend was wearing a black pantsuit that looked as no-nonsense as the woman. Fleetingly Lorna wondered if Brittan had ever worn frills. Lorna could imagine a five-year-old Brittan looking her mother in the eyes and saying, "Frills are not logical, Mommy."

Lorna caught Brittan's eye and then gazed toward the sanctuary. The greeter was thankfully busy with others and didn't notice the two friends make eye contact. Lorna glided into the massive sanctuary just as a small orchestra began the preliminary music—a lively rendition of "Open the Eyes of My Heart, Lord." Lorna found an isolated seat and settled into one of the padded chairs connected in neat rows. She watched as Brittan found a spot near the back doorway. Heather came in two seconds after the minister of music invited the congregation of around 2,000 to stand and sing. She stepped into the very back row, across the aisle from Lorna.

Halfway through the second song Lorna picked up her purse, slipped out of the sanctuary, and went toward the hallway marked "Church Staff," just as the debutantes had planned last night. Her job was to prowl through the pastor's office. Heather had agreed to snoop in the secretary's office. And Brittan was set to start in the first associate pastor's office. They'd be back to the church as many times as it took to glean as much information as needed—whether through penetrating the offices, casual conversations, or eavesdropping.

Lorna paced down the hallway and glanced over her shoulder before passing a doorway marked "Trent Devenport, Senior Pastor." She continued walking to the emergency exit at the end of the hallway. She loitered a bit, turned around, and reapproached the office door. After glancing toward the foyer, she pulled a linen cloth from her skirt pocket, wrapped it around the knob, and turned. The door didn't budge.

"Man!" Lorna whispered. Simply walking into the pastor's study had been a long shot. Lorna weighed her options. She meandered back down the hallway and scratched the base of her skull beneath the wig's band.

Okay, now what? On a whim Lorna wrapped the linen cloth around the first doorknob she came to and twisted. It opened. Lorna glanced up the hallway again. As she entered the office she read the name plaque: "Sonja Greenfield, Office Manager." Lorna stepped into the dark room, allowed her eyes to adjust to the shadows, and locked the door. The faint smell of gingerbread reminded her of her old nanny's Christmas cookies.

The pale sunlight squeezing through the blinds illuminated the area just enough to reveal a room that looked like it belonged in a magazine ad for office furniture. A large candle sitting on the side of the desk gave off the yummy smell. Lorna stepped toward it, wrapped the linen cloth around it, and held tight. Warmth testified to someone recently blowing it out.

Probably right before the service started, Lorna deduced and relaxed a bit. If Sonja Greenfield were attending the service, she'd be gone an hour or so...if she came back at all. A woman on a mission, Lorna slipped her petite bag's shoulder strap over her head and allowed it to rest beneath her arm on her hip.

She gazed at shelves behind the desk, each laden with neat rows of books and knickknacks. Whoever Sonja was, the woman ran a tight ship. Lorna stuffed the linen cloth into her purse's side pocket, unzipped the center compartment, pulled out a pair of latex gloves, and slipped them on.

When you can't be with the one you love, investigate the one you're with, she thought and squinted. Lorna figured that one would have Heather laughing in her face. But no matter how much she tried, Lorna couldn't conjure the right turn of phrase. *Whatever!* she thought. *I'm in! Let the clichés fall where they may.*

She scanned the room and debated where best to start. A doorway grabbed her attention. Lorna glanced toward the file cabinet near the window, gazed toward the doorway, and decided to go ahead and try it first.

Probably just a storage room, she thought and hurried to the task. But when she opened the door, she discovered a private restroom. *Get outta here!* she thought, and the investigator inside insisted she snoop a bit more. Lorna closed the door behind her, fumbled to lock it, and snapped on the light. She squinted, took in the white walls, the row of mirrors, the automatic towel dispenser, and other bathroom necessities. A door opposite the one she entered proved too tempting to resist. Lorna turned the handle and, once again, it wouldn't budge.

"Wait a minute," she whispered and calculated the distance from the pastor's office. Her eyes widened. This bathroom was shared by the two offices. While she couldn't stand out in the hallway and pick at the lock to the pastor's study, nothing would stop her in here.

"Only problem is, genius, you don't know how to pick a lock," she muttered. Lorna dropped to her knees and examined the doorknob. After ten seconds of contemplating her options, she realized all she had to do was turn the lock. The door was locked from *inside* the restroom. "How ditzy is that?" she muttered and chuckled under her breath. This was *one* revelation Lorna had no plans of sharing with Heather or Brittan.

She stood and opened the door. Just as she'd speculated, the pastor's study was on the other side. Shutting the door, she noted that the knob locked from this side too. She locked it, faced the spacious office, and thrust her fist into the air. "Yes!" she whispered.

Even with the lights off, the office appeared disheveled in the weak light leaking past the curtains. The computer was missing. Files and papers hung out of cabinets. More paper littered the top of the desk. A closet door stood ajar. A jacket lay on the floor. The investigators had left nothing unturned.

Lorna reached inside her purse and pulled a mini flashlight from an inside pocket. She approached the desk and flicked the tiny beam across the pile of papers. Logic insisted the investigators would have removed anything of use. Nevertheless she leafed through the mess. She found old receipts, business correspondence, and a few grocery lists. She settled into the padded chair and pulled out the center drawer. It held all the usual office odds and ends...pens, tape, thumbtacks, a stapler, pencils, erasers, Wite-Out, and a calculator. Nothing incriminating and certainly nothing to exonerate him.

Lorna closed the drawer and sighed. She scanned the desktop once more and spotted a photo in the right corner. Picking up the frame, she pointed the flashlight at the picture. It was a snapshot of Trent Devenport with an attractive brunette and two blond-haired twin toddlers. The contentment in the couple's eyes suggested there could be no greater happiness. Lorna sighed as her heart went out to the man and his wife. If he really were innocent, this was a horrific slam that he might never recover from. Even if he were found innocent, there were still those who'd always view him as guilty. Some churches wouldn't want a pastor who had any hint of child porn attached to his name—no matter how innocent he was. If Brittan and Heather's theories were valid, and Lorna believed they were, this successful pastor might be forced to resign and drop from ministry.

Whoever set him up must hate him, Lorna thought. *And if we find out the pastor's guilty, he's the most innocent-looking child porn dealer I've ever seen.*

She set the photo back on the desk corner and glanced across the room. The closet tugged her attention just as strongly as had the door to the bathroom. Lorna followed her gut and approached the closet. Her high heels slapped against her feet and punctured the silence with staccato rhythm. She paused in front of the open closet and flicked her light across the contents.

Several jackets and a couple of changes of clothing hung in their places. A row of shelves held disheveled boxes, lids off, photos and papers askew. A pair of running shoes sat in the bottom. At closer vantage Lorna realized the coat on the floor was an old leather letterman jacket. She gingerly picked it up and pointed the beam at a red-and-blue monogram that read SMU.

"Hmmm," Lorna said. That was the second time she'd encountered Southern Methodist University today. Michael told her over breakfast he'd attended the highly esteemed school, got his degree in political science in 3 years, then took 18 months to do his master's degree. He'd been in city management and politics ever since, while playing to win in the stock market. Forcing herself to focus on the task at hand, Lorna checked the jacket's pockets. She found nothing. After setting her flashlight on one of the closet shelves, she ran her hand along the inside lining "just in case." The "just in case" paid off. She discovered a hidden pocket along the lining and inside was an old letter. She put the jacket back where she'd found it and reached for her flashlight.

Her fingers had barely wrapped around the light when the hallway doorknob rattled. Lorna stared at the door. She turned off the flashlight. Someone jiggled the knob again...then again. Lorna held her breath, glanced from the closet to the desk to the drapes. The knob turned. The door eased inward. Lorna lurched into the back of the closet and realized in her haste she hadn't shut the door.

SIX

Trent Devenport paced the jail cell and cried out to God with every step. He should've been in the pulpit this morning preaching the Good News. Instead he'd spent the last 48 hours in jail, waiting on his poor wife to somehow pull together the cash needed to get a $15,000 bond that would buy his freedom until his trial. And the way things looked, "trial" was just a politically correct word for "shortcut to prison."

He paused beneath the window, looked to the blue sky, and wondered if Paul and Silas had felt this hopeless during their imprisonment. Trent slumped onto his cot, rested his elbows on his knees, and cradled his head in his hands. He'd been so shocked when the investigators arrived at his office door that he hadn't even seen the handcuffs coming. When he'd protested they must have the wrong man, the officers promptly showed him on his own computer just how sure they were. How all those obscene websites got into in his computer's history was still enough to make Trent's mind go numb for years. He'd always avoided pornography and had kept his marriage pure.

But child porn? How twisted is that! he thought. Trent had two four-year-olds. He'd never entertained the idea of violating boys...

or girls…or anyone else. Thoughts of delving into such perversion made him nauseous.

"Oh God, help me," he groaned. "How did this happen? Lord, you know I'm innocent. Please, please, please…"

Heavy footfalls accompanied by the rattling of keys prompted Trent to lift his head. "Your wife's here for a visit," a dark-skinned officer explained. While the other officers had been sarcastic, rude, and even disgusted with him, Officer Laurette had gazed upon Trent with initial speculation and finally with compassion. He'd given Trent a Bible yesterday without the pastor asking for one. This morning Laurette mentioned he was praying for Trent. Trent knew the officer sensed his innocence but couldn't do anything about it.

The pastor stepped through the opened door and walked past the other incarcerated inmates toward the visitation area. One hairy ogre shouted "Pervert!" as Trent walked past. He'd heard nasty stories about what prisoners did to child molesters and child porn aficionados. This was merely jail, and already word had circulated that Trent was the worst of the worst. He'd barely slept the last two nights because of nightmares of waking up and finding himself surrounded by inmates with pain on their brains.

He kept his head lowered and his focus on the rubber-soled shoes they'd "lent" him to wear. The shoes were every bit as attractive as the dingy white suit he'd been forced to put on.

All he could do was pray Katie hadn't taken the same attitude. In his one phone call to her Friday, Trent heard nothing but shock and pain in her voice. But now he was going to see her face-to-face. If his wife of six years showed any signs of doubting him, Trent knew he'd sink into a pit that would swallow him whole.

Finally he came to a gray room with a glass partition. Katie sat on the other side, her head lowered.

"You've got fifteen minutes," Laurette said.

When he shut the door, Trent winced and waited for what he would find in her expression.

Katie's head snapped up.

All Trent saw in her big, brown eyes was love, anguish, and unfailing trust. She had on the blue suit he'd bought for her, and she was wearing her hair loose and wavy, the way he liked best. He would also wager she wore some of that pomegranate body spray that always made him want to step closer. Everything about his Katie said she believed in him—irrevocably and unconditionally.

Trent collapsed into a chair and placed his flattened hand against the glass. Katie pressed her palm exactly where his rested. Sobs welled up in Trent as a "How in the world did we get here?" echoed from soul to soul. He swallowed the sobs and tried to be strong for Katie, who had tears streaming down her cheeks. Despite his best effort, Trent couldn't stop tears from stinging his eyes.

Lorna bumped into the corner and listened. Someone slipped inside the office. The door faintly snapped shut. Drowning in the musty-smelling darkness, Lorna fought the urge to run toward the pale light that squeezed through the curtains and created a gray puddle on the closet floor. Her logical side squelched the primal instincts.

I've got to stay put, she told herself. *Don't even breathe too heavily.* She pressed her back against the corner and prayed that whoever was walking around the room would go away. A flashlight beam snaked just inside the closet and then vanished. The sound of light footsteps neared. The beam reappeared.

Lorna's eyes bugged. She held her breath. She clenched her fist and wadded the letter she'd found in the jacket. The faint crinkle of paper sounded like a crashing boulder in the stillness. Lorna tried not to gasp but couldn't stifle it. A form stepped into the closet and thrust the beam into Lorna's face. Feeling like a prisoner of war caught escaping, Lorna opened her mouth and let out a pathetic yelp.

"Lorna?" Heather's voice floated past the terror as the flashlight beam met the floor.

"Heather?" Lorna croaked and recognized her blonde friend now that the light was out of her eyes.

"What are you doing here?" the two whispered in unison.

"I was supposed to investigate the pastor's study," Lorna stepped from her corner.

"No, I was," Heather quietly insisted and switched off her light. "Remember? We decided last night. You were supposed to go for the secretary's office."

"I thought you were secretary and I was pastor," Lorna whispered. Her voice as unsteady as her knees, Lorna leaned against the doorjamb.

Heather sighed and shook her head. "I knew you were distracted last night." She wore a pair of black-rimmed glasses, and her hair was in a bun. On top of that, she had on some sort of a trench coat dress that made her look about as interesting as mold. But the garment had so many pockets Lorna doubted Heather had bothered with a handbag.

"I guess I was a little distracted," Lorna admitted and then added, "You look great by the way."

"So do you. Brittan came looking a lot like herself. But I enjoy disguises. Don't you?"

"Well, I hadn't *planned* on the costume route," Lorna said, "but after my picture came out in the paper..."

"The one with you and Michael Hayden?" Heather teased. She crossed her arms while still gripping the flashlight. "And, like, maybe *he* was the reason you were off a bit last night?"

"Yep," Lorna admitted.

"Is there something you'd like to share with the class?" Heather asked.

"I officially met him Friday night," Lorna explained. "Yesterday we had brunch and played golf. This morning we met for breakfast. I was going to tell you guys soon. I didn't want to make a big deal out of it until I knew for sure."

"That's what I told Brittan." Heather nodded.

Lorna glanced toward the door. "How'd you get in here? The door was locked."

Heather pulled a small case from her pocket, flipped it open, turned on the flashlight, and illuminated a collection of needle-like tools ensconced in leather. "These are Duke's. His uncle was a locksmith. He taught Duke how to pick locks a long time ago, and Duke taught me." She shrugged. "I came armed today just in case." She pointed the light toward the doorknob. "That lock is a lot like the one on my suite at home, so I was able to get inside before anyone saw me."

"Get outta here!" Lorna breathed and reached for the tools. "You need to teach me how...and Brittan too."

"I will," Heather agreed. "But I just got the hang of it a few days ago. I've been practicing for awhile now. How'd you get in here?"

"The office manager's door was unlocked. There's a bathroom that connects these two offices. I came in that way." Lorna purposefully left out the part about not realizing she simply needed to unlock the bathroom door. That was so much less glamorous than Heather's grand entrance.

"Well," Heather said. "I guess great minds think alike. So here we are." She gazed around the disheveled office, turned her flashlight on, and allowed the light to caress the room in a slow sweep. "What have you discovered so far?"

"Just this letter in a hidden pocket in a letterman jacket." She pointed toward the jacket still on the floor. "I haven't read it yet." Lorna lifted the envelope.

Heather stepped beside her and directed the beam onto the

front. It was addressed to Trent Devenport. The return address said Katie Lane.

"Looks like an old love letter," Lorna mused. "His wife's name is Katie. Must have been from her before they were married."

"Very likely," Heather agreed. "Why don't you skim it. I'll see if there's anything in these boxes on the shelves."

"Okay. I've already gone through the desk," Lorna explained while twisting on her pen-sized flashlight. "Everything except the side drawers. Might not hurt to check those out if we have time."

"Good."

While Heather perused the boxes, Lorna read the letter that was full of undying love. The words eventually took on a clandestine tone that suggested the relationship should be kept a secret. "The last thing I ever want is for Michael to get hurt," Lorna read quietly as she gradually became more and more enthralled with what appeared to be a love triangle. "But I don't know if there's any way around it. I've never been in such a predicament in my life. I pray daily that God will forgive me and deliver me, and that Michael will end our engagement and make this easy on all of us. Oh God, please help us. Trent, he's your best friend. When he finds out, this is going to kill him."

"Would you look at this?" Heather whispered and nudged a photo into Lorna's view. "It looks like your new friend and Trent Devenport were college buds. Either that's Michael Hayden with Trent or it's his dead ringer."

Lorna's eyes widened. She glanced toward the open box. It contained a jumble of old photos. In this picture Trent Devenport, Michael Hayden, the pretty brunette from the photo on the desk, and a few other young adults sat at a patio table outside a restaurant...or maybe a college cafe. The brunette held Michael's hand and smiled into the camera. Her left hand rested atop the table. A small diamond ring claimed her ring finger.

"Oh my word!" Lorna gasped. "This letter...it's from Katie to

Trent! They're in love and hiding it from Michael." She pointed her flashlight's tiny beam on Katie's ring. "Look. I think she and Michael are engaged. In this letter she's saying she hates to hurt Michael…that he and Trent are best friends and it's going to kill him."

"Yowsa," Heather breathed. "Looks like we've got ourselves a love triangle."

"No wonder Michael…" Lorna trailed off and didn't explain. A couple of times she'd detected a lonely ache in Michael's eyes. She'd assumed that, like her, he'd had a bad experience. And boy had he. If he was really in love with Katie, her marrying his best friend wasn't exactly the dynamics for a fun and fulfilling ride through life. The knowledge of Michael's pain eroded Lorna's last reserves. Maybe God was finally putting someone in her life who would understand her pain because he'd endured betrayal and heartache as well. And maybe she and Michael could pick up the pieces and learn to love together.

Okay. I'm in, she decided. *I'm going to explore this relationship and see where it goes.* For the first time since Chuck Griffith turned into a beast, Lorna believed she was finally on the road to recovery.

※ ※ ※

Michael sat in his apartment with Socks in his lap. He held the Sunday morning paper and read and reread the second lead story until the facts finally seeped into his stunned mind. Apparently news of Trent Devenport's arrest had been in the media since Friday night, but Michael had been so distracted by Lorna he hadn't watched TV or even looked at a paper—at least not until his sister called early this morning, wanting to know about this new woman in the photo with him. Michael retrieved his Sunday morning paper, flipped to Lifestyle, and nearly fell through the floor.

Only after he got home from breakfast with Lorna and was

changing into his Sunday morning best did he notice the second major story on the front of the *Houston Star*. He'd always prided himself on being up on current events and took it even more seriously now that he was mayor. But here was something beyond reach. His former best friend was arrested for child pornography. According to the article, Trent was more than just a viewer, he was also involved in distribution. The scenario couldn't have been more bizarre.

Even though Trent had stooped to stealing his best friend's fiancée, Michael knew Trent wasn't a pervert. No headline could convince Michael otherwise. His first impulse was to call Katie to console her and offer his help.

But no, that wouldn't do. Not ever. They'd pushed him out of their lives the night they confessed the truth to him...that they'd fallen in love, had fought it, had lost the battle. Michael wouldn't forget that night as long as he lived. When the door shut on his apartment his best friend and his fiancée walked out of his life. It was a fate worse than death. Michael saw a counselor and took antidepressants to get through the final days of graduate school. After he graduated he crashed. In the crashing he worked through the pain enough to get on with his life.

The kicker had been that Trent was a seminary student. Men of the cloth weren't supposed to take their friends' women. But the way he and Katie talked, neither of them had *wanted* the whole thing to happen the way it did. But their "we're so sorry" hadn't stopped Michael's pain.

And now Trent was a huge success for a man in his early thirties. At SMU they'd called him and Michael the "Dynamic Duo"—two unusually gifted friends who promised to seriously move the world before age 40. Both were proving the prophecy true—except Trent got the girl and Michael...

He glanced down at Socks. "All I got was a cat," he griped.

Socks meowed and rubbed his head against Michael's arm.

Michael smiled at his bud and then noticed the tie he'd never finished knotting. A quick glimpse of his watch indicated that his astonished trance had cost him the Sunday morning service at church. Michael lowered the paper and scratched Socks' ears. The poor guy didn't even get his albacore this morning.

SEVEN

After a thorough search of the office manager and pastor's offices, Lorna and Heather made a discreet exit. Since the service was nearing an end, they meandered toward separate foyer restrooms. Lorna took her time washing her hands, applying lip balm, and fluffing her blonde wig. When a string of ladies entered the room, the orchestra's rendition of "To God Be the Glory" filtered in with them.

Lorna zipped her handbag and prepared to leave when one of the young gals said, "I just can't believe Pastor Devenport would really—"

A hard look from an older lady stopped the young woman in mid-sentence. Lorna pretended not to hear but felt a few glances go her way. She nonchalantly reapplied lip balm and continued to primp while the ladies made their necessary visits. When no one uttered another word, Lorna meandered out.

She noticed Brittan moseying from the hallway marked "Church Staff." As usual her impassive face revealed nothing. All Lorna and Heather discovered was the love triangle business. Hopefully Brittan uncovered something that might be linked to the pastor's innocence. They planned to meet back at Lorna and Brittan's penthouse apartment, compare notes, and figure out what they were going to do for lunch.

Lorna loitered as long as she could. Eavesdropping along the way, she detected a significant level of shock among the attendees regarding their pastor's arrest. The last comment she heard before stepping into the summer heat was, "I guess this is what he gets for wanting to start a prison ministry. Well, he's got it now!"

She discreetly examined the face of the person making such a statement. He was a tall, skinny man whose narrow face looked like a stretched raisin. His pale-blue eyes were hard, spiteful, full of anything but the love of Christ. Lorna allowed the foyer door to close behind her and shivered despite the heat. Apparently everyone at the church wasn't madly in love with Trent Devenport...or his plans for outreach.

Sashaying toward her rental vehicle, Lorna didn't look for Heather and Brittan until she settled into the vehicle's oven-like heat. She couldn't get the car started soon enough or the air conditioner on high enough. While the AC began to lower the temp, Lorna scanned the grounds filled with people walking to their vehicles.

The raisin-faced man exited with a short, plump woman at his side. Both were dressed in Sunday suits. They appeared to be man and wife. Amazingly, the woman looked as sweet as he was sour. Lorna watched until they got into a white Ford truck with an empty horse trailer attached. The side of the truck read O'Keefe Horse Farm and included their logo, address, and phone number. Lorna dug a pen and notepad from her purse's side pocket and jotted down the truck's license plate number as well as the name "O'Keefe" and the phone number. Given Brittan's expert access to the internet, they'd have more info on the couple soon.

"Then we'll have our first person to investigate," Lorna mumbled with a sly smile.

After noting Brittan and Heather's exiting the church and

getting into their vehicles, Lorna fastened her seat belt, put the car in reverse, and cruised out of the parking lot. She'd barely cleared the first green light when her cell phone rang. Lorna checked the caller ID and saw Michael's name. He'd given her his phone numbers that morning, and Lorna had stored them in her address book. Already he felt like part of her life—and she hadn't known him 48 hours yet.

"Hello, Michael," she purred into the phone.

"Hi there," he responded. "I was thinking about that photo in the paper some more and wanted to let you know again how sorry I am—"

"There's nothing for you to be sorry about," Lorna said and gave the vehicle a bit more gas as the next light turned green. "It was no more your fault than mine."

He sighed. "Well, you left so quickly, I was concerned maybe you were mad or…"

"No…" Lorna hesitated. "I just needed to…I actually had a meeting," she explained and slipped her left foot out of her spiked sandal.

"Oh," Michael stated and then paused.

Lorna cleared her throat. "It was with two friends," she explained. "Brittan Shay and Heather Winslow. We went to church together." *There,* she thought, *it's the truth, and it doesn't leave him thinking I was ditching him.*

"Oh, okay," he replied, his voice taking on a caress. "You didn't have to explain."

Lorna smiled and recalled the way he'd looked at her over breakfast. She'd sensed he wanted to kiss her as much then as he had when she'd fallen out of the golf cart. One part of her was thankful Michael wasn't moving fast, but her risk-taking side wished he'd kissed her this morning…and yesterday on the golf course. She nearly laughed out loud when she thought about how her father would've looked if he'd caught them kissing.

You just met him! she reminded herself. *Take it slow, woman!* She pressed the brakes for a red light at a busy intersection. *Remember the last time you took it too fast?* Despite Lorna's self-warning, the voice of discernment insisted Michael wouldn't violate her boundaries.

Never had silence been so loaded with unspoken energy. Lorna's fingers quivered against the phone. It was almost as if she and Michael each had kisses on the brain and were enjoying the fantasy together.

Michael cleared his throat. "Since our time this morning was cut short, I was wondering if you'd like to come to my place for dinner tomorrow night. My sister and brother-in-law will be here, and also a few other people who were extra supportive during my campaign. I'm cooking," he explained.

"Sure," Lorna agreed. She was so impressed with the fact that he was cooking she barely gave her acceptance a thought.

"Great," Michael said, his voice thick with a grin. "I've purposefully made tomorrow a light day in the office. But once Tuesday hits, you probably won't hear from me much. I'll be snowed under at work for awhile. I'm going to be working on getting a grant for land development tomorrow, and then there's a plastics manufacturer that's looking to build a plant in Houston. I'm meeting with civic leaders and the plant's founder Tuesday. It could bring millions of dollars and hundreds of jobs into our economy. I've got a meeting with the governor tonight."

"Wow! You *are* busy."

"I'm going to be a busy, busy boy for a good while...not as bad on the weekends though. If you'd like, maybe I can count on spending some weekends with *you.*"

"Name the time and place," Lorna rushed and hoped she wasn't sounding too easy. "I'll be there."

"What about *all* the weekends?"

"All the weekends?" Lorna gurgled. "Okay. If that makes you happy. *All* the weekends."

He fell silent.

Lorna dug her thumbnail into the steering wheel. "Michael? Did I lose you?"

"No! I'm here. Just recovering from the dead faint."

She giggled.

"Did I just ask my dream woman to be my steady and hear her agree? Or am I hallucinating?"

"I think I said yes," Lorna answered. "Either that or we've both been eating funny mushrooms."

Michael's heartfelt laugh infected Lorna as well.

"Please don't think I'm always this fast with women," he explained. "I haven't dated anyone in seven years. Not since—" He stopped and Lorna was hard pressed not to say, *Not since Katie Lane dropped you for Trent Devenport?* but she refrained.

"Let's just say I had a really bad experience," Michael explained. "Since then I've immersed myself in college and then work."

"I understand," Lorna stated. "I have a similar story. You're the first one for me in a long time as well."

"Maybe we can both explain tomorrow after dinner—if we get a chance."

"That sounds good...really good."

"Now the only business we need to worry about is what to do about the Houston paparazzi," Michael observed. "If they see us out together enough, we'll be in every newspaper within a 50-mile radius."

Lorna sighed. The layer of perspiration under her wig's lining was every bit as annoying as thoughts of society-page reporters. "I'm planning on having a chat with the owner of the *Star*," she said. "I'm friends with the owner's daughter, Brittan Shay. I'm hoping I can stop them from showing our pictures or at least keep it to a minimum. But I guess it would take an act of congress to completely stop the press."

"I like the plan with the *Star*. As for the rest, why don't we not worry about it?" Michael suggested. "Ignore it. Let them say what they will."

She nodded. "That might be the only way to stay sane. But let me talk to Daddy. He has a way of taking care of these little things."

"So he won't mind that I'm not IBM?"

Lorna snickered. "I have a hunch it won't be a big deal. I had a talk last night with my parents. You're on their very short list of acceptable men to date."

"Oh really?"

"Absolutely." Lorna nodded and checked her speedometer. "Daddy's really impressed with you—believes you'll be president one day."

"Maybe I will. Who knows?" Michael speculated. "But right now I've got to do this mayor thing and do it like a big boy."

Lorna smiled. "Just like a *big* boy, huh?" she teased as if Michael were a two-year-old trying to build a sand castle.

The next few minutes were marked by light flirting that promised tomorrow night would be a landmark evening in their budding relationship. *Maybe the kiss will happen then,* Lorna thought as she ended the call.

The second the phone flipped shut Lorna realized she'd strayed off route and must have taken a wrong turn—*several* wrong turns in fact. What should have been a 20-minute trip to the penthouse wound up taking 35. When she let herself into the fashionable flat, Brittan and Heather's voices drifted from the sunroom. The place smelled like gourmet pizza. Their cook and housekeeper made the masterpieces and always had some ready in the freezer.

Lorna leaned into the sunroom doorway. Her friends were seated at the tall cafe table and appeared to be seriously discussing some papers Brittan was leafing through.

"Hey, I'm here!" Lorna waved. "I'm going to change and get outta this wig." She scratched at the base of her neck. "I'll be right back."

"So nice you could make it," Brittan teased.

"What took you so long?" Heather asked. "I saw you leave right before me. We were starting to get worried." Her hair now hung around her shoulders as usual, and she'd changed into linen slacks and a matching tank top.

"Oh, I...took a wrong turn or two."

"You took a wrong turn?" Brittan's brows raised, and Lorna was starting to feel like a delinquent student facing parental interrogation. Unlike Heather, Brittan *hadn't* changed. And the simple black suit heightened the interrogator impression.

"Michael called," Lorna explained and tried hard not to sound defensive. "I was distracted, and I guess I meandered around some."

"Oh," Brittan and Heather said together.

"Look, I'm sorry I didn't tell you guys about him before," she said. "It's only been a couple of days since I met him, and well, I just didn't know how it would go at first."

"But you know now?" Brittan adjusted her dark-rimmed glasses.

"Sorta, I guess." Lorna nodded. "Yes. I think we might hang out together for awhile...at least every weekend."

"Oh, that's all?" Heather's blue eyes sparkled.

"Sounds serious to me," Brittan stated.

Lorna shrugged. "If it gets that way, you guys will be the first to know."

Brittan nodded and straightened the papers they'd been discussing.

Her curiosity piqued, Lorna stepped into the room. She pointed to the table and said, "What's this?"

"I found an interesting printout in the first associate pastor's office, so I copied it." Brittan lifted the short stack of papers.

"What is it?" Lorna asked and walked to where she could read the first page.

"Apparently Pastor Devenport wanted to start an aggressive prison ministry—and I don't mean just going and visiting in prison. He wanted the congregation to adopt prisoners and work with them until they got out and then bring them into the congregation. He proposed discipling them and helping them get jobs."

"Whoa!" Lorna said. "That explains what I overheard after church. This old guy made some derogatory remarks about the pastor and a prison ministry."

"I can see where some shortsighted people wouldn't want that to happen," Brittan chimed in.

"Especially those who want the church to be more like a social club," Heather added.

"I think I saw the president of the social club today." Lorna set her purse on the table and pulled the license plate number out of the side pocket. "Here's his license plate number and the name and number that was on the truck. Looks like he's got a horse farm."

"You go, girl!" Brittan enthused.

"I figured you could let us know everything about him by sundown, Brittan."

"Maybe sooner."

"Maybe he's on your list already," Heather said.

"List?" Lorna questioned.

"Yes." Brittan lifted the stack of papers. "The first few pages are a prospectus of the prison ministry plan. After that there's a printout of emails and names of those against it. A few were really fighting it with a vengeance."

"Badly enough to arrange for Trent to go to prison?" Lorna asked.

"That's what we're thinking," Heather said.

"How harsh is *that!*" Lorna exclaimed. "I mean, if that's the case, someone hated him enough to smear his name for years. Even if he *is* innocent, this sort of thing puts a fog over a person forever."

"A *cloud* over you," Heather corrected as she smirked.

Lorna rolled her eyes. "You *know* what I mean." She climbed into one of the elevated cafe chairs and removed the wig. "This thing is driving me *nuts*." She loosened her hair from its knot, tousled it with her fingers, and sighed. "That's *much* better."

"I thought you looked kind of cute in it," Brittan said.

"You always say that," Lorna replied.

"And you always say it drives you nuts," Heather said through a grin.

"Anyway..." Brittan lifted the papers. "Heather and I were thinking we should continue to attend church there so we can match names to faces." She wiggled the pages. "And then see if we can link one of these people to what happened to the pastor."

"There's still a chance he might be guilty, you know," Lorna warned and thought of the old love letter she'd read. "If Trent Devenport could double-cross his best friend, he might stoop to other evils as well."

"I told Brittan about what we found," Heather explained.

"It's *awful*," Brittan added. "Has Michael told you about it yet?"

"No." Lorna shook her head. "But he's hinted and mentioned maybe telling me about it tomorrow night." Her friends' silent question insisted Lorna share about "tomorrow night." "He's cooking dinner for a few people who helped his campaign. He asked me to come over too."

"He cooks?" Heather asked.

"Sounds like it." Lorna shrugged.

"All Duke knows how to cook is hamburgers and microwave popcorn," Heather said. "I've already decided when we get married my first household staff member is going to be a cook. I can't cook worth a flip. We'll starve to death the first week."

"I feel your pain. Brittan's the cook here—when Tilley's not around, that is."

"Speaking of which, I need to go check on the pizza." Brittan slipped from her chair. "Here." She passed the papers to Lorna. "You can read over these while I'm gone."

"I think this case is going to take a while," Heather predicted.

"Maybe," Lorna agreed as she flipped to the pages of negative emails.

"You know," Heather placed her elbow on the table and rested her chin in her hand, "I still think Devenport is innocent. I mean, even if he *did* steal his best friend's fiancée, that doesn't mean he would be a pervert. Child porn is a far cry from falling in love with a lady. Maybe Trent and Michael's girlfriend just fell for each other." Heather shrugged. "They couldn't stop it. It happens, you know."

Lorna sighed. "Yes, I know. Maybe you're right." She grimaced. "I think I'm probably projecting some negative stuff on him because of how I know it must've hurt Michael."

"But if Trent and Katie hadn't gotten married, Michael would have married her and *you* wouldn't be planning on having dinner with him tomorrow night." Heather wiggled her brows.

"Good point!" Lorna said through a grin.

The debutantes spent the rest of Sunday compiling their suspect list. The plan was to converge back at the church for the Wednesday night service and put faces with names. From there they'd build profiles on each suspect and hopefully nab the violator or violators.

EIGHT

Lorna pulled her Jeep into the high-rise parking garage. While Heather and Brittan were eaten up with proving Trent's innocence, Lorna was gradually losing trust in Devenport's character. As her trust dwindled, she was becoming aware she was just in for the ride on this one. She loved snooping around and piecing together clues as much as her friends did, but her experience with Chuck Griffith had jaded her. She'd fully trusted Chuck because he came across so low-key and had such an innocent persona—much like Devenport. Chuck had been anything but innocent...and with more women than just Lorna.

She shoved the haunting memories from her mind and focused on Michael. *Now he's one man I can trust,* she thought and recalled the text message he'd sent with instructions on how to get to his place. He'd ended with, "Can't wait to see you!" Even now Lorna relished the thrill that zipped through her. She couldn't wait to see him either.

She drove the Jeep through the labyrinth garage, searching for a vacant slot. Lorna guessed this apartment building was full of upscale professionals—if the sports cars and luxury sedans were anything to go by. As things turned out, Michael's place was only a few minutes from Lorna and Brittan's penthouse. Lorna decided next time she'd take a taxi and not deal with the hassle of finding parking. At last she found a space and headed toward the elevator that would take her to Michael's floor.

Within minutes she stood outside Michael's apartment—number 1802. He'd said the flats near the top of the building were larger. Only one other apartment door claimed this wing of the hallway. Lorna decided his place must be nearly as big as their penthouse. Before knocking Lorna glanced down at her linen blouse and brushed her hand over her ankle-length skirt. She smoothed her layered hair and hoped she'd pass inspection.

Lorna had gained 20 pounds since her tennis days. Given her height, a size 16 made her just a little above her best weight. Nevertheless, she hadn't watched her diet since she'd left pro sports. Now she wished she'd acted like Heather and eaten more bean sprouts and fewer candy bars.

Maybe that's something I need to work on soon, she thought and imagined Heather falling into a shocked coma. She sighed and decided she looked presentable enough—at least Michael seemed to think so every time he saw her. Tonight his sister was supposed to be here, and Lorna wanted to make as good of an impression on his family as he'd made on hers.

She pressed the doorbell and waited. After the second ring she was rewarded with the door's swift opening. Michael stood inside wearing a food-smeared chef's apron over a crisp white shirt and a pair of slacks. His grin was the size of the moon and made Lorna's stomach start that meltdown she'd first experienced in the garden Friday night.

His dark eyes sparkled as he gestured for her to enter and said, "You're the first one here. Come on in."

Lorna stepped inside and scanned the place. It was every bit as spacious as she'd assumed, and the decorator had captured Michael's winning personality with masculine simplicity...right down to the brown leather sofa and the corner wall arrangement that centered around his golf clubs parked beneath it. The shelf full of model airplanes near the TV added another clue to his interests. While the apartment attested to a bachelor's presence, the kitchen aroma smelled like somebody's grandmother had been here all day creating award-winning masterpieces straight from heaven.

Michael closed the door, and Lorna swiveled to face him. Her eyes wide, she said, "Whatever you're cooking, I'll have two." Her stomach rumbled.

He chuckled, grabbed her hand, and invited, "Come on. I'll show you. I can use some help. I've just had a small explosion, actually."

Lorna dropped her purse on the breakfast bar as she entered the kitchen. "An explosion?" she questioned and then noticed the red sauce splattered on the cabinets. Her gaze followed the trail upward and stopped on the ceiling, where red splotches crowned the room. Her focus moved back to Michael. The food stains on his apron matched those on the ceiling...and a few dots in his hair.

She giggled. "You've even got it in your hair! What *happened?*"

"I threw a few fresh tomatoes into the blender to add to the spaghetti sauce and forgot to put the top on. When I turned it on, ka-poo-ee!" Michael gestured toward the ceiling and then followed the length of his body with his hands. Lorna then noticed the tiny red dots along the sleeves of his shirt as well.

"How did you forget to put the top on the blender?" she gurgled.

He squinted and tilted his head. "Do you *really* wantta know?"

"Well, I asked, didn't I?"

"My mind was on something...*someone*...else." His gaze warmed to the point that Lorna had no doubt who that "someone" was. "I'd already pureed a few tomatoes and put a few more in. Then I turned to stir the spaghetti sauce and meandered back over to the blender and pressed the button just like—"

"Just like a *big* boy," she teased.

"Yep." Michael's eyes twinkled.

"Well look, at least let me help you clean up." Lorna grabbed a dishcloth near the sink, dampened it, and approached the cabinets. "I'm no kitchen expert, but maybe I've got what it takes to wipe down the cabinets."

"Seriously? You don't mind?" Michael asked. "I really need to finish the sauce."

"Don't mind in the least," Lorna agreed. "As long as you don't let that stuff erupt on me." She snickered.

"No eruptions, I promise," Michael vowed.

Lorna tackled her task while Michael moved the blender down the counter and pureed some more tomatoes. Once the tomatoes were in the sauce and the water was steaming for the pasta, Lorna had dealt with most of the mess.

"Thanks so much," Michael said. "I'll worry about the ceiling later." He waved away the stains. "I've already got the salad in the fridge and the cheesecake is—"

"You even made cheesecake?" Lorna gaped.

"No." Michael shook his head and glanced down at his stained apron. "I *can*. But I cheated on the cheesecake. I was just going to say it's on the way. My sister's bringing it. I ordered it from a caterer I use a lot. I can't top it. I *did* make the lasagna though." He pointed toward the oven.

"Lasagna?" Lorna moaned. "That's my fave."

"Good." Michael grinned. "It's an old family recipe. My grandmother was full-blooded Italian. She lost hope trying to teach my sister to cook and used me as her second-choice victim."

"Go, Grandma!" Lorna said with an animated smile.

He sighed and lifted his hands. "Look at me! I'd best go change—at least my shirt. The governor's coming. Did I tell you?"

"Dick Terry?" Lorna asked.

"In the flesh." Michael nodded. "Your dad knows him well. Have you ever met him?"

"Oh, in passing, just a time or two," she admitted. "I'm sure he probably won't remember me. Are you and he getting thick?"

Michael laughed and turned to stir the sauce a bit. "I guess you could say that. We've been friends for years. He's planning on making a bid for the presidency in the 2012 election if all his cards line up. Last night he asked me if I'm interested in national politics. If I am he said there'd be a place for me in his administration."

Lorna's mouth fell open. "No joke?"

"No joke." Michael set the spoon aside and faced Lorna again.

"I guess Daddy was right about your being president one day."

Michael lifted both hands. "Who knows where all this will lead. Dick and I discussed my running for the Senate or the House of Representatives in the next election. I'm seriously considering it."

"Wow! Congratulations!" Lorna said as a drop of tomato dripped from Michael's hair to his forehead.

"Ah man!" he groused and wiped at the goo. "I've got this stuff all over me."

On an impulse Lorna stepped forward and used the dishcloth to swipe at another droplet that was threatening to fall.

Michael tilted the top of his head toward her and said, "What do you think? Can we get it out or should I go shower?"

"Is everyone supposed to be here now?" Lorna asked and dubiously examined a few tomato seeds mixed with the liquid dots.

"Not until six-thirty."

She checked her watch and noted that it was six-twenty. "But you told me six."

He lifted his head, looked into her eyes, and smiled. "So I did," he admitted while raising a brow.

Lorna narrowed her eyes. "You're a sneaky one, aren't you?" she accused. "Like showing up at the country club and watching me play tennis before 'accidentally' running into me in the parking lot. Care to share *that* whole story?"

"Oh *that*," Michael said through a sheepish smile. "I thought for awhile you really didn't catch on."

"Oh, I caught on." Lorna laid aside the cloth and folded her arms. "When you asked me if the guy I was playing tennis with was IBM I was positive. I chose not to say anything until now."

Michael lifted both hands. "I've been officially nabbed. What are ya gonna do? Throw me into the slammer?"

"Maybe," Lorna warned.

"So I chased you a little," Michael countered. "And maybe I'll *keep* chasing you." His gaze trailed to her lips and lingered there. "And maybe the reason I blew up the tomatoes was because I was planning my strategy."

Lorna swallowed as she leaned against the counter. She hadn't exactly anticipated their first kiss in a tomato-splattered kitchen, but she also hadn't planned meeting Michael Hayden in the garden Friday night either...or anything else that had happened the past weekend.

He slowly leaned closer, a statement in his eyes that clearly said, "If you aren't ready for this, stop me." But at the same time there was a silent "*Please* don't stop me."

Her pulse pounded in her temples. The last time she kissed a man, he'd turned into a beast and nearly violated her. The terrible scene flashed through her mind in a living-color nightmare. The unexpected flare-up sent her into a tailspin of fear that mingled with the desire to feel Michael close.

I've got to get over this, her logical side insisted. *I can't let that ruin my life. I've got to go forward.* Her counselor had said something very similar numerous times.

Michael's gaze grew cautious, questioning. He stopped centimeters away. "You look frightened," he said. "Am I scaring you?"

Lorna swallowed hard and decided to be honest. "I had a really bad experience a few years ago. I—I—"

He backed away. "I'm taking this too fast?"

"No, it's not—not you," she stammered. "It's *me*. I need to deal with it and get over it. But it's been *so hard*." Her eyes moistened. The room went blurry. Lorna lowered her head.

"Hey…" Michael squeezed her hand. "No pressure, okay?"

"I told you on the phone yesterday that there hadn't been anyone in several years," she said, her voice wobbling. "There was a man who…"

Cold silence enveloped the kitchen. Lorna glanced up. Michael's face had turned an unearthly shade of red and his mouth tightened. But his eyes radiated with concern. "Did he rape you?" he whispered.

"No." Lorna shook her head. "He would have…if a friend hadn't shown up."

Michael's face gradually resumed its natural color. His eyes softened even more.

"Heather heard me screaming. She has a black belt in karate," Lorna explained. "After I whacked him in the face with my tennis racket, she came in and took him down."

"Good for her," Michael said.

"But it's been years now, and I've *got* to move on," Lorna admitted.

Michael took her hands in his and squeezed. "And I'd like nothing more than to be with you on the journey," he said, his voice oozing with understanding, compassion, adoration.

Lorna wobbled out a smile and smudged at the corners of her eyes. "I'd like nothing more too, Mr. President," and on impulse she kissed his cheek in what she assumed would be a chaste gesture of new friendship. But the light brush of her lips created a reaction that made the blender explosion look tame.

Michael's eyes widened. He touched his cheek. "Wow!"

Lorna locked her knees and rode the tide of a chemistry reaction she'd never experienced.

The doorbell's ring did nothing to alter the intensity. Michael ignored it as thoroughly as Lorna did. This time when he neared, Lorna sensed no internal fear—nothing but attraction and a desire to feel Michael's lips on hers. The second brief kiss rocked the kitchen and rattled Lorna's equilibrium.

When the doorbell chimed the third…or fourth time, Michael pulled away. Lorna realized she was gripping the front of his shirt and his arms encircled her.

"I guess I should get that, huh?" he whispered, resting his forehead against hers.

"Yeah…maybe," Lorna answered softly.

"It's probably the governor. I don't guess we should keep him waiting." His voice was full of regret.

"We never did anything about the tomato sauce in your hair." Lorna released his shirt and eyed his hair.

"Oh well. Maybe it will work to our advantage. Let's see."

NINE

Even though he was still Mr. Tomato Head, at least Michael had the presence of mind to wipe off Lorna's lip gloss before opening the door. His younger sister and her husband stood in the hallway, cheesecake in hand.

"Hey, guy!" Carrie chirped. She wore a neon-orange pant-suit and lipstick that was closer to pink than orange. The clash was nearly blinding. Michael didn't know much about women's color fashions, but he'd often wondered if Carrie should get a professional consultation. A few times he even suspected she was color-blind.

Michael motioned them in.

"We were beginning to think we'd gotten our nights mixed up and you weren't home." Rob strode past him. As the regional manager of the Hayden family menswear chain, he dressed the part—right down to the finest in leather loafers.

"No mix-up." Michael closed the door. "I'm home. Just had a disaster in the kitchen." He tilted his head toward them. "I forgot to put the top on the blender."

Rob laughed.

"Oh my word," Carrie said. "You're a mess!" She nudged Michael toward the hallway. "Go jump into the shower. I'll take care of the mess in the kitchen," she said before hustling through the living room.

"But we already—"

Lorna emerged from the kitchen looking like a tall, elegant goddess next to Michael's plump sister.

"Oh!" Carrie stopped and looked at Lorna like she was a new dish she'd never tried—and that would be a rarity indeed. Even though Carrie was no cook, one thing she and Rob had in common was they liked to eat out…a lot…and their extra pounds proved it.

"Lorna, this is my sister, Carrie, and her husband, Rob." Michael moved to Lorna's side. "And this is my new friend Lorna."

"Yes, we saw you in the paper," Carrie said with a teasing smile. "Michael didn't tell us you were going to be here tonight though."

"Nice to meet you." Rob stepped forward and Lorna extended her hand.

"Rob's been better to me than ten brothers," Michael claimed and gripped Rob's shoulder. "He put as many hours into my campaign as I did."

Lorna's smile was as warm as Carrie's.

Michael's brother-in-law came from a solid Italian family. The Haydens had groomed all three of their children to marry nice, Italian mates, preferably Episcopalians. Michael's mother was half Irish, half Italian, and his father was British and Italian, but they clung to their Italian roots.

Lorna wasn't Italian by a long shot. Her brunette hair wasn't quite dark enough and the freckles gave her more of an all-American appeal. But Michael suspected both his parents would shout if he brought home any lady from any gene pool and any Christian persuasion. Katie had her share of Italian genes and had been officially approved as a good Episcopalian girl. When that engagement fell through, his family had grieved nearly as much as he had. Now his mother was constantly telling him all good mayors needed wives and that she was ready for grandchildren. The Hayden clan was nearly as bad as the Houston paparazzi. In the greater family network it was a good time for Michael to get involved with a "nice" woman.

Carrie's smile said she was ready to start wedding plans. Michael was still so blown away by the kiss that he didn't mind thinking toward a wedding either. *Whoa!* his logical side warned. *Don't even go there yet! You're just getting to know each other. Let's take it slow, okay?*

"Okay," Michael said out loud.

Carrie, Rob, and Lorna looked at him.

"Uh, okay!" He rubbed his hands together. "If you guys will man the door for a few minutes, I'll hop into the shower and get rid of this sauce."

"Sure," Lorna said with a smile that was as warm as their kiss.

"The lasagna needs to come out in five minutes." He untied his apron, slipped it over his head, and extended it to Lorna. "Think you could do that for me?"

"I'll be glad to." She took the apron. "Do I put this on now or…"

"No." Michael chuckled. "Just toss it on the counter."

"Will do."

The doorbell rang.

"Here they come." Carrie shooed him toward the hallway again. "We've got the door."

"Just don't say anything stupid to the governor, will ya?" Michael wrinkled his nose at his sister. "He's asked me to be part of his administration if he gets nominated in the 2012 presidential election."

"Congrats!" Rob cheered.

With a huff Carrie placed her hands on her hips and said, "When have I *ever* said anything stupid?"

✳ ✳ ✳

Three hours later Lorna lingered by Michael's side while the last guest prepared to leave, and he just happened to be the governor. As the evening wore on Lorna had gradually gone from one of Michael's guests to being his cohost for the dinner party. Everyone, including Dick Terry, assumed they were an official couple.

Now, with Governor Terry standing near the doorway, Michael took Lorna's hand in his, and she fully felt the part. They *were* an official couple. And she had indeed served as mistress of the manor. Well, cohost of the apartment anyway.

Mr. Terry, a tall man of the premature gray persuasion, smiled his approval at his younger friend. If ever a man looked like he should be called Mr. President, Dick Terry did. Even in his sports shirt and slacks he was the epitome of official. "I was glad to hear you're going to accept my offer, Michael," he said. "I don't think I've met another young man more gifted than you. If I win you'll certainly make your mark."

"Let's see how I survive being mayor first," Michael said through a smile. "And I *do* like the idea of running for the Senate. We'll just take it a step at a time."

"Good." Dick nodded and then eyed Lorna. "It was good to see you again," he said. "Give your father my best."

"Of course," Lorna said and politely shook his hand.

"You know, Hayden," Dick gripped Michael's shoulder, "every good politician needs a good mate." He winked and then pumped Michael's hand.

Lorna lowered her gaze and suffered through a sea of discomfort during the governor's final words. Being an official couple was one thing. Having everyone from the governor to Michael's sister hinting at marriage was another.

We only met Friday, Lorna thought. *Good grief!*

The second the door closed, Michael squeezed Lorna's hand and said, "Sorry 'bout that."

Lorna looked him squarely in the eyes. Regret was mixed with a tinge of embarrassment.

"I didn't put anybody up to any of those hints about marriage. After all, we just met last week." He shrugged. "My sister knows better. I think the governor was just trying to encourage me. I don't think he realizes how new of an item we are." He pointed at her and then himself.

Lorna nodded as relief washed away her discomfort. "It's okay."

"No pressure from this side." Michael lifted his hand.

"Yes...and just in case the same thing happens from my family, ditto from me." Lorna grinned.

"Come on." Michael tugged her toward the huge picture window that offered a breathtaking view of the Houston skyline that was now covered in lights. "I want you to see something."

Lorna followed his lead and soon realized that a sliding glass door made up one side of the window. He opened the door, and they stepped onto a spacious balcony that overlooked the city streets. The balcony was furnished with wicker furniture, and a gas grill claimed one corner. Before Michael shut the door, he flipped on a light switch inside. The balcony lit up in a soft glow that was amazingly cozy—especially with the canvas awning that captured the light.

"This is so cool!" Lorna exclaimed. "I love it."

"Yes, it's my little escape. I can sit out here and see the sunset... and if I sit long enough, the skyline comes on and I relax right through all of it. I love it too."

A welcoming meow came from the corner chair, and Lorna gazed toward a black-and-white cat who observed her with golden eyes.

"Meet Socks," Michael said and stepped forward to scratch his pet between the shoulder blades.

"You have a cat?" Lorna asked and wished she didn't sound so disenchanted.

"Yep. He adopted me a while back. I couldn't shake him, so here he is."

"And he's safe out here on the balcony?"

"Voila!" Michael lifted a thin leash attached to the cat's collar. "The leash is long enough for him to have some freedom," he pointed to a duo-dish of dry cat food and water and a small litter box a few feet away, "but it won't let him go too near the railing. I put him out here if I'm going to have a houseful of company. He likes this more than he would being shut up in my room. He gets a charge out of the occasional bird that comes through. Believe it or not, I've even taught him to walk with me in the park." Michael chuckled. "I'm the only one out there with a cat on a leash, but he loves it."

"Oh." Lorna tried to smile as the unusual image tottered through her mind, but she couldn't. She was too distracted waiting for the beast to snarl at her like most felines did. But all Socks did was meow toward Lorna and squirm onto his back.

"He wants you to rub his tummy," Michael encouraged.

A Goliath flashback whipped through her mind, and Lorna rubbed the scar on her hand. That mean-spirited cat sank his teeth into her tender flesh and refused to let go. Lorna had landed in the emergency room, and Goliath spent the rest of her visit in the utility room.

"Cats usually hate me," she dubiously admitted and didn't add that she usually hated them right back.

"Me too. But Socks is different. I think he's a Christian cat or something. He's got the love of Jesus in him. He loves everybody."

Lorna chuckled and offered Socks an obligatory rub. He purred and squirmed some more.

"See there? He likes you!" Michael exclaimed.

"This is a historic moment," Lorna drawled.

"Come on, boy," Michael said and unhooked the cat's leash. "Let's get you back inside. I don't need any competition out here."

While Michael dealt with his pet, Lorna walked to the railing and rested her hands on the lukewarm metal. She closed her eyes and allowed the evening breeze to wisp away the ten o'clock fatigue as the smells of the city mixed with the scent of the sky. Michael's footsteps stopped nearby, and she opened her eyes. He stood beside her, rested his forearms on the railing, and gazed across the city.

"I really appreciate your coming tonight," he said without looking at her. "You helped in ways I never imagined."

"I helped in ways I never imagined too," Lorna said with a laugh.

"I guess neither one of us expected you to turn into the hostess… or a tomato puree mopper-upper," he said, his voice thick with humor. Michael straightened and pivoted to face her.

Lorna cut him a sideways grin. "It was my honor—after all, you're the future president."

"That's what everybody's saying," Michael said through a wry grin. "I'm beginning to wonder if I have any say in that." He laughed.

"Oh well…que sera sera." She laid her hand on his.

Michael gently grabbed her fingers, kissed the back of her hand, and never broke eye contact.

Lorna relived the earlier kiss in the kitchen and sensed he did the same. A gust of wind whipped her hair around her face, and she fought to control it as much as she grappled to contain her reaction to Michael. Her skirt danced around her weak knees, and Lorna slipped off the killer spikes. She wiggled her aching toes against the warm concrete and fought to maintain her equilibrium.

Michael gazed toward the horizon, and Lorna observed his profile. His Italian genes had blessed him with dark brows, a prominent nose, and deliciously olive skin. Lorna suspected many female voters had been influenced by his looks. If the truth were known, Lorna was in their ranks. She'd voted for Michael herself.

"Looks like maybe a few clouds are rolling across the moon. Is it supposed to rain? Do you know?" he asked.

"Haven't heard," Lorna responded.

He slipped his fingers between hers. "Nice fit," he said.

Lorna grinned. "Yep." She sensed he wanted to say something but didn't quite know how to begin.

"I was...really disturbed about what you said in the kitchen," he admitted. "There's nothing that makes me madder."

Lorna sighed. "I've come so far from when it happened. I think I'm finally going to be able to get on with my life."

"I'm glad. You know..." He hesitated. "I had a similar situation. I mean similar in the shock and having to get over it."

Yes, I know, Lorna thought but kept her face impassive.

"I was engaged seven years ago. But my fiancée and best friend showed up together to tell me *they* were in love. I lost the woman I loved and my best friend in one night."

"How *awful*," Lorna consoled.

"It was," Michael admitted. "But you know what's odd?"

"What?"

"Yesterday's paper. I was in the society pages with a new woman who's got my head spinning, and he was on the front page. He's the pastor they've arrested for pornography."

"Whoa!" Lorna exclaimed and hoped she sounded genuinely shocked.

"So after he and Katie kicked me to the bottom of a pit, he's now in the pit and I'm climbing to the top." A tinge of bitterness tainted his words.

"Does it still hurt?" She flexed her fingers against his.

"A little. Maybe." He shrugged. "I guess. Except if I'd married Katie I wouldn't be here with *you* now." He gazed at Lorna like she was a princess.

Lorna glanced down. Michael had told her she was his dream woman. Lorna hoped she could live up to such a standard.

"And, really, I'm starting to think maybe I'm *glad* it all happened. Whether you know it or not, you've got me thoroughly dazzled. I'm not sure Katie ever had me to the point you've got me already."

"Maybe the years have healed some of your wounds and you've forgotten," Lorna countered and couldn't remember ever sounding this logical. Brittan would be proud. "I'm not perfect, you know," she added on a worried note.

"You're about as close as I've ever seen." Michael winked. "In case you haven't figured it out, I had a *serious* crush on you when you were in pro tennis."

"Really?"

"Yes." Michael's brows arched.

Lorna giggled simply because she didn't know *what* to say. She'd had her share of men make a play for her, but no one had ever been so blatantly spellbound.

"But you were so young and I was so much older that I was embarrassed to even admit it to Rob."

"He's your best friend, isn't he?" Lorna asked.

"Yep. I was the one who introduced him to Carrie. They've only been married two years. Those two ate their way right up to the altar and haven't stopped eating since."

Lorna laughed. "I didn't think they were going to leave any lasagna for me—which was delicious by the way," she added.

"Thanks. Glad you liked it. That might be the last time I cook for a long time. I was in the office today and had to tear myself away. I'm going to be really focusing on work from now until..." He shrugged.

"You'll be the best mayor Houston's ever had," Lorna averred.

"Well, after Katie dumped me, I buried myself in my college work and then in my career. Now here I am buried in mayor business."

"And what a mayor you are!" Lorna's sassy words tumbled out before she could stop them. Her eyes wide, she held Michael's

mirthful gaze, only to see that he was as elated as she was morti-
fied. "I can't believe I just said that," she rushed.

"Neither can I, but I certainly am glad you did." Michael wrapped
his arms around her. "This is going to be one summer I don't think
I'll ever forget," he whispered near her ear.

Lorna closed her eyes and relaxed against Michael. For the first
time in years she felt safe. Really safe.

"You're keeping weekends open for me, right?" he questioned
and began swaying to a tune only he could hear.

"Yes," Lorna whispered.

"I'm too tired right now to suggest anything to do, but I'll call
you Thursday and we can figure it out."

"I enjoyed golf Saturday afternoon," Lorna said.

"Me too."

"Maybe this Saturday we could play a round of golf and then
some tennis."

"Uh-uh!" Vehemently shaking his head, Michael pulled away.
"You're not getting me on the tennis court! I saw what you did to
that poor guy at the country club the other day. I'm not up for that
punishment. At least I have a *chance* in golf."

Lorna laughed. "You may have been born in the dark, but not
last year?" she questioned.

Michael threw back his head and laughed to the stars.

"Oh no," Lorna groaned. "Did I get it wrong?"

"It's 'you may have been born in the dark, but not *last night.*'"

"Ah man...I'm the queen of mixed clichés," she groaned. "Not
long ago I said I was between a rock and a fireplace. How duh is
that?"

His laughter increased. "It's a rock and a *hard* place," he said
between breaths.

"Yeah, I know that...*now!*"

"Oh Lorna," he said through a final round of chuckles, "you
have no idea how you've already brightened my life." He stroked

her cheek, and Lorna relished the chills that danced along her spine. "God knows how I needed this." He rested his forehead against hers and then sealed the evening with a kiss that tilted the skyscraper.

TEN

Brittan swung her feet out of the bed, yawned, and fumbled through the blurry darkness toward the bathroom. She usually made such a trip once during the night. Tonight was no different. She never bothered with her glasses and usually made the trek to the bathroom and back with little memory or disrupted sleep.

Such would have been the case tonight except just as Brittan was crawling back into bed a disturbing thought bombarded her brain. She went rigid and sat straight up. Wide awake she stared with horror into the inky darkness.

She and Heather had sat up until nearly eleven o'clock going over the names she'd copied from the first associate pastor's office. They'd compiled a list of people who'd sent vehement letters and emails of protest against the prison ministry. One congregate even stated he hated the pastor. That one had been placed at the top of their to-do list.

"But maybe there's another name we need to add to the list," Brittan whispered. "Michael Hayden." As her lips formed the words, her heart beat with dread awareness that Hayden had a greater motivation for framing Trent Devenport than any on the church list. Trent had stolen Michael's fiancée. Now Michael was in a position of prominence that lent him an aura of respectability and gave him some power. *Maybe he's waited all these years to take Trent down. Now that he's the mayor he thinks he's in the best position to get away with it.* The possibility seemed more plausible by the second.

She looked toward the digital clock. It was just after four-thirty. Brittan was sure Heather wouldn't appreciate a call at this hour any more than Lorna was going to appreciate her theory about the new mayor.

Brittan flopped back on her pillow and recalled the glow on Lorna's face last night when she'd come home after dinner at Michael's. Forget cloud nine. She'd been on cloud 99. Lorna said she and Michael both had bad relationship experiences and were moving forward for the first time since their hearts had been broken. She'd sat up with her two friends until after twelve and came close to babbling about her whole evening…the exploded tomatoes, the lasagna, the governor, the other prominent guests, and even the guy's cat who loved her, for cryin' out loud.

"Lorna, you hate cats," Brittan whispered to the walls. "Have you lost all sense?" Covering her face, Brittan groaned. This was exactly what Lorna did with Chuck Griffith. She'd babbled on about him like he was Adonis. Both Heather and Brittan had seen the guy was a predator, but Lorna had been so ensnared she'd refused to listen. If Heather hadn't been purposefully hanging close just in case Lorna needed her, she might have been raped and would probably *still* be in therapy.

Yes, but Michael Hayden is the mayor, a practical voice insisted. Brittan opened her eyes, stared toward the ceiling fan whose rotations were barely perceptible in the shadows. "Well, Chuck Griffith was a professional trainer. *He* looked respectable too."

Brittan sighed, rolled over, punched her pillow. *I'll just wait and talk to Heather in the morning,* she thought. *See what she thinks. Maybe I'm overreacting.* She tried to close her rebellious eyes. They popped back open…and stayed open until six-thirty. That's when Brittan threw the covers off and sprang out of bed. She grabbed her phone from the nightstand and pressed Heather's speed dial number. If she wasn't awake, it was time for her to wake up.

Her friend's groggy hello attested she wasn't awake.

"Rise and shine!" Brittan called and sounded more like an army sergeant than a cheerful friend. "I've been awake since four-thirty."

"And so you want me to join you in your misery? Can't you get thrown in jail for being awake so early? What time is it anyway?"

"Six-thirty."

"Have you *lost* your mind!" Heather complained.

"No, but I've had a very disturbing thought," Brittan replied.

"Well, I don't think at six-thirty," Heather shot back.

Brittan ignored the barb. "Of all the people we've considered, who has the biggest motive for hurting Trent Devenport?"

"Umm…"

"Michael Hayden," Brittan said and cautiously glanced toward her open doorway. She tiptoed toward the door and shut it with one faint click. Then she stepped to the settee near the penthouse's window.

"Michael Hayden?" Heather repeated.

"Yes." Brittan flopped onto the settee. "Think about it. Trent Devenport stole Michael's fiancée. Michael has now risen to prominence. What if he's taking down his number one enemy on his way up?" She twisted the tassel on a velvet pillow.

"Power can do some wicked things to people," Heather observed. This time she sounded more alert.

"Exactly. And Lorna says everybody is saying he'll be in national politics one day. Maybe he's feeling invincible and above the law." Brittan tossed the pillow to the settee's corner.

"Man oh man," Heather breathed.

"And you know Lorna's track record with men. Think about

Chuck Griffith. Remember how she acted over him? Is she or is she not acting the same over Michael?"

"Oh man," Heather groaned. "What are we going to do?"

"Like I know?" Brittan lifted her hand and stared at her rumpled satin sheets as if the answer lay tangled in the unmade bed.

"Well, you are 'the Brain'!"

"Yes, but this isn't a computer, and I *do* have my limits." Brittan stood and dug her toes into the plush carpet.

Heather yawned. "There's no way I can go back to sleep now."

"Tell me about it!" Brittan whispered. "I've been wide awake forever."

"Thank you for not calling me then."

Britain meandered to the window and gazed down into streets stirring with the first morning mix of city dwellers. "I guess we need to investigate Michael Hayden too."

"Without letting Lorna know," Heather added. "And then we should just change our names to Benedict Arnold and get it over with. If Lorna finds out, and if he's innocent, we're up a creek."

"Well, if we're sneaky, Lorna won't find out," Brittan asserted. "And if he's *not* innocent, we'll never forgive ourselves for not pursuing the investigation."

Brittan yawned. Now that she'd spilled the information, her adrenalin rush was off. Her mind was telling her eyelids the time had come to shut down. Brittan strolled to the glass of water she kept on a coaster on her dresser in case she wanted a drink in the night. She took a long swallow of the tepid liquid and then yawned again.

"You sound like you're about to go into a coma," Heather noted.

"I think I am," Brittan admitted before collapsing back into the high poster bed and flopping onto her pillow. "I'm going back to sleep for awhile. This has been a wild night."

Heather's sigh was loud...and annoyed. "Okay. Just go back to sleep then. I guess I'll get up and go to the gym."

"You do that, girlfriend," Brittan mumbled before closing her cell.

✳ ✳ ✳

As Michael drove to work, the last few days' headlines were as vivid to him as the steering wheel. Every time his mind flitted toward Lorna, an unseen force flung Trent Devenport into the forefront of his thoughts. Despite everything Trent had done, he had been Michael's best friend since they met at church when they were 10. The two attended the same junior high and high school and decided to stick it out together at SMU. They'd shared many good times and lots of happy memories. Until Trent had fallen in love with Katie, he'd been the best friend Michael could ever ask for.

Michael accelerated around a line of traffic in the right-turn lane and was tempted to loosen his tie. But he couldn't. The day was just starting. Nevertheless, thoughts of Trent sitting in jail constricted his throat as severely as a hangman's noose. The more he pondered the horror, the more tangled he became in the situation. If anyone was innocent, it was Trent. As mayor Michael had some influence with law enforcement, but even his word wouldn't change hard evidence. According to the paper the evidence was convincing.

All that means is that some people know how to set up the innocent, Michael thought. If Trent Devenport said he wasn't guilty, Michael believed him. Trent had his faults, but he was no liar and never had been.

In the midst of his concern for Trent, the new relationship with Lorna made Michael thrilled he'd never married Katie. Lorna was well worth the wait...well worth the heartache of losing Katie. Michael couldn't even imagine being married to Katie now. Last night he'd dug out his old college album. He'd expected at least a twinge of feeling when he saw Katie's photo, but he'd only experienced dull relief.

He gripped the gearshift and relived that kiss on the balcony last night. Fresh attraction enveloped him as fully as the new leather smell of his sporty vehicle. If he'd married Katie somebody else might be kissing Lorna now. "Thank You, God, for having Katie fall in love with Trent!" he mumbled. And the impact of those words nearly made him miss his turn.

As he steered the Mercedes toward Hermann Square and caught a glimpse of City Hall, a hard knot in the center of Michael's soul slowly unraveled. All these years he'd thought he was the one who'd been "done wrong." Now he wondered if God had allowed the betrayal to set him free.

He relived that night when Katie and Trent told him they truly believed their getting married was God's will. At the time Michael had scoffed the very suggestion. Now he was agreeing.

"Trent was probably just telling the truth," Michael muttered. He smiled. Then he laughed and was filled with a joy he hadn't encountered in years.

Once he drove into his reserved parking place and turned off the engine, Michael pulled his cell phone from his belt harness. Before he started his insane schedule, he'd send Lorna a text message. More than anything else, he wanted to remind her of his growing fondness…and make certain he stayed on her mind.

※ ※ ※

Despite Lorna's plans to sleep in, she'd rolled out of bed at eight. By nine she was sitting at their cafe-style table sipping Tilley's fresh coffee and idly reading Heather and Brittan's notes from last night. When she arrived from Michael's, they informed her they'd compiled a list of names of those who opposed the prison ministry. Lorna vaguely remembered their mentioning plans to begin investigating those on the list one by one—starting with the most vehement ones.

She picked up the stack of emails Brittan had retrieved from the first associate pastor's office. Each email was addressed to Trent Devenport and copied to Rich Cooper. Idly Lorna scanned the list to see if they'd written down Rich Cooper as well, but she didn't find his name. She sipped her coffee and considered the motives an associate pastor might have for wanting the senior pastor out of the way.

"Maybe with Devenport out of the way, the associate pastor would step into his position," she mused. "Definitely a short-term advantage. And if he plays his cards right, a long-term advantage." Lorna set aside the list and observed the Monet on the east wall. "Move over so *I* can serve Jesus in your place." She shook her head. "Let's hope that's not the deal," Lorna continued, but gut instinct suggested the possibility shouldn't be dismissed. She placed "Rich Cooper" on her mental list. Then she noticed Brittan's note indicating that a star suggested top suspects. Lorna scanned the starred names:

> Hattie J. Smith, *Head Deaconess*
> Frank R. Bass, *Church Treasurer*
> Conroe Youngblood, *Church Board Member,*
>   *Small Group Leader*
> Libby Youngblood, *Cooper's Wife,*
>   *Sunday School Teacher*
> Evelyn Wright, *Singles Ministry Director*
> David M. O'Keefe, *Head Usher—guy Lorna got*
>   *license number on*

The other 24 names weren't starred. *Let's hope one of these people is the perpetrator and we nab them fast,* Lorna thought. *Otherwise this could take a year.*

She fished through the emails until she found the messages from those whose names were starred. Her eyes widened as she read the venom dripping from them—especially David O'Keefe's. That man point-blank called Devenport crazy and stated the church wasn't meant for scum that landed in prison. It was one thing to minister to them while they were in jail and another thing to actually bring them into the church. O'Keefe went on to say that before long the sanctuary they'd worked so hard to build would be nothing more than a breeding ground for crime and the violation of women and children.

"Yikes!" Lorna said and then read the last lines: "Maybe you're the one who needs to be in prison. Since you want a prison ministry so badly, join them where they are!"

In the face of these leads, Lorna's previous doubts about Devenport's culpability diminished. *Maybe somebody* did *set him up*, she decided.

"Okay, buddy," Lorna said through a sage nod. "You're numero uno. And I get to take you on." Her cell phone produced the chime that usually indicated a text message. Still focused on the list, she reached to her waistband and retrieved her cell. Lorna absently pressed the buttons that opened the text message window and soon saw the name Michael Hayden. She dropped the emails and dismissed O'Keefe and his cronies while devouring Michael's words:

> *Good morning, Lorna! Just wanted 2 let u know I'm thinking about u. I enjoyed last night. Can't wait until this weekend. 2day's insane 4 me. Same 2morrow and the next. I'll keep in touch, but don't think I've forgotten u if I don't. I can't WAIT until the weekend. Polish up ur golf clubs. I'm playing 2 win this time. In case I lose—loser gets a kiss! xoxo...Michael*

Lorna hit the respond button and daringly wrote,

> *I call being loser.* ☺ *LL*

ELEVEN

Trent Devenport walked through the final steel door, stepped into freedom, and into the arms of his Katie. The door clapped shut behind him and ended Trent's six night stay in jail. Katie didn't wait until they were outside the building to cling to him as if she hadn't seen him in months. He buried his face in her soft hair and clung right back.

"I don't know how, but we're going to get through all of this," he said, his voice thick, his eyes stinging. "God is faithful so I know we will."

When he pulled away, he noticed a tall woman behind Katie. Trent extended his hand to the former church member who'd stepped forward with the bond money and the offer to represent Trent at no charge. "I don't know how we'll ever thank you, Stevie," he said.

The lawyer smiled. "If we win, that's thanks enough. It's the least I can do for the best pastor I've ever had."

Katie gripped Trent's hand. "We want to pay the bond money fee back as soon as we—"

Stevie Simon raised her hand and shook her head. "Not a chance," she stated like a woman few argued with. "I just won a huge case and got a big piece of the pie. This is my way of investing a chunk

in the kingdom. 'If one falls down, his friend can help him up,'"
she quoted like a woman who knew her Bible well. "I'm 'his friend'
this time." She motioned toward the glass doorway. "Come on.
We need to have a little meeting with the bondsman and then, if
you're up to it, let's have lunch and start planning our strategy." The
lawyer turned toward the door and marched forward, her shoulders stiff. In her double-breasted jacket she reminded Michael of the
confident, assertive Claire Huxtable from *The Cosby Show*.

Trent glanced toward Katie. "What about the boys?" he asked.

"They're with your mom," Katie replied. Her brown eyes full of
unfailing trust, she was more beautiful than Trent remembered. "I
told them you'd be home this evening. All they know is you've been
away for awhile, and I figure that's all they need to know."

He nodded while they followed Stevie to the parking lot. The
June sunshine blasted Trent with heat he welcomed. Being cooped
up in jail made him appreciate every molecule of fresh oxygen.

"You have no idea what being in jail is like," he commented. "I
felt so degraded. I'm so glad to be *out!*" He stretched his hands from
side to side, lifted his face to the sky, and said, "Thank You, *Jesus!*"

Stevie paused and turned toward them. "Let's make sure you
stay on this side of the bars!" she rapped out like a drill sergeant,
and Trent feared for anyone who crossed her on this case.

"Ma'am, yes, ma'am!" Trent hollered with a salute.

The lawyer laughed. "Come on, you! We're in my Cadillac." She
pointed toward a fiery red chariot that perfectly fit its owner.

Trent squeezed Katie's hand and smiled into her eyes. "We'll
win this case and get it behind us. I promise."

"Yes, we'll win because the jury will be afraid to cross Stevie,"
Katie whispered.

Snickering, Trent followed the lawyer to the red Caddy. From
the first time he'd met her, he sensed Stevie was a fireball in court.
The pit-bull intensity in her dark eyes confirmed he'd made no
mistake. She'd won her share of cases since he met her at the first

church he pastored. The most widely publicized was a racial discrimination case that rocked Houston and made national news. Ironically she'd been representing a white man. The press had been nasty and turned the whole thing into a racial showdown. As a result she'd taken serious criticism from a few African-American organizations, but Stevie stood her ground.

"Discrimination is discrimination," she said every time a microphone was shoved into her face. "It doesn't matter who it's against—man or woman, black or white. It's *wrong!* I stand for equal rights for *everyone.*"

As Trent crawled into the back of the vehicle with Katie at his side, he sensed the undeniable assurance that God had assigned Stevie to his case and that she could prove his innocence if anyone could. Trent slipped his arm around his wife. Even though the vehicle's interior was very hot, Trent wanted her close. She laid her head on his shoulder.

"I missed you so much," she said, her voice unsteady.

"I missed you too," Trent replied and rested his cheek on her head.

Stevie turned on the air conditioner and glanced over her shoulder. "We'll have it cooled off in a few," she declared.

"Thanks." Trent lifted his head and held the lawyer's gaze. "For everything."

"It's my pleasure," she affirmed in a voice that said whoever had done this to her former pastor had better get out of the way.

She switched her attention to driving.

Despite the trickle of sweat slipping down his spine, Trent squeezed Katie closer.

"I'll be here for you no matter what," Katie vowed. "I'll go to my grave believing someone has done this to you out of revenge. You have more integrity than six men, Trent Devenport." With the Caddy cruising from the parking lot, she peered into his eyes and stroked his cheek.

Trent never doubted that marrying Katie had been God's perfect will for them and now he knew why. He wondered how many other women would hold such undying belief in their men.

I just wish the pathway to Katie hadn't been through Michael, Trent thought and rested his cheek on her head once more. That irony never ceased to amaze him. Trent would've cut off his own arm before hurting his best friend. They'd been a team through Little League baseball, junior high drama, high school football, and college debate.

When Michael arrived in their dorm room saying he'd asked Katie Lane to the Christmas banquet, Trent never told him he'd been about to do the same. They'd never discussed Katie, and Trent was shocked Michael had beat him to the task of asking her out. Being the loyal friend he was, Trent backed off. But gradually he fell hard for Katie. Even when Michael announced he was going to propose, Trent kept hoping she'd say no or something would deter Michael.

Then one day he'd run into Katie in the library. The two shared an English class with a killer professor who piled on the work. They'd been stressed beyond insane over a final that loomed bigger than Mt. Everest. Katie said Michael was supposed to help her but had to work. Trent offered to step in. Out of desperation, she readily agreed. They'd found a corner table and spent the next two hours laughing their way through a cram session that left Trent dazzled...and Katie with a thoughtful expression in her eyes. By the next English class, the thoughtfulness had morphed into a spark of attraction.

Trent fought against the inevitable as hard as Katie did. They avoided each other for several days before Katie had a fender bender in the parking lot—with Trent, no less. From that time on they'd both known. And hurting Michael had nearly killed them both. While Trent wanted to marry the woman God had chosen for him, he wondered how his best friend would ever forgive him. Now he wondered if Michael ever had. And to top it off, Michael had never married, unless his success was a prime indicator he'd married his career. Perhaps the betrayal warped him for life.

Despite everything Trent spent his few nights in jail wishing for his former friend. And he wondered if there was any way Michael would consider standing by him during this dark hour. If ever Trent needed character testimonies it was now. And having a popular mayor stand up for him would go a long way in court.

The car hadn't even begun to cool when Stevie pulled into the parking lot of "A-1 Bond Service," one block from the jail. She steered the Caddy to a stop, put the vehicle in park, and swiveled to face the couple.

"The first thing I'm going to ask you for is a list of people who have access to your office. I don't care if you trust them with your life. *Nobody* is above suspicion at this point. Understand?"

Trent nodded.

"This is your *life* and your reputation we're talking about. We're going to play hardball and play it fast. Got it?"

She shifted her gaze to Katie. "There's no friend that's above this in my eyes. So don't try to protect anyone. Just give me the names, and I'll do the rest."

"But—" Katie began.

"No buts." The lawyer lifted her hand, and a diamond wedding band flashed.

Trent knew Stevie's husband well. He was the strong, silent type—a former NFL quarterback who looked like he could and would physically protect Stevie from any force that dared come against her. *And it's a good thing she has him,* Trent thought. *As feisty as she is, she probably stirs up trouble.*

"Most of the people on that list will never know we checked them out," Stevie continued. "If they're innocent, there's nothing lost. But I've been doing this too long not to tell you that it's usually the one everybody trusts who's the culprit. So when I say hold no name back, I mean hold no name back. Got it?"

The couple nodded in unison.

"And while I'm on the subject, let's think about the dynamics of this prison ministry you wanted to start."

"Looks like it's starting off with a bang," Trent drawled. "I've got experience on my side now."

Katie's giggle was laced with a nervous quiver.

Stevie's red-tinted lips barely lifted at one corner. "We know you created a tidal wave with your plan. There's a dissenting camp that shouldn't be ignored."

"This is *awful*," Trent said. "I always want to think the best of everyone. I've had my share of hard-nosed church members, but it's hard to believe any would stoop to *this!*"

"Yes, you Pollyanna types are the ones they always go after," Stevie drawled. "You see the best in everyone, and sometimes you see good that just isn't there." She narrowed her eyes. "There are some very wicked people out there, and some of them are warming church pews."

"If this does turn out to be a church member, and if we ever get out of this, I think we need a sabbatical or two," Katie stated.

"Oh, you're going to get out of this," Stevie vowed, the fire in her soul flickering in her eyes. "I don't care if it costs me my *hide*. I'll find out who's done this and fry him or her."

"In Christian love of course," Trent teased.

"Of course." Stevie's assured smile couldn't have been more promising. "Jesus was tough when it came to confronting sin. He turned over tables for holy justice. He's called me to do the same." She jabbed her index finger against her chest.

"And heaven help anyone who gets in your way," Trent declared.

"Heaven help them is *right!*" She turned off the engine and said, "Let's go!"

TWELVE

Lorna stood in the Houston Heights Community Church's foyer gazing at the glassed-in billboard that announced the church's options for Wednesday night attendees. According to the roster there were numerous support groups and small groups that met. A more traditional Wednesday night prayer service was offered in the main sanctuary. Lorna gambled that Mr. Raisin-face, aka David M. O'Keefe, would show up in the traditional service.

She pulled her petite purse's strap onto her shoulder and walked toward the sanctuary's east entrance. Lorna stepped through the opened doorway and scanned the worship arena. She estimated 200 people present, and they were assembling in the middle front section. Lorna hovered near the wall and searched for Raisin. She spotted him near the west entry greeting people as any head usher would.

Head down, Lorna turned back to the doorway and ducked into the foyer. She navigated around a man pushing a vacuum cleaner and a woman holding the hands of two boys who were more interested in trying to kick each other than cooperating with their mom. Before Lorna arrived at the west entrance, she smoothed a hand over her wig. She wore the same disguise tonight she'd worn Sunday morning...blonde wig, no makeup. But instead of a skirt she wore a snazzy capri pant set with thong sandals.

Lorna adopted an innocent, blank expression and stepped through the west entrance behind a gray-haired couple who glanced toward her like she was the wrong breed of bird for this flock. Lorna noted the sanctuary was occupied by a more mature crowd and estimated herself as the only person there under 50.

She paused near Raisin and waited to receive whatever he was handing out. When her turn came, he smiled into her eyes with a kind, blue gaze that suggested he was somebody's dear ol' grandpa who wouldn't hurt a soul. If his email hadn't proven different, his hateful remarks last Sunday morning did. Lorna smiled into his eyes and accepted the service schedule, replete with a section for notes.

"We're mighty glad you decided to join us here in the big sanctuary," Raisin said, "but there are several small groups in your age group that are meetin' around the church."

"Why, thank you," Lorna crooned in a rich Georgian drawl. She leaned closer and held up her bulletin. "But rally, I *sooooo* prefer a more mature service. You know, folks my age just don't seem to have any depth these days."

"Well, you're in the right place then, young lady," he asserted with a grin that for one second teetered on inappropriate before he switched back to grandfatherly. Keeping her wide-eyed innocent appeal intact, Lorna was shocked at how swiftly the man covered his less-than-pure thoughts.

Hmmm, she thought, *wonder what* his *computer's history might reveal.*

Lorna meandered a few feet from Raisin, found a seat within earshot of his conversations, and settled down. She crossed her legs and placed "Cruise Raisin's computer" on the top of her mental to-do list. She'd have Brittan in tow, who, by this time had penetrated Evelyn Wright's small group. The church billboard said it was for single adults ages 25 to 35. Even though Brittan wasn't quite 25, she could fake it as well as Lorna.

However, neither Brittan nor Heather would ever be able to touch Lorna's ability to feign accents. That was a talent Lorna was born with. Even her college theater teacher had been amazed at her on-the-spot ability. So tonight Lorna was a sweet Georgian gal. Tomorrow she could be British or from inner-city New York. And the next day—or minute—she'd do a Chinese inflection if needed. Brittan couldn't even fake a Chinese accent with Lorna's skill, and she was half Chinese!

Lorna tuned into Raisin's continual monologue. If he welcomed one person, he welcomed 50 with the sincerity of Saint Nicholas himself. Just about the time Lorna was being lulled into tuning him out, a conversation began that made her sit straighter.

"What have you heard about Devenport?" a man asked.

"Out on bond today," Raisin responded under his breath.

Lorna snatched a glance toward the pair. Another mature man dressed in a blue suit stood near Raisin. The two smiled at each other like they were discussing a Houston Astros' game. Lorna grabbed her purse from the floor, discreetly pulled a high tech hearing aid from the side pocket, cradled it in her palm, and nonchalantly tucked the earpiece in her ear. Brittan had come up with three of the units a few months back. Lorna hadn't asked where she'd gotten them and didn't care. The woman had her ways when it came to gadgets and devices. After a minor adjustment, Lorna lowered her head and listened hard. While the special hearing aid upped the room's noise, it also allowed her to pick up low-level conversation five feet away.

"Guess he's washed up...for now," blue suit said.

"Let's hope anyway," Raisin stated. "No church would have...in child porn, and well they shouldn't."

"Have you...what the pastoral committee has decided?"

Lorna turned the hearing device up a fraction and strained for every word.

"My wife's on that...you know."

"Yes, of course."

"They're meeting tonight. The wife is going to suggest that they appoint…Cooper in the interim with a…for hiring him as senior pastor."

"And you conveniently agree, right?" Blue suit's voice held a smile.

"Of course," Raisin said through a chuckle that said Mrs. Raisin better suggest Cooper as an appointee or *else*.

The pianist started a soft rendition of "Amazing Grace" that crashed into the hearing aid with enough gusto to make Lorna jump. She glanced around and saw no one looking her way.

"Well, he *has* done a…job…associate pastor."

Lorna glanced toward the pianist. *Can't you stop already?* she fretted and winced at a high note.

"Yep. And he really knows…listen to the people," Raisin affirmed. "That Devenport wouldn't listen to…mother! With all the people against that prison…he dreamed up, he was still trying like a blasted bulldog to push it through!"

"Whoever heard of actually bringing…into a church like that anyway?" blue suit challenged.

"I say he landed where he deserved." Raisin's growl was as low as a sneaky demon. "If he wants to…prisoners so bad, then let's let him."

Both men's chortles took on a sinister twist, and by the time the service got in full swing Lorna was nauseated.

She was dropping the hearing aid back into her purse when a familiar man slipped in and sat across the aisle from her. Lorna's eyes widened as she recognized Michael. *I had no idea he attended here.* Then she corrected herself. *He can't attend here. He told me Monday he was raised Episcopalian and was still a faithful member.* That tradition had started when his great grandmother had come to America as an Italian immigrant. She'd worked for an Episcopalian family, eventually adopted their beliefs as her own, and ultimately influenced several generations.

Michael glanced across the aisle straight at Lorna. That's when she realized she'd been staring at him since he walked in. A vague recognition flitted across his features, followed by a puzzled squint. Lorna averted her gaze, held her breath, and waited to see if he recognized her. She picked up and opened a hymnal. When she dared glance his way again, his attention was absorbed in the worship leader, who was now directing the group in "The Old Rugged Cross."

Lorna's attention was tangled up in one question: *What is Michael doing here?*

The worship leader faded into a blur; "The Old Rugged Cross" became a distant mantra as Lorna's mind tabulated the facts. *First, Michael Hayden is Trent Devenport's former best friend,* she recited while tapping her index finger against the hymnal. *Second, Katie Devenport is Michael Hayden's former fiancée. They had a bad breakup years ago. What if Michael has revenge in mind?* The question exploded into Lorna's mind. Her eyes widened. She curled her fist into a tight ball.

What if Michael is the one who set up Trent Devenport? Lorna's brow wrinkled. She shook her head. *No! I can't think that! I won't think that! Michael is an honorable man. He'd never do anything like that. I know he wouldn't. I just know it. If anything, he's here to reconcile with his friend. The* Houston Star's *evening edition had an article on Trent posting bond today. Maybe Michael came tonight to run into his old friend.*

Lorna's cell phone vibrated against her waistband. She pulled it out of its harness to find the caller was Heather. Both she and Brittan had tried to call Heather this evening but had gotten no response, which was odd. Heather had been assigned a "Celebrate Recovery" small group that one of the chief prison ministry dissenters, Libby Youngblood, was in charge of. All three friends thought it odd that the leader of "Celebrate Recovery" had been opposed to bringing in people who needed recovery the most.

Oh well, Lorna thought. *Self-focus never has been logical.*

She toyed with whether or not to take the call in the middle of a service. The last time she'd visited her grandmother, the elderly woman had vowed cell phones in church were an instrument of the devil himself. Lorna sighed and decided this was an emergency. After another cautious glance toward Michael, she stood and hustled from the service. When she stepped into the massive foyer, she flipped open her phone.

"Whazzup? Where are you?" she asked and hurried for an outside door. All three of the debutantes had learned to *never* have a conversation with the others anywhere they might be overheard.

"I'm in the woods about a half mile from the school where I volunteer," Heather explained as Lorna opened the door and walked into the evening heat. "You know...where I teach karate?"

"What in the name of common sense are you up to?" Lorna asked. She hadn't realized her nose was so cold until the heat blasted her.

"Looks like I've stumbled onto an animal cruelty case," Heather stated, her voice low.

Lorna walked farther from the building and glanced over her shoulder to assure no one was in earshot. "What? I thought we were focusing on the Devenport business," she whispered.

"Is there some rule that says we can't take on two cases at once?" Heather asked.

"No, but..."

"I was at the school jogging. I heard a cat crying in the woods near the track, and you know me and cats..."

"Right."

"I went looking for her, but she ran from me. Before it was over, she led me to a deserted shack. It's filled with dogs. I think it's some kind of a holding place for a dog fighter. Most of them are pit bulls. There were some animal remains outside the hut. I'll spare you the gory details. It's an *awful* situation. On top of that, I think I got into some poison ivy, and if I did, it's *not* good."

"That stuff never has bothered me."

"All I have to do is look at it and it's all over me! I'm calling the doctor at the first sign of it. Otherwise I'll be a scratching fool for weeks. I'm starting to itch just thinking about it."

Lorna snickered. "Did you catch the cat?"

"No. She went under a dilapidated storage building near the house where the dogs are. I think she's got a litter."

"So what are you going to do?" Lorna gazed toward a jet leaving a white trail across the sky that looked like a huge zipper.

"I'm hanging here another hour...until it's nearly dark," Heather said. "The 'Celebrate Recovery' business will have to wait. Sorry 'bout that. I've taken some photos with my cell phone," she continued without a breath. "Whoever has these dogs tied up has to come feed them. I'm going to see if I can get lucky and maybe catch a photo of them. If I do, I'll try to get a license plate number too. Then I say let's go ahead and turn in the info with a rose. It'll be quick and easy, and we'll get a charge out of it. And the animals will be rescued as well—which is the most impor—" Heather stopped.

"Oh my word," she breathed. "Someone's coming, just like I thought. They're in a black Hummer. Gotta go." The call went silent.

Lorna checked the cell phone screen: "Call ended." She gave a quick prayer for Heather, pivoted to face the church, and mumbled, "You and those cats, Heather. I promise, they're going to get you *killed* one day."

All three friends enjoyed the thrill of their secretive semi "living on the edge" lives. So far they'd escaped having their lives threatened—unless you counted being chased down by a *Houston Star* security guard. Last year after they'd left a rose and clues on Duke Fieldman's desk in the middle of the night, they'd nearly gotten nabbed by a gun-totin' guard who meant business.

Idly Lorna wondered how they would penetrate Raisin's house

without getting caught. All they needed was his computer's IP address so Brittan could access his computer through the internet and then snoop around to her heart's content—as long as his unit was connected to the internet. Lorna wouldn't be one bit surprised to find porn in his computer's history. That flicker of lust tonight hinted at a cesspool not far beneath the surface.

If it was child porn they could seriously link him to what happened to Devenport. Nevertheless, they'd still needed solid proof that Devenport's computer had been tampered with. Even if Raisin did have smut on his computer they had no proof of him planting anything on the pastor's computer.

Maybe we could set a trap, Lorna mused. As she walked back toward the church, her thong sandals slapped against her heels in sequence with the thoughts rapping through her mind. When her fingers curled around the church's door handle, Lorna's thoughts jumped back to Michael and the reason for his being at Houston Heights. On a whim she strolled across the refrigerated foyer toward the ladies' room. She was about to enter the multistalled room when she noticed a family restroom between the men's and ladies' room. Thankful for a more private option, Lorna went inside, closed the door, and locked it. She plopped her purse on the baby changing table, reopened her cell phone, and punched in a quick text message to her new guy.

> *Hey, Michael! Whazzup? Just wanted 2 let u know I'm looking forward 2 this weekend. Can't wait for u to beat me in golf. Grins. My parents want 2 have u over 4 dinner sunday night. r u free? LL*

Lorna sent the text message before she chickened out. Yet the second she hit the send button, she wondered if she was being too forward so soon in their relationship. She leaned against the wall. *Will he answer now or wait until after the service?* She knew her Grandma Leigh would not be happy with her for texting someone in church. *Okay, I promise I won't do it again,* she vowed but shamelessly eyed the screen anyway. Lorna despised herself for suspecting him but at the same time she needed the assurance that his motives for attending the service were honorable.

If he tells me where he is I'll know he's not up to something, she decided and stared hard at the phone. *Come on, Michael. Come on. Text me. Tell me you're at Houston Heights and why.*

The thoughts had barely flitted through her mind when her phone vibrated with an incoming call. The caller ID said Michael Hayden.

Lorna closed her eyes, held her breath, and answered the phone. "Hey, speak of the devil," she teased.

After a soft laugh, Michael said, "I just had the oddest experience. I saw a woman who reminded me of you. Like you with blonde hair maybe...and paler."

"Really?" Lorna asked and gazed at herself in the mirror. While she didn't have the washed out look Heather did without makeup, Lorna was definitely paler—especially with the blonde wig.

"And then you called," he continued. "Do you have a blonde cousin or sister or something?"

"Well, my older sister is blonde. But it's out of a bottle, and she's in Fresno, California, anyway."

"Where did you see me—my lookalike?" Lorna closed her eyes and crossed her fingers.

"At a church I'm visiting. It was funny. Like she was there and then when I walked out to call you, she was gone. Maybe I just dreamed her up because I wanted to see you," he said, his words laced with a smile.

"Well, that's encouraging," Lorna drawled. Her fingers tightened on the phone as she dared to voice the next question. "What church are you visiting?"

"Houston Heights," he said with an easy, I've-got-nothing-to-hide cadence.

Lorna leaned against the door, closed her eyes, and nearly wept.

"You remember Trent Devenport?" he continued.

"Yes."

"This is his church. I don't know…it's odd. I just had the urge to connect with him. You know, moral support and all that. We were friends for so long. I just can't get him off my mind. The newspaper said he posted bond today. I knew it was a long shot, but I wondered if he might be here at his church, ya know?"

"You're one in a million, Michael Hayden," Lorna responded.

He was silent so long Lorna thought she might have lost him. She glanced at her phone's screen to see if the call was still connected.

"You have no idea how much that means to me, Lorna," he finally said, as if she'd just handed him the world on a golden platter.

Lorna's stomach flipped, and she knew then that Michael wasn't just another boyfriend. He was a man she could seriously fall in love with.

"If I weren't on another mission, I'd come over to your place *now*," Michael continued. "When you say stuff like that it makes me want to be with you."

Lorna rubbed her free hand along the front of her blouse. Both palms oozed a cold sweat that wouldn't stop. She swallowed hard knowing Michael was standing mere feet away in the church foyer. If her girlfriends wouldn't assassinate her for blowing her cover, Lorna would have sashayed out of the restroom and into Michael's arms.

"I'm *glad* you want to be with me, Michael," Lorna admitted. "*Really, really* glad."

"I know a cell phone isn't exactly the best way for me to say what I'm about to say, and I know you only just met me, but…" He hesitated.

"Go on," Lorna urged.

"Like I've already told you, I've known you...and admired you... for years. I even saved the *Sports Illustrated* issues that featured you."

Lorna bit her lips together and then mouthed, "Yes!" while pulling her fist to her side.

"And I'd like to ask a favor. If there's no chance of your playing for keeps, then please let me know now...before we go any further. I—I'm not trying to rush you or anything," he hurried. "I just don't want to get hurt later if there's no chance—"

"There's a chance," Lorna blurted. "A big chance." She straightened and rapidly blinked.

He went silent and finally said, "Good!" like a man who'd awakened from the best dream ever, only to discover it wasn't a dream at all. "And your parents want me over Sunday night?"

"Yes. Definitely."

"Even though I'm not IBM?" he said over a chuckle.

"In the face of you, IBM is history with them right now. They just want me happy."

"With someone *they're* happy with?" Michael's voice dripped with mirth.

"Yep, you got it."

"But maybe I'm the ticket for all of you?"

"Maybe," Lorna agreed and slowly nodded.

"Well, my mother used to be worried sick that I wouldn't marry a nice, Italian, Episcopalian gal. But she's gotten *so* past that. Now, to be honest, I think Mom would be thrilled if I dragged home a street woman with one leg, one eye, and one hair sticking out the top of her head."

Lorna giggled.

"She's so worried I'll never find someone, she's getting desperate. Carrie told her all about you, and she and Dad want to meet you ASAP. They live in Austin. Are you game?"

"Of course," Lorna said through a smile. "I'm dragging you to meet my folks. Turn about is fair play, isn't it?"

"Honey," he drawled, "you aren't *dragging* me anywhere. I'm trotting right beside you like your loyal, devoted hound."

"Good then. I'll make sure I bring plenty of doggie biscuits," she said through a gurgle of laughter.

THIRTEEN

The second Lorna flipped her phone shut, a voracious temptation to spy on Michael overtook her. Before she questioned the wisdom of taking a peek, Lorna unlocked the bathroom door and opened it a few inches. Michael stood in the foyer with a smile the size of Antarctica. He looked at the cell phone, tossed it into the air, caught it, and kissed the cover. As he turned toward the sanctuary, Lorna bit her bottom lip and forced herself not to run to him. She strained to catch a last glimpse of him and then shut the door. Lorna leaned against it, closed her eyes, and sighed.

"This is it," she whispered. "He's the one. I just *know* it!" Before she could get too caught up with the fantasy, Lorna opened her eyes, stepped to the mirror, and leveled a hard glare at herself. "Listen," she lectured, "you just met him. Don't get carried away." But despite her attempts to keep her tough face on, Lorna broke into a grin even *she* thought was goofy.

The cell phone vibrating in her hand brought her back to planet Earth. She looked at the ID screen in wild hope the caller might be Michael once more. But Heather's name appeared on the screen.

Lorna was jolted back to her friend's predicament. *She isn't in the safest of situations right now, and here I am flirting.* She flipped open the phone. "Whazzup?" she quizzed.

"Okay. They've come. They've fed the dogs. They've taken four with them. They've gone. I have photos of two men and a woman on my cell. I've got a license plate number. I overheard them talking about fighting, so I know that's what these dogs are being used for. I could call the humane society, and—"

"Right, and you're the regional spokesperson, so they'd hop."

"Exactly. Or we could let 'the Rose' handle this. Your thoughts?"

"The Rose," Lorna stated. "Let's meet back at the penthouse tonight. We'll get Brittan to research the license plate. We can scrape together as many details as possible and then go make a... um...*deposit.*"

"You know the last time we broke into the *Star* and left a rose we nearly got caught," Heather reminded her.

"Yep. And since Duke knows we're 'the Rose,' it kinda takes the fun out of leaving the flower with him."

"The Devenport case is another thing altogether because he and I disagree about whether or not Devenport is guilty. I can't *wait* to leave him a rose on that one. I'd *really like* to notify somebody tonight about these dogs though," Heather continued. "I don't want them to spend another night in these horrible conditions."

"Let's get creative...*more* creative on this one," Lorna said. "If we let the police know tonight, *they'll* take care of any arrests and call the humane society." She straightened and touched the top of her head. "Then we can email Duke the information we give to the police so he can get on the story first thing in the morning."

"I like it," Heather said. "We could attach the photos to the email."

"Sure. But how do we get the info to the police and keep from getting caught? They're open *all night.*"

"I have no idea on that one. See what Brittan thinks. Meanwhile, the cat's out of hiding. I'm going to see if I can catch her."

"And what are you going to do with her when you do?"

"I'm putting her in my car and coming back for the kittens—if there are any. It may be a tom."

"You need to get out of there," Lorna said. "Let the humane society get her when they get the dogs."

"Not on your life," Heather said. "She's a white Persian with blue eyes. Beautiful. Skinny as a rail, but beautiful. She needs me—or maybe *he* needs me. There's not that much difference between six cats and seven anyway."

Lorna lifted her hand. "Okay, that's fine. But don't think I'm running interference on the vet."

"I only asked you to do that one time with Lucky," Heather insisted. "And now you act like you should get a Nobel prize or something."

"At the very *least*," Lorna teased.

"Oh, just stop it, will ya?" Heather said. "I've got to get on with my cat catching. Call Brittan. Tell her what's going on. See if she can be back at your place in an hour."

"Okay, will do," Lorna said and realized Heather had already hung up. She lowered the phone, sighed, and grabbed her purse. Opening the door a few centimeters, Lorna peered out in search of any sign of Michael. All she saw was that poor mother and those two boys heading back the way they'd come. But now the kids had stopped trying to kick each other and were actually walking peacefully with their mom.

Invasion of the body snatchers, Lorna breathed and then snickered. She slipped into the foyer, lowered her head, and hustled toward the exit. By the time she hit the parking lot, she seized upon a new idea about investigating Raisin. Lorna scanned the area for his Ford pickup. When she failed to find it, she cruised the parking lot in her rented Toyota until she spotted his truck. She parked two rows over.

After locking her car Lorna hurried toward the pickup. She squared her shoulders in an attempt to look casual and not sneaky.

Once Lorna drew even with the cab, she cast a cursory glance around the parking lot. So far it remained deserted. She leaned close to the glass and gazed inside. After several seconds she spotted a briefcase resting on the floor between the passenger and driver's seat.

Her eyes widened. *What I wouldn't give to borrow that puppy for an hour or two!* she thought. Lorna eyed the locks. They were down like good little protectors. "Bummer," she mumbled and wondered if the truck had an alarm system. "Well, there's only one way to find out." Lorna balled her fist and prepared to hit the vehicle. If a siren went off, she'd scramble to her car and slip inside before anyone suspected her. Lorna gazed toward her Toyota, parked near a line of green shrubbery. She estimated the distance to be 20 feet. She could duck and weave between the cars with no problem.

Lorna lifted her fist and delivered one hard blow to the side of the truck. She winced in anticipation of the screaming siren. But the only noise in the parking lot was from cars passing on the road on the other side of the church. A dog's yapping erupted from across the street, and Lorna glanced toward the terrier to find he was after a disinterested cat.

"Good thing Heather's not here," she stated under her breath. "You'd have yourself a new home in five minutes, kitty." Ignoring the dog–cat showdown, Lorna gazed toward the church and confirmed she was still on her own. She checked her watch. Thirty minutes had elapsed since the church service started. That meant she had about 30 minutes to figure out how she was going to get that briefcase—20 minutes to be on the safe side.

That's when Lorna spotted the sliding glass windows in the back of the truck cab. Her eyes widened. "I'm not believing this. I wonder if the windows are unlocked."

"It's a long shot," she decided, but one worth taking. She draped her purse strap over her head and shoulder. Then Lorna scurried to the back of the truck. She placed her hands on the hot tailgate and stopped. *Gloves, gloves, gloves,* she reminded herself and dug the latex must-haves from her purse. She wiggled her fingers into the thin plastic and was rewarded with an immediate film of sweat. After roughly rubbing the place she'd pressed with her naked hands, Lorna scrambled over the tailgate and crawled into the pickup bed. On all fours she crept toward four bales of hay shoved against the cab and navigated around a bag of oats sitting near a rumpled stable blanket the size of a horse. Finally she stopped beneath the window and rocked back on her heels.

"Ouch! Ouch! Ouch!" she complained and shook her burning hands. The metal pickup bed testified that it was June in Houston.

After rubbing her stinging knees, she stared at the window to determine the best method of opening it. Finally she decided this wasn't a science. She just needed to do it. Lorna placed both hands on one pane, gritted her teeth, and shoved it to the left as hard as she could. It budged half an inch.

"Yes!" Lorna muttered. She rammed her index and middle fingers through the opening and tugged hard. The window moved another half inch. Sweat trickling down her temples, Lorna scratched at the base of the wig and wished she were bald. She gave the window one more yank. It slid open.

Lorna glanced toward the church and around the parking lot. That poor woman with those two boys came tumbling from the church. This time the kids were both crying like they meant it. The mother looked like she'd been wrestling a couple of bear cubs and was ready for a relief squad.

"Bad night at the zoo," Lorna observed.

She crouched lower in the bed and peeked over the side, waiting until the mother was steering a minivan from the parking lot. Lorna peered around the area one last time and then developed her plan. She calculated she could go through the window head first and reach for the briefcase without having to wedge her whole body through the opening. Lorna slithered halfway through the window, into the cab's suffocating heat, and had her fingers around the briefcase handle in 30 seconds.

There's a benefit to being tall and having long arms, she enthused. But the metal window frame biting into her abdomen spoke of the drawbacks of being a size 16 in a size 14 opening.

The case in hand, Lorna wiggled back into the pickup's bed. She snapped the window closed and suddenly heard a man's angry voice saying, "I don't care what you have to tell them. Tell them I died for all I care. I'm *not* going to deal with those people anymore. The last horse I bought from them died within two weeks, and they did *nothing* about it. Forget it."

Her eyes wide, Lorna gazed toward the voice and confirmed her fears. *The Raisin!* She ducked low and doubled over the brief-case. *He's too early!* she thought and pressed against the cab. But the scorching metal's unforgiving burn forced her to inch away.

As the angry voice neared, she imagined him spotting her with the briefcase. The next image was of her in the back of a police car.

She grabbed for the stable blanket and jerked. The feed bag sagged sideways, but Lorna didn't take time to notice whether the man spotted the movement. She threw the blanket over herself and hunkered down between the bales of hay.

"Tell them I said to forget it, Molly! Goodbye!" he growled before ramming his key into the truck door and opening it.

Lorna held her breath and waited for an indication that he noticed his case was missing.

The truck wobbled as he got in and the door slammed. The engine turned over. The rig started to move forward. Lorna fought the urge to claw from beneath the suffocating blanket and jump out. Only God knew where he would stop and if she'd have time to escape. If he made a trip to some store or even to get gas, she was out of here. If he went all the way home—and Brittan's research indicated that was on some country road in the middle of nowhere—perhaps he would unload the truck and discover her.

Once again came the image of her in a squad car.

Dear God, get me out of this, she prayed. *I promise I'll give the man his case back...turn it in to lost and found at the church...I just need to get out of this truck bed a free woman!*

As sweat oozed from every pore, Lorna closed her eyes against the grit sifting from the blanket. Her nose prickled in protest of the horse hair and accompanying sweat smell. Lorna fought back a sneeze, but the sneeze won. She pinched her nose hard and breathed through her mouth. That was rewarded with a prickly hair that stuck to her lips.

The truck hit a dip and accelerated. The muffled sounds of motors and distant horns indicated they'd merged from the parking lot into traffic.

Here we go! Lorna experienced a new meaning to "pray without ceasing."

A few minutes lapsed before the truck slowed, and Lorna shifted toward the driver's side as the vehicle turned. *Either he's going on to another street or into a parking lot,* she thought and hoped for a parking lot. Sure enough, the vehicle slowed and stopped. The engine was turned off. The driver's door opened.

"Okay, thanks for looking," Raisin said. "I can't imagine where I left it. I thought I had it in the truck with me. Maybe I put it in the back."

Lorna's eyes widened as she imagined him looking straight at the blanket. The feed bag near her head shifted. "Nope. Not here." The man released a few choice expletives. "I hope I didn't set it in the truck bed and somebody took it. It had my credit cards and laptop in it!"

Despite the heat and fear of getting caught, Lorna smiled.

"I know...I know," he snapped. "It's not 1930 and in the country!

You've said that a hundred times. I'm not half as absentminded as you think. Look, I need to get gas now, and I'll have to pay cash because my stinkin' credit cards are in the case!" he exclaimed, sounding like the whole ordeal was the person's fault. "I'm not blaming you! Just stop it," he bellowed, and then he stopped talking.

Lorna imagined him hanging up on the person. *Probably his poor wife,* she conjectured and listened to the telltale noises of his opening the gas cap and inserting the pump nozzle. The faint smell of gas penetrated the musty blanket.

The only movements Lorna allowed herself were random eye-blinks. A few pinpoints of light penetrated the edges of the warm blanket, and sweat now trickled into the corners of Lorna's eyes with a hard sting. Her blinking grew more rapid, and she willed herself not to rub her eyes.

Finally the man removed the nozzle with the sound of metal scraping metal. He screwed the gas cap into place and slammed the tank's small door. The click of the nozzle in the pump was the indicator the deed was done. Lorna dared to move her head and lifted the blanket. She caught one glimpse of his back before the sound of boots gritting on pavement grew faint.

Okay, Lord, this is it! Lorna panted as she slung off the blanket. *Either You go with me or I'm fried!* She clutched the briefcase and her purse and scrambled to the tailgate. Raising her head, she spotted Raisin in line inside. Then she bailed out. Once her feet hit the pavement, Lorna remained hunched until she neared the edge of the truck.

A young redhead dressed in a business suit eyed Lorna from the next pump, where she was filling a sports car. The woman's curious, dark eyes silently asked, *What were you doing in the back of that truck, and who are you hiding from?*

Lorna brushed at the grit on her arm, straightened, and darted an assured smile and nod toward the woman. The redhead glanced down. Lorna tucked the briefcase under her right arm and walked calmly toward the side of the store. She feigned a casual glance or two toward Raisin inside and picked up her pace when she saw him about to exit the station's mini-mart. She stepped around the corner at the same time he exited. Hovering against the brick, Lorna watched him a second before casting a final glance at the redhead. A puzzled look on her face, the woman glanced toward Lorna's pathway and then observed Raisin.

Don't say one word to him! Lorna willed and was hard-pressed not to race around the building. Logic insisted she stay and see what the young woman did—if anything.

Fortunately the redhead's gas tank was full about the time Raisin passed in front of her vehicle. She concentrated on removing the nozzle from her car and didn't look toward the truck again until Raisin was in it. The redhead lifted her hand, stepped toward the pickup, and then shrugged as the vehicle left the curb.

Lorna whipped around and quickly walked to the back of the building. She paused long enough to get her bearings and realized she was within 20 feet of the Home and Garden Center of a Wal-Mart Supercenter. She headed straight to the store and into the humid outer chamber that housed the plants. Once through the glass double doorway, Lorna entered the chilled store.

The sweat around the edges of her wig turned to winter's frost; the thin film of perspiration on her body became cold dew. Lorna was sorely tempted to collapse in one of the lawn chairs on display, but instead she sought the help of the first associate she spotted.

"Where's the nearest restroom?" she croaked.

The blonde clerk with thick glasses mutely pointed toward the front of the store. "On th' other side of tha checkout up frunt," she added as her gaze trailed to Lorna's hair.

"Okay, thanks," Lorna said and smoothed at the wig. *The thing is probably crooked as all get out.* She cut a glance over her shoulder and hurried toward the restroom. Hopefully the redhead hadn't pursued her.

Two minutes later she gazed at her reflection in the ladies' room mirror and nearly laughed out loud. Not only was the wig crooked, but she had a piece of hay sticking out the top and a streak of dust marred her cheek. Her elegant capri set, once cheerfully yellow, was now a crumpled image of its former self. Given the presence of her latex gloves, Lorna figured she'd make even the dullest mind pause to ponder. She set the briefcase and purse between her feet, removed the latex gloves, and shoved them into her purse. Lorna whipped off the wig, and splashed her face with water. She pulled a comb from her purse, loosened her hair from the tight knot, and fluffed it around her face. After removing her wristwatch, she washed her hands and forearms until all traces of grit were gone. Once her hands were dry, Lorna replaced the gold watch and checked the time.

"Eight-fifteen," she whispered. "Brittan is probably wondering what happened to me."

Lorna pulled her phone from her purse and noticed she'd missed a call and a voice mail. She pressed a series of buttons and discovered the caller had been Brittan. No noise had come from the stalls since she entered the restroom, but Lorna looked beneath them to make sure she was alone.

She pressed the redial button. The second Brittan answered, Lorna said, "I'm at the Wal-Mart not far from the church. Remember where it is?"

"Yes," Brittan answered.

"Please come and pick me up *now!* Call me when you get to the parking lot. I'm waiting in the bathroom until then. I'll meet you in front of the Home and Garden Center. Got it?"

"But what—"

"I'll answer all your questions when you get here," Lorna said. "Just come *now,* okay?"

"Okay—okay. I'm on my way."

After disconnecting the call, Lorna put the latex gloves back on and manipulated the sweaty wig into a tight roll. After a wrestle that would make Houdini proud, she shoved the wig into her purse. The glimpse of Raisin's briefcase nearly sent Lorna into an investigative frenzy, but she stopped herself. This was not the time or place. Instead she waited for Brittan's call.

FOURTEEN

The second Lorna plopped into Brittan's rented Dodge, she balanced the briefcase on her lap and popped it open.

"What are you doing here?" Brittan asked. "Whose case is that? How'd you get here? Ooooooooo. And why do you smell like a *horse*?"

"I crawled into David O'Keefe's truck through the back window and got his briefcase out. I'd just landed in the truck bed again when he came out. I hid under a stable blanket in the back until he stopped for gas. That's when I escaped with the briefcase and went straight to Wal-Mart."

Brittan stared at Lorna like she was James Bond's twin sister. "You *go*, girl!" she declared. "I'm *so impressed*."

A horn honked from behind. Lorna jumped and swiveled to see if the person was a redhead in a sports coupe. When she spotted a sour-faced matron in a dilapidated sedan, Lorna covered her heart with her hand and wilted against the seat.

"Let's get out of here," she breathed. "A woman saw me at the gas station, and I've been worried she followed me. She had red hair and was driving a cobalt-blue sports car."

"Haven't seen her," Brittan said and stepped on the gas. "But then I haven't been looking for her either."

Lorna gazed around the parking lot. "I don't see any car like that. I think she shrugged the whole thing off and moseyed on home." She sighed and absorbed the cold air blowing from the vents while eyeing the contents of the briefcase. "I took off my wig in hopes that if she did follow me she wouldn't recognize me.

"Man oh man, I've given new meaning to the word sweat tonight," Lorna continued.

"You *smell* like it," Brittan complained.

Lorna cut her friend a sour glance. "That's the horse blanket, not me."

"Sure, blame it on the animal. He can't defend himself."

"Animals!" Lorna shrieked. "Oh no! I forgot Heather! She's coming to our place—might already be there!"

"What's the deal with her?"

"She stumbled onto an animal cruelty case. We're going to deliver a rose tonight."

"Whew! This day is getting eventful," Brittan said as she steered the vehicle into traffic.

Lorna picked up the laptop and tilted it from side to side. "Look what I got," she bragged in a singsong voice. "Raisin's computer."

"Raisin?"

"You know—David O'Keefe. Don't you remember my telling you his face looks like a raisin?"

"No," Brittan said through a chuckle, "I don't. But if you say so…" She slowed for a stoplight near the church while Lorna gingerly fingered the papers and paraphernalia inside the briefcase.

She spotted the credit cards neatly inserted into slots in the leather lining. "I'm going to have to wait until we get home to dig into this. Once I give it a good go-through, I'll have to get it back to him somehow."

"We could mail it," Brittan said with a shrug.

"Good idea," Lorna agreed. "And if we weigh it ourselves and put regular postage stamps on it, nobody can trace it to us."

"Right," Brittan said. "But we need to make sure we keep gloves on while packaging it and use self-stick stamps. Our saliva has our DNA in it."

"Now she tells me!" Lorna huffed and raised her hand. "And all these years I've been licking Popsicles like crazy. Think of all the DNA I've lost."

Brittan cast an "oh brother" glance at her before turning in to the church parking lot.

Lorna scanned the area and spotted a white Ford pickup parked under the portico. "Oh no!" she said and gripped Brittan's arm. "That's him! He's here!" She shoved the laptop back into the briefcase, snapped it shut, and lowered it to the floor.

"Just keep the briefcase out of sight," Brittan said. "I don't see him anyway. There's no way he'll connect you to his missing case."

Closing her eyes, Lorna took a slow breath and said, "Yes, you're right. He probably came back here to see if he left his case inside. I overheard him on the phone, and he was pretty upset that it was missing."

"Look," Brittan said and steered the vehicle toward the nearest exit, "let's just go home for now. Sounds like Heather's waiting for us anyway. We'll come back later and get your rental car. You can turn it in in the morning."

"All right," Lorna agreed and caught a glimpse of Raisin coming out of the church. She instinctively inched down.

"Stay cool," Brittan warned and revved the engine. The car glided into the merge lane, and they proceeded onto the highway. "Home free!" Brittan called.

Lorna released her breath and cast a final glance toward the church. The white Ford was nowhere to be seen. "I can't believe I just did what I did!"

"Me neither," Brittan said. "Especially not in daylight. We're all getting braver and braver."

"Or dumber and dumber," Lorna countered.

"Whatever." Brittan rested her hand on the gearshift. "All I got tonight was a very strong suspicion that Evelyn Wright is probably not our perpetrator."

"Oh?"

"That woman's so computer illiterate she had to ask for help to run the PowerPoint presentation. And how easy is *that?* I promise, before it was over she had everything *but* the right PowerPoint up there. I don't think she could plant something in somebody's history if she had to."

"Well, maybe she didn't actually do the dirty work herself," Lorna mused. "But that doesn't mean she isn't an accessory."

"Yes, you're right. But I don't know..." She shook her head. " I just don't think she's involved."

"I think Raisin is. You should've seen the way he looked at me tonight. Yuck!" Lorna's mouth turned down, and she shook her head. "I'm betting the old codger has all sorts of porn on his laptop."

"I guess we'll soon see, right?" Brittan replied with a wink.

Lorna's cell phone vibrated in the holster at her waistband. "Someone's calling. My guess is Heather." She retrieved the phone, glanced at the screen, and said, "Bingo."

"She's probably wondering where we are."

"Whazzup?" Lorna said into the receiver.

"Where *are* you guys?" Heather asked. "I've been ringing your doorbell like crazy."

"We're on our way," Lorna said. "I just pulled off a biggie, and it's taken us longer than I thought. We should be there in about 20 minutes."

❊ ❋ ❊

Michael pulled curbside in the tidy neighborhood and gazed at the modest brick home nestled on the corner lot. The large yard

was replete with ferns in the flower beds and geraniums along
the sidewalk. A cheerful wreath hanging on the front door read
"Welcome." Everything indicated Katie's creative, sweet nature and
reminded Michael of their good times. She'd majored in home eco-
nomics and wanted to teach. Michael enjoyed being the "victim" of
all her new recipes. He smiled at the warm memories that brought
back feelings of friendship...and, amazingly, nothing romantic.
The eight-thirty sunshine cast long shadows along the tree-lined
street; likewise, the sun was finally setting on his long-held bitterness. In its place was a desire to support and help his best friend
and former fiancée.

He opened the car door, got out, and noticed the home's front
door opening. Michael snapped the car door closed, held his breath,
and waited. Trent Devenport stepped outside, paused, and glanced
over. His eyes widened. Michael didn't move. An evening breeze
caressed the trees. The leaves whispered of more than a decade of
brotherhood that no pain could erase. Trent closed the house door
and took a step toward his former friend. Propelled by old memories and brotherly love, Michael hurried forward.

The two met halfway. Without a word, Michael extended his
hand and clasped Trent's in a hard shake. The shake turned into
a back-whacking hug. Gripping Trent's shoulder, Michael pulled
away, looked him in the eyes, and said, "I believe in you, man. I
know it's all a lie."

Trent's upper lip quivered. His eyes reddened. He coughed
and pressed his fingers against his eyes. "Thank you so much," he
wheezed. "It *is* a lie! I don't know who's done this to me, but—"

"I'll go to the paper, and issue a statement saying I believe in you,"
Michael declared and was amazed at how resolute such a sponta-
neous decision sounded.

"You'd *do* that?" Trent lowered his hand and stared at his friend
like he was Michael the archangel, not Michael the mayor.

"Yes." Michael nodded.

"So many people think I'm the scum of the earth." Trent laid his hand on his chest. "You'll really be going out on a limb. It might hurt your reputation."

"My rep means nothing next to my friend being sent down the river for something he didn't do." Michael gripped Trent's shoulder again. "It's the least I can do."

The front door banged open. A blond-haired four-year-old stood on the threshold like the king of the neighborhood.

"No, no! Come back here, Todd!" Katie's high-pitched voice floated from inside.

"Daddy!" Todd exclaimed and scurried toward his father.

Katie stepped out onto the porch, holding another blond boy that looked just like the first. "I promise," she fumed, "these guys are worse than two monkeys!"

"I've got him," Trent said and scooped his son into his arms.

"Play train with me, Daddy!" Todd exclaimed.

"Me too!" the other twin piped in and squirmed out of his mother's grasp.

"Tim!" Katie exclaimed, trying to wrestle the child back to her. When he won the contest, she straightened, placed her hands on her hips, and shook her head while he insisted on Trent picking him up as well. That's when Katie spotted Michael. Her eyes widened just like her husband's had.

"Look who's here, honey!" Trent announced, balancing a son in each arm.

"I see!" Katie exclaimed and rushed forward.

Before Michael could stop her, she was hugging him. He was relieved to feel nothing but fondness. "Hello, Katie."

"Oh my goodness!" She placed her hands on either side of her face. "I can't believe this. Would you look at you? You haven't changed a bit!"

"Neither have either of you." Michael included Trent in his appraisal and meant it.

When Katie leaned into Trent and placed her arm around him, the family portrait was complete: father, mother, and the offspring of their love. Each was dressed in shorts and a T-shirt and looked like they should be strolling along the beach during a free-spirited vacation. The dark circles under Katie's eyes attested that their lives were anything but carefree right now.

"Michael's going to issue a statement to the newspaper in support of me," Trent said, his gaze never leaving his friend.

"You'd do that?" Katie asked.

Michael nodded. "I've got to," he admitted and slipped his hands into his pockets. "I couldn't live with myself if I didn't."

"Come on." Katie tugged on his arm. "I've got some fresh coffee, and I've just tried out a new cake recipe. I need some tasters."

"Hey, I'll volunteer!" Trent planted a kiss on each of his son's cheeks. "Want some cake, big boys?"

"Yes!" the twins said in unison. Then they were squirming from Trent's grasp and racing back into the house screaming, "Cake! Cake! Cake!"

"Don't touch that cake!" Katie squawked and raced after them. "I've still got to put the icing on it!"

Trent laughed and shook his head. "Never a dull moment," he said.

Michael chuckled and had never been so thankful to be single. "Two have got to be a handful," he observed.

"Katie's mother had twins, remember?" Trent asked.

"Yep." Michael snapped his fingers. "Katie's older sisters."

"Right." Trent shook his head. "She says if she had a terrible enemy and wanted to wish the worst thing on him she could think of, she'd wish he had twins."

"How cold is *that?*" Michael questioned.

"You ever had twins?" Trent cut his friend a speculative look and awaited the obvious answer.

"Uh, no."

"Well, I wouldn't take anything for either one of mine," Trent admitted. "But they're not twice the work, they're *ten times* the work. Whew! I don't know how Katie managed while I was in jail." A dark expression flitted across his face as the friends strolled toward the house. "And I sure don't know what she'll do if I have to go back and stay a while."

"That's not going to happen," Michael assured. "Not if I can help it."

"Yes, well, you can only go so far," Trent hedged.

"I know. But I'll go as far as I can for you."

The men paused and faced each other in front of the house. "I'll never be able to repay you," Trent admitted.

"You're not supposed to." Michael whacked his friend's back once more. "Now come on!" They tromped into the house like two brothers, and Michael was hit hard with the smell of cake that had to come from heaven. "Wow!" he exclaimed as he gazed around the spotless living room. "It smells like Katie's outdone herself this time."

Trent rubbed his hands together. "It's supposed to be a Dr Pepper cake," he said and motioned Michael through the living room and into a cute breakfast nook. The house was filled with country decor that reminded Michael of some of the magazines his mother always had lying around.

Katie stood in the kitchen and donned a frilly apron while the boys created havoc with the pots and pans they were pulling from the cabinets. "Have a seat," Katie said and motioned toward a trio of high-backed chairs hugging the breakfast bar. As Michael settled into a chair, she gazed toward the ceiling and said, "Let's see, if I remember, you always liked black coffee with your cake."

Michael nodded. "You remember," he said.

"We've even got French vanilla." She lifted a red package that read "Folgers."

"That's even better," Michael agreed and was struck by how soft and childlike Katie's voice was. Back in their college days that sweet voice had woven a spell around Michael's youthful heart. But now he wondered how long it would take for it to get on his nerves. He was tempted to say, "Do you *try* to sound like a six-year-old or does it just come naturally?"

Trent moved from Michael's side and stepped into the kitchen with Katie. The two worked as a team putting the finishing touches to the cake and making a pot of coffee that smelled like something Michael wanted to swim in. The whole time the couple dialogued they appeared to be two halves of a whole, working together in harmony.

When Katie placed the chocolate cake and coffee in front of Michael, she smiled into his eyes. He was stricken with the simplicity of her nature before she turned back to her task. Katie was different than he remembered, but somehow the same. Her brunette hair, brown eyes, and translucent skin had changed little, but Michael didn't remember her being so…uncomplicated. Her figure was certainly trim and showed little fallout of having given birth to twins. She was dressed in an attractive manner, but nothing sparked for Michael. He remembered Lorna in her sequined dress with the moonlight making magic in her hair. Compared to the tidal wave Lorna created in his mind, Katie had been a mere swell.

He picked up his coffee mug and took a sip while Trent leaned in to kiss Katie's cheek. Michael tried to imagine himself as the husband in the kitchen and nearly dropped his mug. Horrible feelings of being trapped swooped his soul. He stared at his cake and panicked to think that *he* could have married Katie. While her winsome ways were perfect for a pastor's wife, she'd have been a royal flop as a politician's wife. She simply didn't have the sparkle and tenacity and grit he saw every time he looked in Lorna's eyes.

And this is the person I've been pining for all these years? he thought and was amazed that he'd wasted so much mental energy on a woman who was so wrong for him.

Trent's voice sounded as if it were from a distance, and Michael shifted his focus to his friend, now settling beside him.

"So how are you enjoying being mayor?" he questioned.

Michael stammered around a few seconds about the ins and outs of the office and then crammed his mouth full of cake. He was washing the first bite down with a gulp of hot coffee when the twins started a screaming fight over the lid to a pot.

"Would you two just *stop* it!" Katie demanded, her little girl voice going shrill. She pulled the lid from their grasp, and that worked like a volume switch. Their wails increased tenfold.

Michael winced and stopped himself short of covering his ears. Just a few minutes with these two blond bombers made him dread the thought of having kids. Apparently Katie's side of the family manufactured twins from one generation to the next. Yet another swirl of terror nearly knocked Michael from his seat. The last thing he was ready for were two identical screamers. While he *did* want a family like any normal guy, right now Socks was enough fulfillment for him.

After passively trying to corral the boys, Katie looked toward Trent with a "what do I do?" look on her face.

"You've got to be firmer with them, dear," Trent admonished. He slid from his chair, knelt beside his sons, placed his face inches from theirs, and said, "Stop this now!"

The volume switched off. The twins stared at their father like they knew the party was over.

Good grief, Michael thought. *She's struggling to manage her own kids. I can't imagine how she'd hold up managing the media.*

Katie placed her hands on her hips. "Why don't I take them out back so you two can visit?" She yanked off her apron and tossed it on the counter.

Trent rose from the floor. "Well, honey, I hate for you to—"

"It's okay." She held up both hands and shook her head. "I know when enough is enough, and this is *enough*." Katie turned to her sons. "Come on, boys," she crooned. "Let's go out back and play in the new pool Mommy got you last week."

The twins cheered and dashed down the hallway on chubby legs, leaving behind the scattered pots and pans.

"You guys help yourself to more coffee and cake," Katie encouraged before following her sons.

Michael barely had time to finish chewing his second bite before he sensed Trent's gaze. He cut his friend a sideways glance and encountered blue eyes full of regret. Michael lifted his brows and waited.

Finally Trent said, "I never meant for the whole thing with Katie to turn out like it did." He shook his head, fell silent, and Michael was taken by his intense honesty.

"I know," Michael said. "But really, I think it was for the best... for both of us." He couldn't stop the relieved laughter bubbling from his soul.

"What?" Trent prompted, raising his hand.

"Oh..." Michael hedged. "I was just thinking about what your mother-in-law said about twins. I think I'm starting to understand."

"And you're glad I'm the one corralling them and not you. Is that it?" Trent jovially challenged.

"Something like that," Michael admitted.

"Well, 'in all things God works for the good of those who love him,'" Trent quoted.

"I believe that more now than ever." Michael picked up his coffee mug and offered a toast. "Here's to God protecting us from ourselves."

Trent picked up his mug and tapped Michael's. "And here's to His protecting us from our enemies." Trent's eyes clouded. "Even when we don't know who they are."

FIFTEEN

The GPS announced, "Turn left." Brittan did as directed, and Lorna eyed the gadget that was taking them straight to the precinct captain's home.

"The number is 691," Heather confirmed from the backseat.

Lorna glanced over her shoulder. Heather's blonde hair hung beneath the dark knit cap that snugly fit her head. In the shadows she reminded Lorna of a beautiful criminal in an action-packed drama who was poised and ready to steal a famous diamond. But the debutantes were interested in restoring justice, not obstructing it.

The three friends had sent Duke Fieldman the information about the animal abuse, replete with digital photos. Then they looked up the Houston Police Department's website, and Brittan hacked away until she got the address of a precinct captain.

Brittan steered the rented Dodge down the dark lane dotted with circles of light from the street lamps. At midnight the neighborhood appeared peaceful.

Lorna's nose was as cold as a tombstone. She reached toward the air vent and shoved it toward Brittan.

"Why do you always have the car so stinkin' cold?" she asked. "My nose is, like, freezing off."

"It's just fine to me," Heather interjected. "Lorna, I promise, you've got reptile blood. You're as cold-blooded as they come."

"It's 30 below in here," Lorna complained and rubbed her gloved hands together. The thin latex at least provided a scrap of insulation from the chill.

Brittan clicked the blower to low. "There. You happy?"

"What? I can't hear you for the ice in my ears."

Rolling her eyes, Brittan adjusted the thermostat as well.

Lorna pressed the button to lower the window and allow some warmer air in the vehicle. Despite the chill, her heart beat with the adrenaline that always accompanied one of their Rose drop-offs.

As they neared the end of the street, the headlights illuminated a large swing set and slide in the next block. Lorna leaned forward and strained to see if it was a neighborhood park. If so, they could leave the vehicle and slip back to the precinct captain's city car that was parked in the driveway. He'd see the rose first thing in the morning when he headed for work.

Two cats dashed in front of their sedan and raced toward the curb. As they jumped the curb, the cats became a tangle of rolling fur balls. High-pitched yowling erupted into the night. A nearby dog joined the upheaval with enough barking to rattle Europe.

"Well, great!" Brittan muttered. "Why don't we just turn on a siren and announce we're here over a megaphone?"

"There's his house!" Heather exclaimed. "On the corner."

"Perfect," Lorna stated as the cat and dog chorus died. "Look straight ahead. I think that's a park. We can leave the car on the other side and walk to the captain's house."

"Works," Brittan stated. While they cruised down the next block and around the corner, she clicked off the headlights, leaving only the parking lights on. "Oh man," Brittan groaned. "What a bummer. There was a jungle gym on this side of the house."

"I told you he was probably married," Heather chided from the backseat.

"But he's *so* got it!" Brittan stated under her breath, and Lorna stopped wondering what had motivated her to choose this guy.

"I didn't think he was all *that*," Heather replied.

"You're blind," Brittan shot over her shoulder, and the dashboard reflection on her glasses reminded Lorna of a computer screen.

"Maybe you're just feeling left out," Lorna teased, "and it's getting the best of you. Heather's engaged. I'm being nabbed by the mayor. And you're still on your own."

"Hey, I'm happy on my own!" Brittan snapped and pushed up her glasses.

"Then why are you pining after Rob Lightly?" Lorna picked up the ziplock bag lying on the seat.

"Who said anything about pining?" Brittan replied. "I just think he's great looking. What's wrong with that?"

"Well, I'm with Heather. I thought the photo on the web was okay, but he didn't look like anybody I'd want to date."

"You two need to have *your eyes* examined," Brittan groused.

"Yes, I can see you involved with a police captain," Lorna teased.

"If he made you mad on your first date, you'd shoot him," Heather added and poked at Brittan's shoulder.

"Ha, ha, ha," Brittan drawled. "It doesn't matter anyway. He's obviously married and has a family."

"Ah well, better luck next time," Lorna encouraged and rolled up her window.

Brittan pulled into the playground's parking area and stopped the vehicle. She turned off the parking lights and the engine. "Okay, here we are," she said and swiveled toward Lorna. "You've got the rose and notes?"

"Got 'em. And the CD with the photos." She lifted the gallon-sized bag that held the goods. "Just like it was when we left your apartment. Nothing's leaked out."

Heather chuckled.

Brittan sighed and lifted her hands. "What I have to put *up* with!" she complained.

Reaching for the door handle Lorna said, "Come on. We need to get this over with." She opened the door.

"Roger that," Heather said.

The summer night wrapped around Lorna like a warm blanket. She rubbed her chilled nose and snapped the door shut. Even though the park was deserted, Lorna could almost hear the echo of children's voices as they laughed and played, ran and tumbled. She recalled her early years. They'd been good. Very good. Her parents were a long way from perfect, but they'd been there for her...taught her good morals...and the love of adventure.

The three friends met at the back of the car and exchanged silent glances. Their plan was simple. They'd walk to Lightly's police car, slip the bag under his windshield wiper, and vanish into the night. Then they'd wait until the information seeped to the public via the press. Reading the follow-up articles and hearing about "the Rose" on radio and local TV stations made their escapades fun and satisfying.

Each was dressed like the other...black slacks and shirt. Each wore a black knit cap, pulled low.

Lorna lifted her hand and wiggled her fingers. "Where are your gloves?"

"Yikes! Mine are still in the car." Brittan whirled back toward the vehicle.

"Glad you mentioned them." Heather pulled her latex gloves from her pocket and slipped her hands into them. "Hope we won't need these." She smoothed her hands together. "You're the one who should do all the touching."

"Right," Lorna agreed. "And you're sure police cars don't have alarms, Brittan?" Lorna questioned as Brittan joined them again.

"I'd say there's a 99 percent chance it doesn't." She gave her gloves a final yank. "Who'd be stupid enough to try to steal a police car or break into one?" She pulled her cap down on both sides. "Most robbers are smarter than that, and most police forces know it. So why spend extra money on every car?"

"Okay." Lorna rubbed her forehead where the knit cap scratched her skin. Despite the former chill, her hands oozed a slight layer of perspiration against the latex. The moment was upon them; her body tensed and heated.

"If all goes well, we should be back here in two minutes," Heather announced while stuffing her hair beneath her cap.

"If all goes well…" Lorna repeated and relived that chase from the *Houston Star's* business offices. That security guard had been armed and ready to shoot, but they'd escaped because Brittan knew all the nooks and crannies of the building her family owned. The security guard never imagined he'd been chasing the daughter of the Shay publishing magnate along with her two best friends.

Lorna scanned the 30 or so yards between the park and the captain's home. Other than a collection of garbage cans near his house, there was no place to hide. And those garbage cans didn't look like a guaranteed refuge at all.

"Look," Brittan stated, "if, by some bizarre long shot we get caught, I'm heading straight to the car. If one of you is cornered, I'll swoop in and you get on board."

"And if *you're* cornered?" Heather challenged.

"I won't be." She sliced her hand through the air. "How hard can this be anyway? His car is right there." She pointed.

"Okay, let's do it," Lorna said, and the two debs fell in beside their friend. The trek to the vehicle was as uneventful as a Sunday afternoon stroll. The night smelled of damp earth and warm summer dew and reminded Lorna of her grandparents' farmhouse where she'd spent summers.

The three sleuths silently slipped through the night like three panthers focused on their mission, determined to succeed.

Lorna reached the police car first. She paused until Heather and Brittan were at her side. Then she reached for the windshield wiper. Even though Brittan insisted the vehicle had no alarm, Lorna planned to handle the wiper with the greatest delicacy. If an alarm were in force, a mere touch or lift of the wiper usually wouldn't set it off. A slap of the wiper against the windshield might, if the alarm's sensitivity was set on high.

Here goes, she thought and gritted her teeth as she lifted the wiper. The sound of distant traffic and the shrill chirps of crickets slipped through the night. Lorna placed the ziplock bag beneath the wiper, making sure the single-stemmed red rose lay at a strategic angle. She gently settled the wiper against the windshield and pulled away from the vehicle. Everything was simple. Easy. Now they only had to walk back to the black Dodge, drive from the neighborhood, and the delivery was complete.

Everything was perfect…predictable…. until those fighting cats darted across the yard and began another screaming duet. The canine backup singer once again piped in.

"Oh no," Heather groaned.

The front porch light flicked on.

"Duck!" Lorna hissed and dropped into a squat.

Her friends joined her in the car's shadow as the door bumped open.

"All right already," a sleepy male voice floated across the yard. "It's just cats anyway." A dog with the bay of a St. Bernard erupted upon the yard and sounded as if he were serious.

Lorna figured he was probably the size of a squirrel and wouldn't know what to do with a cat if he caught one. But that didn't stop him from flinging his attitude all over the far side of the yard.

When the cat rampage ceased, Brittan squeezed Lorna's arm. She glanced to Brittan and then toward Heather. Both friends' expressions said the same thing, *Let's go before the dog loses interest in the cats.*

Lorna inched up until she glimpsed the man's shadowed form in the glassed door. He yawned, scratched his head, and gazed toward the sound of the barking dog. Glancing behind, Lorna scoped the best route out of there. Pointing toward the darkest section of street, Lorna whispered, "Let's get outta here."

Brittan hunched over and led the way. Lorna followed. She scurried across the street to the clump of trees that shielded the street from the lamps' glow. The three friends stepped into the oak patch, pausing long enough to ensure they'd been undetected.

The man still stood in the door. The dog was trotting back from the yard's shadowed edge.

Lorna released her breath and turned toward the park pathway.

"Hurry!" Heather whispered. As she glanced back she saw the dog stop where they'd just been squatting.

"Oh no. It's a German Shepherd," Brittan whispered. "What if he's trained to track?"

"Are you kidding?" Lorna turned. "Of course he is. He's probably an official police dog."

"Yes," Heather whispered, "but unless his owner gives him the order, he probably won't leave the premises. They're *trained*," she emphasized.

"It doesn't sound like he waited for any order to be disturbed over the cats," Brittan whispered.

"Rocky!" a male voice commanded. The man stepped out, and the front door slapped shut.

Lorna's attention shifted to the bare-chested officer. Rob Lightly for sure. His hair was mussed, and he wore pajama bottoms. The dog trotted to his master, who bent to scratch his ears. "What's the matter, boy?" he asked. "This just isn't like you."

The dog wagged his tail but whined.

"Those cats fight all the time," Rob mused and scanned the neighborhood.

Lorna grasped Brittan's hand on one side and Heather's on the other. The silent message between the three friends was *Wait!* The slightest movement could alert the skilled dog.

Rocky's whine escalated into a short bark.

His face drawing into a frown, Lightly strolled toward his car.

Eyes widening, Lorna held her breath as the cop neared the vehicle and stopped. He placed his hands on his hips and studied the windshield. Next he rounded the vehicle and leaned over the ziplock bag. After several seconds of examination, he gingerly pulled the bag from beneath the wiper and opened it. The first object he pulled from the bag was the single-stemmed rose.

"Oh my word!" he exclaimed and whipped around to examine the street. After gazing directly at the clump of trees, he pulled the documents and photos from the bag. Hurrying toward the porch light, he fumbled through the papers and photos before commanding, "Rocky, inside!"

The dog trotted to his master's side and through the door his owner opened. Rob searched the neighborhood once more before closing the door.

"If he's what his reputation says," Brittan whispered, "he'll be back out here in 5 minutes—at the police station in 15."

"Let's scram!" Lorna whispered, and all three hustled toward their vehicle. Within three minutes, they'd cruised to freedom and couldn't wait to see tomorrow's headlines.

SIXTEEN

Michael set his ice water and lasagna on the kitchen table and tossed his suit jacket and tie into a chair. He settled into the opposite chair while buttoning his shirt cuffs. After a quick bite, he snapped open the morning paper and skimmed the headlines. Front and center was an article titled "The Rose strikes again." Michael smiled through a surge of curiosity and wondered who this mysterious sleuth was. Houston would be abuzz once again. This time the case involved animal cruelty.

Sipping his water, Michael eyed Socks, who gobbled his morning albacore. While Michael wasn't an animal fanatic, he respected God's creation and couldn't understand how some people could purposefully abuse or harm critters. Even though he'd hardened his heart against Socks that first day in the parking garage, he'd ultimately been a pushover for the feline's pitiful cries. Looking back, Michael was thankful the cat had been a tom and not a mother cat with six kittens. He'd have been forced to either take them to the animal shelter or find homes with the people at the office.

He turned his attention back to the article and could sense the glee in the columnist's description of the latest Rose escapade. The writer's name was Duke Fieldman. He recounted the Rose's former accomplishments and wrote with a skill that would probably whip up the populace's curiosity. Everyone loved a good mystery…especially when the person uncovering the mysteries was a mystery.

"Humph!" Michael said and decided this Duke Fieldman was the one he should contact regarding his support for Trent. Today Michael would call the reporter and then email him a letter in the afternoon. A worried voice in the back of his mind suggested such a move would harm his popularity. Decent voters hated child molesters and porn distributors. In standing beside Trent, Michael was aligning himself with someone the people were probably frothing at the mouth to see sent away. Michael fully understood that his statement would stir a commotion. He was also sure every advisor from his father to Governor Terry would tell him to stay out of it.

But Michael just couldn't do that. If he were in Trent's position, he'd be begging God for someone to validate his character. Michael would be that someone for Trent.

He lowered the paper and gazed toward the horizontal blinds that allowed thin slits of light to stripe the kitchen table. Memories of last night's meeting with Trent and Katie blotted out his surroundings. The evening had gone well…very well. After the boys had gone to bed, they'd reminisced about old times without a trace of the awkwardness that could have existed. The time together had miraculously enabled Michael to release all vestiges of resentment and pain. And this morning he was more thankful than ever that he hadn't married Katie.

He was completely free and available for Lorna. Even though she'd received a serious setback on the tennis tour, she possessed a certain spark Michael recognized. It was the same determination in his mother's eyes. She'd stood beside Michael's dad in developing the menswear store that had grown into a national chain. Every store manager from Texas to Ohio was in awe of the feisty Italian gal who took nothing off anyone. Even his father had a wary look in his eyes when Edna Hayden had enough.

He thought of Lorna and chuckled. She'd admitted to leaving the imprint of her tennis racket on her attacker's face. Even though her karate friend had come to the rescue, Michael wondered if Lorna might have made the attacker *eat* her tennis racket before it was over.

Chuckling, he set aside the newspaper, sipped his water, and made short work of downing the leftover lasagna. When a dollop of sauce landed on his chin, Michael wiped it off and shamelessly licked his finger. Lasagna was his favorite breakfast, second only to pizza. Lorna had mentioned pizza as a favorite breakfast item as well. He smiled.

After tidying the kitchen Michael checked his watch. He was running an hour early this morning. Lorna woke him up at six. Well, thoughts of Lorna, anyway. He'd been dreaming of their first kiss and awakened to thoughts of their last conversation. She'd said yes...and an *eager* yes...to his asking if their relationship stood a chance.

Thoughts of Lorna ushered in reflections about their weekend dates. Michael decided to head to the office even though he'd be an hour early. *Much to do,* he thought. *If I can cram more in today, maybe I can kick off early tomorrow evening.* The sooner he got off work, the sooner he'd see Lorna. Hopefully the weekend would be all theirs.

After shrugging on his suit jacket and draping his tie around his neck, he grabbed his cell phone from the kitchen counter where he'd left it charging last night. Spotting the phone book nearby, Michael decided to contact Duke Fieldman now. Couldn't hurt. Besides, once he hit the office he'd be sucked into work, and he didn't want the public statement about Trent to slip his mind. His mother told him that when he got focused on something he could forget to breathe. Michael figured he was just like his dad in that respect...and maybe a few other men as well.

After dialing the number, he leaned against the counter, crossed one leg over the other, and eyed Socks. As the phone rang, the cat finished his last bite and sat back for a good paw licking. Finally a receptionist came on the line and stated in monotone, "Houston Star."

"Duke Fieldman please," Michael said.

After a series of clicks, a male voice said, "Yo."

"Duke Fieldman?" Michael asked.

"Speaking," Duke clipped.

Michael grimaced. The guy sounded as cocky as they came.

"Duke, this is Michael Hayden."

Silence. Then Duke said, "The mayor?"

"In the flesh," Michael replied with a harder edge.

"How can I help you?" Duke asked. This time his tone held a hint of respect.

"I'm good friends with Trent Devenport—the pastor who's—"

"The child porn guy?"

"Yes." Michael shook his head. "I mean no," he hurried. "No. He's not. I don't believe he's guilty. He's one of my best friends," he said, his voice firm.

"No joke?"

"No joke," Michael repeated. "I want to make a public statement in support of Trent's character." He uncrossed his legs and stood straight. "I like your style and was wondering if I emailed you a statement this afternoon you'd—"

"Yes!" Duke exclaimed.

Michael bit back a laugh.

"Okay," he said. "If you'll give me your email address, I'll send you my statement sometime..." he mentally reviewed the day's schedule, "—sometime after two o'clock," he said and reminded himself to enter a reminder on his Palm Pilot. "Does that work?"

"Yes." Duke agreed. "I'll go ahead and start putting together an article."

"Good," Michael said.

* ✤ *

Lorna's eyes drooped open. She pulled the covers under her chin and planned to roll over, snuggle in for a few more Zzzzzzs. Before the roll could happen, her gaze rested on the laptop sitting on her dresser. Her eyes opened wide.

Raisin's laptop!

Last night Lorna scanned through the laptop's internet history. Her first look showed no signs of pornography. She and Brittan planned a more thorough perusal, but they'd been sidetracked by Heather's animal cruelty case. After delivering the rose last night, Lorna fell into a post-adrenaline slump and dropped into bed the second she changed into her pj's.

She checked the old-fashioned alarm clock on her nightstand. The ticker belonged to her grandmother and brought back fond memories of long summer days in Texas hill country. She'd seen the old gadget sitting in a storage closet last Christmas and asked her Grandma Leigh if she could have it.

The spry 65-year-old asked, "Whatever for, Cheryl?" She'd wanted Lorna's parents to name her Cheryl and refused to call her anything else.

Lorna smiled, held the clock to her chest, and said, "I like its tick."

"Drives me crazy," Grandma admitted and granted Lorna's wish.

Now Lorna relived each minute of her childhood summers with the clock's every tick.

A soft knock preceded the doorknob's click.

Lorna shifted and gazed toward Brittan, who held up the morning paper. "You awake?" she asked, her hair mussed from the night's sleep.

"Did we make the headlines?" She sat straight up.

"You better believe it!" Brittan said through a broad grin.

Still in her housecoat, she piled onto Lorna's bed and flopped open the paper. The smell of fresh ink accompanied her "Ta da!"

Lorna pushed the hair out of her eyes and perused the article. "'The Rose' strikes again," she read and clapped. "Woo hoo! We struck again!"

"Look." Brittan pointed to the photos. "He printed one of Heather's digitals."

"Of course he did," Lorna said and picked up the paper. "He knows he'd be in hot water if he didn't."

Brittan snickered.

"Three prominent businessmen arrested in multiple cases of animal cruelty," Lorna read. *Animal remains and recently deceased dogs found at the site,* she continued reading to herself and cringed anew over Heather's photo. Sidebar shots included the arrests of the perpetrators. "According to precinct captain Rob Lightly," she read aloud, "he found the photos and a typed document detailing where the site was. A single-stemmed red rose was left with the information. Lightly claims his dog was disturbed at midnight. He discovered the information and rose on his windshield after letting the dog out. He suspected 'the Rose' was still in the area but was so appalled by the information he went inside to immediately call the police station. The arrests happened at four-thirty this morning. The animals have been moved to a local animal shelter." The article went on to venerate 'the Rose.' Duke also mentioned receiving an e-mail from the mysterious sleuth in the wee hours.

Lorna lowered the paper and shared another high five with Brittan.

"Are we having fun or what?" Brittan asked.

"Absolutely! Now we've got to solve the Devenport case!" Lorna exclaimed and swung her feet out of the bed. She hurried to her dresser, put on the latex gloves lying atop the computer, retrieved the laptop, and placed it near Brittan. "Let's go through Raisin's memory and see what we can see."

A muffled version of "Shout to the Lord" erupted from Brittan's pocket. She fished her cell phone from her robe, glanced at the screen, and said "It's Heather" while flipping open the phone.

"Hi, Heather," Brittan said into the phone. "I guess you've seen the paper?" Smiling, she gave Lorna a thumbs-up. "Yes, I agree. We were just opening up O'Keefe's computer."

Lorna reached for the bottled water on her nightstand and enjoyed a few sips while Brittan listened to Heather.

"Really?" Brittan shrieked. "You're kidding?"

Putting down her water, Lorna raised her brows at her friend. Brittan didn't usually get this excited unless something was seriously shocking...or encouraging.

The doorbell's commanding dong announced Tilley's arrival. Lorna started to get up, but Brittan waved her back to the laptop before scurrying from the room. Lorna watched her go and wondered what Heather had told her that had reaped such a response.

Oh well, Lorna thought. *She'll tell me when she gets off the phone.*

Brittan cruised toward the front door. "Just a minute, Heather," she said into the cell. "Tilley's here. I need to let her in. I don't want to be talking about this where she can hear me. As soon as I get her squared away, I'll go to my bedroom and close the door. That way nobody can hear me."

"Okay," Heather agreed.

Brittan glanced over her shoulder to be certain Lorna hadn't followed...or heard. But there was no sign of her.

She opened the door and admitted a short lady with gray hair and twinkling blue eyes. Brittan and Lorna proclaimed Tilley their domestic hero. "Good morning," Brittan said with a smile. She and Lorna made sure their "Domestic Disaster Relief Specialist" knew they appreciated her. Dependable and excellent help like her was hard to find.

"Have you made the coffee yet?" Tilley asked.

"No," Brittan answered and shook her head. "We haven't been up long." She yawned and wiggled her toes in her satin slippers. "I'm sure Lorna is ready for her morning jolt, and I could use one too."

"Coming up," Tilley said and headed toward the kitchen.

Brittan closed the door and walked into her bedroom. After shutting and locking the door on the monstrous room, she mumbled, "Okay, Heather, I can talk now."

"Great."

"So...what do you think his motive is?" Brittan sat on the edge of the settee and tapped her short nails against the back of the phone. "What does Duke think?"

"Duke's taking it at face value, and I didn't hint that he should do otherwise," Heather said. "When I called to tell him how great the article was, he told me about Michael Hayden's call. He was excited about it, of course. Every hot cover story he gets is just another feather in his cap."

"Like he needs it!" Brittan replied and reached for one of the votive candles sitting on the end table. "The way my dad talks about him, he's nearly ready to put him in charge of the paper. He can do no wrong in Dad's eyes."

"My eyes either," Heather said, chuckling.

"Oh, save me, *please*," Brittan complained and would never admit she secretively wished for a relationship like Heather and Duke's.

"It's odd that Michael Hayden would make a public statement supporting Trent if he's really behind having him framed," Heather mused.

Brittan held the peach-scented candle to her nose and inhaled her favorite scent. She rolled the tiny crystal vessel between her thumb and fingers while narrowing her eyes. The immaculate bedroom became a blur of ivory and white as her mind whirled with possibilities. "What if he's making a public statement to support Trent in order to cover his tracks? I mean—who would ever suspect Michael of framing his former best friend if he's stepping into the limelight and taking the risk of supporting him?"

"Okay," Heather drawled. "I can buy that—except he's putting his career on the line. If he really is framing Trent and he *wants* him to go to prison enough to plant smut on his computer, it's political suicide to step forward."

"Maybe he really doesn't care. Maybe he's gotten so engrossed with vengeance it's made him sick so he's willing to risk his career to see Trent go down." Brittan set aside the candle. Standing, she began pacing toward the dresser and back.

"Well…" Heather finally drawled, "I guess maybe…"

"Maybe?" Brittan asked. "You're starting to sound doubtful."

"That's because I *am* doubtful now," Heather admitted. "I mean, the guy is the mayor and he's voluntarily stepping forward to validate Devenport. If he is behind the framing, it's getting twisted."

"Probably because it *is* twisted," Brittan said. "Vengeance can do wicked things to good people."

Heather sighed. "Okay, okay. I give. I just don't want us jumping to conclusions and Lorna getting hurt. She's wild over Michael Hayden."

"Yes, and the sooner we get to the bottom of his real character, the safer she'll be."

"If he is corrupt, we do need to know," Heather admitted. "But really, if you remember, you and Lorna both doubted Duke's character at first. Sometimes I think we analyze things to the point that we don't trust anybody." Heather sighed.

"Well, if Hayden's behind the framing," Brittan snapped, "we'll all be glad I'm analytical."

"I just hope that if he's not behind it, no one gets hurt."

"Nobody's going to get hurt!" Brittan raised her hand. "I just think we need to keep looking at all options."

"Okay, okay…"

"I was the one who first thought Lorna's trainer was a cad. Remember?"

"Okay, I said," Heather huffed. "Let's just be careful."

"I am careful," Brittan insisted and pressed her fingertips against her chest. "You *know* I'm careful."

SEVENTEEN

"Nothing," Lorna commented and shook her head. Raisin's laptop was *clean*. No signs of porn. No signs of anything illegal. Not even one discolored email…other than the hateful one he'd sent to Trent Devenport. According to his laptop, Raisin was the epitome of good character. His main flaw was a bad attitude and a lack of vision for Devenport's prison ministry. Since bad attitudes weren't illegal, the debutantes had hit a wall.

Lorna sighed and shook her head. "I risked my life for an attitude problem," she groused and relived the precarious truck ride from the church to the gas station. *I'm sure I gave my guardian angel a stroke!*

She downed the last drops of water and prepared to shut down the computer. *Brittan might want to take a look,* she thought as the door opened.

Brittan strolled in carrying two mugs of coffee. The smell made Lorna want to howl. She'd developed an increasing attachment to caffeine from any source as of late and wondered if perhaps she was flirting with an addiction. Heather would think so, but when it came to food Heather was so out-of-balance she needed therapy. Lorna reached toward the mug, opening and closing her hand while feigning a toddler's whimper.

"Smells good, doesn't it?" Brittan said. "Tilley's coffee is *the best*."

"I think I have caffeine in my veins these days." Lorna took the warm mug. "Maybe I'd be better off to just hook up an IV." Her generous swallow was accompanied by Brittan's snicker.

"I think you give Heather all kinds of grief," she said.

"Oh, I know." Lorna downed more of the sweet liquid before resting the mug on her thigh. The warmth penetrated her cotton pajamas to the point of discomfort, and she moved the cup to the end table. "But she's a big girl." Lorna winked at Brittan. "She'll deal with it."

"What did you find out?" Brittan pointed to the laptop.

Lorna shook her head and drew a line across her neck. "Nothing. Not one thing." She scooted the computer toward Brittan. "You take a look. You're the computer guru. Maybe you can see something I'm missing." She peeled off the latex gloves, tossed them near the laptop, and reached for her coffee again.

"You're not shabby by any means." Brittan settled on the bed's edge, put on the gloves, and lifted the computer onto her lap.

Lorna's cell phone began playing the classic pop tune "Endless Love." She stopped in mid-sip and plopped down the cup. "That's Michael!" she exclaimed.

"Oh *please*," Brittan complained. "You've assigned him his own ringtone now?"

"Of course." Lorna's smile nearly hurt. She flipped open the phone and said "Good morning" with an eagerness even she suspected was over the top.

"Hey, beautiful!" Michael replied.

Lorna's face warmed; so did her heart. She glanced toward Brittan who was studying the laptop. The phone call from the previous evening flashed through Lorna's mind. Michael had point-blank asked her to break it off if she didn't think they had a chance for something permanent. Then she'd spied him kissing the phone after they hung up. Even though their relationship was new, Lorna hoped it would last...and last...and last. She stood, reclaimed her coffee, and meandered from the room. No sense giving Brittan anything to roll her eyes over again. Sometimes that woman was a downer. She could analyze the trunk off an elephant and never change her expression.

"Lorna?" Michael asked. "Did I lose you?"

"No, I'm here," Lorna replied as she emerged into the living room. "I was just stepping from my bedroom. My roommate was there. I love her to death but didn't want an audience, if you know what I mean." She pushed aside the sofa's pillows and settled into the corner.

"Of course," Michael replied. "Her name's Brittan, right?"

"Yes. Brittan Shay. Her father owns the *Houston Star*." Lorna set her mug on the marble-topped coffee table.

"Ah yes...and half the publishing empire in the U.S. as well, right?"

"You got it."

"Well, how about that. He was a contributor to my campaign. Not nearly the support your parents were by any means, but still, I was glad for his help."

"You impressed the greatest," Lorna purred and slid her finger-tips along the couch's armrest.

Michael chuckled. "I hope you're one of them."

"Well, I wouldn't say I'm the *greatest*—"

"I would," Michael stated and the caress in his voice triggered a vivid memory of their first kiss. Lorna's heart began a slow hammering. She reached for a pillow and squeezed it tightly.

"Say..." Michael's voice sounded a bit raspy, and Lorna wondered if he was thinking of that kiss as well. "I'm on my way to work and wanted to let you know the latest. I don't want you to be surprised."

"Oh?" Lorna stifled an unexpected yawn. She checked the huge, brass clock hanging on the far wall and noted it wasn't quite eight. After flopping at two, Lorna had gotten nearly six whole hours of sleep. The yawn won.

"Sorry," she mumbled and eyed the coffee. "I didn't get a lot of sleep last night."

"Hope you were thinking of me," Michael teased.

Lorna stopped herself before blurting something about the precinct captain, his German Shepherd, and the rose under his windshield wiper. When her mind was tired, she could reveal all sorts of secrets without realizing what she'd done.

"Oh...um...of course," she said through another yawn and did recall fleeting thoughts of Michael before she went into a "coma."

"Wow," he drawled. "You don't have to sound so enthused."

Lorna giggled. "I'm just really groggy," she explained, yet even in her hazy exhaustion her curiosity was piqued by Michael's "latest," whatever that was.

"Okay, I won't keep you," he rushed.

"No, I wasn't—"

"Really, it's okay," Michael insisted. "I'm about to pull into City Hall anyway. I don't have too much longer. I'm coming in early today because I want to take off early tomorrow. I thought we might be able to get an early start on the weekend. Is it okay if I call you later about details?"

"Yes. Absolutely!" Lorna agreed and assumed this must be his "latest."

"Good. Okay. Oh, the reason I called is...you know I went to Trent's church last night, right?"

"Yes," Lorna said and realized she'd jumped to the wrong conclusion about the "latest."

"Well, I went to his house last night after church and we—for lack of a better word—reconciled."

"You did?" Lorna's eyes bugged.

"Yes. I visited with him and Katie."

"You mean the woman you almost married?" Lorna tossed the pillow aside.

"In the flesh."

"Weird," Lorna said before she could check herself.

Michael laughed. "Yes, I guess it is a little weird. But then, when God wants to heal a rift, He does it right. I felt absolutely nothing for Katie—except relief that I didn't marry her. She's about as suited to me as a timid mouse."

Lorna's husky laugh wouldn't stop.

"I like that," Michael said.

"What?"

"Your laugh. I like it a lot."

"Good," Lorna quipped. "I like to laugh."

"Great," Michael shot back. "You can laugh with me anytime— all the time."

"I just might do that," she purred.

Michael's chuckle was low and inviting. "Okay, woman, you keep getting me off the subject!"

"Oops. Sorry."

"Anyway..." he drawled. "Remember Trent was arrested for that child porn business?"

"Yes." Lorna nodded.

"Well, I've decided to make a public statement in support of him."

"You're kidding!" She sat upright.

"No. I'm serious." Michael's words were firm.

"But—but—" Lorna stuttered. "Aren't you worried about how this will affect your career?"

"That crossed my mind," Michael admitted. "But I've decided I've got to do what I've got to do. I don't believe he's guilty. Not for one second. I haven't since the first time I read about it in the paper. If I were in his shoes, I'd be praying for character witnesses to come forward. I've got to do this. Whatever happens with the career happens. Who knows? Maybe God put me here at this place and this time just for Trent. If I perish, I perish."

"Do I start calling you Queen Esther now?" Lorna asked.

Michael snickered. "You know your Bible!"

"Yes. And I think this speaking up for Trent is an honorable thing," Lorna admitted. She hoped he'd never guess she'd doubted him for a few minutes last night. "This guy was your best friend. He repaid your friendship by stealing your woman, and you're repaying him by putting your career on the line for him." She reached for her mug.

Michael sighed. "I never really thought about it like that. All I know is the longer I think about it, the more I believe this is God at work. I've got to do what I feel my gut is telling me to do. End of discussion. Besides," he added, "I've gotten to the point that I'm *thrilled* Trent married Katie. I think my marrying her would have been a mistake. I'm talking a *huge mistake.*"

"So there's not even a flicker of love for her?" Lorna asked and wished the tinge of doubt weren't in her voice.

"*Not at all!*" Michael affirmed, his words thick with a grin. "Why? Are you jealous?"

"Who me?" Lorna squeaked before sipping the cooling liquid.

He laughed. "I love it!"

"Oh stop it!" she huffed. "You'd feel the exact same way and you know it!"

"Nope. You've got it all wrong, honey." He paused. "I'd be ten times *worse!*"

Lorna laughed and then downed one fourth of the lukewarm coffee.

"Anyway," he continued, "I called a reporter at the *Houston Star*—the same guy who did that front page write-up on 'the Rose.'"

"You called Duke Fieldman?" Lorna blurted and clamped down on her bottom lip. *I can't believe I just said that,* she groaned. Lorna slumped back and rested her head against the couch. The last thing she needed was Michael suspecting she was too familiar with "the Rose" by being too familiar with the journalist who wrote about her.

"Oh good. So you've seen the paper this morning?"

"Yes. I—I read the article on 'the Rose,'" she rushed. "And I know Duke. He's my friend Heather's fiancé. Remember my mentioning her?"

"She's the one whose family is Shelby Oil, right?"

"Yes. She's engaged to Duke."

"No joke?"

"No." *Whew!* she thought. *That covers my tracks.*

"How'd a newspaper reporter land an oil heiress?" Michael asked.

"They met when he interviewed her at her debutante ball. Heather thinks he's wonderful!" Lorna said.

"On the phone he seemed a little cocky."

"Yes, he can be sometimes." She propped her bare feet on the table and wiggled her painted toes. "But he's really a nice guy overall."

"He's a good writer, that's for sure."

"Yes...I think he's about to sell a mystery novel to one of Brittan's dad's publishers in New York."

"You guys are tight too, aren't you?"

"*Very.*" Lorna nodded. "We're like family in a lot of ways."

"So..." Michael hesitated. "Has Duke ever told Heather or you if he knows who 'the Rose' is?"

Lorna choked over another sip of her brew and coughed for several seconds. "Sorry," she wheezed and set the mug on the end table before her heaves created a spill. "I'm drinking coffee and it slipped down the wrong way. Duke's never told me he knows who 'the Rose' is." She was thankful it was the absolute truth and that the hacking broke up any hints she might give otherwise.

Michael sighed. "Ah well, I was just curious. I think all of Houston is ready to pull their hair out in suspense."

"Yep," Lorna agreed and magnified the inevitable yawn. "It's certainly a sensation when it hits the press," she added and tried to sound as bored as a half-dead earthworm.

"I can tell you're not a 'Rose' fan. I guess you've got other things to think about. Mainly me, I hope."

"Yep," Lorna agreed and didn't stop her enthusiasm.

"I think tomorrow's front page will feature my public statement. I'm emailing Duke a letter this afternoon. I just wanted to let you know what's up."

"And you think you'll still be available tomorrow night?" Lorna questioned. "This might create enough uproar to keep you busy for a year."

"If it does, it does," Michael replied. "I've still got to eat...and go out with my lady."

Lorna's grin wouldn't quit. "Maybe we should meet somewhere out of town—*way* out of town. The Houston paparazzi will drive you nuts for awhile."

"How would you feel about a flight to Dallas?" Michael suggested.

"Sounds good if you can find an airline with seats left."

"Oh there are seats left," he said. "Four to be exact. I own a Cessna Skyhawk."

"You're a pilot?"

"Yes. I started taking lessons when I was 12. I did my first solo at 15. Bought the plane used a few years ago. I've never shared it with another woman. Want to be the first?"

"You *bet!*" Lorna agreed.

"It's not anything as fancy as your dad's business jet—"

"Sounds just right," Lorna injected. "I don't need fancy."

He chuckled. "Good. We can fly midafternoon and be home by midnight. We could make it an evening...dine at the Hyatt restaurant in Reunion Tower."

"That's the one that looks like a giant lighted ball and rotates, right?"

"Yes. Have you been there?"

"Once. A long time ago."

"Then you're due another trip. The view of the skyline is unbelievable. There's also a park close. Maybe we could go there for a walk...and a kiss," he added.

"This is starting to sound too romantic for words." Lorna fiddled with a button on her pj's.

"That's because it is," Michael said. "All I need is for you to give the nod."

"Well, I'm nodding...a lot."

"Okay. I'll text you later with the details. I'll have to call the airport tower and get a departure time. Let's take separate cars to the airport, okay?"

EIGHTEEN

Lorna flipped her cell shut. This time *she* was the one kissing her phone. "I can't wait," she whispered.

"Hello in there!" Brittan's voice invaded Lorna's reverie.

Blinking, Lorna looked up at her friend.

"I called your name three times, and you never heard me," Brittan said through a smile. "I guess that was Mr. Mayor on the phone?"

"Yep." Lorna tossed the phone into the air and caught it. "He's flying me to Dallas tomorrow night for a date. He's a pilot. Has his own plane—a Cessna Skyhawk. How sweet is that?"

"You're going by yourself?" Brittan asked.

"No, I'm going with Michael!"

"Do you think that's safe?" Brittan placed her hands on her hips.

"G-i-r-l..." Lorna dragged out the word. "*Puleeze!* Michael Hayden is *not* like Chuck Griffith. He's the mayor, remember? If he had those kinds of skeletons in his closet, the press would have eaten him alive, and he'd have never been elected."

"Well, there's always a first time." Brittan crossed her arms.

"Get over it, sister." Lorna stood, slipped the cell into her pajama pocket. She walked past Brittan and didn't do a very good job of hiding her exasperation. "You're as protective as a wet hen."

Brittan laughed outright. Lorna stopped, narrowed her eyes, and pivoted to face her friend.

"It's as *mad* as a wet hen—or as *protective* as a mother hen." Brittan smoothed the back of her mussed hair and laughed some more.

"Oh whatever." Lorna waved her hand and stepped toward the hallway. "You know what I mean."

Nearing, Brittan rested her arm around Lorna's waist. "I'm protective because I love you, girlfriend," she admitted with a squeeze.

"To be perfectly honest, Brittan," Lorna said, "I think that attack by Craig affected you as much—if not more—than me. Really, I'm starting to get over it. But it's like you're sure the next guy I develop a relationship with is going to need a psychiatrist." She rested her hand against her chest. "I do have a few scraps of good judgment left, ya know."

"Okay, okay." Brittan raised her hand and shook her head. "I won't say anything else."

"I know you mean well. But even my parents approve of him, and you *know* how hard-nosed they can be."

A flicker of doubt fluttered across Brittan's features. "Your parents know him?"

"Duh!" Lorna said. "My dad was up to his eyeballs in his campaign. Why do you think I was roped into going to the inauguration business?"

"Okay, right," Brittan said. "I knew that. I just forgot."

"The world is coming to an end. 'The Brain' forgot something," Lorna teased.

Brittan's smile was less tense than the last one. "Duke called Heather this morning and told her Michael Hayden is going to make a public statement—"

"In support of Trent Devenport," Lorna finished.

After gaping a second, Brittan asked, "How'd you know? Oh. Michael told you."

Lorna gave her a thumbs-up. "He's got to have the strongest character of any man I've ever met. There are very few men who would put their necks on the line for the guy who took his woman."

"I agree. That's remarkable," Brittan admitted.

Narrowing her eyes, Lorna examined her friend.

Brittan was by far the best roommate she could ever share a place with. She'd been a wonderful support. They'd lived together since they finished college. Lorna hadn't wanted to be alone after what happened with Chuck, but she didn't want to live with her folks either. Unlike Heather's setup at the Winslow castle, Lorna wouldn't have had the privacy of a wing to herself or a separate entrance. Lorna had jumped at Brittan's offer to share a place. Their personalities complemented each other. Brittan was a bit low key; Lorna was a bit feisty. Brittan kept her territory immaculate but didn't gripe at Lorna when she failed in that department. She usually stayed out of Lorna's business and supported her like crazy. Lorna tried to do the same.

But sometimes Brittan could be downright odd. Lorna had long ago stopped trying to figure her out. How Brittan could seem so unimpressed with Michael was an unknown that Lorna decided to chalk up to the odd-zone and let go of.

"I'm going to hit the shower," Lorna said. After three steps in that direction she pivoted to face her friend. "What about the laptop? Find anything?"

Brittan created a circle with her forefinger and thumb. "A big fat zero," she stated. "Let's put an X by his name and move on to someone else."

"I agree." Lorna unfastened the bottom button on her pj's top.

"We'll keep an eye on him. Just because his computer is clean doesn't mean he's totally innocent. He could have left tracks elsewhere."

"You're right." Lorna hoped they uncovered the culprit soon. Michael was about to put his neck…and his career on the chopping block. She prayed that Trent was as innocent as Michael believed he was.

Michael was putting the final touches to the plane's interior and awaiting Lorna's call. The lemony smell of the leather cleaner heightened his desire to "get out of Dodge"...or at least out of Houston. His public statement had been printed as planned. His secretary was aghast, as was the city manager. Even Lorna's father, Oliver, had sent an email right away. After only two readings, every word was blazoned on Michael's mind.

> *Hayden...I just read the paper. What were you thinking? I want to trust your judgment, but I'm afraid you're committing political suicide. I wish you'd called me before doing this. If you really believed you must, maybe there was another way. I had high hopes in your climb to the top. Maybe you can recover from this error, but too many more like this, and your career won't fly.*
>
> *Oliver Leigh*

A similar message had arrived from the governor before lunch. Michael kept his office door shut and dodged phone calls until noon. Then he slipped away from City Hall, managed to sneak home, and changed into a ratty pair of jeans and a worn-out T-shirt. That, along with the tattered baseball cap and sunglasses, got him out to his plane without anyone noticing him. Whatever happened, happened, but he would lie low all weekend and be available Monday. Hopefully the news would fade by then or be eclipsed by something else.

When he'd annihilated every hint of dust from the plane's interior, he stopped the rubdown, stashed the cleaner and used cloth under the backseat, and relaxed in the pilot's seat. The leather wrapped around him like an old friend as Michael gazed toward the hangars and planes. A few planes like his awaited their turn on the runway while several business jets were periodically taking off and landing. Just 20 miles from downtown Houston, this airport was small enough to offer freedom from congested traffic but large enough to suit Michael's needs...and that of dozens of other aircraft owners.

The day couldn't be more perfect for flying. The June heat wave had relinquished and granted them weather in the mid eighties. The sun was bright; not a cloud to be seen. According to radar, Dallas was just as nice.

Michael smiled and checked the time on his phone. He'd texted Lorna this morning to meet him at two. It was 15 till, and he still hadn't heard a peep out of her. *If she doesn't call in the next 5, I'll call her,* he decided and toyed around with also phoning Trent.

He'd expected a call from his friend shortly after the paper hit, but that hadn't happened. Michael left his cell number with Trent Wednesday night, so the guy certainly knew how to reach him. He rubbed his fingertips along the plane's yoke and hoped Trent fully comprehended the magnitude of what he'd done on his behalf.

His cell phone burst into a high-energy jazz tune that would rattle the teeth of a dinosaur. Michael smiled when he saw Trent's name on the screen. He answered with an eagerness fueled by years of separation.

"Sorry I haven't called before now," Trent said. "Your statement has thrown my morning into a tailspin. I've had reporters on my lawn and a meeting with my lawyer. She's ready to kiss your feet!" Trent's excited words flowed. "Don't even be tempted to think this is going to hurt your career either. Stevie Simon and her husband have stacks of money, and she's already talking about supporting you in your next campaign—whatever that is. She says great character like yours is unheard of these days. I agree."

Michael's mouth sagged open.

"They have all sorts of influence. Do you remember her husband? He's a former NFL player—Conley Simon."

"Yes, I recognize the name. He was a Super Bowl MVP." Michael shifted and swung his legs out of the single-engined plane. Two steps on the short ladder landed him on the ground. "So far everybody I've talked to thinks I'm crazy—including Lorna's dad."

"Lorna?" Trent questioned, and Michael realized he hadn't mentioned Lorna or her family to Trent.

"Yes, Lorna's my girlfriend," he explained with an assurance that suggested they'd been an item much longer than a week. But she'd been his "private item" for years. Michael still had moments when he wondered if he was dreaming.

"Her father is Oliver Leigh," Michael continued. "He owns stores in Houston, including several national chains, some hotels, country clubs, and the like. Oliver contributed heavily to my campaign before Lorna and I met. He thinks I've lost my mind and career potential." Michael's voice took on a worried undertone despite himself.

"Just wait!" Trent exclaimed. "You'll be the town hero when this is over. I know you will be. God will reward you for this, Mike. Please don't lose heart. Lots of good is going to come—and is already coming."

"All I know is that it's great to hear your voice right now." Michael stroked away a smudge of dust from the plane's wing. "It's been a tough morning."

"What, Katie?" Trent questioned. "She's on the phone now? *Again?*"

While Trent talked with his wife, Michael noticed a red Jeep in the distance. He smiled.

"Listen, my lawyer's on the other phone. I've got to go. Thanks again, Mike—"

"Win your case!" Michael encouraged. "And let me know if you need anything else."

"I promise. I won't let you down. I'll call later."

"Sure thing." Michael flipped shut the phone and eyed the Jeep as it pulled into the west parking lot, a hundred yards from where his plane was parked. The slow thrill that oozed into his soul suggested this evening would be one he'd never forget.

His phone erupted again. As suspected Lorna's name scrolled across the screen. "I'm here," she said the second he answered.

"Good. I'm waiting," Michael replied, and the sun's balmy glow was matched by the warmth of his heart. "Ready and waiting," he added with an inviting undertone that reaped him that low, husky chuckle that made his heart crazy. The stress of the morning vanished, and Michael wished they were flying to Paris for their honeymoon. He blinked and tightened his gut. *Whoa! I just thought honeymoon and Paris!* he thought and knew in that instant he was irrevocably Lorna Leigh's. The sky was waiting…and so was their future.

NINETEEN

Before Lorna left with Michael, Brittan was consumed with memories of Heather's City Hall escapade last year. Dressed like a cleaning woman, Heather had sneaked in to investigate the mayor's murder. Her undercover operation had been daring... risky...but led to the arrest of the criminals.

When Lorna left for the airport Brittan knew she was going to repeat Heather's disguise. But this time she hoped to discover secrets that would reveal the new mayor's duplicity. Despite Lorna's insistence Michael was a prince and Heather's reservations about his guilt, Brittan had him at the top of her suspect list. And she wouldn't remove him until her investigation proved his innocence.

By three o'clock she'd exited Target loaded with the necessary supplies for sleuthing: cleaning scrubs, hairnet, thick-soled shoes, a portable vacuum. She'd then stopped at a convenience store on the way, changed, and donned the pair of glasses she'd bought last year "just in case" she needed them for undercover work. The frames were as thick and black as they came and made her look like a nerd. The hairnet heightened the effect.

Brittan rolled the vacuum cleaner down the City Hall corridor toward an ajar door marked "Michael Hayden, Mayor." She scratched the top of her ear as thoroughly as the latex gloves would allow and shoved at the hairnet. Pausing outside the door, Brittan ran her fingers along her waistband. She'd left her Glock in the rental vehicle due to the security scanners at the entrance. Interestingly enough, Brittan had never used the tiny gun for self-defense and hoped she'd never have to. But having it went a long way toward upping her bravado.

I guess I'll have to be brave without it, she noted. *Here goes.* Brittan rolled the vacuum into the executive secretary's office. A dark-skinned matron sat behind the desk marked "Frances Rousseau." She eyed Brittan like she was every bit the imposter she was and then rapped out, "So you finally decide to show up." Her steely eyes added to her interrogator persona.

Brittan blinked and scrounged around for the best Asian inflection she could muster. Even though her grandmother and mom spoke fluent Chinese, Brittan struggled to sound anything other than Midwestern.

"I vacuum," she said and pointed to the apparatus she'd purchased an hour ago. As the words left her mouth, she imagined Lorna rolling her eyes. When it came to accents, Lorna had it down and could rightfully mock Brittan's best efforts.

"Yes, you vacuum," Frances said and pursed her lips in a way that insisted she ran this office on a tight schedule. "I called someone two days ago. The head of housekeeping should be *fired*. He's slower than Christmas!" She pointed to the room's corner where dirt marred the cream-colored carpet around an erect, although ruffled, fichus tree.

This couldn't have worked out better if I planned it, Brittan thought and suppressed a smile.

She dutifully rolled the vacuum to the corner and plugged it in. Fortunately, she'd run a vacuum at home enough to know the routine...unlike Lorna who'd probably suck herself up. Brittan hid another smile. As the whirring vacuum gobbled the dirt, she cut a few discreet glances toward the closed door behind the secretary's desk. The nameplate read "Michael D. Hayden."

Brittan decided the best tactic was to play ignorant and vacuum every nook and cranny in every room that had a door that would open. She eyed the doorknob and prayed it wasn't locked. Keeping her head bent, Brittan ran the Eureka from wall-to-wall, only avoiding the secretary's corner. When she bumped into Michael's door, she turned off the unit.

"Well, I must say you're making up for the delay." The woman's frown diminished as she straightened her business jacket.

Beaming, Brittan said, "I vacuum."

"Yes, and you're doing a *way* better job than the other lady they're always cursing me with. What's your name anyway?" Frances looked at Brittan's chest where a name tag should have been.

"I vacuum!" Brittan smiled and rapidly nodded like she had no clue what the woman was saying.

"Humph," Rousseau said. "Whatever. Who cares if you don't understand as long as you do a good job." The phone rang, and the secretary dutifully answered it.

Deciding to take her chances, Brittan scurried to unplug the Eureka and darted back to the mayor's office door. She twisted the knob and nearly went into a swoon when the door swung open.

Rousseau glanced toward Brittan, bobbed her head up and down while saying, "Please wait while I check his schedule."

Returning the smile, Brittan nodded. She rolled the unit inside, clicked on the light, and snapped the door closed. Holding her breath she waited to see if the secretary reopened it. But all she heard was the woman's muffled voice as she arranged an appointment for her boss. Brittan twisted the lock on the knob and connected the vacuum cord into the first plug she spotted.

With another glance toward the locked door, Brittan turned on the vacuum and left it in the middle of the room while she hustled to Michael's desk. She checked her watch and gave herself exactly seven minutes to find clues. Brittan settled into the over-sized leather seat and whipped open the desk drawer that usually held pens, pencils, paper clips, and the like. And that's exactly what she found. Nothing else.

Brittan moved to the side drawers. The massive cherrywood desk had large drawers. Each drawer was such a jumble of files and odds and ends that only God Himself would understand the filing system. She nearly laughed out loud. The guy appeared to be a neat freak on the surface, but underneath was an organization-ally challenged soul.

After rifling through the files, she closed the final drawer, glanced toward the classic bookshelves, typical file cabinets, and an entertainment center or armoire along the south wall. The latter promised a higher chance of clues than the stoic file cabinets.

She checked her watch. Half her time had lapsed. Brittan's stomach fluttered. She eyed the vacuum, still merrily whirring its heart out. *Good girl,* she thought and decided to spend the rest of her time on the polished cabinet.

Standing, she inched the desk chair back to the exact spot she'd found it and hurried across the room. With a tug on the handle, the door sagged open and Brittan discovered a portable closet. Several changes of clothing hung on the rack to the left while four deep drawers claimed the right. The faint aroma of masculine cologne smelled deliciously expensive. Brittan ignored the appeal and searched the pockets of two suits, several shirts, and a pair of golfing shorts. She came up empty.

"Man!" she whispered. Wincing, Brittan checked the cheap Timex she'd bought as an afterthought on her way out of Target. She glanced toward the door and lunged into the drawers with the hunger of a desperate detective.

If I don't find something soon, I'll have to give up, she despaired, and was prepared to do exactly that...until she opened the bottom drawer.

✳ ❋ ✳

Lorna stood in the lobby of the Hyatt Regency on Reunion Street, home of the famous Reunion Tower, and awaited Michael's return from upstairs. He'd requested the use of a small room long enough to change, and the hotel had granted him permission for a minimal fee. Lorna had been surprised to find him looking like a street bum when he'd met her at the airplane and felt overdressed in her slinky, Christian Dior pantsuit. But Michael explained he'd wanted to keep a low profile until they got to Reunion Tower, when he'd change into something more suitable.

Settling into the corner of the settee, Lorna crossed her legs and observed the upscale hotel's plant-filled foyer. She'd been in more facilities like this one than she could recall. Her father owned a few. Lorna appreciated the architecture, from the finely chiseled marble to the waterfall that cascaded across a brass barrier in a liquid wall as thin as glass. The splash mingled with the noisy flow of pedestrians, the occasional call for the concierge, and the opening and closing sigh of the building's glass doors.

Lorna idly swung her foot and watched the row of elevators for the first signs of Michael. While he looked ruggedly handsome in his scraggly clothes, Lorna recalled the night in the garden when he'd been dressed up. She hadn't questioned why he'd been featured as one of Houston's most eligible bachelors last year. The garden shadows had heightened the effect of dark eyes and hair...and a man who was made for tailored clothing and the finest in leather shoes. Lorna pressed her hand into the couch arm and recalled the indulgent grin he'd greeted her with when he met her at the small airport's entry. His expression had been that of a college kid tangled in first love, and Lorna had lost her breath.

One of the elevators slid open, and Lorna's waiting was rewarded. Michael emerged dressed in a charcoal-colored suit. After strolling a few feet, he paused, scanned the crowd, and shifted his duffel bag from one hand to the other. A klatch of short-skirted twenty-somethings passed and didn't bother to keep their glances discreet. Lorna would have been a bit exasperated except she had to admit that if she were them she'd be doing the same thing. Lorna realized why so many in Michael's circle were making comments about the senate and, eventually, the presidency. He possessed a VIP air that few men had.

Lorna smiled and waited until his gaze scanned her direction. When he spotted her, she lifted her hand and wiggled her fingers. He broke into a grin and moved toward her like iron caught in a magnetic field.

Standing, Lorna picked up her sequined bag, walked toward him, and tried to recall why she'd been so hesitant to give him her number at their first meeting. Right now she entertained having it tattooed on the back of his hand. With every meeting Lorna was slipping closer to the precipice of complete fascination.

Michael Hayden was a man who knew who he was. He had the gifts to do what God wanted him to do and the heart to rescue a stray cat.

"Hi," he said and reached for her hand. "Hope I didn't keep you waiting too long."

"It was worth the wait," Lorna purred and wondered if her eyes expressed the meltdown in her stomach.

He chuckled. "I think we've got our script wrong. It's usually the lady keeping the gentleman waiting, and the gentleman says, 'You're worth the wait.'"

"Remind me to keep *you* waiting next time then," she teased.

"You've already kept me waiting," he flirted. "I've been waiting for years for you to wake up and realize I'm here."

Lorna looped her arm through his, and they walked toward the concierge desk. "Well, believe me, I'm awake!"

Michael smiled into her eyes and silently promised their next kiss would be soon. He paused at the counter and handed his bag to a uniformed young man ready to serve. "Is it possible for me to check this until we get ready to leave?"

"Absolutely."

Once the bag had been tagged and stored, Lorna and Michael strolled through the foyer, to the exit that led to Reunion Tower. Soon they boarded one of the glass elevators and hovered near the handrail, watching the streets of Dallas slip into the distance as they ascended 55 stories. A few seconds into the lift, Lorna sensed that Michael had stopped watching the scenery and turned his attention to her. As much as she wanted to play it cool and keep her focus on the skyline, Lorna couldn't stop from turning to him.

"You're so beautiful," he whispered.

Lorna swallowed and attempted to stammer a thank you, but she couldn't get out anything but garbled noise. Michael stroked her cheek, and Lorna closed her eyes and leaned into his caress. The thrill of his lips on hers mixed with the heady rush of the elevator's upward climb. When the kiss ended, Lorna opened her eyes and realized she was clinging to his lapels. His eyes, only inches away, hinted at future promises...and an evening Lorna would never forget.

The door dinged and opened so swiftly Lorna barely had time to inch away. A low wolf whistle sent a rush of heat to her cheeks as she turned to encounter a group of college guys bent on showing their maturity...or lack of it. A second guy said, "Woo! Woo! Woo! He's scoring!" The friends' laughter was anything but appropriate.

Michael grabbed Lorna's hand, glared the men down, and hustled onto the Tower's lowest deck called "The Lookout." While the guys filed into the elevator they'd exited, one of them belched an expletive and then added, "He looked just like the mayor of Houston. I just did a current events project on that guy."

Lorna glanced up at Michael, who smiled down at her. They moved down *The Lookout* as the elevator doors swished shut.

✳ ✳ ✳

When Brittan picked up the phone book and looked beneath it, she gasped. At first glance the leather-covered book looked like a journal. When she opened it, she flipped through several pages of masculine scrawl that promised much information. Nevertheless, she hesitated. She closed the journal, rubbed her gloved fingers across the front, and debated whether she should take it. The journal probably held Michael's deepest, most honest thoughts.

And that's what you need to determine his guilt or innocence, a practical voice insisted. *But it's private,* another voice countered. Brittan glanced at the motionless doorknob and then to the vacuum cleaner, still droning with a vengeance. She wondered what would happen if Lorna discovered she'd taken Michael's journal.

But Lorna took David O'Keefe's laptop, she reasoned. They'd gone through his belongings and shipped the whole thing back to him this morning. *This is what investigators do,* she justified. *This is the way we discover criminals. There's no way around it.*

A repetitious thud overpowered the vacuum's roar. Brittan's eyes widened. She shoved the bottom drawer back into place, closed the armoire, and hustled to the vacuum cleaner. She turned it off. The doorknob rattled again and the knocking began anew.

"Open the door!" Frances Rousseau demanded, her French accent prominent. "Open it *now!*"

Brittan clutched the journal as her mind darted in a dozen directions. Short of stuffing the journal inside her waistband, she couldn't think of another way to get it out without being seen. But she feared it might slip and make walking impossible. She stared at the montage of airplane prints filling the north wall and wished one would zoom from the frame and give her a magical lift out of this fix.

Urging herself to action, she ran to the plug and yanked it out of the socket while Frances's exasperated voice penetrated the door.

"I don't know what's going on in there, but I don't think she's up to any good."

Okay, she's got somebody out there with her. Not good, Brittan noted. "Jus' minute!" she bellowed. "I vacuum!"

"I vacuum!" Frances screamed. *"I vacuum?* Don't give me that! The lady who's supposed to vacuum is out here. And the head of maintenance is on the way. Who are you? Open this door *now!"* More pounding followed.

Brittan gaped at the door and was at a loss about what to do now. *This could get ugly,* she decided, and imagined herself being ushered to the police station by City Hall security guards.

Panting, Brittan loosely wrapped the cord around the unit's upright handle. Her heart beat faster as her adrenaline skyrocketed. And she still hadn't decided what to do with the journal. She examined the vacuum cleaner for an answer. The bag's zipper posed a swift and logical solution. Brittan unzipped the bag, slipped the journal between the outer layer and the dust bag, and pulled the zipper closed.

The knob rattled. Her hands oozed sweat. The cleaning scrubs clung to her clammy body. *You need a plan,* her frenzied mind insisted. She wished for her Glock, but then fully understood that pointing a handgun at the mayor's secretary would definitely land her in jail.

Heather would just kick her way out. She decided to do her best to make the element of surprise weigh in her favor. She was miles removed from Heather's polished fighting skills, but Brittan did have a brother, and she'd delivered her share of blows when needed.

Okay, here goes! She pushed the vacuum toward the locked door.

Frances was body-slamming the door, screaming, "Let me in or I'm calling security!"

Brittan did what she asked. She unlocked the knob and measured the rhythm of the woman's pounding. When the momentary lull guaranteed a new body slam, Brittan twisted the knob and yanked open the door. Frances Rousseau sprawled into the room and crashed against the mayor's desk with a yell and an "umph!"

Brittan rammed the vacuum in front of her and sidestepped a shocked housekeeper who looked old enough to be Noah's grandmother. When a balding bulldog-of-a-maintenance man hustled into the room and tried to block the doorway, Brittan kicked him in the groin with every ounce of strength she had. He doubled and howled.

"Come back here!" Frances screamed.

"No comprende!" Brittan yelled and raced into the hallway. She was rounding the corner before she realized she'd used the wrong language. Her crazed mind suggested she'd laugh about that in the future, but right now *nothing* was funny. She careened down the hallway, shoving the vacuum cleaner in front of her like it was her lifeline. Her body had gone from clammy to dripping sweat. One droplet trickled from her hairline and stung her eye. Brittan ignored it.

The elevators loomed ahead, and her first instinct was not to take them. That was too obvious, too easy, too direct. The yelling down the hall insisted Frances was on her trail. The stairs seemed the more logical option. In movies spies were always taking stairs when trying to escape. Brittan paused a few seconds. She hit the down arrow and then unzipped the vacuum cleaner and pulled out the journal. She opened the stairwell door, shoved the vacuum inside, closed the door, and moved to the elevator just as it dinged on her floor. The door opened. Brittan glanced down the hall. No Frances yet. Brittan lunged in past a lone man walking out. She pounded the button for the fourth floor just as Frances came into sight. The maid limped behind.

"Stop that elevator!" Frances screamed as the doors slid shut.

Slumping against the wall, Brittan prayed the woman didn't make it to the down button before the elevator started moving.

The ancient lift's first lunge left Brittan sagging against the handrail. "Thank You, God," she murmured and imagined the secretary taking the other elevator down.

When the elevator bell dinged and the door opened Brittan exited like a bullet and knocked her way through a trio of businesswomen who protested her intrusion.

Brittan hit the door marked "Stairs" and raced down four flights. By the time she reached the lobby, she was feeling her freedom. Puffing for air, she casually glanced over her shoulder but saw no sign of Rousseau, the decrepit cleaning lady, or the yelping maintenance man.

She ran into the parking lot, jumped into the rented Ford sedan, and cruised to safety with the journal claiming the passenger seat.

TWENTY

"You did *what?*" Heather squeaked into the cell phone.

"I got into Michael's office and found his journal," Brittan repeated. She related the whole story. "You were my inspiration," she said when she finished her tale. The cell phone shook against her ear as fiercely as her limbs shook, and Brittan wondered how she'd *ever* pulled this one off. As she'd told Lorna after the joyride in O'Keefe's pickup, the debutantes were getting braver and braver.

"Oh my word!" Heather breathed. "Brittan! If Lorna finds out—"

"How's she going to find out?" Brittan challenged and hoped her strong front hid her inner misgivings. "Besides, anytime we've investigated someone we've taken a peek at something personal. That's how we found out the other mayor had a mistress before he was murdered, remember? We'd already investigated the old mayor's files. We're just going to take a look at the new mayor's journal. It's all part of the job." Brittan shrugged. "Nobody's above suspicion at this point. If the journal comes up clean, I'll replace it…somehow…and no one will ever know. I've got it here with me now." She picked up the leather book and propped it on her Jaguar's steering wheel. The journal shook in her hand as severely as the phone next to her ear.

"Look," Brittan continued, "can I come to your place to read it?

I'd rather leave it there with you until we can replace it or we turn it in as evidence."

"Well, now that you've gotten it, I guess we've got to read it," Heather said as hesitancy mingled with curiosity.

"That's right, Heather." Brittan nodded and eyed a silver Toyota pulling into the car rental's parking lot. It stopped near the Ford she's just returned. She set aside the journal and cranked her Jaguar's engine. "Just think about it. If there *is* some evidence in the journal, we'll be *so glad* we dared. And wouldn't *you* want to know if the guy you were falling for would stoop to framing someone else and destroying his life?"

"Absolutely," Heather agreed.

"Okay then. I'm heading over now."

"I'm waiting."

✳ ✺ ✳

"This evening has been perfect," Lorna said and smiled up at Michael in a way that made him feel like her hero. "And I've never enjoyed smoked salmon so much." As they stepped from the Hyatt, she wrapped both hands around his, and Michael squeezed tight. Her eyes insisted that the enjoyment was 99 percent because of him and 1 percent due to the salmon. Michael's ego swelled a tad, and he didn't bother to stop it.

"Well, if you think the evening has been good so far..." He pointed toward the horsedrawn carriage waiting at the curb just as he'd planned. Michael couldn't have been more pleased with the expression in Lorna's eyes.

"You think of everything, don't you?" she asked.

"I try," he said and felt smug.

Bathed in evening sunshine, the open coach looked as if it had rolled out of the pages of a fairy tale...right down to the driver's brass-buttoned uniform.

All we need is some snow, Michael thought. He tugged Lorna's hand and said, "Come on. The sooner we get in, the sooner I can steal another kiss."

Her usually husky laugh held an excited quaver that suggested Michael wouldn't have to resort to stealing. He'd barely been able to eat his meal after the kiss in the elevator that swayed the tower. Michael wondered how the carriage would hold up under the influence of a repeat.

He confirmed with the driver that this was the ride he'd hired and helped Lorna in. He settled beside her, draped his arm across her shoulders, and announced, "We're supposed to get a one-hour tour of downtown Dallas. I know we've both been here before, but—"

"It doesn't matter if I've seen it a hundred times," Lorna interjected. "It will all be new." Her enamored gaze suggested she was falling as hard and fast as Michael, and that she really didn't care what the tour involved as long as they were together.

Not wanting the night to end, Michael decided to add one more element before they flew home. He leaned toward her ear and whispered, "When we get through, let's go back up the tower to The Lookout. It should be dark then, and the skyline will look like a million stars." The daytime effect they'd admired before dinner couldn't compete with the night lights.

She rested her head on his shoulder and said, "Okay."

The trust and expectation wrapped in that one word sent Michael's heart into hard thudding that he was sure rocked the carriage. He anticipated the coming evening...the coming weeks... the coming years. As the carriage started moving, he was overcome with a renewed sense of thankfulness that Trent had married Katie. All those years of pain and avoiding the temptation toward vengeance had been rewarded with a woman who was perfect— absolutely perfect. He'd yet to see one flaw in Lorna Leigh. Hopefully his ring would be on her finger within six months.

On an impulse he thought about popping the question tonight—now—while the carriage rolled through the streets and the evening sunshine warmed their faces as thoroughly as budding love warmed Michael's heart. Yet he resisted. She hadn't known him that long, and he didn't want to rush her. And besides, the beginning of a lifelong relationship should be like slowly savoring a creamy latte. If you downed the latte in two or three gulps, you'd miss the pleasure of every drop. As the carriage drove into the shadow of a skyscraper, Michael inhaled the aroma of Lorna's sweet perfume and savored the first few sips of lasting love.

Brittan steered the Jaguar along the private lane that sliced through the Winslow estate and led to the castle that had once been featured in *Southern Living* magazine. When Heather and her mother toured Scotland years ago, Marilyn Winslow fell in love with the whole castle idea and ordered one tailor-made for their family. Brittan turned the final curve and the castle came into view. The place sprawled around the edges of a lake, surrounded by several acres of grass too green not to have been babied to good health. The woods began a couple of acres behind the house and provided the backdrop for the perfect medieval royalty look.

She took the left fork in the lane and drove to the back entry, which provided direct access to Heather's wing. By the time she got to the door, Heather was opening it. Her wide, blue gaze oozed with a mixture of awe, misgiving, and unbridled curiosity.

"Look at you!" Heather exclaimed. "You're still in your cleaning lady gear." Her honker of a laugh echoed in the hallway. "And *where* did you get those glasses? You look like a total nerd!"

"Thanks, I love you too," Brittan said drily and adjusted the thick-framed spectacles. "Here. Take this while I get my duffel bag. It's got my real clothes in it. I'll change while I'm here." She extended the journal to Heather who reached for it. Brittan jerked it back. "No! You're not wearing gloves."

"Yikes!" Heather lifted both hands like the journal was a viper. "Sorry. Let me get your duffel. You go on inside. I'll get my gloves while you're changing."

"Okeydokey." Brittan stepped into the corridor and hungrily eyed the journal. Her growing curiosity over Michael's thoughts overshadowed the echoes in her conscience.

Within ten minutes Brittan exited Heather's bedroom where she'd changed into designer jeans and a snug-fitting T-shirt. Wearing her regular glasses, she started feeling more like her normal self and less like a spy.

Heather looked up from her place in the middle of the leather sofa and patted the pillow next to her. She wore latex gloves and held the open journal.

"You're already reading it?" Brittan dropped her duffel near a chair. Her high-heeled sandals tapped against the stone floor as she hurried across the palatial den.

"Just skimming," Heather admitted. "Looks like this journal only goes back four years. That was several years after the breakup, so he might not even mention it. It also doesn't look like he wrote in it every day, so there's probably lots of his life that's missing."

"If he had vengeance on the brain, let's hope he mentioned it." Brittan settled next to her friend.

Heather shifted the journal so the two of them could read it together. Brittan skimmed through a good bit of spiritual commentary and was simultaneously relieved and disappointed. If Michael was as concerned about eternal issues as his words depicted, he would be a good match for Lorna. But that would also mean they were getting nowhere fast on finding the person who framed Trent. Every lead was a dead end.

Heather turned the page. Brittan skimmed anew when Heather gasped and plopped her finger underneath a line. "Look!"

"I wish I could get Katie out of my mind," Brittan read aloud. "I can't seem to get interested in any other woman. The only one who's grabbed me in years is Lorna Leigh, and every guy in America knows what a babe she is."

"Hello!" Heather said.

"Wow! Sounds like he's really had a thing for Lorna for awhile," Brittan mused.

"Do you think it's an obsession?" Heather asked.

"You mean like a psycho thing?"

"Yes."

Relaxing against the sofa, Brittan gazed up at the relief panels in the ceiling. So much of this castle had been imported from the finest sources worldwide. A few items, like the carved ceiling panels, came from an ancient Scottish castle that had deteriorated past the point of use. The Winslows bought the place, salvaged what they could, and sold what was left, including the land. The whole shebang helped fund the new castle.

"Oh, I don't know," Brittan finally said. "He doesn't really look psycho to me. I see him as more the cold revenge type."

Heather sighed. "He seems to be moving so fast."

Brittan flipped a few more pages and picked up details about a grandfather's death, a friend who had cancer, and more spiritual insights. "He's more spiritual than I had him pegged," she mumbled.

"Me too," Heather agreed, her words tinged with guilt. She pulled at the neck of her lacy blouse.

"Don't go soft on me, Heather." Brittan peered into her friend's eyes and hardened her own heart. "We don't have a choice. It's what we do. *Nobody's* above suspicion."

"Here." Heather released her claim on the journal. "You do the reading. I'll go fix us some tea."

"Okay," Brittan agreed. "I'll have some of that blueberry you fixed last time." She slipped her feet out of her gold sandals, snuggled into the corner, and stretched her legs along the couch. For the next several minutes Brittan skimmed page after page of Michael's thoughts. Occasionally he mentioned Katie in a lamenting tone but never with a nuance of hatred. Lorna's name crept in a few times, and Brittan grew increasingly thankful none of the notations sounded even close to psychotic. Apparently he'd been enamored with Lorna when she was a tennis pro.

Brittan was on the verge of doubting Michael's guilt by the time Heather arrived with the herbal tea. She laid the journal on the marble-topped coffee table, accepted the tea, and swung her feet to floor. The Persian rug felt like royal cotton beneath her toes, and Brittan didn't think she'd ever lose her appreciation for life's finer things. By the time she'd downed her third sip, Heather was reading the journal again.

"Did you find anything?" Brittan asked.

"No. Same sort of stuff," Heather admitted.

"You look like you've repented of the guilt." Brittan eyed her friend's intense profile and grinned.

Heather waved her comment aside. "I think I found something!"

Brittan plopped her tea mug on the table and scooted closer. "Where? What?"

"Here. Last year. In the spring. Look." Heather ran her polished nail along a section that Brittan devoured.

I saw Trent's photo in the paper today. It was a real shocker. He's apparently taken a senior pastorate in a church that runs about 2,000 people. There was a big article about how he was the youngest pastor they've ever had and how the whole congregation thinks he's the next Billy Graham. Katie was right there in the mix. There was a photo of her and him together. I thought I was doing so well. Seemed like it lately anyway. But seeing them so successful and so happy brings back a lot of bad feelings. I wish I could be more spiritual and say I've never wished something

bad would happen to those two, but I can't. I remember the first
few weeks after they walked out of my life. I wanted something
awful to happen to them. Every time I'd think something like that,
I'd ask God to forgive me. It was terrible being trapped by such
thoughts. And I haven't thought anything like that in years—
until today. God, please help me! God, forgive me! I wished his
success would go down the drain. How horrible is that?

"Wow," Brittan whispered as she continued to skim. The next entry was weeks later and didn't mention Trent or Katie.

The two friends lifted their gazes from the journal and stared at each other before Brittan spoke. "I wonder if there's any way we could get into his apartment?"

TWENTY-ONE

The flight from Dallas to Houston was a perfect conclusion to a perfect evening. Lorna relaxed in the small plane's passenger seat and enjoyed watching Michael's mastery of the flying process. He'd taken off his tie and jacket and tossed them on the backseat before claiming the pilot's seat. When they left he communicated with the control tower like a pro. He constantly checked the two colorful monitors that were about ten inches square. The digital displays offered information ranging from weather radar to facts about their flight. Lorna felt as safe—or maybe safer—in the sporty Skyhawk as she did in her father's business jet.

By the time they landed at the Houston airport, midnight was looming. Once the plane was safely in its hangar, Michael stowed his coat and tie in his duffel bag and assisted Lorna from her seat to the ground.

He smiled into her eyes and said, "What do you think? Do I pass as a pilot?"

"You scored 100!" Lorna allowed him to lead her from the hangar and into the balmy night.

"Good." Michael adjusted his duffel bag on his shoulder and said, "I guess those obnoxious guys were right. I did score points." His grin was as audacious as they came. "One hundred, to be exact."

Lorna punched him on the arm. "Don't get too sassy," she warned.

"Yow!" Michael rubbed his arm with a fierceness that said he'd been mortally wounded. Through plenty of chuckles, he draped his arm around Lorna's shoulders. They strolled through the small airport and into the parking lot.

The private airport was far enough away from the Houston lights to allow a glimpse or two of stars twinkling on the horizon. The midnight moon bathed them in a gauzy glow, and the parking lot lights increased the effect. A sporadic breeze whipped at Lorna's big-legged pants before scurrying away again. Lorna was pleasantly tired but hated the night to end.

If we were married, it wouldn't have to end, she thought and kept her head ducked lest Michael read her expression. While she knew he wasn't interested in a passing flirtation, they hadn't been seeing each other nearly long enough to think about matrimony. Nevertheless, the thoughts wouldn't stop...especially when she imagined Michael standing at the altar in a black tuxedo. He looked every bit as handsome as he had when he exited the elevator earlier this evening.

They found her Jeep, and Michael paused while Lorna dug her keys out of her evening bag. She sensed his wanting to linger as much as she, but it was midnight. They'd just spent ten hours together. The spiked sandals were a long way from a comfortable pair of tennis shoes, and her feet were telling her how angry they were over the torment. Lorna tried to swallow the yawn that bulged up her throat but lost the battle.

Michael's corresponding yawn landed them in a puddle of chuckles. "The power of suggestion," he said and stroked her cheek. "I hate to go, but I guess it's late. Still wantta spend some time together tomorrow afternoon?"

"Absolutely!" Lorna agreed. "Then Sunday night we're still on for dinner with my parents, right?"

"Sure thing," Michael said through a white-toothed smile. The parking lot shadows were as good to him as those in the garden had been. The flutter in Lorna's stomach began as his gaze trailed to her lips. The goodbye kiss was their third—and sweetest—of the evening. The brief kiss matured into a heartfelt hug that filled Lorna's senses with the scent of sophisticated masculinity and the essence of a passionate man. Michael held on as tightly as she until, at last, their embrace came to an end.

With regret playing on his features, Michael helped her into the Jeep. "Did I mention I'm going to be out of town next week?" he asked, his forehead wrinkling.

"No." Lorna shook her head and snapped her seat belt.

"I'm going to be in Kansas. I leave Tuesday and won't be back until Saturday. That's my birthday, by the way, so keep your calendar open. We'll celebrate!"

"Sounds great," Lorna replied and wondered what she should get him. "What do you do with Socks when you're gone?" she heard herself ask. Lorna never thought she'd see the day when she worried about the welfare of a cat. But this wasn't just somebody. It was Michael. And his cat was important because *he* was important.

"Sometimes I put him in a cattery, but he doesn't like it. He pouts for several days after I get back home. Sometimes I get my sister to feed and walk him, but she gripes like it's killing her. A time or two I've had my housekeeper do the honors, but this time she's out of town. I'm seriously thinking about calling an animal sitter."

"I'll check on him for you," Lorna heard herself offer.

Michael blinked. "You?"

"Sure." She shrugged and realized she really didn't mind. Socks wasn't all that bad for a fur ball.

"Wow!" Michael rubbed his forehead. "That would be great. One less thing for me to worry about. Would you mind taking him for his walk in the park too?" He lifted his hand. "If you have time and all."

"No, don't mind at all." Lorna shook her head and nearly laughed out loud over the image of her in the park with a cat on a leash. "But I bet Heather and Brittan will think I've lost it!"

"Hey, when am I going to meet them?" Michael asked, his eyes alight with interest. "You mention them so much…"

"Here's a photo." Lorna reached toward a flat plastic frame hanging from her rearview mirror by a ribbon. She removed the ribbon from the mirror and passed the picture to Michael. "At least you can see what they look like until you get to meet them," she explained as he peered at the three ladies standing outside a villa in France. "We went to France together a couple of years ago," she explained and pointed to the villa. "The blonde is Heather, and this is Brittan."

"Ah, you never mentioned Brittan was Asian."

"Yes, half Chinese. I think Heather's genes are all Swedish."

"Who'd have guessed it?" Michael teased and handed the photo back to Lorna.

"Anyway, like I was saying, these guys will think I've lost it when I tell them I'm going to take care of Socks." She hung the photo back around her rearview mirror, leaned back in her seat, and gazed into Michael's dancing eyes.

And maybe I have, she debated and gripped the leather-covered steering wheel. "Should I check on him every day or…"

"Do you mind?"

"No. How often do you walk him?"

His sheepish smile suggested that was a daily ritual as well.

"Man oh man," Lorna teased and shook her head. "This has to be the most spoiled cat in the south. Didn't you tell me you mostly feed him albacore tuna?"

"That's almost all he'll eat!" Michael protested.

"Socks has *you* trained *really well.*"

"At least you know I'm trainable," Michael responded with a lift of his chin. "That's more than some men can say."

Lorna giggled. "Why are you going to Kansas?"

"There's a plastics manufacturer looking to build a plant somewhere." He slipped his hand into his slacks pocket and adjusted the duffel on his shoulder. "We're doing some serious lobbying for Houston. I'm going to see if I can lay the charm on thick, ya know?"

"I'm sure if they locate here that will be a serious feather in your cap," Lorna noted. "How many jobs would it create?"

"Nearly a thousand. After today's paper hit, I need lots of feathers."

Lorna hadn't mentioned the statement in the paper because she sensed Michael left his troubles in Houston for the evening and wanted to keep them there. Her father had called this morning, eaten up with concern over Michael's popularity. According to Oliver Leigh, if Michael wasn't careful he'd commit political suicide.

"I still think it's very brave and honorable." Lorna dared to stroke his face. "And I'm sure your friend is ecstatic."

"That's not even the word for it," Michael admitted. "The good thing is his lawyer's rolling in dough and is saying she and her husband will be major supporters in my next campaign—whatever I choose to run for."

"See there—not everybody's against you."

"Well, when I left the office this morning, I'd already gotten some serious emails from your dad and the governor, and my secretary thinks I've lost my mind. She's already left several voice mails on my cell. I'm ignoring them for now. I don't even want to think about what she might be reporting."

Lorna recalled Michael's grimace when he turned his phone off before dinner. She'd wondered about it.

"I almost hate to check my email when I get to work Monday. And I'm sure there will be some press wanting to cram mics in my face." He sighed.

"You have to face everyone and let them know you did what your conscience told you to do. My dad's not as gruff as his eyebrows make him look anyway." Lorna smiled and toyed with her shell necklace. "He's really impressed with you and wants you to succeed. When he called me this morning he sounded more worried than anything else."

Michael nodded, lowered his head, and rubbed the base of his neck. "Yes, that's what I know," he said. "I don't regret stepping up to the plate, and I'd have done it even if I knew it was going to hamper my career. But at the same time I hope it won't." He lifted his face, peered into her eyes, and she responded to his silent request for support.

She squeezed Michael's hand with both of hers and held on tight. "I'll pray it won't be," she encouraged and rubbed his forearm. "I think God already has everything planned, and I know it's going to be all right."

Michael lifted her hand to his lips and pressed it against them. In the night his eyes appeared as dark as his onyx cufflinks. He closed his eyes and hung on for several seconds. When he lowered her hand, he opened his eyes. "Thanks."

Her heavy lids drooping, Lorna smiled. "It's my pleasure."

"And I have kept you out late enough, girl," he teased and backed away. Michael gripped the handle on the Jeep's door. "Let's plan another round of golf tomorrow afternoon. Maybe this time I can beat you."

"You're on, buddy. And don't hold your breath on beating me. I always play to win. And I mean *always*." Lorna sliced her hand through the air.

"We'll just see about that." Michael wagged his head from side to side. "I was on the golf team in high school, and I'm still just as good as I was then."

"Did your team always lose?"

"Oh!" Michael clutched his chest. "That was a low, low blow."

Lorna giggled and inserted her key into the ignition. His smile as big as hers, Michael shut the door and stepped back while she pulled out of the parking space. He waved again, and Lorna returned the gesture before driving toward the exit. With a final glance in her rearview mirror, she confirmed that he was getting into his Mercedes. Lorna smiled again and couldn't wait until tomorrow afternoon.

By the time she paid her parking fee, he'd pulled up behind her and honked. She waved into her sideview mirror. He waved back. For a few seconds Lorna toyed with the idea of letting him win at golf tomorrow. *No way!* she thought and laughed out loud.

✳ ❁ ✳

Michael rolled over in bed Saturday morning and tried to block out the annoying ringing that wouldn't stop. As if that weren't bad enough, a cold paw pressed his cheek, followed by an icy nose. Michael shoved at Socks, pulled the pillow over his head, and wished the phone would fall out the window. Finally it stopped, only to resume again 30 seconds later.

"All right already!" Michael grumbled. He shoved the pillow off, reached from beneath the covers, and fumbled for the cordless phone on his nightstand. Not even bothering to read the caller ID he mumbled a dry-mouthed "Hello" into the receiver and noted the digital clock on his nightstand. It was almost ten. Michael's eyes bugged as Frances Rousseau's voice came over the line.

"Mayor Hayden," she said like an interrogator, "I've been trying to reach you since last night. Apparently you've sworn off checking your voice mail."

Michael covered his eyes and rested his head back on the pillow. "Frances," he mumbled while his fuzzy brain suggested there might be something wrong. "What is it?"

"We had a break-in yesterday afternoon in your office."

He sat up. "What?"

"A woman locked herself in your office," she said and detailed the whole story, right down to her chasing the intruder into the elevator. "We lost her after that," Frances admitted.

"Did she take anything?" Michael asked and tossed aside the covers.

"Nothing that I could tell," Frances said. "But I thought you might want to go to your office and see. If there's something missing, we'll need to add it to our report for security."

"What are they saying?"

"They have no clue, as usual," Frances mocked. "Duh!"

Michael stood. "Do you have any idea what it might be linked to?"

"Well," Frances drawled, "you did make a public statement yesterday."

"Yes, but…" Michael trailed off and marched toward his closet. His clothes from last night lay draped over the chair in the corner, but he went for a pair of shorts and a polo shirt hanging in the closet.

"But?" Frances prompted.

"Surely this can't be related."

"You have stirred up a hornet's nest." Frances enunciated each word. "Our office phone rang all day yesterday, and *I* had to deal with the fallout," she accused.

Michael sighed. If the woman weren't pretty much perfect at her job, he'd fire her. Instead he bit his tongue and calmly said, "I know you're old enough to be my mother, but…" He allowed the rest to go unsaid.

After a lengthy pause Frances said, "I'm sorry."

"I flew to Dallas last night and was late getting in, so I slept late. I'm hitting the shower now. I should be at the office within an hour."

"Do you want me to meet you there?"

"If you don't mind," Michael said as his hazy mind tried to comprehend this latest turn of events.

"Then I'll see you in an hour."

Michael turned the phone off, tossed it onto the bed, and kicked the closet door closed. A series of crashing thuds followed the closet's closing. "Oh shoot," Michael mumbled and reopened the door. One bowling ball rolled toward his feet while three more were caught in the mix on the closet floor. A fifth one plopped from the slanted shelf and crashed into the others.

"Shoot!" he repeated. "Shoot, shoot, shoot!" Michael dropped his clothes on the bed and began picking up the balls. If they didn't have sentimental value, Michael would've tossed them. But when his sister said she no longer wanted their grandfather's collection she'd inherited, Michael took it. He hunted for a place to store them and finally made room on his closet shelves. But the shelves were slightly slanted for shoes. While the lip usually held the balls in place, if he slammed the door too hard or bumped one, they all jumped off the shelf for a bowling-ball fest on the closet floor. He was beginning to understand why his sister had passed them on to him.

He and Carrie had spent some fun times bowling with their grandfather. As Michael placed the blue one back on the shelf he recalled his grandfather's fingers in the ball, his hand wrapped around for a sure strike. Sighing, Michael decided to do the logical thing and try to find another spot for the balls…just not today.

"Okay," he mumbled, "stay put this time." He gently shut the door, picked up his clothing, and walked toward the bathroom.

He gazed at himself in the bathroom mirror and grimaced. His hair looked like a porcupine. He was sporting some serious morning stubble. And the right side of his face had a sheet imprint on it. Frowning against the taste in his mouth, Michael set aside his clothes and grabbed his toothbrush.

TWENTY-TWO

Two hours later Michael stood in the middle of his office with his hands on his hips. He shook his head and shrugged toward Frances. "I can't find anything missing. I've gone through my files, my desk, and even my armoire." He motioned toward the elegant piece he'd had delivered two weeks before.

Frances sighed and crossed her arms. Her shoulders relaxed, and she rested her hand on her chest. "I'm so relieved. I was the one in charge, and I was the one who let that woman go into your office. If anything important was gone…" She shook her head and remained silent.

Michael stepped toward his secretary, wrapped his arm around her shoulders, and squeezed. "Don't worry," he encouraged. "You're like my own personal bulldog. I know if that gal got past you, she had to have been slyer than a fox. It's not your fault, okay?"

Rousseau looked up and smiled into his face. In her blue jeans and T-shirt, she looked far less intimidating than she usually did in her crisp business suits. Michael was certain her clothes stood at attention and said, "Ma'am, yes ma'am!" before she put them on every morning. She lacked her usual perfume and smelled oddly of baby powder. For a second or two Michael saw past her firm exterior to the big heart that viewed protecting his interest as a serious assignment.

"Look." Michael pulled out his billfold and offered her a 20. "Go have lunch on me," he said. "You deserve it after I stood you up on the phone and for coming in today. I don't know what that woman was up to, but maybe it isn't as big of a deal as we're all thinking. She might have just been a confused employee from a cleaning service they hired in another building."

Frances looked at the 20 and then up at Michael. "I don't think so."

Michael tucked the 20 in Frances' hand. "I don't know what else it would be." He smiled and tilted his head. "Maybe she was just an admirer who wanted a lock of my hair," he teased.

"Oh brother," Frances said and shoved the 20 back at him. "You must've been out with Lorna last night."

Michael fumbled to stop the bill from sashaying toward the floor. "Why would you say that?" he asked as he finally clutched the money.

"You're too easy," Frances said and marched from the room with her shoulders squared. "You've turned into a Santa Claus who doesn't care if his whole office is turned upside down."

"Now you're exaggerating," Michael accused through a smile as he followed her into the outer office.

Rousseau glared at him while he locked his door and rounded her desk. "Are you going to call security?"

"Yes. That's what I'm doing now." She picked up the phone. "They're waiting to file a full report. They just needed to know if anything was missing."

Michael glanced at his watch. He still had two hours before meeting Lorna. He'd grab a bite to eat and then warm up at the country club. No way was he going to let Lorna beat him this time.

✳ ✳ ✳

Sunday morning Lorna settled on the church pew and silently observed the crowd gathering for worship. In just the few times she'd frequented Houston Heights, she was beginning to recognize several familiar faces—not counting Brittan who sat in the center, six rows from the front, and Heather, who claimed the last row of the south section of chairs. Lorna was in the north section, not as far back as Heather.

The plan for today was to infiltrate the space of another suspect on their list. They'd moved David O'Keefe and Evelyn Wright to the questionable list. Brittan remained firm about thinking Evelyn Wright was not involved in framing Devenport because the woman couldn't manage a computer. All three planned to revisit David O'Keefe if no other probes proved viable.

This morning the friends were focusing on Hattie J. Smith, a deaconess, and Frank R. Bass, the church treasurer. Last night when Lorna arrived home from her date with Michael, Brittan had accessed the church's website and retrieved photos of everyone on their suspect list. Now Lorna scanned the crowd for a tall redhead and a short fellow who resembled Sugar Ray Leonard.

She spotted Frank Bass walking down the center aisle. He paused to greet several people with a smile that was polished. Lorna cut a glance toward Heather, whose gaze was focused on the stocky churchman. As kind and considerate as he appeared, no one would ever guess the venom in his email to Devenport. The longer Lorna watched him, the more her skin crawled. He was what she called a snake. His high-dollar suit spoke of worldly success. His manners hinted that he was a master of deceit.

Lorna glanced toward Heather again. The two made eye contact and transferred leagues of silent communication. Both had just placed Bass on their "hot" list. He was their next serious pursuit. Lorna waited until he settled three rows from the front and discreetly moved to a chair behind him.

She cast a glance toward Brittan, whose nod was barely visible, and then to Heather, who held her gaze a few seconds and then glanced away. Today Brittan was wearing the thick-framed glasses again and a simple, navy pantsuit. Heather had her hair in a bun, wore no makeup, and had donned a pair of wire-rimmed glasses. The trench coat dress was the same one she wore last week. Lorna scratched at the base of her blonde wig and flipped the long hair over her shoulder. When she examined her appearance in the mirror this morning, her short-waisted jacket and matching skirt coupled with the blonde wig had made her appear closer to 18 than 24.

While Lorna kept her attention tuned to Bass, her mind wandered to the past couple of days. Despite her best effort, Michael had soundly beaten her at golf yesterday, and she'd insisted he cheated. When Michael asked her how, she'd reverted to, "You just did!" and crossed her arms with a huff. Of course it hadn't taken her long to remind him that the loser got a kiss; it hadn't taken Michael long to accommodate the loser.

They'd talked about everything during their golf session, including issues of faith. Michael wanted to know about Lorna's denominational persuasion. Lorna told him she'd been raised Methodist but presently attended a nondenominational church. Her parents were about as "thrilled" as Heather and Brittan's over the church all three attended. Meeting in a gym wasn't sophisticated enough. But the debutantes could be themselves in their little church that met in north Houston. It was real with no pretentiousness. Just a group of people who loved the Lord and wanted to share His love. Lorna knew there were folks like that at the church her parents attended, but she also needed this independence as much as her friends did. Sleuthing at Houston Heights Community Church made Lorna miss her own congregation. She would tell her friends she was going to her home church next Sunday no matter what.

Lorna shifted in her seat, eyed the back of Frank Bass' head, and tried to tune in on the final song before the associate pastor's message, but her mind turned back to Michael. He'd given her a key to his house yesterday, after asking her again if she minded taking care of Socks. Lorna had gone home last night, placed the key on a long, golden chain, and now wore it under her blouse. When she thought of the key, Lorna felt simultaneously elated and foolish. Her adult side suggested the act was nothing short of juvenile. She felt for the key beneath her blouse while her mind whispered she was holding the key to Michael's apartment...and his heart.

When Rich Cooper claimed his position behind the pulpit, Lorna's mind shifted solely to him. She crossed her legs, smoothed her skirt, and revisited the possibility of the associate pastor's having a strong motive to get rid of Devenport. Even though his name wasn't on the list of those who'd sent hate mail to Devenport, he was the one who'd been holding copies of the emails. *Maybe he's the inciter sort,* Lorna mused. *He craftily corrals the opposition and has them do his dirty work.* She rested her elbow on the back of the upholstered seat next to her.

Cooper was at least 40. His dark hair and eyes, hawk nose, and winged brows made him look more like a bird of prey than a minister. He was dressed in a typical black suit and grabbed the sides of the pulpit as if he were driving it. This morning's sermon centered upon the necessity of Christians having solid ethical character in all they do.

"Remember, Scripture says every deed done in secret will be revealed!" he bellowed.

Yikes! That's a direct hit, Lorna thought while half the congregation said "Amen," and Frank Bass stood to his feet to clap, along with half a dozen other members. They sat down.

Encouraged by the support, Cooper continued, "Don't think you'll get away with hidden sins. They'll come back to haunt you. I don't care who you are or what position you hold in the church, you can't hide from God or His all-seeing eyes! He will ensure that you are revealed for who you really are!"

Lorna winced and straightened while Bass and even more members again rose to their feet with applause. While the clapping swelled and died, cold reality set in upon Lorna. *This is starting to feel more like a cult than a church,* she thought. *And maybe Cooper is the central leader.* Bass reclaimed his seat, and Lorna stared at the back of his head. *Or Frank Bass,* she added to herself. *Poor Devenport was probably just trying to act like Jesus and those in "the cult" wanted none of it. So they crucified him.* Her stomach clenched into a twist. *They destroyed his life just to get rid of him. I wonder how many of them collaborated to pull it off?* Her gaze darted from one face to the other. Some were as incensed as the minister. A few looked somewhat bewildered, while several left the sanctuary. Lorna wondered if those leaving were sensing what she was.

Lorna's reeling mind fleetingly suggested that if some congregants would stoop to destroying someone's character, they might cross the line to something more serious.

"And with God it doesn't matter who stands up for you," Cooper railed. "*He's* the supreme judge! Not the president, not the governor, and certainly not the mayor."

Lorna's blood went cold. *This message is propaganda!*

The man gripped the pulpit with renewed vengeance and shouted, "God requires us to keep our hearts holy and pure before Him. Anything less will get us thrown in the lake of fire, where there is weeping and gnashing of teeth." By this point his face was as red as the lake of fire.

So much for grace, Lorna thought and was amazed at the difference in this week's service versus last week's. But of course, they'd had a guest missionary last Sunday. Cooper had merely stood in as ministerial official.

She was so focused upon Cooper and his gall that she nearly missed Frank Bass' swift exit up the aisle. He was passing her before Lorna noticed. She caught sight of a silver cell phone in his hand.

My grandmother wouldn't be happy with you, Frank Bass, Lorna thought.

She counted to three, reached to the floor, gripped her leather bag, and stood. By the time she entered the aisle, Bass was hitting the swinging doors that lead to the foyer. Lorna kept her face impassive while she strolled as swiftly as possible without alerting suspicion. Most the attendees were focused on Cooper's performance.

She made brief eye contact with Heather before exiting the sanctuary seconds after Bass. When Lorna entered the foyer, she glanced to the left, then the right, and glimpsed Bass' green sport coat as he ducked down a hallway. A movement on the foyer's other side caught her eye. Heather stepped from the sanctuary, glanced toward Lorna, and turned away as if she hadn't even seen her.

Okay, Heather, you've been my bodyguard once. I guess I'll let you again, Lorna decided as she followed Bass down the hallway.

TWENTY-THREE

Trent Devenport sat on his back deck, cell phone in hand. He and Katie had gone to early church today with her folks, who were presently the only link between them and financial disaster. Katie's parents never believed Trent was guilty, and he was more thankful every day for the support network God provided.

He'd come home to a voice mail from Frank Bass and had returned it immediately. As the phone droned out its fourth ring, Trent prepared to leave a voice mail while eyeing the bushes along the back privacy fence. They needed trimming again, and Trent planned to use this down time to take care of some home and yard upkeep he'd let slide.

Finally Frank picked up on the fifth ring. "Trent my man!" his mellow voice sang over the line.

"*Frank*," Trent replied and kicked at the beach ball the kids bounced from the pool to the deck, "it's so good to hear your voice." Even though Stevie insisted Trent should trust no one and guard his conversations, he couldn't resist returning Frank's call. The church treasurer had been such a strong friend. He'd even wept the day Trent was arrested.

"Hey, man," Frank said, "I was just calling to see how you were doing. The wife and I went to early church this morning and were wanting to touch base with you. How's everything going?"

"Well, I've had better days," Trent said through a smile, "but things look promising." He closed his eyes, lifted his face to the sun, and hesitated before discussing details about his case. Finally he decided it wouldn't hurt to mention the stuff everyone already knew about. He opened his eyes, shifted in his lawn chair, and waved at the twins who screamed, "Watch, Daddy!" as they bounced from the pool's short ladder into the water.

"I'm sure you've already seen Friday's paper," Trent said as their mutt meandered from his post near the pool and plopped at his feet.

"Yep. The whole church is buzzing about it," Frank assured. "Awesome that the mayor would do that for you!"

"I've had a lot of emails and calls from members in the last few days." He reached down to scratch Poochy's ears and decided the dog-pound refugee looked like a big, gray mop. "The ones calling me are saying they know I'm innocent. I hope they represent the majority." Trent rubbed at his forehead, beading in perspiration.

"Well, you know Latrice and I are behind you," Frank stated.

"Thanks so much." Trent stood and paced to the edge of the deck. He paused near a plant rack loaded with ivies and pinched at a dried leaf. "How's Rich doing without me?"

"Seems to be fine," Frank said. "He didn't preach last Sunday, but he did today. He did a good job. I'm sure he's wishing you were back. Your shoes are big ones to fill."

Trent chuckled and said, "Thanks," while Frank's compliment warmed his heart.

"Is there any word on your case?" Frank questioned. "Is the lawyer getting anywhere on who set you up?"

"Uh…" Trent hedged and had a flashback to Stevie Simon's dark eyes peering into his while she said, "Do not discuss one inch of this case with anyone. It's not anybody's business what we're doing or what stones we're turning."

But this is Frank! Trent argued as the kids splashed the chlorine-laden water toward the deck. Trent jumped away before the water slapped the boards where he'd been standing.

"Just a minute, Frank," Trent said and was thankful for the diversion. "My kids are in the pool and trying to baptize me."

"Sure, man," Frank replied through a chuckle.

Trent covered the phone's mouthpiece and said, "Hey, guys, I'm glad you're enjoying the pool, but don't throw any more water at me, okay? I'm in new shorts, here, and don't want the chlorine to spot them." Katie said she'd gotten the pool to distract the boys while he was in jail. It was only 18 feet wide, but the boys acted like it was an Olympic-sized dream pool.

"Come on, Daddy!" Todd cried and rubbed at the water in his eyes.

"Get in with us!" Tim encouraged before flipping the water into a tiny splash that lapped over the pool's edge.

Trent hesitated. One of the things he'd reflected upon in jail was the amount of time he was allotting to his sons. He'd spent too much family time at the church.

"Okay!" Trent removed his hand from the phone's mouthpiece. "Listen, Frank," he said, "looks like I'm in for a swim with the kids. We can catch up later, okay?"

"Oh, sure thing," Frank agreed, a wilt to his words.

"Sorry," Trent said and hoped his smile translated over the line. Before he had the chance to utter another syllable, his call waiting beeper erupted. "Whoops. Looks like somebody's beeping at me anyway," Trent said. "Might be my lawyer. Look, call me later, okay?"

"Will do."

Trent glanced at the screen and confirmed Stevie's name before answering the waiting call.

"Trent," she said, her voice as hard as a glacier, "I've had a report from your church this morning."

"A report?" Trent asked.

"Yes. I've planted some eyes there."

"Okaaaaay," Trent said, raising his brows. Every time he talked to Stevie, he learned new information about her tactics.

"It's not good," Stevie said.

Trent placed his hand on his hip and said, "What happened?"

"There's a reason I told you not to trust anybody. My contacts said Cooper's sermon this morning was loaded with double meanings—mostly negative—about you."

"Me?" Trent squeaked and swallowed against the dismay. Along with Frank Bass, Rich Cooper was on Trent's short list of those he trusted.

"Yes, *you*," Stevie insisted. "Have you heard from anyone at church recently?"

"Yes, I was just on the phone with Frank Bass." Poochy moved to Trent's leg and leaned against him.

"You didn't tell him anything did you?"

"Nothing that's not public knowledge." Trent's heart went cold. "Not him too!" he rasped and eyed the dog who gazed up at him trustingly. *Too bad my human friends aren't this loyal.*

"My spy says Bass was applauding Cooper before he walked out of the service."

"When was that?" Trent bent to rub the long-haired dog's ears.

"About 15 minutes ago."

Trent straightened. "He left the service to take my call? I was returning his call. Frank usually goes to early church, so I figured he'd be through. He *told* me he went to early church this morning. And he said Cooper gave a good sermon today."

"Well, either he went to both services or he lied," Stevie said. "And Cooper certainly isn't supporting you. This is the reason I told you not—"

"Not to trust anyone. I know, I know." Trent sighed as his spirits hit the deck. Frank Bass and Rich Cooper were two men he considered among his best friends. And Stevie had just placed them at the top of her suspect list.

"Why would they do something like this to me?" he croaked.

"If you're talking Cooper, I'd say jealousy," Stevie replied.

"Jealousy?" Trent echoed and tried to wrap his mind around the idea. While he had his share of weaknesses, Trent didn't usually struggle with envy.

"Jealousy makes people do awful things," she affirmed. "Joseph's brothers shoved him in a pit and sold him as a slave. King Saul tried to kill David. The Jewish leaders were jealous of Jesus' following."

"So they crucified Him," Trent finished.

"Yes. And someone is trying to crucify you. If it's Cooper, his motive is to nab your position. From what I understand, the membership committee is looking at appointing him soon. Frank has probably been his crony all along. Don't be surprised what happens after this—or who we uncover. Just brace yourself, okay?"

Trent sighed. "Okay, I'm braced. But if Rich is the ringleader do you think he'd take shots at me in church—even underhanded shots?"

"If he was *smart* he wouldn't," Stevie stated. "Some people are so convinced they won't get caught they're careless to the point of stupidity."

※ ※ ※

Lorna lowered her head and pretended to dig through her purse as she strolled up the hallway. Frank was returning toward the sanctuary now. When she passed him, Lorna cut a keen glance out of the corner of her eyes to see if he noticed her. The man kept walking as if he had no clue a woman had been eavesdropping on him. Lorna slowed and glanced back. Bass strolled forward like a man of character, never wavering in his step.

You're about as loyal as a viper, Lorna determined and couldn't believe how convincingly kind he'd been to Trent after applauding Cooper.

Before Bass was out of sight, Heather stepped from a Sunday school room and shot Lorna a glance before meandering back toward the foyer.

Once Bass was gone Lorna turned around and strolled up the hallway. Back in the foyer, she wandered toward the billboard and caught Heather's eye. Without a word they mutually agreed to put Hattie Smith on the "later" list. Today was going to be dedicated to Cooper. Last Sunday morning Brittan investigated Cooper's office and came up with the stack of emails that had triggered their suspect list. This morning Lorna itched to give his office another peek. She wondered if Heather might agree.

Trusting her friend to follow, Lorna walked toward the hallway marked "Church Staff." Cooper's office was on the other side of the office manager's. Lorna doubted the office was unlocked. She opened her purse, dug past her ever-present latex gloves, and retrieved a tissue from the pack she always carried. Glancing up the hallway, Lorna wrapped the tissue around the knob and turned. The knob resisted the pressure.

"Locked," she whispered and figured finding the office manager's door unlocked last week was a fluke.

Heather appeared at the hall's end. Lorna made eye contact, shook her head, and strolled toward Heather. The two passed, giving impersonal nods to each other. Lorna noticed Heather pulling out a small, plastic case from her dress pocket. Lorna recognized the case as Heather's lock-picking tools.

The girlfriend has it going on. Lorna nearly laughed.

The staff hall dead-ended at an emergency exit door, so Lorna didn't worry about anyone entering the hall from that way. The foyer opening was another thing altogether. She posted herself at a glass case near the staff hallway and read a memorial list while keeping an eye out for Heather. If someone approached, Lorna would stroll into the hall and cough obnoxiously loud. Hopefully Heather would take the hint and break away from the lock-picking.

Her cell phone vibrated. Lorna retrieved it and glanced at the screen. The text message icon indicated she had a new note. Casting a protective eye around the area, Lorna opened the message and discovered it was from Heather.

"In the office. Join me."

Whoa, you're a fast one! Lorna flipped the phone shut.

She strolled back down the hallway, slowed near Cooper's door, and looked over her shoulder before wrapping the tissue around the knob, opening the door, and stepping inside. The second the door snapped shut, Heather gripped Lorna's arm.

Lorna jumped and covered her chest.

"Just me," Heather breathed and reached to lock the door.

"I can't believe Cooper's gall!" Lorna hissed and glanced around the shadowed office.

"Neither can I," Heather replied. "He's an idiot, whether he's innocent or guilty. Either way you look at it, he's incriminating himself."

"Yes, and I just heard Frank Bass lie to Trent Devenport. He acted as supportive as all-get-out and then asked him about the case."

Heather gasped. "Do you think Devenport told him anything?"

Lorna shook her head. "The call ended right after that. From the sound of it, I'd say Devenport was interrupted and had to go."

"Good. I hope he has the sense not to confide in anyone." Heather turned on a mini flashlight and checked her gold watch. "It's ten 'til twelve." She adjusted her glove. "We've got to work fast and get outta here."

"Right." Lorna scratched the base of the blonde wig and was looking forward to taking it off. She pulled her set of thin gloves from her purse, slipped them on, and retrieved her own flashlight.

Silently the women each chose a section of the room and went to work. Lorna perused a file cabinet while Heather claimed Cooper's desk. The first two drawers Lorna opened contained church business and produced no leads.

The third one contained personal files that smelled a bit musty. The long ago dates on some of the files attributed to the mustiness. One read "Grandma's photos," and featured pictures that dated back to Moses.

Nevertheless, all the files were not so archaic. She gripped the miniature flashlight between her teeth and pulled an unmarked manila envelope from the back of a drawer. Lorna opened it and removed a document with a cover sheet that read "Ten Year Goals." Like a bloodhound on the trail of a new scent, Lorna eagerly flipped to the next page, dated nine years ago. Her attention riveted, she skimmed the list of achievements Cooper planned to accomplish. Some goals, like owning a home, were common. Others, such as having several ministry-related books published, were more prodigious.

Lorna noticed that a good number of the list items were checked. She deduced that those were the ones Cooper had accomplished. She checked her watch, noted five minutes had lapsed, and glanced toward the desktop copy machine nearby. Within two minutes, she'd copied the document and was inserting it back into the file.

Heather neared from the desk. "Find something?" she whispered.

"Maybe." Lorna folded the document and slipped it into her handbag. "We'll see."

"We need to get going," Heather urged.

"Yep." Lorna nodded and was turning toward the door when the knob rattled. Her eyes widened. She stopped breathing and gazed at Heather for two stunned seconds.

"The closet!" Heather pointed to a closet she hoped was identical to the one in Devenport's office.

The friends dove at the door. Lorna opened it and cast a final glance toward the office door before following Heather inside.

The knob rattled again. The door squeaked open. Cooper's booming voice erupted into the room as Lorna entered the darkness and silently shut the door. She maneuvered past a couple of coats and a choir robe and then hugged the back wall near Heather.

"Okay, Mom," Cooper agreed, his voice edgy. "I will." The office door clapped. "You don't have to remind me every day. I know Dad's in the nursing home, and I know he wants to see me. Lay off! I've got a church to run."

With Heather on her heels, Lorna inched deeper into the closet until she met a stack of boxes wedged in the corner. Heather squeezed her hand. Lorna held her breath and prayed Cooper's mission would be short-lived and that he wouldn't open the closet.

TWENTY-FOUR

Brittan strolled from the sanctuary and mingled with the crowd in the foyer. She'd seen Lorna exit the service on Frank Bass' heels. The next time she checked Heather's presence in the sanctuary, she was gone as well. Brittan deduced that Heather had followed Lorna as a backup, so she decided to stay in the service.

One of them needed to hear everything Cooper was spewing. After his initial round of dart-throwing, he'd focused on Scripture. His chosen references had been on divine punishment for wrongs but he ignored references to grace and forgiveness. For Brittan, the amazing thing was the crowd's positive responses. And that made her miss her own church all the more.

As Brittan navigated through the crowd, she wondered if Devenport had been such a legalistic preacher. Something in her spirit whispered he couldn't have been if he were so set upon offering grace and opportunities to former prisoners. The stark differences between Devenport's view and the hard-nosed rigidity of some of the members were impossible to miss. Whether or not some members had framed him was still to be seen.

Several times Lorna mentioned she thought Cooper might be the culprit. But Brittan couldn't believe anybody would be stupid enough to make such blatant remarks from the pulpit if he'd been involved in framing Devenport. For Brittan, Cooper's brazen blows were evidence that he probably didn't set up Devenport. She couldn't imagine anyone being obtuse enough to commit the crime and then make public statements that made himself appear vengeful or hinted at what he would gain from Trent's demise.

She tugged her purse strap onto her shoulder and inserted her hand into her slacks pocket. Pausing near the glass doors, Brittan scanned the crowd for her friends while continuing her analysis of the case. She still believed Michael was a stronger suspect than Cooper. She and Heather had discussed accessing Hayden's apartment but had yet to determine when. Heather said she was willing to try picking his apartment's lock, but that she doubted her skills were sophisticated enough to pull off an outside door. From what Heather had learned from Duke, they usually weren't as simple as inside doors.

Brittan crossed her arms and tapped her toe. She checked her watch and noticed the crowd was thinning. With every person who exited the building, warm air wafted inside. Finally Brittan stepped outside and decided to peruse the grounds. Maybe her friends had already left and didn't bother notifying her. She stopped, scanned the parking lot filled with hundreds of cars, and realized the futility of her mission. Neither of her friends had told her what vehicles they'd rented this morning. And they had a pact. None of them were to leave without notifying the others. This allowed them to cover each other.

Amazed at her own oversight, Brittan strolled around a corner and walked toward a large bed filled with geraniums. After a discreet glance around the grounds, she pulled her cell phone from her purse and dialed Lorna's number.

Lorna's phone vibrated in the holster clipped to her waistband. The vibration startled her, and she jumped. Heather's hand tightened around hers. The light seeping from beneath the doorway offered the only illumination in the dark closet. Lorna peered at her friend, straining to see her silhouette.

Finally she leaned in and whispered, "My cell phone's vibrating," hoping she was somewhere near Heather's ear.

She released her friend's hand and pulled the cell from her holster. Brittan's name appeared on the screen. Lorna tilted the phone toward Heather. The phone's light illuminated Heather's features with an eerie play of shadows. With her hair in a bun and the wire-framed glasses, the shadows made Heather look sinister.

The friends understood Brittan's concern. Now that the service was over, she was probably waiting on them, wondering where they might be. The debs had a deal. None of them left the others without some type of notification. But Lorna and Heather were stuck in Rich Cooper's closet while his desk chair squeaked and his computer keyboard clicked. The telltale signals suggested he might be checking his email. After he'd barked at his own mother, no telling who he was "blessing" now. The man was certainly *not* the epitome of suave.

Lorna flipped open her phone and pressed the button that ended Brittan's call. Then she texted her friend a message that read "Stuck in Cooper's office closet. Cooper here. Help!" Lorna had no idea what Brittan could do to help, but she was sure if anyone could come up with something, it would be Brittan Shay.

She left the cell open and welcomed the scrap of illumination the phone proffered. As the seconds ticked by the closet became more stifling. The beads of perspiration dotting Lorna's upper lip multiplied with the growing knot of anxiety in her gut. The only thing worse than Cooper's finding them was his long-term presence in the office.

The phone's vibration alerted Lorna to a return message from Brittan. Her friend's note pierced the darkness with a ray of relief.

"I'm on it," Lorna read as Heather squeezed closer to glimpse the message. "Be ready!"

Lorna lifted her attention to Heather. The two nodded in sequence and waited for whatever Brittan had planned.

Brittan strolled back into the church and was thankful the foyer was nearly empty. That made her deed much simpler. Every public building she'd ever been in had one of those little red boxes that said "Break glass and pull lever in case of fire only." She also knew from experience what happened when someone pulled the handle. When her brother was 12, he couldn't resist pulling the lever. The result had been a horrid clanging that could jar someone out of a coma. Brittan assumed the same clanging would jolt Cooper from his office.

She spotted the telltale box between the men's room and the family restroom. Head bent, Brittan strolled toward it, looking up only long enough to make sure no one was around. Thankfully, the only people left were still in the sanctuary. Figuring her window of opportunity was short-lived, she first checked the door to the family bathroom and found it unlocked. She left it ajar. Taking a tissue from her purse, she gripped the tiny metal hammer that was chained to the mechanism, and tapped the glass. It shattered. Her fingers still shielded by the tissue, Brittan grabbed the bar and yanked. The fire alarm responded as she planned. Brittan hustled into the family restroom. The shocked calls in the foyer attested to the alarm's effectiveness.

"Oh my word!" Cooper exclaimed. "Fire!" The chair squeaked and bumped. His footsteps thumped toward the doorway.

Lorna gripped Heather's hand and never thought she'd ever be so thankful to hear a fire alarm. The office door banged open, and with it came the sounds of alarmed voices mixed with the clanging.

"Let's go!" Heather hissed.

Lorna stumbled forward, cracked the door, eyed the office, and affirmed that Cooper was gone. "Hurry!" she whispered over her shoulder. The two friends bustled from the closet, and Heather snapped the door shut.

Lorna stopped at the edge of the hallway, glanced to the left, toward the foyer, and then to the right. The emergency exit offered the only logical option.

"Let's hit the emergency exit!" Heather urged.

With Heather on her heels, Lorna trotted toward it, glancing behind every few steps. Other than a glimpse or two of people darting across the foyer, she saw no one. Before opening the emergency exit, Lorna glimpsed a warning that indicated an alarm would sound when they opened the door.

Lorna hit the metal bar and figured the alarm would provide a nice duet for the current one. The noon-time heat struck her sweating torso as Heather shut the door behind them. Panting, Lorna gripped her handbag and gazed around the parking lot like a cornered feline facing vicious dogs. She took off the latex gloves.

Even though Lorna's mind reeled with the aftermath of their close call and the door's alarm, the parking lot appeared amazingly calm. Nothing had changed. The highway streamed with traffic. A few cars rolled from the church parking lot. Several birds fluttered toward a nearby oak.

"Whew, I guess we just walk to our cars now," Heather said, pulling off her gloves.

"Yep." Lorna eyed Heather, who looked as hot and bothered as Lorna felt. "Just remember, if anyone approaches us, we tell them the truth. When we heard the alarm, we ran down the hall and used the emergency exit."

"Works for me," Heather said.

"Where'd you park?" Lorna asked and flipped the long hair away from her face.

Heather nodded to the left. "I'm in the blue Mustang."

"I'm over there." Lorna pointed straight ahead toward a white Chevrolet.

"Let's get in our cars and wait for Brittan," Heather said.

"Okay." Lorna nodded. "Once I get in the car, I'll text her and see where she's at." She struck out across the parking lot and forced herself to maintain a moderate stride. When she cut a discreet glance toward Heather, Lorna marveled at how her friend appeared to be casually strolling to her vehicle as if nothing unusual had happened.

Brittan debated how best to escape. The fire alarm still blasted while men's voices boomed through the doorway.

"...can't find a fire anywhere."

"Let's get the alarm off!" Cooper hollered.

"It was probably kids," a nasal voice suggested.

"Should we call the fire department?" a woman queried. "Won't they be on their way?"

"Good point," another man confirmed. "Would you take care of that, Hattie?"

"Sure. I can use my cell."

Brittan looked up at the ceiling. Hattie was the head deaconess, so she'd cancel the fire department's arrival. Good. Brittan weighed her options. Either she could stay put until everyone exited and risk the chance of getting locked in the building—or worse, they'd realize someone was in the bathroom and suspect she was the culprit. She could exit now and offer an act worthy of an Oscar to avoid suspicion. But she had to act soon to show her surprise. Brittan rubbed the damp palm along the front of her blazer and took her chance on the Oscar. She flung open the bathroom door and rushed out.

An elderly gentleman in a gray suit spotted her.

"My word! Is there a fire?" Brittan yelped. She darted her gaze around the room while kneading her purse strap. "Where do I go? What do I do?"

"Ma'am, don't worry!" He stepped to her side and placed an assuring hand on her shoulder. "It was a false alarm."

"Oh," Brittan heaved and covered her chest with her hand.

"Did you see anyone—any kids around the box before you went into the bathroom?" he asked. After a yank on his necktie, he unbuttoned his shirt's top button.

"N–no." Brittan stuttered. When she realized people were looking at her, she squirmed inside but managed to keep her expression as innocent as a terrified three year old. She shook her head from side to side and even offered a wide-eyed stare at Cooper. He assessed her with his keen brown eyes, and then turned his back and strolled toward Hattie, who was on her cell. Brittan nearly sank to her knees, but she kept her innocent and frightened demeanor intact. At least she was telling the truth. She hadn't seen children near the little red box.

"Okay, well, the coast is clear," the man assured and waved toward the exit.

"Thanks." Brittan heaved a big sigh. "I guess I'll go home then." Without a backward glance, she hurried across the foyer. When she emerged into the summer heat, Brittan restrained herself against racing to her vehicle. She kept her pace to a brisk stroll.

Lorna scratched at the wig's elastic band and arrived at the Chevrolet without compulsively ripping the hairpiece off. *It's like wearing a blonde mop*, she fumed and plopped into the auto-oven otherwise known as a car.

She couldn't turn the engine on and activate the air conditioner fast enough. With the cool air blasting her sweaty face, she picked up her cell phone to text Brittan. The phone vibrated against her palm. Caller ID indicated Brittan was already on the line.

"We're out!" she said into the receiver.

"Good. So am I," Brittan said. "I should get an Oscar on this one. I'll tell all as soon as we get home. I'm about to get into my car. Are you in yours?"

"I'm in."

"What about Heather?"

Lorna strained to catch a glimpse of her friend but was at the wrong angle. "Hang on," she said, putting the car in reverse. "I'm going to cruise her way and see." Lorna pulled from her parking place and motored toward Heather's area. She spotted the blonde opening the Mustang's door. With a final glance toward the church, Heather sat in the driver's seat.

"She's in," Lorna affirmed.

"Good. I'm pulling out now."

"See you at our place after I switch cars," Lorna said.

"Sounds good."

"I'll call Heather and make sure that works for her."

"Okay. If I don't hear back from you, I'll see you at home."

Within a minute Lorna confirmed the meeting with Heather. By the time she pulled onto the freeway and headed home, she was consumed with the desire to pull Cooper's goals from her purse and sneak a peek while driving. But her flawless driving record was spotless for a reason, and Lorna decided to stick to safety. The list could wait until she turned in the rental vehicle and picked up her Jeep.

TWENTY-FIVE

Lorna plopped onto the couch, kicked off her spiked sandals, and rubbed her feet against the posh carpet while rereading Cooper's goal list. She'd skimmed it when she picked up her Jeep and had been convinced more than ever that the associate pastor was a major suspect. The main goal that stood out was his desire to become a senior pastor. The original date on the ten-year goals was nine-and-a-half years ago. Now in his early forties, Cooper was still an associate pastor.

She lowered the paper and stared at the oversized clock hanging across the room. Lorna imagined the exasperation of an ambitious man whose boss was nearly a decade younger than he was. With every tick of the second hand Lorna's gut whispered, "He's the one. He's the one. He's the one." She knew it. End of discussion.

The electronic lock on the penthouse door beeped, and Lorna waited through Brittan's pressing in the combination that unlocked the door. On the sixth beep Brittan breezed in with Heather close behind. "Look who I picked up on the way," she said through a grin, jutting her thumb toward Heather.

Lorna wiggled her fingers at them both and then dropped Cooper's list on the coffee table. "Looks like we've got our man," she predicted. "I think Cooper's as guilty as all get out."

"Oh really?" Brittan asked and hurried to the list. She picked it up, and Heather peered over her shoulder.

"Yep." Lorna crossed her arms. "One of his top goals is to be a senior pastor. Well, he's not. And I'm thinking he just might be ambitious enough to take down Devenport to make it happen."

Brittan looked up from the list while Heather reached for it. Brittan passed it on and placed her hands on her hips. "Really, Lorna, I have my doubts."

Lorna's eyes widened. "Even after this morning's sermon?"

Adjusting her glasses, Brittan meandered to the window and pulled on the curtain cord. The drapes sashayed open and shuddered to a stop while a blast of sunshine invaded the room. "I can't imagine that anybody who is involved would be dumb enough to say some of the things he said this morning."

"Honestly, Lorna, the more I think about it," Heather admitted, "the more I think Brittan has a solid point. I do think the man incriminated himself, but it's too obvious." She shrugged and placed the goals on the table. "If he planted the links on Devenport's computer, he should be doing everything in his power to cover his tracks—not make himself look guilty."

"I was hoping there was something more direct on his list," Brittan admitted. "But just having that goal isn't enough for me."

Lorna wrinkled her brow. "You guys are serious, aren't you?" she queried and gazed from one to the other.

Brittan shrugged and gazed toward Heather.

"I think we need to put him on our 'maybe' list and look into the other suspects," Heather said. "Maybe we'll see it differently in a week...or find more evidence."

Lorna sighed and propped her feet on the coffee table. "Okay. Whatever you guys say. I'm out-voted. But I'll be as honest as both of you. I think he's our man. I think he's meaner than a junkyard cat and not overly bright."

Brittan laughed outright.

Lorna narrowed her eyes.

"Don't you mean junkyard *dog?*" Heather drawled.

"What*ever!*" Lorna snapped. "You get my drift. The bottom line is, I'm ready to dig deeper." She gazed straight at Brittan, whose eyes still glimmered with humor. "I think people have a tendency to project their own insights and abilities and thoughts upon others," she said. "Brittan, you're thinking that since Cooper's moves are stupid he can't be guilty because you're assuming nobody could be that dumb because you aren't. But there *are* people that dense. That's how criminals get caught. They make mistakes...open their mouths...think they're invincible." She lifted her hand and gave a twist. "Then they trap themselves. I think if we can get into Cooper's house, we'll find enough evidence to hang him."

"Okay," Heather stated. "Let's say if we don't find any stronger leads in a week, we do exactly that. While he's at church, we investigate his house." She shrugged and gazed at Brittan. "What's it going to hurt?"

Brittan sighed and adjusted her glasses. "Okay," she agreed. "But I hate to see us barking up the wrong tree."

"Isn't that barking up the wrong *bush?*" Lorna teased.

"No. It's meowing up the wrong ladder," Heather shot back.

Lorna threw a couch pillow at her and hit her smack in the face "Hey!" Heather shrieked and slung the pillow back at Lorna. She caught it and stood.

"I've got to go change," she said and checked her watch. "I'm meeting Michael for lunch in, like, 30 minutes. After lunch we're going to the park for awhile and then having dinner with my parents." She turned to Brittan and pointed at her. "By the way, thanks for the fire alarm. That was brilliant. You really bailed us out. We owe you big."

"Just don't forget it," Brittan said through a huge smile.

Lorna walked into her room and closed the door. She pondered Brittan and Heather's lack of insight, rolled her eyes, and huffed.

If they want to wait a week, fine, she decided and slipped out of her skirt. *But I'm going to start prowling tomorrow.* Lorna laid the skirt on the end of the bed and decided she'd start by digging into his background, and do it long before Sunday. When she slipped off her knit blouse, Michael's key caught in the tangle, and Lorna looped it over her dresser mirror. By the time she changed into the wide-legged slacks and matching blouse, Lorna knew the second she found valid evidence she'd present it to her friends, do her share of "proper" gloating, and then they could all do "the Rose" thing.

Lorna believed people who viewed God as a stringent judge who gleefully punished people were more likely to see themselves as His arm of punishment upon those they disagreed with. She imagined that in Cooper's twisted mind he might be thinking Devenport deserved being framed because he'd purposefully blocked Cooper's career. People like Cooper often invented or imagined all sorts of scenarios to validate their actions.

Checking her appearance in the mirror and then glancing at her watch, Lorna realized she was running a tad late and better call Michael on the way to the restaurant. The afternoon stretched before her like a dream, and she couldn't wait to be with the man she was falling in love with. She dabbed an extra dot of perfume on her wrists. Her father had the fragrance custom made for her last Christmas. The name "Lorna" was scripted in gold across the burgundy bottle. She'd been as thrilled with the sporty scent in December as she was now. It suited her like no other.

She grabbed her purse, called a quick goodbye to Heather and Brittan, and hurried out the door. Lorna was halfway to the parking garage before she realized she'd left Michael's apartment key hanging on her dresser mirror. Tempted to go back and get it, she decided not to. It would take time and wearing it was a whimsical idea anyway.

Brittan gazed at Heather, who'd plopped in the chair like she was going to be there a while. "Don't you and Duke have plans for lunch?" Brittan asked.

"No, we're doing dinner," Heather explained and covered a yawn. "I think the adrenaline rush is off now. I'm coming down."

"Yep." Brittan tucked her hair behind her ear. "You should have been where I was. I came out of the bathroom and acted like I was just this sweet little innocent bystander terrified by the commotion. They were still running around, calling the fire department, and trying to find out who triggered the false alarm. They asked me if I'd seen any kids. I told them no because—"

"Because you hadn't!" Heather threw back her head and laughed.

"Exactly," Brittan said through a snicker. "Anyway, we all had a tight squeeze today." She plopped onto the couch, rested her head on the back, and smiled. "But it was fun, wasn't it?"

"Loads," Heather agreed. "I love it!"

"Wantta go get some lunch?" Brittan asked and lifted her head.

"Sure. I was about to ask you the same thing. I could do some serious damage to a salad bar somewhere." Heather reached toward her bun, pulled out several pins, and allowed her hair to fall around her shoulders. "And I have no earthly idea why I'm still wearing these glasses," she mumbled and removed them.

"But you looked so teacherly," Brittan commented.

"And you look like a geek," Heather shot back. "You're still wearing your spy glasses too."

Brittan touched the side of the thick frames and laughed. "I guess I am." She stood and slipped off the navy blazer. "I'm going to change into some jeans."

Heather looked down at her dress.

"Did you bring something to change into?" Brittan asked.

She shook her head.

"Come on." Brittan waved her toward the hallway. "We're close enough to the same size; I'm sure I've got something you can wear."

With Heather on her heels, Brittan passed Lorna's room and casually glanced inside. When her gaze landed on the key hanging from the mirror on the long gold chain, she stopped.

"What?" Heather asked.

Her eyes wide, Brittan gazed into Heather's blue eyes. "Lorna left the key to Michael's apartment," she said and pointed inside. "She told me he'd given it to her and she'd put it on a chain."

Heather gazed into Lorna's bedroom, and her mouth fell open.

"We could get it duplicated while we're out to lunch," Brittan suggested. "Lorna and Michael are out for the rest of the day, so we have time. And Lorna said Michael's going to be out of town next week. It's the perfect opportunity."

Shaking her head, Heather eyed Brittan. "I—I can't."

"What?" Brittan exclaimed. "I thought we decided—"

"We did. But I've been thinking about it, Brittan, and I just can't." Heather squared her shoulders and lifted her chin. "Really. I'd rather spend my time on Frank Bass. He seems like a more likely suspect than Cooper or Michael. Lorna heard him on the phone outright lying to Trent Devenport. He's *got* to be involved."

"But we can't ignore other leads. What if Michael is the one?" Brittan pressured and squelched the twinge in her own conscience.

"Really, Brittan, the more I think about it, I have big problems with thinking Michael would make a public statement to support Devenport if he's the one who framed him. I think silence would be smarter. I mean, if Michael's motive is to see Devenport go to prison, publicly affirming him is like shooting himself in the foot." She wrinkled her brow and shook her head. "Either way he loses. If Devenport is convicted, Michael has committed political suicide. If Devenport goes free, he's thwarting his own plans."

"I know. I know." Brittan rubbed the back of her neck. "I've already thought of all the angles, but I just can't get away from thinking he's a strong suspect. I think part of the problem is that Lorna doesn't have that great of a track record when it comes to men. I mean, the last guy tried to rape her, for cryin' out loud."

"But one mistake doesn't mean she's going to always pick bad apples," Heather insisted.

Brittan sighed and stared at the floor. Finally she shrugged and said, "Okay, fine, Heather. If you don't want to check out his apartment, I won't push you. But I'm going to because I have to for my own conscience. If Michael Hayden is a scoundrel in disguise, I'll never forgive myself for not pushing the envelope. Lorna is worth it."

"Okay. That's fine," Heather said and lifted both hands, palms out. "My hands are off. I just hope Lorna never finds out."

"How will she find out?" Brittan said and stepped toward the key.

✳ ✺ ✳

Sunday evening Lorna preceded Michael into his apartment and smiled as Socks trotted from the kitchen to check them out. After a welcoming meow, the cat rubbed against Lorna's leg. Even though his tail got trapped beneath her long skirt, he went in for another rub.

"I can't believe how he's taken to you," Michael commented and closed the door. "He's usually much more aloof."

Bending down, Lorna scooped the cat into her arms and scratched his ears. "Listen, buddy," she teased, "we're going to be an item starting Tuesday. Are you ready?"

Socks purred and gently kneaded her arm with his paws.

"Hey, what about me?" Michael said and pressed his hands against his chest. "I'm starting to get jealous here."

The cat lifted a paw and rested it on Lorna's face.

She and Michael laughed while he scratched the cat's ears.

"Come on," he said and motioned toward the kitchen. "I'll

show you where his food is." Michael slipped off his sport coat and dropped it on the back of the sofa.

"What about his litter box?" Lorna asked.

Michael made a sour face and shook his head. "That's in the utility room. I don't expect you to deal with that. I'll change it before I leave, and it will be fine until I get back. Besides, when you take him to the park, he'll take care of some business then as well."

Lorna chuckled and rubbed her cheek against Socks' head. "Are you sure he's not part dog?" she asked. "Because I'm really starting to wonder. Dogs usually like me; cats hate me. If Socks is part dog that explains that...and the park thing."

Michael opened the cabinet and turned to Lorna with a mischievous smile. "Well, he *did* bark a few nights ago. Maybe his true colors are coming out."

Lorna chuckled again and enjoyed the light in Michael's eyes. "Did you bark, Sockies," she asked in a singsong voice, "or is Michael telling stories on you?"

The cat meowed, and Michael and Lorna laughed all over again.

The evening with her parents had been as free and easy as their conversation about Socks. Since her parents were founding members of the Michael Hayden Admiration Society, their accepting him as Lorna's man wasn't that big of a leap. Lorna's mom even cornered her and asked if they should start shopping for a wedding dress soon. Lorna assured her that was premature, but she'd let her know if anything changed.

Lorna gazed at Socks and reminded herself she was willingly holding a cat and actually enjoying it. And she was even looking forward to caring for the guy. *This must be true love,* she thought. Only true love could overcome her lifelong hatred for felines. She sighed and allowed the bad memory of Goliath to unravel. *Maybe all cats aren't that bad,* she reasoned. *Socks certainly seems sweet.*

"Okay," Michael said in his taking-care-of-business voice, "here's his albacore."

Lorna moved in closer as Michael pointed to a pile of tuna pouches. "Just give him one pouch of this a day and make sure his water bowl stays full." Michael pointed toward two red dishes sitting near the refrigerator. "After he gets through with his tuna, you can give him a scoop of this." He pulled out a small bag of Meow Chow. "It's not his favorite, but it gives him something to munch on. Tell you what..." Michael placed five packages of tuna beside the bag, "I'm going to set it all out so it's easy for you."

"Sure. No problem."

Michael closed the cabinet, turned to face Lorna, and reached for Socks. "Come here, you," he said and pulled the cat into his arms. "What gives with this anyway?" he fussed. "Are you switching allegiance on me?" Socks struggled against Michael and leaned back toward Lorna.

"Oh, oh, oh," she said, "looks like you've got competition!"

The cat strained toward the floor, and Michael put him down. "Well, at least I know he likes you."

"Yep. Looks like he likes me as much as my parents like you. You had them purring tonight." Lorna threw in a saucy wink.

"Hard not to," Michael admitted. "They're great people, and your dad's been such a huge support."

"I heard him talking to you about Trent Devenport." Lorna crossed her arms and leaned against the cabinet.

"Yes." Michael opened a cabinet and pulled out two tumblers. "He's worried sick that Trent will be convicted and I'll look really bad." Michael shrugged and began rolling up the sleeves of his dress shirt. "But that's a chance I took," he admitted. "And like I already told you, I knew when I made the statement I was taking a risk."

"Have you heard any more from Trent? Are they making progress?" Lorna asked.

"He called right before I got to your folks' house," Michael said. "He's not supposed to talk to anyone about the case, but he did me and made me promise not to tell anyone anything."

"Oh," Lorna said. "I guess I'm 'anyone' then, right?" She toyed with the top button of her linen blouse and tried to hide her intense interest.

"Technically yes," Michael said with an apologetic smile.

As unquenchable curiosity raged through Lorna she eyed the colored rhinestones decorating her sandals and feigned a nonchalance she was far from feeling. Any information Michael leaked would be a bonus nugget for "the Rose."

"You know," she mused, "it's really none of my business, but I've wondered if maybe there's, like, an associate pastor in the mix who might want Trent to go away so he can be senior pastor. You know, let me stab you in the back and get rid of you so *I* can serve Jesus." Lorna squared her shoulders, bobbed her head from side to side, and gazed into Michael's eyes for any hint of affirmation.

He looked down and slipped his hands into his pockets. Silence marched into the kitchen and sat a while. Finally Michael lifted his head and said, "Like I said, I'm sworn to secrecy," but his eyes affirmed everything she'd said.

Then Michael smiled, clapped his hands, and rubbed them together. "So...Saturday I'm the birthday boy!" he said. "Since I probably won't see you between now and then, why don't we make our plans now?"

Lorna smiled and sang, "Happy birthday to you..."

"So what *are* your plans for me?" he teased. "Wantta take me out to eat and give me a big birthday kiss? Or maybe I'll just get my big kiss early?" He leaned in and smacked her on the lips.

Laughing, Lorna returned the quick kiss and said, "Why don't you let me surprise you?" She wiggled her eyebrows. "You never know what I might come up with."

Michael doubled his fist and gently nudged her on the chin. "Well,

I guess we'll just see then. But remember, now you've got my hopes up."

Lorna's mind whirled with possibilities. Some options like the diamond cuff links she'd seen last week would let him know just how much she was smitten.

Michael had barely lowered his hand when a peculiar expression cloaked his face. He stared across the room for a full 15 seconds as his expression went from thoughtful to perturbed to horrified.

"That's it!" he said and balled his fists at his side. "My journal. That's what's missing!"

"What?" Lorna asked and stared in the direction he was gazing. She only saw the kitchen blinds.

Michael snapped his attention to her. His eyes wide, he said, "Remember when I met you for golf I told you someone pretended to be a cleaning lady and locked herself in my office for a while? Well, I didn't think anything was missing, but somehow...just now..." he pressed his fingertips against his forehead, "it flashed into my mind. I remember looking in the bottom drawer of the armoire and the phone book was in there, but the journal wasn't." He shook his head and rubbed his face. "At least I don't think it was."

"Well, do you want to check it out? I'll go with you," Lorna said.

Michael straightened. "Yes," he said. "Do you mind?"

"Not in the least." Lorna shook her head. "This is important." She grabbed his hand and pulled. "Come on," she ordered as her sandals clapped against the kitchen tile.

"Yesterday I thought the whole break-in was a fluke, but maybe it wasn't. But I was so focused on seeing you and winning our golf game...I couldn't let you beat me twice." A slight smile tilted the corners of his mouth.

"And don't think I'm going to let it happen again," Lorna

challenged and playfully stuck out her tongue. "You cheated anyway."

"I did not!"

"Did too." She grabbed her purse from the couch before they bustled out the door amid more banter.

TWENTY-SIX

Michael opened his office, hurried inside with Lorna on his heels, and flipped on the light. Normally, he allowed her to go first, but this time he was so focused on the journal he forgot. "Sorry," he said and darted a smile over his shoulder as he hurried to the armoire. "I'm not being very gentlemanly right now."

"I don't expect you to be," Lorna said and stopped near the armoire.

Michael flung open the doors, squatted, pulled out the bottom drawer, and picked up the fat phone book. "No journal," he said and rocked back on his heels. "She took my journal. Oh man!"

Lorna knelt beside him. "Was there anything important in it?" she asked and then pressed her fingertips against her temple. "That was boneheaded," she mumbled. "No, there was absolutely nothing important in it. Just my deepest most inner thoughts." Lorna lifted her hand.

"Yes." Michael chewed on his lip and shook his head. "If I weren't the mayor, I wouldn't be as upset, but right now I'm seeing the headline: 'Mayor's secret journal revealed.' I promise, sometimes the *Houston Star* is more like the *National Enquirer*."

Lorna reached for his hand and squeezed it. "Did your secretary get a good description of the lady?"

Michael sighed and rubbed his face. "She said she was either Hispanic or Asian or both. She wore thick-framed glasses and a hairnet. Other than that, Frances didn't look at her all that closely until she was chasing her down the hallway, and then that was from behind. She said at first she thought the woman was Asian, but the lady said, 'No comprende' when she left." He released Lorna's hand, moved to his knees, and rubbed his face. "Oh man," he groaned. "I can't believe this."

"We're going to have to pray that God will protect you in this," Lorna encouraged.

"What if the journal is sold to the press, and they print my struggles? I used to really fight feelings of vengeance over what Katie and Trent did. That's going to link me to them even more and make me look really bad."

Lorna's shoulders sagged. "Oh Michael, who wouldn't struggle with feelings like that? It's normal. You're human."

"Yes, but the press will eat me *alive*, Lorna! Your dad's fear will be fulfilled. It will be my political death. The governor will find another person to mentor, and I can kiss national politics goodbye!" Michael plopped onto the floor, propped his elbows on his knees, and cradled his head in his hands. He scrunched his hair in his fists and thought about giving it a good yank.

"Look," Lorna said and squeezed his arm, "let's not borrow trouble, okay?"

Michael lifted his head. She stroked his face, smiled into his soul, and those green eyes of hers had never been so full of kindness...and new love.

His despair eased a bit as his logical side agreed with Lorna and insisted he go forward, business as usual. "Maybe I took it to my apartment and forgot," he reasoned.

"Right!" Lorna shook her head and her smile further eased his anxiety. "Just go home and see if you can find it. Maybe it's in your nightstand."

His gut relaxed, and Michael prayed Lorna was right. *She is so good for me,* he affirmed. "One day I'm going to ask you to marry me, Lorna Leigh," he said and was stunned at the admission. But Michael was about as discombobulated as could be right now and had little control over his own tongue. "You're the best thing that's ever happened to me."

Lorna's freckled cheeks turned a lovely shade of pink, which only urged Michael to seal his promise with a kiss. He reached for her, and she took encouragement to a new level…a level that hinted she just might say "yes" when he proposed.

※ ※ ※

Friday evening Brittan opened the door to Michael's apartment for the second time that week. After Lorna indicated he had indeed left on his trip, Brittan made her first visit to his home Wednesday morning. She got up early and spent three hours searching Michael's flat. She'd found nothing that incriminated him—unless an obsession with airplanes was incriminating. Further prowling had uncovered a stack of *Sports Illustrated Magazines* in a basket near his TV. Interestingly enough, numerous copies featured Lorna. Those were at the top of the pile.

The search had been anticlimactic, to say the least. Brittan wouldn't have returned were it not for the journal she held under her arm. Like the apartment, the journal revealed nothing except a few references to Michael's struggling with feelings of vengeance. But nothing indicated he'd acted on them. After discussing everything with Heather, Brittan was finally convinced Michael was innocent. She could only pray neither Lorna nor he ever suspected she'd pried into his background.

She pocketed the key, shut the door, turned the deadbolt, and walked toward the hallway. When she'd searched the house Wednesday, she hadn't been through perusing the journal and planned then to return the diary today. She'd even chosen the best spot to place it. According to Lorna, Michael was due back in town tomorrow. So today was the perfect time.

Brittan knew Michael had missed the journal. She'd caught snatches of one of Lorna's conversations two days ago in which Michael apparently admitted being worried about it. Brittan strolled through the living room and was entering Michael's room when she saw the black-and-white cat lying in the center of his bed.

"Hi, kitty, kitty," she said in an attempt not to disturb him as she had Wednesday.

The cat lifted his head, jumped straight up, arched his back, and darted from the bed. Tail straight, he whizzed past Brittan and down the hall, just like last time.

"Okaaaaay," Brittan said through a chuckle and scanned Michael's room. The bold Chippendale furniture revealed a man of good taste. The room was clean except for several items of clothing draped on a chair. Paperwork cluttered a corner desk.

She knelt beside the nightstand and slid the diary behind it, making sure a corner showed out so Michael would eventually notice it. Brittan was standing up when the front door clapped shut. A hot wave of panic stiffened her. She held her breath and listened while footsteps tapped across the tile entryway. Brittan spotted Michael's closet, and it proved the only logical choice. She whipped around the bed and halted in front of the closet door. Silently she turned the knob, stepped past the neat row of designer suits and the hanging shoe sorter, and into a tangle of trophies and sports paraphernalia and stacks of magazines. She worriedly eyed a collection of bowling balls precariously perched on slanted shelves, closed the door, and hoped nothing in the closet could bite her.

Lorna kicked the apartment door closed, placed her purse and canvas totes on the floor, and hustled to the coffee table with the massive balloon bouquet she'd ordered for Michael. The plastic weight on the bottom held the shiny balloons in place while they stretched to the ceiling. The biggest one cresting the top said, "Happy Birthday!"

She smiled and rested her hands on her hips. "Perfect!" she proclaimed.

The place was clean, as usual, and smelled as if the cleaning lady had just left. Lorna had yet to investigate Michael's closets, but she suspected they were all color coordinated or alphabetized, depending on the need. The man was the epitome of organization—a skill Lorna desperately needed to learn.

A low growl erupted from across the room, and Lorna spotted Socks' yellow eyes glowing in the shadows. "Socks!" Lorna scolded. "Why are you growling at me? I thought we were buddies." She stepped toward the feline, who crept from beneath the table and cautiously rubbed against her leg.

She bent to scoop him up, but the quick movement sent him scurrying back to his hiding place. Before he ducked into the shadows, Lorna realized every hair on his tail was standing straight out.

"That's odd," she mumbled as a low rumble of thunder testified to the downpour outside. "Oh!" Lorna waved toward the closed drapes. "The rain, of course. You're scared of thunder."

Lorna neared the cat, knelt beside the table, pulled him out, and scooped him into her arms. "Come on, Socks," she crooned. "I brought you a can of sardines. I didn't want to leave you out of the celebration. Once you smell these guys, you'll forget all about that ol' storm."

She snuggled the cat close while turning to lock the door. Lorna retrieved her purse and canvas bags and walked into the kitchen, all the while reassuring Socks. By the time she opened the sardines, the cat's tail hair was smooth and he was meowing in his normal voice. Lorna deduced that the storm was distant history in the face of dozens of tiny fish that smelled like ocean heaven.

With Socks devouring his treat, Lorna began unpacking her

bags onto the counter. Michael had called last night and said he was coming home a day early. His business was complete, and he'd been able to move his flight to today. Lorna had risen this morning even before Brittan and had spent the day preparing for tonight. Along with the diamond cuff links she'd bought and a card, she'd also included sparkling grape juice for two, along with a set of fine cutlery, crystal, and china, which the salesclerk had carefully wrapped in tissue. The delicate, handwoven tablecloth was last.

The caterer said they could supply the china and crystal, but Lorna wanted to bring her own. She'd purchased the pieces and planned to leave them with Michael as a reminder of their special evening...and more to come. The caterer was scheduled to arrive in 5 minutes. The violinist, in 15. Between the smothered steak, baby potatoes, Caesar salad, and the violin serenade, Michael should feel like the sheik of Houston. According to his new schedule, he was due in about 30 minutes.

Lorna set aside the flower arrangement and brass candleholders in the center of the dining table. Michael took the extension leaves out when there was no company, so the cherrywood table was just the right size for two to four people. With the cloth in place, Lorna strode back toward the kitchen cabinet, unwrapped the crystal and china, and carefully placed them on the table. She finished the effect by replacing the brass candleholders. Lorna stood back and observed the arrangement. The candleholders were a perfect foil for the china's gold rims.

"Nice," she stated and walked toward the large window. Lorna pulled the drapes open, and the evening sun poured into the room like liquid gold. The effect looked like something in one of the home magazines her mother lived by.

A hard thud from across the living room jerked Lorna from her reverie. She waited, wondering if she'd really heard something. She slipped back into the kitchen. Socks had suspended the sardine pursuit. He hunched down, glared toward the living room, and softly growled. Something was definitely amiss. Lorna's heart raced. Her lips trembled. Logic insisted Socks' earlier disturbance had nothing to do with the storm and everything to do with another presence in the apartment. She was a long way removed from Heather's tough karate or Brittan's sharp shooting. Her mind flashed to the night she'd nearly been raped. Right before Heather crashed into the room, Lorna had gotten her hand around her tennis racket and slammed it against Chuck's face with the power of a killer serve. Heather's attack from behind had sealed his doom. When the police hauled him off, his face still carried the tennis racket's checker imprint.

While she didn't recall seeing any tennis rackets in Michael's place, she did remember the golf clubs in the living room corner. They were part of the decoration scheme, but very obviously well-used by the owner. Lorna tiptoed toward the living room. She paused on the threshold, eyed the golf clubs, and then scanned the living room and the part of the hallway she could see. The path was clear to the golf clubs.

She held her breath and waited for any other noise. When none came, Lorna wondered if perhaps she'd only heard a dull roll of thunder. Socks' worried growl insisted it was no thunder.

Lorna dashed forward, secured a nine iron, and tiptoed toward the hallway. She pressed herself along the wall, held her breath, and listened. After a desperate prayer for help, she rounded the corner to come face to face with...nothing.

Yet another thud from Michael's room attested there was something...or someone...in this apartment. Lorna lifted the golf club higher and crept into Michael's bedroom. At a glance, the room held only furniture and Michael's personal items. Lorna's gaze darted into every corner, landing on a huge print of an eagle in flight above his bed.

She twisted around and stared down the hallway, wondering if the noises were coming from the guest bedroom. Then another thump erupted, and Lorna was certain it came from the closet. Wild thoughts darted through her mind while a rash of cold sweat swept her body. She debated her options—proceed or retreat and call the police.

Before Lorna could make one move, the closet door eased open. Lorna lifted the club, caught her breath, braced her legs, and prepared to deliver a blow that would knock the intruder out cold.

TWENTY-SEVEN

As the dark-haired villain exited the closet backward, Lorna gritted her teeth and was about to swing the club when the woman turned and spotted her.

Brittan hollered. Lorna yelped and lowered the club.

"Oh my word!" Brittan gasped. "What are *you* doing here?"

"What am *I* doing here!" Lorna exclaimed. Squinting, she shook her head from side to side. "What are *you* doing here?"

"Before or after I was attacked by bowling balls?" Brittan asked and limped to Michael's bed. She sat down and rubbed the top of her foot.

"So *that's* what I heard."

"Yes. I accidentally bumped one, and they all started falling. That place is dangerous," she said, pointing to the closet. "Once I got them stabilized, I was trying to sneak out before it got worse. I promise, the man is a closet slob!"

"No way! Really?" Lorna opened the closet and gazed into a jumble of disorder. The only things in place were his extensive wardrobe and the organizer bag that hung from the rod and held his shoes. The rest was a jungle.

"Go figure," she muttered and closed the door. "I thought his closets were perfect."

"Yes, but that would make him perfect," Brittan reasoned. "And nobody's perfect."

Lorna sighed and crossed her arms. "So what are you doing here?" she repeated. As Lorna grappled with this strange turn of events, Brittan gazed up at her and a silent confession finally danced between them.

Lorna knitted her brows. "Brittan? How did you get in here? There was no sign of tampering with the lock. And there's a deadbolt. Can you even pick a deadbolt?" Lorna shook her head as the first droplets of Brittan's betrayal tainted her spirit. "Did you somehow get a copy of the key I have?"

Brittan looked down.

Realizing her friend was dressed in the dark "Goodwill Special" pants and T-shirts they usually wore for investigations, Lorna deduced her deed. "You were investigating Michael!" she accused. "*Why?*"

Brittan lifted her head and stared Lorna in the eyes. "I wondered if maybe *he* set up Trent Devenport," she confessed, "because of the Katie business."

"What?" Lorna squeaked.

"I was worried about you as well," Brittan admitted. "The last time you got serious about a man, well..." She shrugged.

"So you're saying you don't trust my judgment *at all*. Is that it?"

Brittan silently looked at Lorna.

"So you've been sneaking behind my back? How *could* you?"

"I did it because I care about you," Brittan insisted.

"But Michael Hayden is the *mayor!*" Lorna placed her hand on her hip and waved the golf club with the other. "If anybody's honorable—"

"Oh, you mean a politician?" Brittan defended.

"He's not just a politician!" Lorna snapped. "He's a solid Christian who wants to serve God and the community. So tell me, what dirt did you find that says otherwise?"

More silence.

"You didn't find one thing, did you?"

Brittan sighed. "No," she admitted.

"I'll tell you who I think set up Trent Devenport!" Lorna exclaimed. "Rich Cooper, that's who! And I've tried to tell you more than once, but you wouldn't listen because you were so focused on trying to smear Michael. Well, I've been doing some digging on my own. And Cooper isn't exactly the epitome of St. Frances."

The front doorknob rattled. A faint thump against the door followed.

Lorna stared toward the hallway and then back to her friend. "I think that's Michael," she whispered and checked her watch. "He's a little early. You've *got* to hide!" She pointed to the closet and grabbed Brittan's arm.

"No!" Brittan hissed. "The bowling balls!"

"Come on, then, the hall closet!" Lorna whispered.

Both friends dove toward the tiny closet. Lorna opened it, and Brittan scrambled inside. Lorna tossed the golf club in after her. The last thing she saw before shutting the door was Brittan fighting to maintain her balance while jackets and flannel shirts wildly swayed on their hangers.

Trembling from head to toe, Lorna hurried into the living room and flipped on the light just as Michael stepped into the apartment.

"Surprise!" she said as the caterer pushed a cart behind Michael. He glanced over his shoulder and then back to Lorna.

"What's all this?" he asked, a huge grin dimpling his cheeks.

"Happy birthday!" Lorna cheered and wished she didn't sound so brittle.

"Who's this guy?" Manhandling his luggage, Michael stepped further into the apartment and turned toward the man dressed in white.

"He's our caterer!" Lorna exclaimed and extended her arm toward the man like he was a celebrity. "You're early, Michael!" she continued. She wondered if her cheeks were as red as they were hot. "You weren't supposed to be home until *after* he got everything set up."

"For once the flight was early," he explained. "We caught a tail wind. Then, when I got to Houston, traffic wasn't so bad." He winked. "I thought you forgot my birthday!"

"Absolutely *not!*" Lorna placed her hands on her hips.

"If you'll just show me where I'm supposed to set up…" The caterer pointed to the cart he'd parked in the hallway. As Lorna directed him to the dining area, the smells of the gourmet meal wafted through the apartment.

"I'm *not* believing this," Michael said as soon as Lorna stepped back into the living room. He set his briefcase on the couch near his luggage, removed his suit coat, loosened his tie.

"Believe it!" Lorna moved to his side and kissed his cheek. She glanced toward the hallway and hoped he didn't sense her dread discomfort.

Socks meandered from the kitchen, licking his mouth like he'd just eaten a whole tuna.

"I gave Socks some sardines," she babbled. "I hope that was okay."

"Not only are you spoiling *me,* you're also spoiling my cat." Michael's gaze was more indulgent than Lorna had ever seen it.

Her pleasure was nearly enough to make her forget Brittan in the closet. But when Michael picked up his briefcase and headed toward the hallway, Lorna's memory was jolted. That closet was so small there was no place to actually hide. Her friend was crammed in, and when you opened the door she was visible.

"Here!" she exclaimed. "Let me take that for you. You need to sit down, put your feet up, relax." She pointed toward the sofa and tried to relieve him of his briefcase. She didn't know if he planned on depositing it in the hall closet, but Lorna didn't want to take any chances.

"No, that's okay," Michael insisted. "I'm going to change. I want to get out of what's left of these soaked clothes. He picked up his coat and tie, and then glanced down at Lorna's designer jeans and cotton blouse, both decorated in bling. "Since you're in jeans, there's no sense in my staying in this monkey suit." He planted a kiss on her forehead and said, "You're incredible! Thanks so much!" His eyes shone as he looked toward the balloons. "You thought of everything."

A knock at the door testified that the final guest had arrived. "Oh! That's probably the violinist," Lorna said.

"Violinist?" Michael echoed.

"Yes. I hired her for tonight."

"You *really did* think of everything!"

"Why don't you get the door, and I'll put your coat and brief-case up."

"To be perfectly honest, nature is calling. Do you mind?"

"No…th–that's okay," Lorna stammered. *Oh dear God,* she prayed all the way to the door, *please don't let Michael open the hall closet. Oh God, please help me to somehow get Brittan out. Please, oh please, don't let him find out she's here!*

She opened the door to a blonde-haired woman dressed in a black tuxedo. The musician carried a violin case and wore a professional smile. Lorna fumbled through introducing herself and on her way to the dining room, cast a worried glance toward the hallway. From this vantage, the closet door was still closed. Lorna flung herself into another round of panic-driven prayer and had little room in her emotions for the exasperation that nibbled at her mind. However, if she survived this and got Brittan out, Lorna wasn't sure she'd *ever* get over the slow-burning anger simmering in her soul. She could only imagine what would happen if Michael found Brittan. Lorna wanted to melt into a heap of mortification at the very thought.

When Lorna stepped back into the living room and saw Michael entering from the hallway, she knew her worst fears had been realized.

"Lorna?" he questioned and jutted his thumb over his shoulder.

Brittan stepped into the living room close behind Michael and mouthed, "I'm so sorry."

Michael pivoted to face her.

"I opened the closet to put up my briefcase and found your friend," he stated. "At first I didn't recognize her, and then I remembered the picture you showed me and asked her if she was Brittan Shay. Does this have something to do with my birthday or..." His brow wrinkling, he shook his head and looked quizzical.

"I..." Lorna croaked as the tension in the room mounted.

"Is this the reason you kept wanting to take my briefcase and coat?" he pressed. "I thought that was a little odd, but chalked it up to my birthday. Now..."

Lorna's face was as cold as a corpse.

"Did you know she was in the closet?"

"Uh..."

"You did, didn't you?" Michael asked. "What's the deal here?"

Both women stared at Michael in silence. Finally Brittan spoke up. "I guess I should be going."

"Oh no you don't!" Michael said. "This is *weird!* Both of you are acting like kids caught stealing gum, and I'm not letting you go until we get to the bottom of this." The incredible dark eyes that looked at Lorna with such adoration only minutes before had now gone dark and suspicious.

"Lorna, was this whole birthday shebang some kind of cover for—"

"No!" Lorna exclaimed. "I didn't even know she was here until just before you came."

"How did she get in?"

"I have my ways," Brittan supplied, her face and voice emotionless.

"You have your ways?" Michael repeated, his face stiff. He turned back to Lorna. "Did you give her a key to my place?"

"Absolutely not!" Lorna stated and crossed her arms.

"What were you doing in here, Brittan?" Michael demanded.

Brittan sighed and lowered her head.

And that's when Lorna's panic moved over and made room for fury. "I'll tell you what she was doing here!" she blurted.

"No, Lorna! You can't!" Brittan barked.

"Excuse me?" the caterer's voice floated from the kitchen doorway. "Is there a problem?"

"Yes, there is," Lorna stated and faced the man. "Would you and the musician mind waiting in the downstairs lobby for a few minutes? We need a little privacy."

"Well…" the man glanced at Michael, "sure. Okay. But I'm sched-uled to leave here by seven." He checked his watch. "I have another job after this."

"It's okay." Lorna waved away the worries. "You'll still get paid no matter what happens, and you can still leave at seven."

He shrugged. "All right."

"Please take the violinist with you, okay?"

"Okay," the man said. His expression said, *This is the most bizarre business I've ever run into in my life.*

Within seconds the door closed behind them, and Lorna turned back around. Hands on hips, she blurted, "We're 'the Rose'!"

"Aaah!" Brittan shrieked. "How *could* you?"

"How could I? Heather told Duke!" She bobbed her head from side to side. "How is this different?"

"He figured it out!" Brittan lifted both hands. "That's a big dif-ference!"

"You two? 'The Rose'?" Michael's eyes grew big.

"Yes. And our friend Heather." Lorna nodded. "The blonde in the picture with us." She pointed to Brittan and herself.

"Are you *serious?*"

"Absolutely." Lorna held Michael's gaze. "Remember when you saw that blonde at Trent Devenport's church you said looked like me?"

He nodded.

"That *was* me. We were investigating. We believe someone framed him, and we're trying to get to the bottom of it. And remember the animal cruelty case that just hit the press?"

He nodded. Lorna pointed to herself and Brittan. "We're the ones who left the rose with the precinct captain and leaked the info to the *Star*."

"And the cases last year?"

"Yes." Lorna nodded.

Michael shook his head and gazed from one to the other. "So this is what you do in your spare time?" He frowned.

Sock's meow pierced the thick silence.

He pointed at Brittan and said, "You were in my closet because..."

The answer to his question hung between them. As Lorna's anger began to subside, she wondered if her honesty had created a greater problem.

"Were you *investigating* me?" Michael prompted.

"I was mainly worried about Lorna," Brittan said, her words as rigid as her face. "She had one bad experience with a man," she explained, tapping her toe, "and I didn't want her to get hurt again. Especially if you were involved in—" She stopped.

"Involved in what?" Michael demanded.

"You don't want to know," Lorna ground out.

"Did you know about any of this?" Michael swiveled to face her. "I've a good mind to call security and have you *both* thrown in jail!"

Lorna gasped. "But I wasn't—"

"What exactly *were* you doing here, Lorna?"

"Oh no," Brittan groaned.

"I was waiting for you." She pointed toward the balloons. "And then I heard something in your room and went in there and found her. We were talking when you arrived. That's when she hid in the closet."

"How do I know all this wasn't some sort of diversion to cover her!" He waved toward the balloons. "Maybe you were here digging through my belongings as well!"

"Michael!" Lorna exclaimed as tears stung her eyes.

"Maybe the only reason you even showed an interest in me was so you and 'the Rose,'" he waved toward Brittan, "could see what kind of smut you could dig up and then ruin me in the press."

"Oh my word!" Brittan gasped.

"That's not true!" Lorna cried.

"I trusted one woman and she betrayed me," Michael continued. "And now it looks like I've been taken again."

"Michael!" Lorna hollered. Doubling her fists, she stepped toward him. "If you'd just listen! I promise before God I did *not* know she was here or that she was investigating you!"

Michael backed away and gazed at Lorna like she was a serpent.

"Does her being here have anything to do with Trent Devenport?" he asked.

"Why would you ask that?" Lorna queried.

Michael pressed the heels of his hands against his forehead. "I—I don't know," he replied. "I just thought... It just came to me. It makes perfect sense. You were at his church investigating because you think he was framed." He lowered his hands. "Oh dear God, help me," he slowly stated. "Do you think I..." He put his hand on his chest.

"I can't believe this," Brittan croaked.

"Listen to me, Michael!" Lorna stepped to his side and gripped his arm. "I don't believe that for one minute. You're the most decent and honest man I've ever met!"

He jerked away. His haunted gaze shifted from Lorna, to Brittan, and back again. "Just leave!" he finally commanded. "Both of you. Get out of my apartment."

"But Michael!" Lorna protested.

"She's telling you the truth," Brittan asserted. "She didn't know what I was up to and had no idea I was in here."

"What a mess!" Lorna groaned through a sob. She covered her face and shook from head to foot. "All I—all I wanted was to have a wonderful birthday surprise for you," she gasped.

"Lorna, I'm—I'm *so sorry*," Brittan said, "for everything. I guess I got a little carried away."

Michael sighed.

Lorna lifted her face and rubbed at the hot tears. "I'm going!" She marched toward the corner table and grabbed her purse.

"Lorna?" Michael questioned.

She pivoted to face him.

"Either you trust me or you don't, Michael. I can't stay in a relationship where I'm blindly accused of things I haven't done."

He rubbed his forehead and finally asked, "So you never doubted me? Not once?"

On the verge of vehemently shaking her head, Lorna recalled those few minutes in the Wednesday night prayer meeting when she had indeed suspected Michael. But the doubts had been so short lived she tried to convince herself that denying them wouldn't really be a lie. After all, Michael had vindicated himself in telling her he was there to meet Trent. Lorna opened her mouth to speak a firm no but couldn't get the word out. No matter how she rationalized, a lie was a lie. And what kind of a relationship was based on lies?

"Michael, I—" she rasped as tears filled her eyes.

A pallid veil started at Michael's chin and crept up his face. His eyes clouded with disenchantment, disillusionment, pain. His shoulders sagged. He gazed at the floor and finally said, "I was wrong, wasn't I, Lorna? You aren't perfect."

"I tried to tell you I'm not!" Lorna hugged herself as the room grew colder by the second. "But for what—whatever it's worth, I'm still not—not guilty of what you're accusing me of."

He shoved his hands into his pockets. "This is all such a shock."

"Well, it's been a shock for me too," Lorna said, her voice thick. "I'll tell the caterer and violinist they can go home. They'll probably have to come back up for their stuff." Lorna scrubbed aside the tear trickling down her cheek and gave in to the survival instinct she could no longer squelch. She hurried to the door, whipped it open, and slammed it in her wake.

Lorna ran to the elevator, frantically pressed the button, and was rewarded with a swift ding and opening. She lunged inside, pounded the first floor button, and wilted against the handrail. Never had she felt so alone...betrayed...bereft. One of her best friends had gone behind her back and investigated her boyfriend. And her boyfriend had accused her of not caring and being deceitful. She'd had to admit to him that she'd doubted him. And two relationships she believed would last forever crumbled into a heap of distrust. She was able to moderately hold herself together until she paid the caterer and violinist. But by the time Lorna reached her Jeep, uncontrollable sobs shook her body.

TWENTY-EIGHT

Michael eyed Brittan, who silently stared back. The room was increasingly growing too small for both of them, and Michael was finding it hard not to yell. He was on the verge of telling her to get out again when she finally spoke up.

"As bad as it makes me look, Michael, I was telling you the truth. Lorna had nothing to do with my being here. She had no idea I was here or investigating you."

Rubbing his eyes, Michael moved to the couch and sat on the edge. He placed his elbows on his knees, rested his forehead against his hands, and forced his breathing to steady.

"I know that...now," he admitted, but his words came out like a low-key growl. Even though the smell of gourmet food testified to Lorna's honest intent, he still fought fury over her doubting his integrity. "Still...she admitted she doubted me."

"Yes...and *you doubted her*," Brittan stated with a punch.

Michael lifted his head, narrowed his eyes, and stared into her impassive face. Only the twitch of her lip indicated she was experiencing emotions.

"Sounds to me like you have some trust problems going," she continued.

He did his best not to glare at the woman, but he wasn't sure he managed to curb it. "*I* have trust problems?" he prodded. "Who's breaking into people's apartments trying to dig up who-knows-what on them?"

Brittan looked down and fumbled with nothing. "Maybe I got a little carried away," she mumbled.

"A *little?*" His laugh held no mirth.

"Well, what would *you* think in my shoes?" Brittan went to the chair opposite him and plopped down. "All three of us totally believe someone is framing Trent Devenport, and then we find out he double-crossed his former best friend. Doesn't that leave room for a strong motive?"

"Yes, I guess," Michael admitted and blindly stared toward the sound system, "except I'm that former best friend and I'd *never* do that to anyone." He pierced her with a gaze he hoped put her in her place and kept her there. "Especially not with child porn! I wouldn't touch that stuff to frame the devil! How sick did you think I was?" Michael hollered.

"But none of us has known you that long, and..." Brittan hesitated and broke eye contact. "I look really bad, don't I?"

Michael shook his head. "If you weren't Lorna's friend, I don't know what I'd do."

"I probably need to go." Brittan stood. "One more thing...If I were you, I'd chase Lorna down and beg her to come back. She's falling in love with you. You won't find a better woman anywhere."

Michael clamped his teeth and gazed up at the petite female who'd violated every boundary of friendship he knew.

"In one breath you admit you're investigating me like I'm a criminal, and in the next you encourage me to chase Lorna down and beg her back? Explain that, will you?"

"Well..." Brittan hedged. "The deal is, I now know you are innocent! And now that Lorna's hurt, I want to do whatever I can to try to help you see that—"

"Help *me* see?" Michael snapped. "*You're* the one who started this!

If you hadn't sneaked in here in the first place, none of this blowup would have happened!"

"So now you're blaming me for your lack of trust in her?" Brittan challenged and crossed her arms.

"No, not totally, but I will say that I'm not the only one who hurt her. What you did took a lot of audacity."

"Yes, but audacity is what solves cases."

Michael stood as well. "Which brings us back to the fact that you're 'the Rose.' Right?"

"I still can't believe she told you." Brittan gripped the base of her neck. "But I think she was so mad she'd have given our names, ranks, serial numbers, addresses, and anything else she could think of!" She observed Michael with a silent plea and added, "It would mean a lot if you wouldn't tell anyone. You're the mayor. All you'd have to do is make one public statement, and our cover would be blown. Since nobody knows who we are, we're free to act like spoiled rich women during the day and—"

"Charlie's Angels by night?" Michael asked. Despite the irritation, the image brought back fond memories. He and Trent had spent their adolescence watching *Charlie's Angels* reruns. While Trent had been infatuated with Farrah Fawcett, Michael hadn't thought she could touch Kate Jackson. Now he'd had his chance with his own "Kate Jackson," and it was over.

"Why don't you guys get a job or something?" Michael groused. "I'm sure that once you take the right courses, the Houston police would hire you on their investigative team if you're so bent on—"

"Do you think our families would *allow* that?" Brittan asked. "They'd make us miserable! Mine is the most open-minded about a career. But Heather and Lorna's folks wouldn't permit anything but upper-management in their respective family empires."

"Or pro tennis?" Michael interjected.

"Well, yes. Something like that."

"But all that aside," Brittan said, "we've got more money than we'll ever spend. We're doing this for the love of the chase and justice. We set our own schedules and choose our own cases. We like it this way."

"And I guess you like making Houston stand on its ear with those roses."

"Now why would you say that?" Brittan smiled.

Despite the night's upheaval, Michael wanted to smile, but all he could manage was less of a frown. Nevertheless, these three women had to be the most spunky trio he'd ever encountered. He relived the second he opened the closet door and spotted Brittan staring at him. Her hair was still a spiked mess. Michael shook his head and inserted his hands into his pockets.

"If this weren't so wacky and you weren't such good friends with Lorna, I'd probably have you arrested," he stated, his tone serious enough to underscore his sincerity.

"Well, that's encouraging," Brittan drawled.

A knock at the door ushered in the caterer, and a fresh round of agitation seized him as Brittan glided out the door without a backward glance. Once the caterer and musician retrieved their gear, Michael was left alone with smothered beef tips, new potatoes, and enough Caesar salad for half of Houston. He wasn't hungry and the sight of the special china and crystal nauseated him.

"The woman came over to give me the best birthday ever, and now it's over," he mumbled. As hard as Michael tried to heap all the blame upon himself, he couldn't. The idea that Lorna had considered him a suspect in framing Trent exasperated him. Just a normal "frame" would be bad enough, but she'd suspected him of handling child pornography! Michael shivered and almost barfed.

When Michael found the black velvet box with a card beneath it on the kitchen counter, he nearly fell to his knees. His common sense told him not to open the box, but his fingers worked of their own accord. The lid sprang up to reveal a pair of diamond cuff links that were perfect for those high-profile dinners that dotted his schedule.

Michael swallowed against the bulge in his throat. He hadn't thought the situation could get any worse until he opened the card and read a touching message about friendship and romance that hinted at love without coming right out and saying the obvious. He dropped the box on the counter and released the card as if it were dripping arsenic.

His dream woman had come into his life. He'd believed her to be the epitome of perfection, only to discover she was far from it. Eyeing the diamonds, he was tempted to lambaste himself for falsely accusing her, but he still couldn't get past the idea that she'd doubted his integrity in the most degrading way. He felt like he was awakening from the best dream ever, only to realize Lorna really was just an abstract ideal in a *Sports Illustrated* magazine... and that was all she was ever going to be. The real Lorna simply didn't measure up.

* ※ *

By the time Lorna got home, she managed to stop crying enough to call Heather. She was so distraught over Brittan's invasion she didn't want to see her. So she packed a bag with enough clothing for three days and planned to crash at Heather's place, if she'd let her. The cell phone trembled in her hand as she threw her hair dryer into the suitcase and shut it.

Heather's cheerful, "Hey, girlfriend," sent a new sting to her eyes. Lorna swallowed and caught a glimpse of her swollen-eyed self in the mirror. She winced and croaked, "Heather..."

"What's wrong?" she asked. "You sound like you've been crying."

Lorna sniffed. "I have been," she whispered. "Are you home?"

"Yes."

"May I come over? Like now?"

"Of course," Heather confirmed. "Lorna, did someone die or..."

"N–no," Lorna stammered. "It's—it's Brittan. She broke into Michael's apartment and—"

"Oh no," Heather groaned. "How did you find out?"

"I caught her there—today—not long ago," Lorna explained. "And I want to get out of here before she gets back home. I'm so mad and so hurt!" Lorna zipped her suitcase, grabbed her purse, and manhandled both of them while gripping the cell phone.

"Oh no," Heather repeated. "I told her I didn't think she should—"

"You *knew* about it?" Lorna squeaked and stopped halfway down the hallway.

"Well..." Heather hesitated. "I knew she really suspected him. And to be honest, I did too at first, but after we read through his journal I really didn't think—"

"You read his journal!" Lorna bellowed and dropped her bag and purse.

"I can't believe I said that!" Heather moaned.

"Aha! That's it!" Lorna paced to the end of the hallway and started back. "Brittan is the one who broke into Michael's office and took his journal, isn't she? His secretary said she thought she was someone Asian or Hispanic. Well, hello!" Lorna pressed the heel of her hand against her forehead. "Brittan is Asian!"

Heather sighed. "She was returning the journal today," she explained and paused while Lorna leaned against the wall and tried to absorb the sordid mess. "Brittan believes Michael is totally innocent now. I do too."

"I feel *so betrayed*," Lorna wheezed.

"We did it because we really were worried about you, Lorna. We didn't want Michael to hurt you, and I guess we..."

"Went nutso!" Lorna straightened and wiped her forehead. "That's what you did!"

"Well, for whatever it's worth, I told Brittan I didn't think it was a good idea for her to go into his apartment. But she felt she had to make doubly sure he was on the up and up."

The front door's beeping indicated Brittan was entering the apartment. Lorna stiffened. She'd hoped to be gone before Brittan arrived.

"Look, I think Brittan's home. I don't know what I'm going to do right now. I'll call you if I decide to come over. Right now I'm thinking I might be better off at my mom's...or maybe looking for my own place."

"Lorna, *please!*" Heather begged. "I'm sorry. I really am. If I'd known all this was going to blow up on us, I'd have never—"

"Michael Hayden is the most decent man I've ever met, and we were falling in love. My parents loved him. His parents couldn't wait to meet me. Now it's over, Heather. And it's because of Brittan and this whole mess." Lorna scraped back the hair that was falling into her face.

"But the most awful part is—you and Brittan weren't the only ones who doubted him," she admitted. "I did too—not much and not for long—but I *did*. And now he knows that too."

"Oh no. I'm so sorry," Heather whispered.

Lorna sagged into the wall and hugged herself. "Then—then—I just blurted out and told him we're 'the Rose.'"

"This can't get any worse!" Heather croaked.

"This has got to be one of the worst days of my life!"

When Lorna looked up, Brittan was standing in the hallway.

Her eyes brimming with tears, she doubled her fists at her sides and said, "I—I'm sorry, Lorna."

"Brittan's here. I've gotta go," Lorna said and closed her phone.

As much as she wanted to remain furious, Brittan's tear-streamed face crumbled her resolve. As her friend neared, Lorna reached out and so did Brittan. The two hugged and wept together.

TWENTY-NINE

🌹 If Lorna hadn't seen it with her own eyes, she'd have vowed she was hallucinating. But there Heather was, removing a half gallon of German chocolate ice cream from a bag that read "Braum's." She plopped the ice cream on the kitchen counter and said, "Sometimes, you just gotta splurge."

"Oh my word!" Lorna gasped. "Do you have a fever? Are you possessed?" She leaned closer and stared into Heather's eyes. They were as blue and clear as always.

"Stop it, you!" Heather pushed Lorna away. She'd called back after Brittan and Lorna had their joint sob session and announced she was coming over. Little did Lorna know she would come loaded.

"What's this?" Brittan asked from the kitchen doorway.

"Heather brought German chocolate ice cream from Braum's," Lorna explained.

Brittan's swollen eyes widened. "Are you on drugs or something?"

With a huff, Heather rolled her eyes and said, "Somebody just get the bowls and spoons before I change my mind and leave."

Lorna opened the cabinet, reached past their guest china, and pulled out the cut crystal bowls that her parents had given her last Christmas. They were perfect for the occasion—salvaging friendships was definitely an occasion worth celebrating. It was hard to hold a grudge against Brittan when she was sobbing so fiercely. However, she still experienced the ache of betrayal and the haunting loneliness of "no Michael." She doubted the guy would call her again. And as one of Houston's most eligible bachelors, she also knew he'd have no trouble finding a new lady. Lorna could only hope she didn't have to read about it in the *Houston Star*, but imagined that was inevitable too.

She plopped the bowls on the marble-topped breakfast bar and dropped a silver spoon in each one.

He'll never call me again! Lorna wailed inwardly. *My friend invaded his privacy in the worst way, and I admitted I doubted his integrity.* The more she thought of that weak moment when she'd suspected him, the more Lorna wanted to dissolve. The magnitude of his framing someone was bad enough, but his using child porn to do it was unthinkable!

When Heather set the ice cream on the bar, Lorna's stomach lurched. Even though German chocolate was one of her favorites, thoughts of food added to her discomfort. Nevertheless, she didn't want to disappoint Heather. The fact that she'd lowered her dietary standards all the way to German chocolate meant she truly was sorry for any part she played in the fiasco. As Heather proudly scooped up generous helpings in each bowl, Lorna eyed the ice cream and decided maybe she wouldn't have that big of a problem downing her share once she got started.

She crawled onto the middle bar stool and looked down at the jeans and blouse she still wore. Lorna had bought the flashy set especially for Michael's birthday party. Her eyes stung and she swallowed hard while the memory of his saying she wasn't perfect slammed her anew.

I never was perfect, she fretted. *I tried to tell you that, Michael!*

Their spoons clicked against the bowls as the three friends indulged in the coconut-laden dessert. Initially Lorna's stomach did better than cooperate. It demanded more with the chewing of every pecan. Lorna obliged.

Eventually she drifted away from her own thoughts long enough to realize their silence was stiff. She cut a glance toward Brittan, who'd showered and changed into a pair of fashionably torn jeans and a Princeton T-shirt. With no makeup and reddened eyes, Brittan looked like a 16-year-old who'd just had a good cry because of teenage angst.

Lorna stroked her puffy eyelids. The bathroom mirror had testified that her eyes were as swollen as Brittan's. When she relived the evening's events, her stomach tightened. She sighed and put down her spoon. Even though her dish was still half full of the dessert, Lorna couldn't force another bite.

She stared across the living room to the large window that lined the penthouse's wall. The window faced south, but the sunset's final glow was not lost. Lorna wondered where Michael was, what he was thinking, if he'd found the cuff links. She sighed and toyed with her spoon.

When she glanced away, Lorna sensed Heather was looking toward her. She eyed her friend, only to realize Heather was gazing past her to Brittan. Caught in the act, Heather studied her ice cream, and her blonde hair swung forward in a curtain that covered her expression.

Too distracted to care, Lorna propped her elbow on the bar, rested her chin in her hand, and thought about the splendor of last Friday night. Michael had flown her to Dallas, kissed her in Reunion Tower...and on the carriage ride. Little did she suspect a mere one week later she'd be singing the blues and Heather, of all people, would bring her ice cream.

"We're really sorry," Brittan mumbled.

"I know." Lorna tried to smile at her friend. "It's okay. Really."

"Actually, it's not," Heather said. "And it never will be—not unless you two get back together."

"The good thing is, I don't think he suspects we read his journal," Brittan encouraged.

"Did you know he had a thing going for you years ago?" Heather asked.

"He wrote that?" Lorna questioned and stroked one of the rhinestones on her jeans.

"Yes, he mentioned you several times," Brittan affirmed.

"Yes," Lorna nodded, "he did tell me that, actually."

"He's also way more spiritual than we had him pegged," Heather admitted.

"I could have told you that," Lorna defended. Another stretch of silence sent Lorna into a stare, and she wished she hadn't blurted the first thing that came to her mind. Her friends felt bad enough.

"Well, maybe he'll find the journal and never know," Heather said, her voice a bit shrill.

"At least we can hope," Lorna drawled. "He's *very smart* though."

"I put it behind his nightstand so it looks like it fell off."

"That's a good move," Heather said.

"What do you think he'll do if he finds out we read it?" Brittan worried.

"Ah, I don't know," Lorna said. "Probably hire an ax murderer or something."

Heather's snicker sent Lorna into an unexpected chortle. Brittan followed and then shoved aside her bowl, placed both elbows on the bar, and rested her forehead against the heels of her hands.

"You should have been with me in that closet," she said. "Those bowling balls started falling and, I promise, I couldn't get them to stop."

Full-blown laughter erupted from Heather. Lorna's nerves were too shot for her to have the willpower to stop from getting sucked into the attack of delirium. She covered her face and imagined Brittan in a shower of bowling balls.

"Then…then…kung-fu Lorna, here, comes through with a golf club," Brittan wheezed.

"We're *so bad*," Lorna said and wished the comment were not so true. "It's by the grace of God we don't get ourselves killed."

"Well, at least we do solve cases," Heather said and then exclaimed, "Oh man! I just dropped chocolate on my blouse." She looked down at the flimsy satin number that matched her linen shorts.

"Off with her head!" Lorna teased.

"Now you're starting to sound like Rich Cooper." Heather slid from her seat and went for the roll of paper towels mounted beneath the cabinet.

"Speaking of which," Lorna said, "I've been doing some digging on that man."

"You mentioned that at Michael's…earlier, I mean," Brittan corrected.

"What did you find out?" Heather asked as she walked back toward her friends.

"I went back to church Wednesday night and hung out and asked a few questions. I found out he moved here from a small town in Arkansas called Greenbrier, not far from Conway. He was the associate pastor of a smaller church there. I got the name of the church out of Hattie Smith. You remember her? She's the head deaconess."

"Yes, I remember," Heather said and sat back down.

Brittan nodded.

"She likes to talk—*a lot*," Lorna added. "For what it's worth, I don't think she's involved. She doesn't seem like the type. More a closed-minded grandmother than anything else." She tucked her hair behind her ear and continued, "Anyway, I got there early Wednesday night and sat by her. Found out all sorts of stuff, including the fact that she had her appendix out in 1973, right after the birth of her third child."

"That's TMI," Brittan said. "Too much information."

Lorna picked up her spoon and toyed with the ice cream. "I called the church in Greenbrier several times yesterday and finally got the receptionist after lunch. I think she was related to Hattie Smith...or at least she talked like it."

"So what did you find out?" Heather leaned toward Lorna.

"I found out Rich Cooper was 'allowed' to leave that church two years ago without having charges pressed." Lorna raised her brows and looked Heather squarely in the eyes.

"Charges for what?" Brittan pressed.

"That's what I don't know," Lorna explained with a shrug. "And when I tried to get it out of the receptionist, she told me she'd already said more than she was supposed to and hung up. I tried to call back, but she didn't answer."

"Maybe we could go online and see if that town's newspaper has their back issues archived," Heather suggested.

"Good idea," Brittan said.

"I already started that and found the site but ran out of time. I was planning on starting back up tomorrow morning. Today I was too busy..." Lorna trailed off into another round of awkward silence.

"Why didn't you tell us this before now?" Heather finally asked.

Lorna lifted her brows. "The last time we talked about Cooper being a suspect both of you dismissed him and acted like you thought I was daft for bringing it up."

Heather looked down and sighed. "I guess we underestimated you, didn't we?"

"I guess," Lorna said. She tried not to sound miffed but failed.

"This has not been a good week for us, has it?" Brittan asked.

"I think that's an understatement," Heather groused.

"If you want to quit us, Lorna, we understand." Brittan laid her hand on Lorna's shoulder.

She covered her friend's hand with her own. "Nice try, but you'll *never* get that lucky."

❈ ❈ ❈

Michael couldn't explain the desire to be with Trent. He didn't even bother to resist the temptation to drive to his home. As he parked the car he silently prayed that Trent was home. Their minivan graced the garage. Beside it sat twin tricycles.

Michael winced and thought, *Two!* He shook his head and figured if he ever had twins he'd probably love them as much as Trent loved his. But until then Michael hoped for one at a time—if he ever got married, that is. The way things were going lately, he wondered if he would ever date again.

Images of Lorna danced through his mind, and Michael slid out of the Mercedes and slammed the door on the car...and Lorna. The evening air engulfed him in balmy moisture. The rain earlier had upped the humidity to the point of discomfort. Michael pulled at the neck of his polo shirt and walked up the sidewalk. The sounds of children playing across the street mingled with the smell of somebody's freshly baked cake, and Michael hoped that somebody was Katie. He could eat a whole slab of the cake she'd fed him the other night.

Lorna sashayed into his thoughts once more, but Michael refused to give in. He was here to make sense of what happened tonight. He forced himself to think logically. The last thing he needed to be remembering was how beautiful *she* looked in the sequined evening gown the first night he met her.

Tonight had been a nightmare. The only salvation came when he found his journal behind his nightstand. All Michael could figure was that he must have brought it home from work and placed it on his nightstand and Socks knocked it off. He hadn't had time to write in the diary since his campaign started, but he planned to start again soon.

He neared the front door, rang the doorbell, and waited. The matching white rocking chairs claiming the front porch invited him to rest a while. Even though sitting in a rocker did hold appeal, Michael wasn't certain how long he could stay still right now. After a second ring, the sound of blood-curdling screaming neared the door before Trent opened it. In his arms was a red-faced twin bellowing like his arm had been cut off.

"Michael, it's you!" Trent exclaimed, and by some miracle Michael heard him over the shrieks.

He wanted to wince but stopped himself.

"Sorry," Trent said. "He's mad because I found him digging in my toolbox. He had my hammer and was about to go after the coffee table with it."

"Oh, that's all," Michael said.

"Another night in the pigpen," Trent said through a smile, and Michael noticed he was wearing a paint-stained shirt and shorts. "Come on in!" He opened the door and then set his son down.

Michael stepped in and welcomed the cooler air.

Trent squatted and looked his son eye to eye. "Now listen, Tim. If I ever catch you with that hammer again, you won't swim in the pool for a whole day. Do you understand?"

The red-faced child nodded while rubbing his eyes with the backs of his hands.

"Okay, go on and play with your brother." Trent stood and gave Tim a gentle pat on the behind. The boy trotted off.

"So what brings you here, Michael?" Trent asked.

"I need to talk." Michael gripped the back of his neck and stared at the floor while Trent closed the door. The smell of fresh paint explained the off-white dots on Trent's cheeks and clothes. "I know you've got problems of your own, but..." Michael gazed at his lifetime friend and couldn't believe he'd made it seven whole years without his fellowship.

"Ah, but my problems are soon to be over!" Trent rubbed his hands together and looked like he was ready to perform a few flips.

"What happened?" Michael asked.

THIRTY

Her mouth opened, Lorna read the article she'd pulled up on her laptop after an hour of surfing. Heather and Brittan stood on each side of her.

"Unbelievable!" Brittan mumbled.

"What frustrates me," Heather said, "is that Devenport was arrested. His name has been smeared all over Houston. And he's pretty much being treated like he's guilty until proven innocent. Isn't it supposed to be the other way around?"

"Yep, it's supposed to be," Brittan said.

"All anyone had to do was a little digging," Lorna said, shaking her head. "Given the way Cooper acted Sunday morning, this article is enough to make anyone question his integrity. But ironically he was given the benefit of doubt in Arkansas." After skimming the article, she scrolled back up and reread the headline: "Local minister fired under suspicion of pornography." The article went on to say that Rich Cooper vowed the rumors were false but that he was stepping down to save the church from further embarrassment. The church refused to make a statement. The person accusing Cooper was the pastor of a neighboring church. The newspaper reported the pastor's comments that he walked in on Cooper while he was viewing the porn on his computer. It also included

Cooper's claim that the other pastor was jealous of the larger church's success and that he was lying.

"This is strong," Brittan said, "but it's still only circumstantial."

"It does make Cooper look suspicious," Heather mused, "but Brittan's right."

"I wonder if there's someone at Houston Heights who could be motivated into revealing the truth." Lorna tapped the edge of the laptop.

"Assuming Cooper had an accomplice." Brittan adjusted her glasses.

"I think he did," Lorna said. "If he's as big of a moron as I think he is, I'd even hazard he had someone else do the dirty work so he could hide behind him or her."

"Yes, or at least a collaborator," Brittan added.

"What about Frank Bass?" Heather crossed her arms.

"I'd say he's in up to his neck." Lorna leaned back in her chair and toyed with a pen lying near the laptop while Brittan went to close the drapes.

Lorna swiveled and glimpsed the darkened skyline, bedecked in lights, before the drapes swished into place. "Remember when I eavesdropped on his conversation? He lied to Trent Devenport."

"Yes, and we let that one slip through the cracks, didn't we?" Heather admitted.

"Yep," Brittan agreed and rubbed her cheek. "We've had a *really* bad week."

"So…what would happen if we got Frank Bass to talk?" Lorna wondered aloud.

"Sure!" Heather walked toward the overstuffed chair and plopped down. "We could just arrange an interview with him and 'the Rose,'" she said with a sarcastic smirk. "I'm sure he'd tell all." She rested her head against the back of the chair and stared at the ceiling.

"Maybe that guy in Arkansas would talk," Lorna said and slipped from her chair. "He wouldn't have to know we were 'the Rose.'

I'd be glad to get my dad's pilot to fly us there. I'd wear a disguise. Maybe he'll talk to me. I could even develop a pseudonym, create a business card, and tell him I'm investigating Rich Cooper."

"Hmmm..." Brittan crossed her arms and tapped her foot. "As eager as he was to talk to that reporter, I bet he'll be glad to open up to an investigator."

"I'll use the name my grandmother always calls me," Lorna continued. "Cheryl...and my middle name Saunders. It's my mom's maiden name actually."

"I like it." Heather sat up and scooted to the edge of her chair. "Cheryl Saunders."

"Let's do a little more digging first," Brittan said and moved toward the laptop. "We need to make sure that pastor is still in Greenbrier. What did the article say his name was?"

"Wayne something or other," Lorna supplied.

"It was Smith wasn't it?" Heather stood. "Wayne Smith."

"That's a really unusual name," Brittan drawled. "Maybe he'll get *really* original and change it to John Doe."

"Didn't the article mention what church he was with?" Lorna noted.

With a few clicks the debs had pulled up the church's website and accessed the staff page. Wayne Smith was still listed as senior pastor.

"Bingo!" Brittan said.

"Once we get our facts straight," Lorna mused, "why not go ahead and leak it to the press? Maybe if Frank Bass is involved he'll get scared by the publicity and confess."

"*If* he really is involved," Heather corrected and drummed her fingernails against the breakfast bar.

"I think he acts too guilty not to be involved," Brittan decided. "I initially thought he was a more likely suspect than Cooper anyway. Cooper has probably promised Bass he can have a position in his 'kingdom.'" Brittan drew invisible quote marks in the air.

"Well, here goes!" Lorna said and swiveled from the laptop. She grabbed both friends' hands and squeezed tight. "Let's get started!"

"Why don't we pray together?" Heather suggested and reached for Brittan's hand. "This case hasn't exactly gone as smoothly as the others."

"Right," Brittan agreed as the circle closed.

"The way we're fumbling, we need all the prayer we can get," Lorna concurred.

✳ ❊ ✳

"So what's going on with your case?" Michael asked and set aside his own worries in the face of Trent's jubilant expression.

"Well," Trent hedged and broke eye contact. "You know I'm really not supposed to talk about it, but…" He glanced over his shoulder and whispered, "Katie's in the kitchen—baking another cake. If she overhears me, she'll kill me. We've got to be careful." Trent motioned toward the couch.

Michael picked up a whiff of fresh cake mingling with the odor of wet paint. "I think I smelled her cake when I was walking up the sidewalk."

"Probably," Trent agreed. "When the exhaust fan is on the whole neighborhood gets blessed."

Michael settled on the couch and Trent dragged the wooden rocking chair close. He darted another glance toward the hallway and whispered, "I'm going to tell you this, but you've got to promise you won't leak one drop."

"Okay." Michael nodded.

"Like I told you the other day, my lawyer has pegged Rich Cooper, my associate pastor. She's almost certain he's the one who framed me. I've known Rich for years. He's a friend of my older brother's," Trent explained. "I hired him after I came to Houston Heights. He came with a supposedly clean resume. I didn't look deeply into his past because, well," Trent shrugged, "I'd known him for years and didn't know I needed to."

"Right." Michael shook his head and didn't have the heart to tell Trent he was repeating himself.

"After last Sunday's sermon, Stevie started digging. She found out he left his last church after accusations involving pornography."

Michael leaned forward.

"The church allowed him to resign. Pornography isn't illegal, and, at the time, there was no child pornography accusation. It looks *very* suspicious though considering what's happening here."

"Yes..." Michael said as he recalled what Lorna had said earlier. After she admitted she and her friends were 'the Rose,' she'd said she suspected Rich Cooper.

"My lawyer is *the best*. She's got cases stacking up." Trent lifted his hand to shoulder height. "But she's sticking with me and insisting I don't pay for anything. Her staff's maxed right now, and she's wanting to hire a private investigator to go to Greenbrier, Arkansas, to talk to that pastor who claims Rich was into porn. She contacted him, and he's agreed to talk. So far I haven't had to put any money out for this case, but she's not hired any outside help either."

He rested his elbows on his knees, tightly clasped his hands, and looked at Michael.

The integrity Michael saw was as fierce as what burned in his own soul.

"And really, I just *can't* let her do this," Trent continued. "I'm insisting on hiring the investigator. She's trying to argue me down, but I'm sticking to my guns."

"I know someone who will help you for free," Michael burst out and immediately doubted the wisdom of his words. He stared at Trent as his mind clicked in sequence with the grandfather clock in the corner: *The Rose. The Rose. The Rose.* He stood, paced the room, paused, and gazed into a mountainous landscape print that invited him to climb in and enjoy the scenery. The mountains blurred as a plan tromped through Michael's mind.

Apparently 'the Rose' was already turning stones and finding some answers. *But I shouldn't tell anyone who they are,* he reminded himself and simultaneously wondered why he felt the need to keep their secret. Brittan certainly hadn't minded invading *his* secrets. *But if I tell Trent and his lawyer who they are, Lorna and her friends will know, and they'd probably get so mad they wouldn't help. Besides,* he added, *I still don't want to betray Lorna.*

Michael swiveled toward Trent. "Will you give me the man's contact info?" he asked.

"You're sure this investigator is reputable?" Trent stood.

"Oh yeah," Michael said through a laugh. "I also don't know if I've ever met anyone more determined or...or...scrappy." The image of Brittan huddling in his closet reinforced his claim.

"Who is it?" Trent questioned.

Michael looked down at his Nikes and debated how best to answer. Finally he lifted his gaze to Trent's and said, "That I can't tell you. Just trust me on this, okay?"

Bewilderment clouded Trent's eyes. "You can't tell me?"

"No." Michael pressed his lips together. "Just don't ask any questions, okay?" He lifted his hands.

"Well..." Trent shook his head.

"Look, I *promise*," Michael vowed, "I don't think you'll be sorry. If you'll just give me the guy's name and number, my contact will take it from there. If this person is as...uh...aggressive as I believe... uh...anyway, the case can be wrapped up in a few days."

Okay...well...will he, like, call me or Stevie?"

Michael scratched at his ear and gazed toward the carpet. "Somehow I don't think you'll have to worry about any phone calls," he said. "You'll know when the case is solved."

"This is weird." Trent tilted his head. "Are you sure?"

Chuckling, Michael said, "I've never been surer of anything in my life."

"Well, okay. I just got the man's info from Stevie this morning. It's in my study." He pointed toward the back of the house. "I'll give it to you before you leave."

"Trent?" Katie's voice floated up the hallway, and she soon appeared in the living room. "Oh hi, Michael," she cooed. "I thought I heard someone come in but wasn't sure. It's great to see you again." She neared and offered a discreet hug from the side.

"Same here," Michael said and noticed her voice wasn't grating on him as badly this time. But he was still as thankful as ever that she was Trent's wife and not his. Whatever happened with Lorna, he'd learned a lot about himself through that relationship.

"Looks like you've got my cake schedule down to a fine art." Katie rubbed her hands across the front of her terrycloth apron. "I just pulled another one out of the oven."

"That's what I was counting on," Michael said through a broad grin.

"Good. Give it time to cool and then I'll ice it."

"I was wondering if you'd let us eat it hot without the icing." Trent rubbed his hands together and wiggled his eyebrows. "You know that's my favorite way."

Katie eyed her husband like a playful shrew and then finally gave in, "Oh, okay, you. Come on." She motioned for the men to follow her, and Michael fell in behind Trent.

Within minutes the men settled in a cozy sunroom that overlooked the backyard deck and the kids' new above-ground pool. The room was filled with plants and wicker furniture and offered the exact comfort level and privacy Michael needed for discussing his current problem.

When he was certain Katie was out of earshot, he said, "I actually came over for some brotherly advice."

"Oh?" Trent asked as he crammed his mouth full of chocolate cake.

"I'm having woman problems," Michael said and then wondered how in the world he would relate the story to Trent without revealing the sordid mess. Then he realized he'd just have to gloss over it. Going into too much detail about tonight's episode might lead to information Lorna begged him not to reveal. But he feared glossing it wouldn't give Trent enough information to offer sound advice.

With a sigh Michael said, "Have I mentioned Lorna Leigh to you?"

"Yes, but only briefly," Trent said before downing a sip of coffee. "And I saw you in the paper with her...along with the rest of Houston." He winked. "She's the ex-tennis pro, right?"

"Yep." Michael nodded and rubbed his brow. "Right—and we've hit a rough spot. I can't go into many details," he hedged, "but we've both made some pretty bad slams at each other. One part of me hates the whole thing and wants to make it right no matter what, and the other part is so mad over what she said that I don't ever want to see her again."

"What'd she say?" Trent questioned.

He sighed and examined a potted fern. "She seriously insulted my character."

"Ouch!"

"And I guess...maybe...I insulted hers too."

"Double whammy," Trent said, his words muffled as he downed a huge mouthful of cake.

"Are you mad at that cake, man?" Michael asked and reached for his mug of coffee.

"Absolutely!" Trent exclaimed. "And if you don't eat yours," he pointed to the saucer on the glass-topped table, "I'll show you how mad I am at it!"

"Here." Michael picked up the cake and extended it. "Just take it." His appetite had vanished somewhere between entering the home and admitting that he'd attacked Lorna's character just as thoroughly as she had his.

"No!" Trent held up his hand. "I'm joking. I'll get myself another piece in a minute."

Michael set the cake down and didn't bother to argue. "What a mess," he said and wondered if he and Lorna would ever salvage their budding romance...or if Lorna even wanted to try.

"Do you think you're in love with Lorna?" Trent asked.

"Yes," Michael acknowledged and sipped his hot black coffee. "And I think I have been for a long time too."

"So you've known each other for awhile?"

"No. We haven't actually known each other all that long," Michael admitted. "But I've admired her from afar for years. I've had a serious thing for her since she nearly won the U.S. Open several years ago. I thought she was the perfect woman, but..." Michael waved away the very suggestion and threw in a scornful laugh.

"Ah." Trent set aside his mug, placed his elbows on the chair's armrests, and made a tent of his fingers. "I see," he drawled like an all-knowing sage.

"What?" Michael asked.

"There's no such thing as the perfect woman...or the perfect man either, for that matter."

Michael blinked and absorbed the fact of what Trent was saying.

"Sounds to me like you've been in love with the *image*, not the real woman."

"What?" Michael stood and paced toward the row of windows. The backyard lighting illuminated the spacious lawn and the boys' pool. The shimmering water rippled with the summer breeze and appeared as tumultuous as Michael's emotions.

"Maybe you've created this dream woman in your mind, and

now that you've hit some imperfections, you're ready to go hang yourself...and her too," Trent suggested.

Michael pivoted to face his friend as Trent's words sank to the bottom of his soul and rang with a truth he couldn't deny. "Did you take psychology classes somewhere because—"

"Yes, as a matter of fact I did," Trent admitted and resumed his coffee sipping.

Michael turned back to the view of the yard and pondered the implications of Trent's observations. As the coffee warmed his stomach, the reality of Trent's words chilled his soul. If he was right, Lorna hadn't stood a chance from day one.

THIRTY-ONE

Lorna wouldn't have crawled out of bed by eight, except she'd gone to sleep weeping and woke up doing the same. Her pillow was wet. Her eyes were more swollen than they were last night. And her teeth ached from all the sinus pressure. She showered and dressed in a soft pair of capri pants and an oversized denim shirt. Piling back into bed, Lorna sat with her Bible and a hot cup of tea.

During her intermittent sleep, she'd begged God for another chance with Michael, but she couldn't find the faith to believe that would actually happen. Lorna couldn't imagine a man as honorable as Michael ever aligning himself with a woman who'd doubted him to the level she had.

Of course, he doubted me as well, she reminded herself. But in the morning light Lorna saw clearly just how easily that mistake could have happened. After all, her best friend was in his closet while Lorna was setting up a "surprise."

She put her cup on the nightstand and scrunched back under the covers. Brittan had to be the hottest chick in the south. Even at a compromise temperature in the apartment, she froze Lorna out—in June, no less.

While Lorna flipped through God's Word, her mind replayed

a snatch of Scripture that had come to her in the night: "My grace is sufficient." The words had revolved through her mind over and over again until Lorna decided to track down the verse. Finally she turned to her concordance and scanned the words until her finger rested on the reference. She turned to 2 Corinthians 12:9 and whispered, "He said to me, 'My grace is sufficient for you, for my power is made perfect in weakness.'" She closed her eyes and prayed, *God, I'm weak...so weak. I need your grace.* Lorna thought of Rich Cooper's scorching sermon...of the graceless, vengeful God he depicted, and she prayed she never slipped into such a mentality.

"I need grace," she whispered and closed her eyes. "We all need grace." Lorna rested her head against the pillows she'd propped behind her. "Lord, please help Michael give me grace too."

Her cell phone began playing "Endless Love" from the nightstand, and Lorna's eyes popped open. She held her breath and waited to make sure she wasn't imagining the tune. She gazed at the thin-line phone, alight with signs of a call.

Lorna picked up the phone and noted Michael's name on the ID screen. She flipped it open, and said, "Hello, this is Lorna," and was amazed at how calm she sounded...as if she had no idea who the caller might be.

"Hi, Lorna, it's me," Michael's voice floated over the line.

She closed her eyes, swallowed hard, and said, "Hello, Michael."

"I was...wondering if you'd meet me for a few minutes this morning. There's...some information I got last night I think you might be interested in. It has to do with the flower you mentioned yesterday evening in my apartment."

"Fl—flower?" Lorna croaked and opened her eyes.

"Yes, the *flower*," Michael stressed.

Lorna wadded the sheet in her hand, and her mind scrambled for the right details. The sound of Michael's voice blotted out everything. When she answered, she'd expected...no hoped for...

something altogether different than his no-nonsense tone and the request to meet and discuss flowers.

"*Lorna!*" Michael insisted. "*You know!* What you and Brittan were talking about? Come on! Wake up and smell the roses!"

"Oh!" Lorna swung her feet out of bed and stood. "Oh, I see!" she exclaimed and hurried to the dresser mirror. Her first instinct was to run to wherever Michael wanted to meet and glean whatever information he offered. Since he was good friends with Trent Devenport, she thought the pastor may have passed on some information. But the woman who stared back at her was in dire need of some care before entering the real world...let alone meeting Michael. Lorna wore no makeup and her hair was still damp from the shower. She looked like a wet rat with puffy eyes and a red nose.

"Will you meet me?" Michael asked.

"Y–yes," Lorna rasped. "Can you give me an hour?"

"Of course. I won't take much of your time, and I wouldn't even bother you except this is kind of *important*. I don't want to say any more over the phone."

"Okay," Lorna agreed and didn't bother to tell him that she and her friends discussed cases on their phones all the time. At least she'd get to see him. Lorna grabbed the silver-plated hairbrush and attacked her hair. It looked like this was going to be a ponytail day.

"Would you meet me at..."

"Let's meet at the country club," she offered and immediately questioned the wisdom of her offer. That was where they'd shared their first date.

"Sounds good," Michael agreed. "Like I said, I won't keep you long. But I think this will be worth your time."

"Right," she replied and tried to come across as businesslike as he did. He sounded about as romantic as a toadstool. Apparently this was about whatever clues he'd stumbled across and nothing else.

"Let's meet in the parking lot," Michael suggested. "I'll be waiting."

"Sure." She hung up and gave herself a hard stare. "Just the facts, ma'am. Just the facts," she insisted and wondered how she'd survive this meeting.

The key hanging by the gold chain on her dresser mirror mocked her worries. Lorna removed it and draped it over her head. She wrapped her hand around the key, closed her eyes, and whispered, "Please, God, *please!*"

✳ ✳ ✳

Michael sat in the country club's parking lot and watched the tennis buffs as they slammed the ball back and forth and darted in sequence with the game's rhythm. He recalled the day he'd watched Lorna playing a match and how he'd worried about that tanned tennis whiz who looked like he was ready to grab her and kiss her. Michael had been as jealous as all get out and had wasted no time zooming in for a "chance" meeting.

He rested his head on his steering wheel, closed his gritty eyes, and revisited what Trent said last night. He'd spent half the night thinking about Trent's words of wisdom.

This meeting with Lorna was twofold. Michael could have given Lorna the information over the phone, but he preferred seeing her. When she didn't question his request for a meeting, Michael hoped that was an indicator she would give him a chance to talk about what happened yesterday.

The light tap on his window made him jump and lift his head. He saw Lorna looking like a million bucks. Her hair was in a ponytail. Her makeup was fresh. And she wore spotless white shorts and a pullover shirt.

He glanced down at his slacks, shirt, and Italian loafers. Even at his family's wholesale prices, these pieces had cost Michael a mint.

He'd chosen them on purpose this morning in hopes she'd think he cared because he looked his best.

But she hadn't even bothered to dress up. Fleetingly Michael wondered if she planned to meet that tanned tennis turbo after he gave her the contact information. A fresh twist of jealousy tightened his gut.

He picked up the slip of paper with Wayne Smith's name, phone number, address, and email on it. He opened the door and got out. Michael briefly peered into Lorna's eyes and searched for any sign that he should discuss last night. All he saw was a pair of gorgeous green eyes veiled in caution. In some ways she looked like a gazelle ready to run if he spoke too loudly.

Michael extended the information to her and nearly dropped to his knees when he caught a whiff of her perfume. She smelled as beautiful as she looked. "I wouldn't have bothered you, except this is nearly life and death for my best friend," he explained. "And I know you and your friends are already on the case."

"Yes." Lorna accepted the piece of paper and examined the name.

"That guy is a pastor in the town where Cooper used to live," Michael explained.

"And he publicly accused Cooper of being involved in pornography. Right?"

"Yes. How'd you know?" Michael asked.

Lorna lifted her head. "We're already on it. We got his contact info off the church's website last night after reading the newspaper article in the online archives. We're planning on flying up there this evening or tomorrow and seeing if he'll talk."

"Oh, he'll talk," Michael confirmed. "Trent's lawyer, Stevie Simon, has already made the connection and was planning to send a private eye. I told him I knew someone—"

Her eyes widened. "Did you tell him who we are?" she gasped.

"No way." Michael shook his head. "I wouldn't do that," he added with a defensive edge.

"Oh—I didn't mean to imply…" Lorna covered her mouth with her fingertips and looked down. She'd changed clothes three times and put on more makeup than usual to cover the evidence of tears. Michael's immaculate attire made her feel underdressed and somewhat intimidated. His expression hinted at nothing but business, and his dark eyes were as hard as onyx. Apparently he'd meant this meeting for what it was—the passing of information—and nothing more. He'd also made certain that she understood he wouldn't have requested the meeting if it weren't for his friend's welfare.

"It's good that the man is expecting a contact," she finally croaked and folded the paper. "That makes it easier for us. Thanks." She slipped the information into her pocket and stepped back.

Michael broke eye contact and gazed toward the tennis courts.

To Lorna it looked like he couldn't wait to get away. She decided to make his day. "Well, thanks again," she said and strolled across the parking lot without a backward glance. By the time she crawled into her Jeep, she glimpsed Michael's Mercedes pulling from the parking lot. Lorna bit her trembling lips as she fully realized her relationship with Michael was irrevocably over. She pulled the key from beneath her shirt, yanked it from her neck, and hurled it across the Jeep. It hit the passenger window and dropped to the floor as swiftly as Lorna's hopes sank into a dismal sea of regrets.

THIRTY-TWO

Wayne Smith had been more than happy to give Lorna an appointment. He never questioned her identity. When she told him she was investigating Rich Cooper, he'd been eager to meet. The flight to Arkansas had been smooth and effortless. The interview with Wayne Smith confirmed the pornography charge against Rich Cooper. Wayne's honest gray eyes underscored his credibility. Now, at three o'clock Monday morning, the debutantes had prepared the facts and were ready for 'the Rose' delivery.

Lorna had spent the last two days solely focused upon the case and forced traces of Michael from her mind. Otherwise, she would have crumpled into a heap of despair. Her friends avoided any mention of him, and Lorna was grateful. Their detective work this weekend had offered enough distraction to keep her attention off her failed love life. The flight Saturday night, early interview Sunday morning, and return flight that afternoon had exhausted all three women. They'd crashed Sunday evening for a long nap.

Lorna still had a hard time keeping her eyes open. She yawned, covered her mouth, and knew the jet lag had yet to be chased away. She slowed her Jeep as they neared Duke's duplex in a tidy neighborhood full of young professionals. Brittan passed the manila envelope from the backseat and said, "Go girl."

"You better believe I will!" Heather agreed and accepted the envelope that contained the written and recorded interview and a single-stemmed red rose. The dashboard lights illuminated Heather's satisfied smile before she turned and winked at Lorna. "I can't wait," she exclaimed.

The three friends had agreed this delivery belonged to Heather since she and Duke had argued over Trent's innocence from the start.

"Is Duke still determined that Devenport's guilty even after Michael's endorsement?" Brittan asked. Lorna glanced at Brittan through the rearview mirror. In the shadows the Asian looked like a prowler.

"Michael's statement did take the edge off some," Heather admitted, "but he still has his doubts. Duke can be a pessimist sometimes."

"Well, maybe you'll be the cure for that," Lorna teased.

"Let's hope so!" Heather offered the thumbs-up sign.

Since Duke already knew their identity, there was no reason for the friends to be worried about getting caught. So they'd all piled into Lorna's Jeep rather than bothering with a rented vehicle. Lorna stopped in front of Duke's place and turned off her lights.

"Go to it, tiger," she challenged.

Heather's snicker sounded like a smug "I told you so, Duke," before she opened the Jeep's door.

The muffled sound of sporadic traffic on the freeway blended with the low hum of Lorna's air conditioner. The summer night oozed into the Jeep, bringing with it the smell of fresh dew. Lorna watched while Heather approached Duke's front door and inserted the envelope through his mail slot. She was back in the vehicle within a minute.

The three friends exchanged a high-five. While this had been their most simple delivery yet, the exhilaration of finally starting the pendulum swinging in favor of Trent made them cheer for a whole block.

Once the story hit, their next move involved a call to Frank Bass.

✳ ✺ ✳

"You know 'the Rose'?" Trent Devenport's voice exploded into Michael's ear. He winced and pulled his cell phone away from his face.

"What?" Michael asked and placed his briefcase on his desk before plopping into his chair. He'd barely had time to process Trent's question before Frances Rousseau laid a stack of papers on his desk. Tuesday morning was starting with a vengeance.

"You have a call waiting on line two," she whispered.

"Have you looked at the morning paper?" Trent asked.

"I am now. Give me a minute." Michael picked up the rag from his desk's edge, where Frances always placed it. Using his left hand, he flipped it open and eyed the front page. The headline read, "Another pastor at Houston Heights Church marred by pornography." The first line read, "'The Rose' makes her mark on the Devenport case." Michael's eyes widened as he skimmed the story. The writer claimed to have received factual information regarding Rich Cooper's past from "the Rose." Wayne Smith claimed to have caught Cooper in the act of viewing online pornography two years ago in his former assignment. Duke Fieldman closed the article by mentioning that the senior pastor, Trent Devenport, had vehemently claimed the child porn was planted on his computer and that Mayor Michael Hayden defended Devenport's honor. The underlying implication was clear.

"That's who you put on my case, isn't it?" Trent asked. "'The Rose'? That's why you were so evasive."

Michael lowered the paper and eyed the blinking light on his desk phone. "Trent, I'm not at liberty to—"

"Ha!" Trent laughed out loud and then laughed some more. "I absolutely *do not* believe this! You put 'the Rose' on my case!"

"Look, I never said—"

"Don't give me that!" he challenged. "It's not just coincidental, and you know it. You said I'd know it when the investigator released the information, and now I know why!"

"I guess I did, didn't I?" Michael said.

"So you admit it?"

"I'm not admitting anything." He released the paper. "Just be glad some wheels are turning, will ya?"

"There's no way I'll ever be able to repay you, Michael!" Trent exclaimed.

"Your friendship is payment enough," he asserted as the blinking light called. "Listen, I'm going to have to go now," Michael said. "I think the city manager is calling. We've got a major industry looking at moving to Houston."

"Sure! Sure! Go on and do your job. I've got to go turn cartwheels anyway."

Michael closed his cell and mumbled, "Way to go, Lorna!" yet the ache in his heart tinged his sentiment. As tempted as Michael was to call her, he reminded himself she'd practically run away from him Saturday morning.

He picked up the phone, pressed the blinking button, and allowed his job to suck him into a relentless day that extended into an empty evening.

※ ❋ ※

Her shoulders tense, Lorna approached the phone booth in downtown Houston and slipped inside. She closed the door. The smells of exhaust and baking pavement followed her inside, and

Lorna hacked against the invasion on her lungs. Even though there was no reason for anyone to follow her, watch her, or suspect what she was up to, she still cast a cautious, discreet glance in all directions. The pedestrians filed by the phone booth without a glance. The traffic slipped by without anyone noticing. The ever-present skyscrapers stretched to the clouds as a testimony to this ordinary day with a woman in a phone booth taking care of an ordinary task.

Lorna relaxed and blotted at the dots of perspiration on her upper lip. A Houston phone booth at six o'clock on a late June evening wasn't exactly the coolest place to be. But if Bass had caller ID, then this was the safest place for Lorna to phone him from.

She lifted the receiver, inserted the appropriate change, and dialed the number on the slip of paper. Frank Bass' contact information had been available through the online church directory. Lorna hoped the man was home. She counted the rings and was thinking this effort was going to be a no-go when Frank's voice boomed over the line.

"Hello, Monsieur Bass," Lorna said in the thickest French accent she could muster. "I am calling you about de man who is named Pastor Cooper. Oui, Pastor Rich Cooper, I believe. Do you know him?"

"Uh..." Bass hedged.

"Monsieur Bass," Lorna continued. "We've been watching you... *closely*," she added and paused for dramatic effect. "We're sure you've seen today's paper?"

"Who are you?" he growled.

"If you know of things this Pastor Cooper has done to Pastor Devenport to, shall we say, incriminate him, we suggest you go to the police before they discover your involvement." Lorna wrapped her fingers around the metal phone cord and turned her back to a bedraggled man who glanced her way. "They say the police go easier on those who...how you say it...plea bargain?"

"I don't know what you're talking about!" Bass bellowed and slammed down the phone.

Lorna pulled the receiver away from her ear and smiled at it. "Ah, but Monsieur," she stated through a satisfied smile, "we *so* think you do."

✳ ✳ ✳

Michael stood on the street corner and waited until Lorna exited the phone booth. He'd followed her after cruising around her building to build up the courage to stop and go in. Michael had been surprised to see her exit and strike out on foot. She'd been dressed for the journey in running shoes and shorts and had walked with purpose for two blocks before entering the phone booth with a determination that piqued Michael's curiosity. Whatever she was up to, he wondered if it had to do with 'the Rose.' He had to give it to those three women—they were determined.

He was here because of Trent, who'd shown up at noon and insisted on taking Michael to lunch. When the conversation had turned to Lorna, he looked Michael squarely in the eyes and said, "Just go see her, for cryin' out loud! If you don't, I'm going to haul you over there myself."

"Okay, okay," Michael mumbled as if Trent were still with him. "I'm here. Are ya happy?" He pulled on his shirt collar and wished it were 20 degrees cooler. The countless vehicles releasing warm exhaust didn't help matters. Michael had shed his suit coat and tie and left them in his car that was parked around the corner. He couldn't imagine how hot he'd be with them on.

With her task complete, Lorna strolled in his direction, her head held high like a woman who knew who she was and the things she wanted out of life. Michael could only pray that he was one of those things. Her cheeks were flushed with the heat; her hair swept up into a ponytail. In the crisp shorts and polo shirt she looked like she'd just walked away from winning another championship.

When he got within three feet of her, Michael called, "Lorna?" as if he'd never suspected her presence.

She stopped and gazed at him like he was a hologram. "Michael!" she finally replied, and her flushed cheeks went a shade deeper.

He slipped his hands into his pockets and realized his script ended there. Michael had been so intent on following her, he'd not rehearsed what to say once he caught up with her. "So...how have you been s–since...Saturday?" he asked and scratched his ear.

She glanced down. "Fine."

Michael eyed the pedestrians walking around them. A couple of well-groomed women looked him square in the eyes and then gaped at Lorna. He groaned inwardly and realized they were sitting ducks for the Houston paparazzi.

"Look, my car is parked right around the corner. Would you like to go for a ride?" He dared to let his mask slip all the way off and earnestly appraised her, "Because if you would, Lorna, I'd really like to talk."

A silent nod was her only communication. Michael turned and they fell into step beside each other. When he opened the car door for her, she readily slid inside.

By the time he settled into his seat and turned on the engine, Michael knew what his next line would be. "I'm sorry for every-thing, Lorna." He gripped the gearshift while the air conditioner released an initial blast of warm air that soon grew cool.

"I'm *so* sorry too," she gasped and covered her face. "I really don't think you're a pervert!"

Michael didn't expect the laughter, but it burst forth without his permission and defied control.

She lowered her hands and gazed at him like he was nuts. "Is this funny?"

He reached for her hand and shook his head as the chuckles

kept rolling. "I don't know," he admitted. "I have no idea why I'm laughing. It's just that…" He bit down hard on his lips, but to no avail. "I haven't slept for days," he confessed, "and I think I'm losing it."

"Oh…" Lorna's word wobbled out.

"Ah Lorna," Michael said, "it's so good to see you. I wanted to talk Saturday but didn't have the nerve."

"Me too."

"Well, you sure didn't act like it," Michael stated.

She faced him. "Like *you* did?"

He laughed again. "I was afraid to! You looked like you were ready to bite my head off."

"Well, you weren't exactly Mr. Congeniality." Lorna crossed her arms.

"But I so wanted to be." Michael pressed his fingertips against his chest.

"Well, if you *had* been…"

"Or if *you* had been…" he echoed. "Oh, what does it matter? I've missed you so much. How did we make such a mess of something so good?"

"I don't know," she squeaked and helplessly observed him.

That's when Michael noticed the blemish on her chin. "You've got a zit," he said, and Lorna touched the imperfection.

"You're certainly full of compliments," she said with a grimace.

"I love it!" he exclaimed and pulled her hand away.

"Have you lost your *mind?*" Lorna pressed.

"No! It's just that I've realized I really expected you to be something you could never be."

"You mean perfect?" she questioned.

"Yes!" Michael admitted and also noticed for the first time that her eyebrows weren't an exact match either. "But you really aren't perfect and never will be."

"No. I need grace—and lots of it." She creased the hem of her shorts.

"Don't we all," Michael admitted. He touched the wisp of hair falling loose from her ponytail. "By the way, thanks so much for the cuff links," he said. "You shouldn't have—"

"But I wanted to," Lorna said. "They were perfect for you."

"Well, just so you know, I won't be bested," he admitted. "Be warned! You've got a diamond or two coming."

"Oh no!" She teased. *"Please* no diamonds!"

Michael laughed. "You beat me in golf. I can't let you beat me in diamonds too."

After sharing chuckles, Michael sobered. "Trent says I've been in love with your image—not with the real you. I've been so busy idolizing the Lorna Leigh in the magazines, I missed getting to know the *human* Lorna Leigh."

She released a long sigh and rested her head against the seat. "Honestly, it scared me for you to think I was so perfect." She lifted her head and observed him with those candid green eyes that made Michael's world spin. "I'm human. And no human can ever be perfect."

"Yes, I know," Michael admitted. "I couldn't see that until…"

"Until I really blew it?"

He took her hand. "We *both* blew it, Lorna."

"The only time I doubted you was for about five minutes on that Wednesday night you saw me at Houston Heights," she admitted. "And the only reason I doubted you then was because you showed up at church. At that point we were questioning everybody's motives. But when you told me you were at the church and were trying to see Trent, I totally knew you were okay because you weren't trying to hide a thing. And I kicked myself good for even *thinking*—"

"It's okay," Michael said and swept away her concern. "After seeing the way you three operate, I'm shocked one of you didn't tie me up and interrogate me with a blinding spotlight." He laughed again. "You women are something else."

"I guess you saw the paper?" Lorna asked.

"Yep. Who hasn't? And really, I think Brittan has exonerated herself. She's part of the reason my best friend is going to go free. Of course, it's not official yet, but the way things are stacking up…" Michael adjusted his cooling vent toward Lorna.

"Yes, they're stacking up all right," Lorna agreed. "I was just calling someone we think is up to his neck in this whole thing—a man named Frank Bass. I told him that if he was involved in setting up Trent he should go to the police and plea bargain. We aren't certain he's an accomplice, but if he is we're hoping that call and the article will be the nudge that starts the dominoes falling."

"You have no idea how ecstatic Trent is. You three are really making a difference in the lives of a lot of people."

"We hope so," she admitted. "That's why we do this."

Michael observed the thinning traffic and prepared to put his vehicle into drive. "Let's get something to eat, okay? I'm starving all of a sudden. I haven't eaten in days."

"Me neither," Lorna admitted. "But before we go, there's one other thing I need to say."

He leaned closer, gave her his full attention, and said, "What?" never expecting her to grab his shirt and put a lip-lock on him that left him gasping. After the whole city whirled for ten seconds, Lorna backed away and Michael gasped. "Whoa! Remind me to chase you down more often!"

"Chase me down?" she queried as her brows puckered.

"Whoops!" he said and went in for another kiss before Lorna could ask more questions.

❊ ❊ ❊

HOUSTON'S MAYOR OFF THE MARKET?

by Duke Fieldman

Rumors are flying about Mayor Michael Hayden and his latest flame, former tennis pro Lorna Leigh. After being seen around town together for the last few months, there's talk of an engagement. Miss Leigh is now wearing a sizable engagement ring. As Hayden's popularity increased with Lorna Leigh, so has his popularity skyrocketed with Houston residents.

When Hayden stepped forward in June to defend his friend, Pastor Trent Devenport, accused of involvement in child pornography, the town reeled. But Hayden's judgment proved correct. Devenport's name has been completely cleared, thanks to undercover work by "the Rose."

Associate pastor Rich Cooper has been convicted as a sex offender. Houston Heights Community Church member Frank Bass, in exchange for a plea bargain, testified against Cooper.

When asked what he thought about the outcome of the case, Mayor Hayden responded, "I knew my friend was innocent from the start. I never doubted him. I'm just glad the real criminal has been found guilty."

As for a wedding date? Hayden and Leigh are making no comment.

ABOUT THE AUTHOR

※ ❀ ※

Debra White Smith continues to impact and entertain readers with her life-changing books, including *Romancing Your Husband*, *Romancing Your Wife*, The Sisters Suspense series, The Austen series, and now The Debutantes series. She's an award-winning author, including such honors as Top-10 Reader Favorite, Gold Medallion finalist, and Retailer's Choice Award finalist. Debra has more than 50 books to her credit and over a million books in print.

The founder of Real Life Ministries, Debra recently launched Real Life Minute, which airs on radio stations nationwide. She also speaks passionately with insight and humor at ministry events across the nation. Debra has been featured on a variety of media, including *The 700 Club*, *At Home Life*, *Getting Together*, *Moody Broadcasting Network*, *Fox News*, *Viewpoint*, and *America's Family Coaches*. She holds an M.A. in English.

Debra lives in small-town America with her husband, two children, and a herd of cats.

To write Debra or contact her for speaking engagements, check out her website:

www.debrawhitesmith.com

or send mail to

Real Life Ministries
Daniel W. Smith, Ministry Manager
PO Box 1482
Jacksonville, TX 75766

or call

1-866-211-3400 (toll free)

More Great Books
by Debra White Smith

FICTION

The Austen Series

Amanda

Central Park

First Impressions

Northpointe Chalet

Possibilities

Reason & Romance

The Debutantes

Heather

Lorna

Brittan (coming July 2008)

The Seven Sisters Series/
Sisters Suspense Series

Second Chances

The Awakening/Picture Perfect

A Shelter in the Storm

To Rome with Love

For Your Eyes Only

This Time Around

Let's Begin Again

Fiction/Parable

The Richest Person in the World (with Stan Toler)

NONFICTION

Romancing Your Husband

Romancing Your Wife

What Jane Austen Taught Me About Love and Romance

∽ THE DEBUTANTES ∽

Three contemporary women who tackle mysteries and love.

Heather, an engaging blonde with a black belt in karate.
Lorna, a brunette athlete with unquenchable enthusiasm.
Brittan, a black-haired genius with a creative streak.

BOOK 1
HEATHER

When socialite Heather Winslow succumbs to her mother's push for a "coming out" ball after her college graduation, she grudgingly agrees to be interviewed by Duke Fieldman. Put off by the newspaperman's disdain but attracted by his good looks, Heather startles him by arranging a date. When she learns of Duke's desire to be a "real" reporter, she's intrigued. Can she help him?

Part of the Debutantes, Heather and her friends solve high-profile crimes. Presenting the evidence anonymously, along with a long-stemmed rose, the Debs become known as "the Rose." When they take on a murder case, they cross paths with Duke, who wants to uncover the Rose's identity. The more Duke investigates, the more infatuated he becomes.

As Heather, Lorna, and Brittan dig into the case, can Heather keep her involvement a secret while dating Duke? How will she compete with his mystery-woman fascination?

BOOK 2
LORNA

Attending a welcome-the-new-mayor party, Lorna Leigh counters boredom by escaping to the garden...only to realize she's not alone. The dashing 30-something mayor is getting fresh air too. Sparks fly even as Lorna fights her attraction to this handsome bachelor. She's still not ready to date after last time...

When Pastor Trent Devenport is arrested for pornography, debutantes Lorna, Heather, and Brittan take the case. Convinced the pastor was set up, the gutsy amateur detectives investigate. But when the clues reveal Trent's wife was engaged to Michael, Lorna's heart is torn. Is Michael using his new position to get revenge for a failed romance? Are there others in the church who want Pastor Devenport gone?

As Lorna and Michael struggle with their dating demons from the past, they must decide if they're willing to risk everything for love and justice.

BOOK 3
BRITTAN
(coming July 2008)

THE AUSTEN SERIES

AMANDA

Smart, funny, and generous, Amanda Priebe is a great friend to have...until the matchmaking bug bites. Deciding that her secretary, Haley, needs a beau, Amanda dreams up the perfect match—Pastor Mason Eldridge. Never mind that Haley is seeing Roger, a respectable dairy farmer. And it doesn't really matter that Mason might be attracted to someone else.

When it comes to her own heart, Amanda can't seem to make up her mind what she wants to do. The handsome and debonair Franklyn West is available...so is the ever-present Nate Knighton.

In this tangled web of best-laid plans, who will end up with whom? Will Haley find true love? Will Amanda realize what her heart's known all along?

A lively tale of plans gone awry, affection in unexpected places, and the ultimate power of faith and love.

CENTRAL PARK

Wrenched from her family, young Francine is terrified by her new life with her aunt and uncle in New York City. But their foster son, Ethan, comes to Francine's rescue. As the years pass, the bond between the two deepens...and they spend many hours enjoying the serenity of Central Park. When Ethan goes to Paris for a missions trip, Francine realizes affection has transformed into love. She dreams of the day Ethan will arrive home and share her love.

But when Ethan returns, he brings his new love, the beautiful Carrie Casper. And Carrie's playboy brother, Hugh, falls for Francine. Will Ethan realize the jewel he has in his friendship with Francine? Should Francine stay true to a love that will never be?

FIRST IMPRESSIONS

When Eddi Boswick is cast as Elizabeth, the female lead in a local production of *Pride and Prejudice*, she hesitates. Dave, the handsome young rancher cast as Darcy, seems arrogant and unpredictable. Accepting the challenge of playing opposite him, Eddi soon realizes that he is difficult to work with on and off the set.

But when a tornado springs out of nowhere, Dave protects Eddi...much to her chagrin. And he is shocked to discover an attraction for the feisty lawyer he can't deny. Sparks fly when Eddi misinterprets his interest and discovers the truth he's trying to hide.

Will Eddi's passionate faith, fierce independence, and quick wit keep Dave from discovering the secret to love...and the key to her heart?

NORTHPOINTE CHALET

Texas native Kathy Moore loves her new home in Northpointe, Colorado. The 22-year-old's bookstore is thriving. And her social life is picking up. New friends Liza and her brother, Ron, an unrepentant heartbreaker, are constant visitors. It's her personal life that needs a dramatic twist—like the ones in the thrillers she devours.

Then one dark and stormy night, a kind stranger takes refuge in Kathy's store. When she learns he's Ben Tilman, one of the residents of the mysterious chalet overlooking Northpointe, Kathy is smitten. But Ben's reserved behavior suggests she's too young and flamboyant to be relationship material for him, an established pastor.

Suddenly, like in one of her suspense novels, an old man corners Kathy with warnings about the murderous Tilman patriarch—warnings she must investigate. Will Kathy's growing suspicions and topsy-turvy investigation put an end to her deepening relationship with the man of Northpointe Chalet?

POSSIBILITIES

"A yardman?" Landon's thin eyebrows arched. "You want to marry a yardman?" Her blue eyes couldn't have been wider...or more disdainful.

Practical, down-to-earth Allie is the daughter of Willis Elton, a wealthy, respected gentleman farmer. Although allowed to attend college and obtain a master's degree in horticulture, she is expected to marry well and take her place in society. But Allie has a problem. She's in love with the handsome Frederick Wently—the yardman.

Yielding to family pressure, she withdraws from the relationship. But as the years pass, her heart refuses to surrender. When Frederick turns up on the arm of a close family friend, Allie struggles with jealousy and heartbreak. What can she do to get him back? And should she even try?

An intriguing look at the twists and turns of love.

REASON AND ROMANCE

Sense and sensibility collide when love comes calling for sisters Elaina and Anna Woods...

Ruled by reason, Elaina remains calm in every situation—even when she meets Ted Farris. Although attracted by his charming personality, she refuses to be swept away by love. Accused of never listening to her heart, Elaina finally gives in to her feelings. As her relationship with Ted develops into something magical, they seem destined to be together—except for one tiny detail. Will Lorna Starr keep them apart?

Anna longs for the day she'll meet her prince. When she's rescued by the handsome Willis Kenney, has her dream turned into reality? Inseparable from the start, neither of them worries about the past. Anna, refusing to listen to her sister's cautious voice of reason, lets her romantic heart run wild. Caught in an emotional whirlwind, she and Willis revel in the hope of two passionate hearts. Will their impulsive love endure despite the mistakes of yesterday?

Romance and reason merge in this captivating story about the joys and follies of infatuation and how faith in God reveals true love.

ROMANCING YOUR HUSBAND

Early days in a relationship are exhilarating, but they can't touch the thrilling love affair you can have now. Cutting through traditional misconceptions and exploring every facet of the Bible's message on marriage, *Romancing Your Husband* reveals how you can create a union others only dream about. From making Jesus an active part of your marriage to arranging fantastic romantic interludes, you'll discover how to—

- make romance a reality
- "knock your husband's socks off"
- become a lover-wife, not a mother-wife
- find freedom in forgiving
- cultivate a sacred romance with God.

Experience fulfillment through romancing your husband...and don't be surprised when he romances you back!

ROMANCING YOUR WIFE

by Debra White Smith and Daniel W. Smith

Do you want your husband to surprise you and put more romance in your relationship? *Romancing Your Wife* can help! Give this book to your hubby, and he'll discover ways to create an exciting, enthusiastic marriage.

Debra and her husband, Daniel, offer biblical wisdom and practical advice that when put into practice will help your husband mentally, emotionally, and physically improve his relationship with you. He'll discover tools to build a dynamite marriage, including how to—

- communicate his love more effectively
- make you feel cherished
- better understand your needs and wants
- create a unity of spirit and mind
- increase the passion in your marriage

From insights on little things that jazz up a marriage to more than 20 "Endearing Encounters," *Romancing Your Wife* sets the stage for love and romance.